DELILAH S. DAWSON

WICKED AS THEY COME

A BLUD NOVEL

Pocket Books

New York   London   Toronto   Sydney   New Delhi

Pocket Books
A Division of Simon & Schuster, Inc.
1230 Avenue of the Americas
New York, NY 10020

This book is a work of fiction. Names, characters, places, and incidents either are products of the author's imagination or are used fictitiously. Any resemblance to actual events or locales or persons, living or dead, is entirely coincidental.

First Pocket Books paperback edition April 2012

POCKET and colophon are registered trademarks of Simon & Schuster, Inc.

For information about special discounts for bulk purchases, please contact Simon & Schuster Special Sales at 1-866-506-1949 or business@simonandschuster.com.

The Simon & Schuster Speakers Bureau can bring authors to your live event. For more information or to book an event contact the Simon & Schuster Speakers Bureau at 1-866-248-3049 or visit our website at www.simonspeakers.com.

Designed by Jacquelynne Hudson

Manufactured in the United States of America

10 9 8 7 6 5 4 3 2 1

ISBN 978-1-4516-5788-3
ISBN 978-1-4516-5789-0 (ebook)

"You don't feel safe anymore, do you?" Criminy asked.

"Don't worry, Letitia. Nothing can harm you so long as you're with me."

"But what happens when I leave you?" I asked him. "You can't spend all your time following me around and strangling bludbunnies."

"Don't tempt me," he said.

I watched him playing with the long blades of grass, weaving them into patterns as he hummed an unfamiliar song, a waltz.

"What are you doing?" I asked him.

"I'm letting you get used to the idea of me," he said idly. "I'm pretending to be harmless. Is it working?"

"Until you smile," I said weakly, and he smiled again, his face radiant.

"Can't help that, love," he said. "Not around you."

"Just so you know," I said, "I just ended a bad relationship, and I'm not really looking for another."

"You may not be looking for it," he said. "But maybe it's come looking for you."

***

"*WICKED AS THEY COME* is as good as it gets!"
—*New York Times* bestselling author Nancy Holder

Wicked as They Come is also available as an eBook

To my husband, Craig.
The first one was always for you. Only you.

ACKNOWLEDGMENTS

Huge thanks and cupcakes go to:

My husband, Craig. Thanks for making me write that first book, putting up with an unruly helpmeet, and indulging my muse. I would say he's a saint, but as you can tell by Criminy Stain, I'm not much into saints.

My family. Thanks to my parents and grandparents for their support and love even though I'm the weirdest person in the family.

My children. Thanks for rewiring my brain and being awesome.

My fabulous editor, Abby Zidle, her assistant, Parisa Zolfaghari, and the entire Pocket/Gallery team for an amazing first publishing experience. Thanks to Tony Mauro for an incredible book cover. And thanks to Jen Heddle for falling in love with Blud.

My rock star agent, Kate McKean. Thanks for lifting me out of the slush, indulging my freak-outs, and killing my darlings. When I doubt myself, I open the first email you ever sent and get all twitterpated. Dude, you rock! Here's to many more!

My beta readers. Ericka Axelsson, Carrie Damen, Debbie Pascoe, Austin Lewis, Charis Collins, Kathy Epling, Justina

Ireland, and Brent Taylor. My first audience and my cheer-leaders, I thank you.

Janet Herron, for help with the nursing bits of the book.

Simon Effendi of Artistic Moments Photography in Atlanta, GA, for six years of stunning images.

Literary agents Joanna Stampfel-Volpe and Jim McCarthy. Thank you for taking the time to reject me kindly and offer advice. It meant the world. And to Jennifer Laughran, just thanks. You rock. You know why.

The people who helped me become a writer. To my eleventh-grade AP English teacher, Karen Lanning. To Liz Gumbinner, Kristen Chase, and the whole team at www.CoolMomPicks.com.

My dear friend and mentor, Jan Gibbons. I miss you every day.

The Hush Sound, Villainess Soaps, and Black Phoenix Alchemy Lab for inspiration.

All my real-life friends, my Facebook buddies, my Tweeps, and the people who follow my blog—thank you! If I ever run a magical carnival, I hope you'll all run away with me.

WICKED
AS THEY
COME

1

I was the one who found Mrs. Stein's body two weeks ago. Now here I was, pawing through her things, finally free to explore her creepy old house. It wasn't personal, though—I had barely known her. And the estate sale was probably her idea, anyway, one last attempt to infuriate her children.

The second I saw the sign, I had to stop. She had been surprisingly paranoid for a hospice patient, and I had never seen anything of her historic Victorian home beyond the downstairs bedroom where she had chosen to spend her remaining days. The chance to explore was just too interesting to pass up. Plus, I'd said good-bye to most of my worldly possessions when I left Jeff, and I had an hour to kill until my next patient.

I was starting over from scratch and didn't have the money or the lifestyle for priceless antiques, but I always had room for treasure. Knickknacks, odd paintings, or costume jewelry would help liven up my empty apartment. Best of all, though, the sun-dappled attic upstairs was wall-to-wall books. For me, that was heaven.

When I first saw the chain hanging from the top of the old tome, I didn't know what to think. I tugged it up. As the flat locket slid from between the pages, I got a little rush of excitement, like when pulling the prize out of a box of cereal. Sure, it was tarnished and grimy, but it was a prize nonetheless. Maybe my luck was finally changing.

I let the locket dangle in a sunbeam, charmed by its age and strangeness. I could picture it shining on some young lady's neck, part of an epic story full of romance and a Prince Charming who didn't turn out to be an overbearing, soul-sucking jerk. Not that I was bitter or anything. I just wanted to start over fresh, make that good-bye really mean something positive.

It's funny how a relationship can sneak up on you like that. It starts with a whirlwind courtship, dozens of roses and poetry and dancing. He buys you a toothbrush, gives you a drawer. You move in. You give in on little things, just to make him happy. The curtains. Your hair, which he thinks you should grow out. Then it's bigger things. The checkbook. Your job. And the one big-big thing, the baby that you lose, the gift he wasn't ready to give you. His relief at your pain kills something inside you, the hardest good-bye of all.

And then one day, you realize that you're basically a plaything and property to a man who's charmed you out of your pants and into the perfect wedding ring he had picked out before he even met you. That he's not making plans *with* you, he's making you fit into *his* plans, no matter what the cost. You realize that you've become a paper doll with paper thoughts, that it was all too easy to give up control. And then one night, he hits you, and you pull your dignity off the floor and kick the bastard to the curb.

You say good-bye. And then you leave. And then you get somewhere else and learn how to say hello again.

"Hello," I said to the locket, trying it out.

Just looking at it made me happy in a way I had forgotten. A feeling of hope, of indulgence. I'd forgotten how good it felt to choose something for myself, to see an object and say, "I'm going to make that mine."

It was pretty in such a Gothic, old-fashioned way. One side had a large, flat stone—maybe a ruby or maybe just glass. And the other side of the oval had indecipherable writing around the edge with a compass rose in the center. I breathed on the metal and rubbed it on my scrub pants, but its secrets remained safe under eons of muck.

Just as I was about to head downstairs to pay for the locket, a little old lady appeared at my elbow and said, "Excuse me, miss. Can you read this?"

"I'd be glad to try," I said with a smile.

She handed me a crusty old saltcellar, and I read the smudged grease-pencil price. I was like a magnet for old people. Maybe because I was accustomed to helping them at work. Maybe because I looked kind. Or maybe because every time I looked at an elderly person, I thought of my grandmother and couldn't help smiling.

Taking care of my grandmother was one of my greatest joys and greatest sorrows. I got to be with her and help her, take care of all of the nursing tasks that she would be mortified to impose on a stranger. But I also had to watch her die, and it broke my heart. With my mom gone and my dad remarried across the country, she was all the family I had. The hours I spent with her every day were precious to me, and I couldn't believe how much time I had lost with her by wasting time with Jeff in Birmingham.

This old lady had the same sort of fire that made my grandmother special, a mix of manners and moxie that I hoped I had inherited. Watching her eyes narrow at the offending saltcellar reminded me of going antiques shopping with Nana when I was little, popping jelly beans one by one as she haggled. Still, I didn't have much time until I was expected at Mr. Rathbin's house, and after that, I had four more hospice patients waiting. Old people get really cranky when you're late.

I was just opening my mouth to apologize and slip away when my beeper went off. It was my case manager, followed by 911.

"Excuse me," I said, rushing past the surprised old woman and down the narrow staircase.

"Must be a doctor," I heard her remark to someone else before I was out of earshot.

Coulda, woulda, shoulda, I thought, remembering the night that Jeff tore up my applications to medical school and threw them into the trash. Then I corrected myself.

I can still be a doctor if I want to. Nothing's stopping me, dammit. I can be anything and anyone I want to be. No one's going to tell me what to be ever again.

Back in my car, I reached into my pocket for my cell phone to call the office. Instead, I found the locket. Staring at it, I reminded myself that I was not a thief, that I had never stolen anything in my life . . . on purpose.

But something I couldn't explain kept me from going back inside and making things right. The busy woman running the estate sale probably didn't even know the locket existed. And the recently deceased Mrs. Stein wouldn't miss it. There wasn't a price on it. Still, I couldn't help imagining police cars with blinking lights surrounding my little sedan in the driveway as officers with guns ordered me to put my hands up. So much of the last three years of my life had been based on fear.

I tugged the chain over my head and pulled my long dark hair out from under it. I couldn't help giving myself a sly grin in the pull-down mirror. The locket was heavy, and it hung exactly over my heart, much lower than most of my necklaces. I tucked it under my T-shirt and scrub top, enjoying the dull weight against my skin and wondering what sort of metal lurked under the tarnish. Maybe once it was cleaned, I could have the chain shortened.

Or maybe I'd keep it a secret, just because I could.

2

"What's this thing made of—Kryptonite?" I muttered to myself. "It's useless."

Nana didn't even glance up from her crossword puzzle to ask, "What's useless?"

"Getting this locket clean. I've tried everything under your sink. It's making me crazy."

I looked at the array of cleaners and scrubby things cluttering the kitchen table. I'd tried them all. Up next: a jackhammer.

One corner of her mouth twitched up, and the other puckered down. "Tish, honey, please tell me you didn't just put bleach on a valuable piece of antique jewelry."

"Yep," I said.

"Lordy loo, sugar," she said from her wheelchair, her face all crumpled up like a dried-out apple. "You're going to ruin it. You have to be careful with old things. Show some respect."

"What would you recommend?" I asked her. If she didn't have a good old Southern recipe for hope, no one did.

"Patience," she said with a smile. "Take it to a jewelry store tomorrow, before you muck it up. You're too impetuous. Have you opened it yet?"

"I've been too busy trying to clean it to see what's inside," I said. To be honest, though, I was saving that for later, when I was alone. I wanted to savor it, keep it my own little secret.

When she turned back to her crossword, I tried the bleach one more time, just in case. In the silence of my scrubbing, I heard it. The sound I hated most. Nana's labored breathing. She was having a tough night, but she wouldn't admit it. I had arranged it so she was the last call on my rounds, so that I would always have plenty of time for her. I logged all of my nursing duties, making sure she had her chemo meds and antinausea drugs. And after that, I heated up her dinner, helped her tie the scarf around what was left of her hair, and tucked her into bed. She couldn't climb into it anymore on her own, and she hated that.

"Do you need more Demerol, Nana?" I asked softly.

Her mouth turned down again, and her eyes narrowed. "No, I don't need any more, thank you very much, missy," she said. "Don't you go telling me how I feel." She'd been prickly after the latest relapse. We had thought she was in remission, but apparently, her cancer thought the third time was the charm.

"I just want you to be comfortable," I said. "Because I love you."

"I'd rather be me than be doped up," she said, fire in her eyes. "If I don't have much time left, you're darned tootin' I'm going to spend it awake and raising heck."

"But it's bedtime, Nana," I said with a soft laugh. "You need your sleep."

"You're the one who needs it, sugar," she said. "Old bones don't sleep so easy. Now, why don't you get me ready so you can go out and enjoy being young?"

"I'm twenty-five," I said. "That's not very young."

"I'm eighty-four," she said. "You'll have to be young for both of us. Go to a party, or whatever it is you do. Go meet a nice young man."

"I don't think I'm ready for that," I said.

The last nice young man I'd met had nearly broken me. I wasn't ready to be tied down again. And I wasn't ready to share what was left of myself yet, either.

I thought about it as I went through our nightly ritual. Thought about bars and bookstores, online dating, handing out little cards to attractive men. None of it was appealing. And it wasn't as if I was going to meet any eligible bachelors at work. All of my patients were older than seventy except one, who was thirty and a vegetable.

As I pulled the covers over my grandmother's shrunken arms and bloated stomach, I gave her my brightest smile. I made sure she had her remote controls, her crossword book and pen, her cordless phone, and her "I've fallen, and I can't get up" button.

"Good night, Nana. I'll see you in the morning. I love you," I said.

"Quit saying that like it's the last time you're going to say it," she said peevishly. "Somebody besides me has to pretend I'll live forever."

"You'll live forever," I said. "Until I'm as old as you are, and then you'll finally teach me how to make your famous chocolate pie."

"Maybe," she said. "If you're good."

I'd be back at her house at eight in the morning to help her out of bed and into her remote-control wheelchair. She could do almost everything else for herself and didn't want to give up her independence and move into a home. I was happy to help. After I had left Jeff, she was the first one I called, standing at a pay phone, crying in the freezing cold. I'd left my cell phone behind, not wanting to give him a way to find me.

"Just come home, Tish," she had said. "Us Everett women can get through anything. Just come home."

And I had. I'd lived with her for a few weeks before she offered to give me money for the deposit on my apartment. I was touched that she understood how much I needed space of my own, space to find myself. I was broke, and she'd called it an early inheritance. Since then, we'd anchored each other and developed a friendly, loving relationship with only one rule: we never talked about her illness or my past.

Driving home, I browsed through my CD case. Sure, I had an iPod full of music, but it was all stuff Jeff had picked out, things we had listened to together. I wanted my old favorites, songs that made me feel powerful and pretty and wild and young. The sort of music Jeff had called immature and part of the "old Tish." I rolled down my windows to the balmy spring night and sang at the top of my lungs, loving the wind in my hair and the thump of the locket against my heart in time with the drums. He wouldn't have liked that, either. Would have asked me, with that plaintive voice, if I didn't prefer the diamonds he had given me.

Nope. That's why I'd dumped them down the garbage disposal on my way out and flicked the switch.

Back at my little apartment, I felt lighthearted for the first time in a long time. As if taking the locket had soothed me, become another choice that further defined who I was. I liked loud music. I took care of my grandmother. I had a good book and a rescued cat named Mr.

Surly. I was having cheese toast and tomato soup for dinner. And I had stolen an antique locket from my dead patient's attic.

As I undressed and put on my pajamas, my eyes didn't leave the locket's reflection in the dresser mirror. I didn't want to take it off. There was something exciting about it, about having something I wasn't supposed to have.

It was time to open it. I felt around the edge opposite the hinge but couldn't find a clasp. Then I tried to work it open with my fingers, but it didn't budge. I went to the bathroom and tried to use a nail file to pry it open like an oyster, but it was very unwilling to produce its pearl. Mr. Surly watched me from the counter, tail twitching. He seemed amused.

With a weary sigh, I waggled my fingers at it and said, "Locket, reveal thy secrets!"

Of course, that didn't work. That sort of thing never does.

I ran my fingers over it. There had to be a way. Then I pressed the jewel on the front, and the locket popped open.

I gasped as red liquid burst from inside, splattering my hand with scarlet drops.

Whatever it was, it burned, and I dropped the locket onto the counter, where it spun for a second, scattering a constellation of red on the bathroom counter.

I ran my hand under the cold water. The stains stopped burning but didn't wash away. I lathered up with antibacterial soap, but they didn't budge, so I got out the nail brush. Looking up at the mirror, I saw myself standing there in a ragged tank top and baggy pajama pants, scrubbing my hand until it was raw and pink. The stains seemed somehow brighter, so I gave up.

I couldn't help but wonder, what sort of ancient prankster filled a locket with staining red acid and then hid it in a book? It was its own antitheft device.

The locket lay innocently on the bathroom counter amid more pesky red spots. *No point in scrubbing those right now.*

Then I looked closer and noticed that the red drops had made tiny pockmarks in the granite. Little red holes, eaten into solid rock. I ran my finger over them, puzzled. It didn't make sense—I should have been full of holes, too. But I wasn't.

I didn't think too hard about it. I was more curious about the locket itself, which was finally open. The red stuff had drained out, so I picked it up and held it under the light.

Inside, trapped under glass, was a delicate portrait in watercolor. The man was fascinating, and I was transfixed by his piercing eyes, which challenged me from under delicate but sharp brows. His long dark hair looked as if it had been yanked from a tidy queue just moments before and left rebelliously loose to annoy the painter. His mouth was small and somewhat cruel, quirked up into a knowing smirk. His cheekbones could have cut paper. He wore a high white collar that was carelessly open, an indigo cravat hanging untied.

I loved Jane Austen, so this rogue in a cravat was right up my alley, like an extra-naughty Mr. Darcy. He was the complete opposite of stocky, clean-cut, all-American Jeff— another point in the mystery man's favor.

I could almost see a thought bubble rising above his head. *I dare you.*

"Dare me to what?" I said.

He didn't have an answer for that.

I tore my eyes from the image and considered the other side of the locket, looking for the portrait of his lady.

Instead, there were words engraved there, and I could almost make them out.

"*Viernes toa meo,*" I whispered, tracing the letters. I knew a smattering of French and Spanish, just enough to order a sandwich and find the bathroom, and the words seemed oddly familiar but made no sense. Portuguese, maybe? Or Esperanto?

"Who are you?" I said out loud. "And who carried you over her heart?"

He didn't have an answer to that, either. I would probably never know, unless I went back to the estate sale and dug around in the attic for clues. Maybe there was a larger portrait that I had missed lurking somewhere in the house, or something written in the book. Between the old lady and the locket, I hadn't even cracked the spine or looked at the cover. But it would be easy enough to spot—a deep, oxblood red that stood out from the other, dusty brown tomes, which is why I'd noticed it in the first place. I made up my mind to go back to the estate sale the next day, then snapped the locket shut and slipped it back over my head and under my tank top. I felt a little silly.

Now that the locket's mystery was solved, real life seeped back into my thoughts. After my time with Nana, I was more bothered than ever. If she was in more pain and not telling me, was she telling her doctor? Was the cancer getting worse, or were the chemo drugs the problem? Worst of all, where would she be if I hadn't come back from Alabama right when I had? Sometimes I thought I was the only thing willing her to live.

I've always fallen asleep instantly, and my dreams were a fertile place for solving problems. I hoped to find the answers I needed that night.

3

I was cold and reached for my blanket. There was nothing there.

My tank top and pants weren't there, either.

Neither was my bed.

Now, that was curious.

I opened my eyes as I pressed myself up from the chilly stone. I was completely naked. Except for the locket, which hung against my heart. But it was no longer crusted with age and grime. It was shining and perfect, the brilliant gold glinting in the deep blue stillness of early morning.

I was frantic for a moment, my arms crossed over my chest, my eyes searching the strangely quiet woods around me. The stone slab was in a foggy clearing surrounded by a ghostly ring of birch trees. A few birds began to sing, breaking the silence. But their songs were somehow wrong.

Then I laughed to myself.

I was dreaming, of course.

Just another one of my crazy lucid dreams.

I'd had realistic, colorful, full-sensory dreams my entire life, and I was quite accustomed to this moment. In my dreams, I left behind the self-doubt and worry that had dogged me for the past few years. I was stripped down to the essential Tish—the me I wanted to be. I reveled in the lack of consequences. In my dreams, I was free. And yes, frequently naked.

No big deal. I could do anything I wanted to.

Time to explore the world.

After hopping off the stone, I dusted off my dream-butt. I spun slowly in a circle, looking for a path to follow, some sign of where the dream would lead.

I was startled when I saw him there, leaning against a birch tree. Seconds before, I was sure I was alone, and then he appeared as if by magic.

It was the man from the locket. He had the same insolent, daredevil, knowing smile, the same unruly hair. One tall black boot was kicked up against the tree behind him, and his arms were crossed over his chest, stretching the shoulders of his black tailcoat.

"You're here," he said simply.

"Do I know you?" I asked, which came out more haughtily than I had intended.

"You will," he answered, kicking off the tree and walking toward me. "After all, you're wearing my locket. And I've been waiting for you."

His accent was clipped and British, just as I would have expected.

"I imagined you with more clothes," he said.

"And I imagined that you ended at the collarbone," I said.

He threw back his head and laughed, a laugh so full of fierce joy that it was unsettling. No one laughed like that in the real world. They were too self-conscious of what people would say. I hadn't laughed that way in a long, long time.

"Come along, then, love, and let's get you covered," he said, and he began to unbutton his coat.

"I don't normally talk to strangers," I said, arms crossed.

"And I don't normally escort naked hoydens about the countryside," he said. "But if you stand around here uncovered for too long, something even more dangerous than me is going to find you. Besides, I can't take you home like this. It has to be respectable."

"What has to be respectable? And where do you think you're taking me?" I asked, but he was already shrugging out of his coat and holding it out to me.

"Go on," he said. Then he grinned like a wolf, showing his teeth. "It won't bite."

I wasn't too worried about being naked, but if he wanted me to wear his coat, that was fine. The air was chill and clammy, raising gooseflesh on my arms. I shrugged into the coat, and he buttoned it up to my neck. As he twisted the top button right under my chin, our eyes met, and I had to blush and look down. Too intense, his gaze. He was just a little taller than I, rangy but muscled, as I could see through the open neck of his shirt.

I wasn't used to things tight around my neck, and I struggled to unbutton the top button.

"Mustn't," he said, his glove catching my hand. "That's the most important one."

"Don't tell me what to do." I growled as he swatted my hand again. "What is this—Victorian England? No one buttons anything up to the neck, unless it's snowing," I complained. But I left the button alone.

"Victorian England?" he said. "Never heard of it. But showing your neck is dangerous here. Showing any skin, really. If it were anyone but me, you'd most likely be dead."

He held out his arm, and for lack of options, I took it. His black coat was worn but thick and beautiful, fitted and darted in a way that made me feel curvy and pretty, even with nothing else on. His own shirt fluttered in the breeze, the scarlet waistcoat enhancing the paleness of his skin.

As we began to walk, I breathed in the scent of his coat. It smelled lovely, like berries and wine and something sharp and green. I got a little light-headed, drawing in the aroma.

He was watching me, and he chuckled. "Do you know how a man tames a wolf?" he asked me.

"No," I said.

"You get some clothing you've been wearing for a while, and you toss it in with her. In the cage or the cavern, where she sleeps. That first one, she rips up, shreds it to nothing. The second one, she just mouths it a bit, gets a taste. Inhales, like you're doing there. The third bit of clothing, she starts dragging it around, loving on it, sleeping with it. And then you've got her under your spell. She's got the scent of you, wants to keep it around. She'll follow you anywhere."

"Are you calling me a wolf?" I asked.

"Are you calling me a man?" he said.

"What else would you be?"

He shot me a wicked grin full of pointy teeth. I started and then shook it off.

"I'm not scared," I said. "It's my dream. Nothing can harm me."

"A dream?" he said, one arched eyebrow raised. "You think this is a dream?"

"I know it is," I said coolly.

He grinned. "Sweetheart, you couldn't conjure me if you tried."

We glared at each other then, a battle of wills.

Motion caught my eye, and I looked down to see a small brown rabbit tenderly nosing out from the wood. It hopped and halted, hopped and halted, almost to us.

"Did you dream that?" he said.

"The rabbit? Sure, I suppose I did," I said. "He's a cutie. Probably represents my kindness. Or innocence. Something like that."

The rabbit sniffed my foot, nose twitching, eyes bright. I smiled.

And then it bit me, sinking fangs into my bare ankle.

I shrieked and, without thinking, kicked it. It shrieked, too, tumbling head over fluffy white tail through the air and landing with a thump in the grass. When it finally righted itself, it turned to hiss at me before darting back into the underbrush.

Hmm. That was different.

I looked down. My ankle was bleeding from two puncture wounds. And it hurt. Bad.

"You'll have to watch out for that one now," the man said with another sly grin. "He's got a taste for you."

"Still not scared," I said. "Just a bunny, fangs or not. It's all in my head."

"He's got friends," the man said. "And they'll be back, and they all have fangs. And you're bleeding. If you think you're strong enough to fight off a warren of bludbunnies, I assure you that you're wrong. You'd better come with me. Now."

I wasn't buying it. I needed to take control of the dream. I held out a hand with fingers splayed and focused my will.

"Zzzzzzzssssst! Pshew! Zzzzist!" I said. But nothing happened.

"What in Sang are you doing, love?" he asked.

My arm dropped to my side. "I was trying to shoot lightning bolts out of my fingertips," I said. Then, quietly, "It usually works."

"Told you it wasn't a dream. Do you want to try flying, too?"

Sheepishly, I gave a little hop, but my feet came back down to the ground.

"No," I said, feeling sullen and embarrassed and on the verge of outright panic. Things weren't going at all the way they usually did. He should have exploded in a ball of blue lightning by now.

"If you're done playing around," he said, "we really should get moving before something smells that blood on your ankle."

Again, the glove waited for my hand. I considered.

It was just a dream, whether or not the usual tricks worked. Might as well see where it went. He couldn't be more dangerous than a pack of deranged, bloodthirsty rabbits. I took his arm again, and we began to walk down a strange sort of path formed of two deep ruts in the earth. They were about six feet apart and very straight, cut as if by a machine.

The sky hung too low over a landscape of bleak, endless grasses and small copses and woods. It made me think of *The Hound of the Baskervilles*. The air was hazy, almost smoggy, but that went with my dreams, where things were often obscured or blurry until I was right up on them.

As we walked, something began to form in the sunrise haze ahead, dark shadows standing stark against the pearly lavender clouds.

"That'll be the caravan," the man said conversationally. "*My* caravan."

"Ah," I said, unsure what to say.

The silence between us deepened. He seemed pleased about something, but I was suspicious of his good humor. There was something going on, something obvious that I was missing, that he wasn't telling me. Squinting into the haze, I saw smoke rising from the caravan and tried to puzzle out the shapes.

"Is it a train?" I asked.

"You've never seen a caravan?" he asked. "Oh, love, you slay me. You're like a babe in the woods, trying to pet the bludbunnies."

His accent was growing on me, something close to British but with a touch of pirate growl. Very musical. I wanted him to talk more, even if what he said made no sense.

"Why does half of what you say start with 'blood'?" I asked him.

He didn't answer for a moment, just smiled at the nearing caravan. "I keep forgetting," he said, almost an apology. "You don't know."

"I don't know what?"

"Anything, really," he said with another deep chuckle.

OK, that was just annoying.

"Are you just trying to make me feel like an idiot?" I asked.

"I'm not trying anything," was his response, but it was clear that his mind was elsewhere.

We were close enough now to pick out the individual features of a strange parade of wagons, all attached in a line. The first one looked like a cross between an old-fashioned locomotive, a brass pipe organ, and a chemistry set full of bubbling green liquid and black smoke, and the last one was a little red caboose. The ruts that we were following terminated in the wheels of the caboose, where a capuchin monkey in a red fez sat, looking bored.

I sniffed the air, but all I smelled was smoke. That was when I realized that I didn't see a single creature, except for the monkey on the caboose. No horses or cows or pigs, as I would expect outside a circus, and no accompanying stink. Not even an elephant or a giraffe. *Peculiar.*

"I suppose I should tell you everything," he said. "So you'll know what to expect when you meet everyone. We should be safe, this close to the wagons."

He led me back down the path to a little copse we had just passed. A wide, gnarled tree stump surrounded by leggy little saplings rose from the long grass, and he bowed to me and gestured to the stump.

"Milady," he said.

I looked at the stump and tucked the coat behind me, quite sure that I didn't want to sit my lily-white fundament on a pile of splinters and bloodthirsty ant larvae, even in a dream. Seeing my reticence, he reached into an outside pocket of the coat and pulled out a brilliant crimson handkerchief. And then a yellow. And then an emerald. And then a vivid violet. And then a live dove, which flapped toward the caravan in a flurry of feathers.

I laughed, and he grinned. "Abracadabra," he said quietly. Then he spread the big fabric squares out until they covered the stump.

I sat with a mumbled "Thanks."

As I settled myself, he started pacing, his high boots swishing through the grass.

"Where to begin?" he asked himself.

"The beginning?" I said sweetly.

"Yes, but which one?"

As I waited, a rabbit shyly lolloped out from the grass. I pulled my legs up onto the stump.

"Shoo! Bad rabbit!"

Looking up in irritation from the apparent war in his head, the man picked up the rabbit by the scruff of its neck and twisted its head until it popped. He threw the limp body back into the grass and continued pacing, deep in thought.

I was speechless. I didn't relish another fang bite, but I recoiled from the thoughtless, swift brutality of the action.

"Doesn't matter," he said to me. "It would have eaten the meat off your bones, given the chance. Appearances can be deceiving, you know. Nature is cruel."

Then he stopped and loosened his already-loose collar and looked into my eyes.

"All right. What's your name?" he asked.

"Why does it matter?" I shot back. "I thought we were here so you could give me answers."

"I'm sorry," he said softly. "You still think this is some dream, that the spirits are trying to give you clever little answers to your problems. Don't you?"

"That's usually how it works," I admitted.

"It's not. And I need to know your name. So we can speak as civilized people."

"What's your name, then?"

"My name is Criminy Stain," he said with a bow.

He said his first name so that it rhymed with Jiminy Cricket. It was outlandish, and I almost giggled, but the look in his eyes made it clear that giggling would be a very bad idea.

"Now you know who I am. What's your name, then, love?"

"Tish Everett," I said.

He almost giggled, but the answering glare in my eyes stopped him.

"Tishefferett?" he said. "That's quite strange."

"No," I said. "Tish. Short for Letitia. Letitia Paisley Everett." I enunciated clearly and paused between the words.

"That's a lot of names," he said. "You must be quite important."

"Not really," I said. "First name, middle name, last name."

"I don't see a ring." He tried to say it lightly, but I could tell that he was more than curious.

"No rings," I answered, holding up a hand and remembering the fascinating noise my diamonds had made in the disposal. "Just a locket."

My hand went to the place where the locket rested, heavy, beneath the coat. A slow smile spread across the man's—Criminy's—face.

"Yes. My locket. Let's see it, then."

His gloved fingers shot down the back of the coat's neck and pulled up the heavy chain, bringing the locket out and laying it on top of the fabric.

"It's just as I remember it," he said. "Where did you find it?"

"In an old book at an estate sale," I said.

"How much did it cost you?" he asked.

"Um." I fidgeted. But it was my dream; no point in lying to myself. "I didn't actually pay for it."

"Ha!" he crowed. "I knew it would work. I knew it would find the right one." He was almost giddy.

"I didn't mean to steal it. It was an accident," I said, annoyed. "Back to you, though. What is it that I need to know? What's the deal with the caravan?"

"We're getting there," he said. "It's all part of the story. It started with the locket, you see. I bewitched it and sent it out to find you and mark you as mine. To bring you to me."

He caught my hand in his glove and traced the random gathering of red dots on my skin. Except that they were no longer random, as they had been when I was awake. Now they were aligned into a sort of compass on the palm of my left hand, a central dot with elegant arrows snaking off in four directions, with half marks between them.

"OK, that's really strange," I said. "It looks like a compass now."

"Of course it's a compass," he said. "How else would you find me, with all of Sang to navigate?"

"But I didn't find you, and I don't know where Sang is. You found me, remember?"

There was a cocky gleam in his eyes. I wanted to hate it, but, well, it looked great on him. "If I found you, then why were you sleeping on a blood altar in the nude a mile from my caravan? Exactly when I was out for a walk? Out of the entire world and every moment in time, why were you there at that exact moment?"

"Touché," I said. "But I don't know how I got there. That's where the dream started."

"Wrong," he said. "That's where the dream ended."

But before I could ask what that meant, I heard hoofbeats, and he shoved me to the ground.

4

"What?" I spluttered from an undignified heap by the stump.

He ignored me and sprinkled something over my head while muttering under his breath. I was overtaken with a chill and sat up to draw my legs under the coat, and that's when I noticed that I was mostly see-through.

The hoofbeats were louder now, and two terrifying horses skidded to a stop almost on top of me, their black coats frothy and their eyes wild. I scooted closer to the stump. One giant, metal-covered muzzle plunged into my shoulder with a painful thud, and a plate-sized hoof pawed where I'd just been sitting, barely missing me. The horse couldn't see me, but it could definitely stomp me to death.

"Good day to you, sirs," Criminy said in a respectful but playful voice.

"Stand back, Bludman!" came a muffled shout, and I looked up at a man dressed all in coppery brown leather from the top of his Sherlock Holmes hat to the toes of his high boots. The only exposed skin on his entire body was his face, which was dominated by a waxed black mustache.

Criminy took a step back, hands held up innocently. "Of course, sir," he said. "Can I be of any help to you?"

"You know what we seek."

"My caravan is just over the hill, and our papers are all in order, sir," Criminy answered. Sweeping up the hand-kerchiefs from the stump, he said, "I was just practicing my legerdemain. But I'd be glad to escort you to the head accountant, if you please. We haven't had a biter in over ten years, I'm proud to say, although we had to let the wolfboy go for excessive licking."

"We don't care about your little freak show, Bluddy," the man spat. "We're looking for a Stranger."

"A Stranger? Out here on the moors?" Criminy said in disbelief. "Oh, he wouldn't last long out here, sirs. Blud-bunnies everywhere this morning."

"You know it's a high crime to aid and abet a Stranger, do you not?" said the other man, who was identical to the first save for a pair of wire-rimmed glasses and a spade-shaped goatee.

"Yes, sir, we've got the notices posted, same as every-where," Criminy answered. "Although I've never under-stood why strangers are so threatening." His eyes flicked to me so quickly that I barely saw it, but I could tell that he wanted me to mark what I heard.

"Dangerous," growled the first man. "Enemies of the Kingdom. By order of the Magistrate."

"Yes, but why?" He paused dramatically. "Sir."

The man with the mustache was furious, and his face turned red. His horse jigged in place, digging up divots with its hooves. I crowded back against Criminy's legs. The horse's great black head came down, the bloodred, white-rimmed eye inches from my face. The creature whuffed against the silver cap over its nose and mouth. These men and their mounts had to be more dangerous than anything they sought.

"How dare you question the Magistrate?" the first man said, his voice low and deadly. "By order of the Copper Equilibrium Consortium, I could have you drained."

"But then you'd miss the show, my lord!" Criminy said, and he pulled a bright red playbill from his vest. "Please, won't you accept these deluxe tickets from a humble Bludman who meant no offense?"

"We shouldn't," said the first man gruffly, but the second man reached down to accept the flier.

"I haven't seen a caravan in ten years," he said, longing clear in his voice. "They never come to town anymore. Surely it can't hurt? His question was innocent, I'll wager. And if there are Strangers about, we'd have found them by now. The bludmares are never wrong."

Did he say bloodmares? Did that mean that these nightmare horses were like the bloodthirsty bunnies? Were there actually fangs under their metal muzzles? And, more important, could they smell me? I scooted behind Criminy's legs, as far away from the bludmares as possible. His hand briefly caressed my invisible head.

"Something's strange, Ferling," said the first man. "I can feel it."

He pulled a brass tube from his pocket and pushed a button, and it extended into a spyglass. A softly whirring spyglass with a blinking green light. He scanned the horizon and frowned.

There was a charged silence broken only by the pawing and snorting of the horses. Criminy's grin grew strained as the men had an argument with their eyes.

Finally, the second man said, "I think we can let the

question go, Rodvey. He didn't mean any disrespect, I'm sure. And he's right—I've never seen so many bludbunnies about. A Stranger wouldn't last till breakfast."

The first man, Rodvey, wasn't happy as he glared at Ferling. His waxed mustache trembled with anger as he yanked back on his reins and barked, "Fine! But we keep searching until we find a Stranger or bones. You're lucky, Bluddy. You're awfully lucky."

He turned his horse and galloped away, and the second man gave a little salute and followed him. Criminy watched them go, his face frozen with rage.

"Blasted Coppers," he said. "All the skin in the world doesn't make me half as bloodthirsty as those bastards."

"Can you hear me?" I said from the ground. "Am I still invisible?"

"Sorry, love," he said, waving a hand over me and muttering something.

A warm, melty sensation trickled over me, and then I was visible again.

He reached down a hand to help me up, saying, "Sorry, where were we?"

"But you have to explain that. Those were Coppers? And the Stranger—that's me, right? They're looking for me? How do they know I'm here? And they said their horses were bloodmares? So horses can drink blood, and those guys are looking for me, and you invited them to the carnival? Because that sounds a little insane."

"You're a quick study," he said with approval. He spun me around in an odd little dance step and helped me back onto the stump. "That's all quite true. But we were talking about us. About how you think this is all a dream. That's the important bit."

"The weirder it gets, the more it seems like a dream," I admitted.

"How do you know that it's not the other way around, pet?"

"What—that my other life is the dream, and this is my real life?" I asked.

"Makes as much sense as the contrary," he said, gracefully slipping to the ground and reclining to look up at me.

"Aren't you worried about the bunnies?" I asked.

"Oh, no. They won't bother me," he said.

"Why not? They just like naked women?"

"They like naked anybody. But I'm not to their taste."

Looking down at him in the watery morning sun, I began to notice little details that I'd overlooked on our walk. He seemed to be in his early thirties, but his skin was unusually smooth. His dark, glossy hair didn't have a single strand of gray. And no stubble. He smiled brightly then, showing me his teeth.

They were very pointy.

"What are you?" I asked, my voice low. I wasn't sure I wanted to know.

"What do you think I am?" he asked, still smiling.

"A vampire," I said.

"What's that?" he asked. As if he'd never heard the word and couldn't decide if it was an insult or not.

"How have you never heard of vampires? It's like we're speaking two different languages," I said, bemused to see him finally acting anything less than smug.

"You're smart," he said. "And you heard him call me Bludman. Surely you understand."

"Fine. You're a man. But there's something different about you."

"You're starting to piece it together, love," he said. "This is a different world from yours, which means that there are different rules. Your world must be a soft one. Nearly everything here runs on blood. That's why it's called Sang, I think."

"The world is called Sang, or this country is called Sang?"

"The everything is called Sang. We're now on an island called Sangland, approaching the city of Manchester. There are villages and cities, mayors and Coppers, Pinkies and Bludmen, but the name of it all is Sang."

"Sang," I mused to myself. "In the past tense. I like that. But what's a Pinky?"

"You're a Pinky, darling," he said with a fond smile. "You eat plants and animals and drink water, and your blood is all meaty and hot and fragrant, bringing pink to your cheeks. The cities are full of your kind, of all different colors and sorts. But they all taste about the same."

"You eat people?" I said with an involuntary shiver.

"Eat people? Chew them up, like a cannibal?" He laughed, another crystal-clear sound ringing through the silence. "Never. Just drink of them. And not directly, not anymore. From vials, mostly."

"So that's what a Bludman is?" I asked, pronouncing it as he had, like "blood-mun."

"I am," he said with a bow of the head. "My kind can be born or made, and I'm born."

"Are you dead?" I asked. I had to know.

"Do I look dead?" He chuckled. "Honestly, where did you hear such tales? I'm alive; my body just works differently from yours. I'm a predator, see. And you're the prey."

"What about that rabbit?" I asked. "Are you saying that's a vampire bunny?"

He followed my pointing finger to the offending creature and held out his finger to it. This one was an albino with bright blue eyes, and in my world, it wouldn't have lasted five minutes before a hawk or a fox scooped it up. Here, it was bold as brass. The rabbit sniffed him and hissed, then hopped away in a sulk.

"That was a bludbunny," he said. "And they start out sucking blood, then eating flesh, then cracking bones until they're round as balls. There are no real rabbits left, munching on carrots and flowers. But there are bludrats and bluddeer and bludhogs. Pretty much all of the wild animals are blood drinkers, outside of the old-fashioned predators—wolves and the like. They keep the eating animals, the cattle and chickens and pigs and such, contained inside the cities. To keep them pure. And in one piece."

"Oh," I said. I suddenly felt like a bit of watermelon at a picnic, with untold armies of ants marching in, unstoppable and overwhelming.

"You don't feel safe anymore, do you?" he asked. "Don't worry. Nothing can harm you so long as you're with me."

"But what happens when I leave you?" I asked him. "You can't spend all your time following me around and strangling rabbits."

He laughed and pulled at the grass. "Don't tempt me, woman," he said.

I watched him playing with the long blades of grass, weaving them into patterns as he hummed an unfamiliar song, a waltz.

"What are you doing?" I asked him.

"I'm letting you get used to the idea of me," he said idly. "I'm pretending to be harmless. Is it working?"

"Until you smile," I said weakly, and he smiled again, his face radiant.

"Can't help that, love," he said. "Not around you."

"You sound like a lovesick puppy," I chided. "Or is it a lovesick bludpuppy?"

That garnered a laugh, and I felt as if I'd won a prize.

"Lovesick bludpuppy," he said. "Oh, I like that."

I couldn't look into his eyes anymore, because I could see a sort of adoration in them that made me nervous. I traced whorls on the stump with my finger.

"Just so you know," I said, "I just ended a bad relationship, and I'm not really looking for another."

"You may not be looking for it," he said, "but maybe it's come looking for you."

"In a dream?" I asked. "My brain probably conjured you up because you're the exact opposite of my old fiancé. I may not be taken, but that doesn't mean I'm available. I can't have you looking at me like that. But you seem . . . nice enough."

I didn't really have words for what he seemed.

He chuckled to himself, low in his throat. There was something sinister there, roiling under the surface like eels in a lake, dark and dangerous. But there was something wildly attractive about it, too.

"What?" I said.

"You're buying it," he said. "You may say it's a dream, but you're empathizing, trying to make me feel better. I am no longer a figment of your imagination."

"I'm not buying anything—I'm playing by the rules,"

I said, feeling a bit prickly. "No point in dreaming if you don't dream the dream."

"There's a bit of poetry in that," he said, smiling at the grass in his hands.

Then I felt his full focus on me. I tensed.

"Look into my eyes, Letitia."

"Call me Tish," I said out of habit.

"Never," he said fiercely.

I looked down into his eyes. I couldn't help it, couldn't stop myself.

His eyes were the color of the ocean, a shifting grayish-brownish-greenish, alternately cloudy and clear. They didn't blink. The stare was so intense that a bolt of recognition and understanding shot through me, settling in my belly like a jigger of whiskey, hot and sweet.

My eyes snapped shut.

"I can't feel this way. Whatever magic you're using, stop it."

"My magic won't work on your heart," he said. "Or else I'd have used it already, had you dancing back to my wagon like a marionette on a string."

"That doesn't seem very fair," I said.

"Truer words were never spoken," he said, although I felt that we had agreed on different things.

"My name is Tish Everett. I'm a nurse, and I take care of my grandmother, and I live in an apartment, and I have a cat. This is a dream. Any moment, I'm going to wake up," I said behind closed eyes, my heart beating in my ears.

I needed to be free. I needed time to find myself in the safe little cocoon I'd created in my world. I needed to take care of my grandmother, my responsibilities. I didn't want to feel a pull like this mystifying longing for a dangerous stranger in his bizarre, bloodthirsty world. It scared me.

Until he spoke.

Damn him and his sexy accent.

"Look at it this way, love. If it's a dream, then whatever you do here doesn't count. Dreams are for experiencing things you can't in real life. You can feel, love, kill with impunity. Nothing matters; dreams are your heart's playground," he said, his voice musical and low.

"And if you're in another world entirely, then your grandmother and your cat aren't here. You may never get back. You don't know how to get back, anyway. You might as well do the best you can here, make whatever life you can. You don't want to be alone in Sang, believe me."

He must have sensed my resolve weakening. The smooth voice went on, insinuating itself into my ears and settling in, growing roots.

I wanted so badly to give in.

"Either way, your best bet is to trust me. Come with me. Join me."

His voice dropped so low that I could barely hear it.

"Be my love," he said.

I couldn't tell if it was a question or a command.

"But why?" I asked. "Why you? Why me?"

"Let's just say that we both have our dreams," he answered. "And sometimes, they take a very long time indeed to come true."

The few birds sang in the silence, and I wondered if they, too, craved flesh. The grass rustled. Someone began playing a flute near the caravan, and the eerie trill danced through the air between us.

"It doesn't matter which part is the dream or who is

dreaming whom. My heart is my own, and I'm not looking to share it," I said finally.

I felt as if I was standing on a precipice, and I had to take a stand. I had sworn that no man was going to tell me what to do ever again, even if he was just telling me to love him in return.

"Whatever you think I may eventually feel for you, for right now, you're going to have to back off."

"I don't like following orders," he said quietly.

"Neither do I," I said.

5

The flute song rose and fell between us, breaking the tension into ripples. I watched him shred the little web of grass he had woven. It fluttered away in the breeze.

"It would appear we've reached an impasse," he said.

"So what now?"

He tossed the last bit of grass to the ground and inspected his green-stained gloves, then shook himself like a dog. When he met my eyes again, the charged power of his gaze was gone, replaced by a mask of bright, manic energy. He leaped to his feet and did a strange little jig, then held out his hand with a flourish. A bouquet of flowers appeared there. When I reached to take it, it disappeared, and a little cloud of confetti burst from his sleeve and settled over me.

I clapped slowly and sarcastically but couldn't help grinning at him.

"We go to Criminy's Clockwork Caravan," he said. "We'll find some clothes for you, feed you, introduce you around. The crew's about half Bludmen, half Pinky, so you'll feel at home. And there's a very strict order of things, in the caravan."

He smiled crookedly and held out his arm. "Your blood is safe with us."

I didn't feel safe, neither in body nor in heart. Why was I drawn to this odd, inhuman man? I had felt his tug when I opened the locket, but I had thought it was fancy and romance, the impossible longing for something noble and beautiful from long ago. I thought it was the same sort of harmless yearning I felt for Mr. Darcy. But here, near him, smelling him, I recognized the feeling for what it was. Attraction. And passion. And maybe fear—the exciting kind.

He was right, though. I had nowhere else to go, no one else to turn to. I found myself committing to the world of Sang, whether as a dream or as an alternative dimension. Maybe I had a head injury and was lying on my bathroom floor in a puddle of blood, dreaming strange dreams as Nana left message after frantic message on my voice mail.

That thought made me shiver, and he turned to look at me.

"All right, love? You look as if a goose has walked over your grave."

I tried to play it off as a joke. "You have geese here? Or are they bludgeese?"

"Birds drinking blood?" He chuckled. "Do they have teeth where you come from? Because here, it's just ruddy little beaks. I suppose they could peck you to death, if you held still long enough."

We had reached the caravan again, and I braced myself for further bewilderment. Everything seemed slightly off-kilter, and I was walking into an unfamiliar place full of strangers and people who wanted to drink my blood. Still, nothing moved except for tendrils of smoke on the breeze, and it was eerie. I could see the same monkey in the same fez, sitting perfectly still on the caboose. I was amazed that any animal could sit still that long.

"What's with the monkey?" I asked. "He must be really well trained."

"Well trained? Love, you're a riot," he said, laughing again. I was powerfully drawn to that laugh, and I barely even knew the man. Or inhuman monster. Or apex predator. Whatever he claimed to be.

"Pemberly, wake!" he called.

A flash of green light surged over the monkey's open eyes, and they blinked several times. It leaped into the air and did a little jig on its back legs, its tail forming a perfect question mark.

"Pemberly, come," Criminy called, and the monkey swung down to the ground and ran to his outstretched arm, climbing up to sit on his shoulder, tail curling around his bicep.

The monkey turned to look at me, and I realized that the coppery fur was actually cunningly crafted metal. I could hear a subtle ticking from within, and when the eyes blinked, there was a metallic click.

"Letitia, my dear, this is Pemberly. Pemberly, this is your new mistress," Criminy said. The monkey extended a dainty black paw, and Criminy nodded to me, saying, "Mustn't be rude."

I shook the little hand, which was cold and smooth. The monkey's mouth turned up at the corners in a comical grin, revealing silver teeth.

"She likes you," Criminy said.

"How do you know it's a she?" I said.

"Because when Murdoch built her, I specifically requested a female," he said, as if it was the most natural thing in the world.

"Is she a pet or part of the caravan?" I asked.

"Both, of course," he said. "She's whatever I need her to be."

"Where I come from, we don't have anything like that."

"Well, we're quite lucky to have an excellent builder and mechanic on staff. A Pinky and a hermit but quite talented. He keeps the clockworks running, although we're having a spot of trouble lately with the Bolted Burlesque. The red-head keeps shorting out in the middle of a striptease, and then everyone wants their blood back."

"But . . . why?"

"I expect a patron got too touchy," he said with a shrug. "Happens."

"No, I mean . . . why don't you have real animals? A real burlesque? This is a circus, right?"

He sighed and chucked me under the chin, saying, "I already told you, pet. Almost all of the wild animals are blood drinkers, and no Pinky in her right mind would stand around in her skivvies. Can you imagine what a blood-hungry pachyderm could do to a fragile little body like yours? No one's seen a living monkey in decades. And most of the city dogs and cats have been drained by blud-rats. The clockworks make good enough pets and guards."

"So that's why she was holding so still," I said.

"Guard mode. Can't be too safe, these days. I'll have Murdoch build something lovely for you, don't worry."

I looked up and down the caravan, hunting for the Bolted Burlesque, but no sexbots were cavorting in plain sight. We stood for a few heartbeats in front of the wagons, and I felt as if he was waiting for some sort of reaction from me. I honestly didn't have one. He sighed and held out his hand to sling the monkey to the ground, saying, "Pemberly, guard."

She skittered back onto the caboose and sank down on

her haunches as I had originally seen her, seemingly bored, her wide eyes gazing into the distance. A red light flashed intermittently in the irises.

Beyond the metal monkey, the vast, hazy moors stretched, haunted and sad, to the horizon. I still hadn't seen another person, except for the Coppers. Dream or not, it was unsettling.

"Where is everyone?"

"Oh, they're having breakfast," he said, checking a pocket watch. "Practice won't begin until ten."

"What do they practice?" I asked. "I guess I don't really understand what a caravan is. Or what *this* caravan is."

He let go of my hand and blocked my path.

His lovely, lilting voice rose and took on the tones of an old-fashioned barker, and a cane somehow appeared in one hand, a top hat in the other. He grinned, and his pointed teeth glittered madly.

"This, my lady, is a traveling circus. Death-defying acts, sideshow freaks, games of chance, and mystifying clock-work exhibitions to fool even the most steadfast Copper. Step right up! Test your mettle! See Veruca the amazing Abyssinian, Torno the strong man, and Herr Sigebert the juggling polanda bear!"

The top hat flew up into the air, followed by the cane. In a motion so quick I barely saw it, he snatched a sneaky little rabbit from my feet and threw that into the air, too, juggling the three objects effortlessly, his manic eyes never leaving mine.

Around and around, the hat chased the cane chased the hissing rabbit, in circles, then figure eights. Then the rabbit and the cane disappeared into the hat, which landed delicately on Criminy's head. He wasn't even winded, and his eyes were sparkling. I could tell that he loved performing, loved his art. I clapped in admiration.

He cut a deep bow, and the rabbit fell out of the hat and squatted by his boots, stunned. He stomped on it with a sickening crunch, picked it up by the ears, and lobbed it under the caboose.

"We make magic, you see. We're the last of the gypsies, and we keep the world's treasures safe in jars, masquerading as chicanery."

"You're talking in puzzles," I said.

His energy faded to a thoughtful silence, and he bowed to me. "I do that, when I'm maudlin."

He led me to a shining wagon of deep burgundy. It reminded me of an old-fashioned Pullman car with brass fittings and hand-painted curlicues, but there were no windows.

Criminy Stain, Gypsy King was painted along the side in ornate gold script.

Underneath that, much smaller, it said, *Specializing in all sorts of magic and legerdemain.*

"Impressive," I said.

"Ah, but we're not going in there," he said. "Not until you've got some clothes on. Like I said, respectable."

I rolled my eyes and tucked my arms into the armpits of the coat. It barely covered my important bits in front but overshot my back end by quite a bit. If I didn't raise my arms, I could probably pass for respectable.

We passed several other wagons.

Torno the Strong Man.

Abilene The Bearded Lady.

Eblick the Lizard Boy.

Catarrh and Quincy the Siamese Twins.

I must remember not to make anyone angry, I thought. *These people sound terrifying.*

The next wagon read, *Costuming & Accounts, Carnivalleros Only.*

Underneath that, in tiny letters, it said, *Or else.*

Or else? I took a step back.

"Here we go, love," Criminy said, and I stopped him with a hand on his arm before he could open the door.

"I understand that there might be something here," I said, knowing that he knew what I meant. "And I get that you don't like taking orders. But maybe you should stop calling me 'love' all the time?"

"It's a colloquialism," he said. "Love, bird, pet, poppet, sweeting, although that one really only works for pirates. Terms of endearment, but nothing sneaky-like."

"If you say so," I said, and he raised his eyebrows in feigned innocence as he reached for the handle of the lime-green door. Before he could touch it, it crashed open, banging against the wood.

"Whozat?" screeched a grating female voice from within. "I can hear you out there!"

"It's me, Mrs. Cleavers," he called. "And I've brought a guest."

"Oh, sir, I'm so sorry. I thought it was maybe C and Q trying to sneak a peek again. The twins are randier than a pack of bludbunnies on a full moon. I found them last week up to their chins in petticoats, doing something I won't mention in front of this . . . er . . . lady."

As I entered the dimness within, she came into focus. A small woman wrapped in a violet shawl, with a beaky nose and a ridiculous hat. She reminded me of a baby vulture. She sniffed the air as she blinked at me.

"Ooh, smell her! She smells like—"

"I know what she smells like," he snapped.

"And she needs clothes, sir."

"I know that, too."

"So the spell worked, then?"

"If you value your job and your neck, shut your trap," he growled, and she snorted.

"Hello," I said, timid, and stuck out my hand.

She shrank back, fidgeting with her black, scale-covered hands like bird's claws, muttering, "My gloves, my gloves. Where'd I lay them down?"

I politely averted my eyes. The wagon was crowded with cloth and spangles and lace and ribbons, racks upon racks of clothes and dress dummies in all sizes stuck full of pins and thread. The costumes were stunning and detailed in a way that had fallen out of style in my world. Everything looked deeply uncomfortable.

When Criminy touched my back, I startled and felt blood rush to my cheeks at the light pressure of his hand. I turned to find Mrs. Cleavers staring at me again, a gloved hand held out hopefully. I shook it, and we smiled. Then she erupted into a flurry of activity, buzzing around in trunks and closets.

"Let's see, let's see. What do we need? Petticoats, that's for sure. Corset. Dress and shawl, oh, yes. Look here, dear. What color are your eyes?"

She pulled a chain out from under her jacket and used the attached brass opera glasses to look at my eyes from several feet away.

"Hmm," she muttered. "Murky blue. That won't do at all."

I felt the sudden need to apologize for my eyes, but she

was upside down in another chest, her tiny feet fluttering off the ground in knee-high lace-up boots.

She hooted in what I had to assume was triumph and emerged holding a puddle of deep burgundy fabric.

"That's perfect," Criminy said.

"Step outside, sir, if you please," she chirped. "A lady's got to be respectable."

He obediently went out the door, whistling as it shut behind him.

She focused on me. Her eyes narrowed, and the jovial subservience flashed into all business. "Off with the coat, then," she snapped. "I haven't got all day."

Shyly, I started unbuttoning the coat at the neck, and when my throat was exposed, she gasped. I turned away from her as I undid the buttons and shrugged off the coat, holding it back for her. She draped something over my arm.

"That's your drawers," she said, her voice croaky. "Go fast, now. That's simply too much skin. Saint Crispin, girl! They'll smell you for miles."

Looking down at the frothy black skirts, I was puzzled. If they could make robots, what was so hard about making underwear? I stepped into the petticoats and pulled them up to my waist, tying the drawstring at what seemed like a comfortable tightness.

I held out my hand, and a black satin corset appeared.

"Um," I said. "I've never worn one of these before. Sorry."

I had never told anyone, but I had actually bought one once, on a whim at the mall. It was purple satin with black lace, and it had just caught my eye. When I shyly showed it to Jeff, he demanded that I take it back because it looked, and I quote, "Outlandish."

Well, guess, what, Jeff? I'm in Vampireland, putting on a corset, so screw you.

She slapped it around me and laced it with lightning-fast fingers, very careful not to touch my skin, even with her gloves.

"Hold on to that post," she said.

There was a conveniently placed post nearby, so I wrapped my arms around it, thinking about Scarlett O'Hara. The first yank on the lacing was still shocking, and the tugging didn't stop until I felt as if my lungs were going to explode. Little bars dug into my stomach and pressed against my chest.

"Is this really necessary?" I asked breathlessly.

She blew air out of her nose like a bored horse and lifted her shawl to show a tiny hourglass waist.

"I don't know where you're from," she said, "But in this world, sweetheart, a lady's worth nothing but the size of her waist."

"I hope the food isn't very good, then," I said, and she cackled.

Next came the dress, which had ties and embroidery over every inch. I fumbled around with it but couldn't figure out where my head went. It seemed to have three sleeves. Mrs. Cleavers sighed heavily before snatching it back and holding it out to me with the smallest sleeve—which was actually the neck—open. I ducked through it and pulled it down. It was heavy and thick, and I felt as if I were putting on a twenty-pound wetsuit. The sleeves went all the way to my knuckles and hooked over my thumbs. Along the wrists, another set of laces waited for my costumer's merciless tugging.

She laced and pulled all of the ties. The dress was snug against every inch of my skin until it met my hips, where it flared out and in like a mermaid's tail. A waterfall of ruffles cascaded off my bum. She dragged me to a full-length mirror and tilted it to show my full figure.

I had been transformed into a curvy Victorian bombshell. Or Gothic bombshell, maybe, because even for a garment that covered every inch of skin, there was something decidedly dark and sexy about the thing.

I smiled and ran my hands down my perfectly curved waist.

"Don't get on your high horse yet, child," she chided me, reading my mind. "You've still got hair and makeup to do. And boots. Boots first."

She threw back the top of another chest, and the smell of leather drifted out. I slipped on the pair of gray stockings she handed me, and she started flinging boots to the floor at my feet, urging me to try on pair after pair until I found the ones that fit like a glove. They were calf-high and black with a kicky little heel. Once the boots were laced all the way up and cruelly tightened by my personal costume buzzard, I checked the mirror again and smiled.

Firm hands forced me into a chair. My dark, wavy hair was loose and rumpled, and she began dragging a silver brush through the tangles without mercy. I grunted in pain. She laughed.

A tiny dish of metal pins appeared and were twisted open in her mouth and jabbed into my skull. Against its natural inclination, my wild hair was molded into a proper sort of updo. She nearly singed my nose with a pair of brass tongs as she created little curls with the leftover feathery bits of hair around my face and ears that normally made my life hell.

As the *pièce de résistance*, she produced a long, metal fork with a bunch of black feathers and doodads attached and stabbed it into the glossy pile of hair. I turned my head to admire the effect and saw a polished rabbit skull nestled among peacock feathers and ribbons.

"You look like you've never seen a fascinator," she said.

"What's a fascinator?" I asked.

"Fascinator? I hardly know 'er!" she cried, then laughed until she was wheezing.

I didn't want to laugh, but I couldn't help myself. She'd probably been waiting ten years to use that joke on an idiot like me.

"You Strangers slay me, lass," she said, dabbing at her eyes with a handkerchief.

"So am I done now?" I asked.

"Little bit of paint first," she muttered as she jabbed my tender eyeballs with a sharpened pencil that she moistened with her tongue.

"I don't generally wear much makeup," I said.

"You'll learn."

She lined my eyes and smudged black all around them, then produced a glass jar of white powder.

"That's not lead, is it?" I asked, remembering some choice stories from my high school history class about the ridiculous things women used to do for beauty.

"Lead? Certainly not," she said. "It's chalk and belladonna."

I lurched backward as the brush approached my face.

"Belladonna is poison, too," I said. "I don't want it."

"You'll have it," she said, stepping toward me menacingly.

"I won't."

"You will."

"I refuse."

"I'll tell the master," she warned.

"Fine. Tell him I don't want to die. See what he says."

Her lower lip started trembling, and then she burst out laughing again. These bizarre people and their laughter were starting to get to me. I'd only met two carnivalleros so far, and they had both cackled maniacally within moments of meeting me. Jeff would have hated it, but I was starting to crave it.

Her tiny boots clicked over to the door, and she stuck her head out and hollered, "Master Stain, the lady don't want powder. Says it's poison, and she don't want to die." I could hear his elegant guffaws carrying through the crack in the door.

"If she doesn't want powder, then don't use powder!" he shouted.

"But sir—"

"No buts, Cleavers. It's her choice. She'll stand out no matter what she does. Being unfashionably tawny is the least of her troubles."

When she turned back to glare at me, I smiled smugly.

"Fine," she snapped. "No powder. But you're wearing rouge."

"Fine," I said. "So long as it's not made of battery acid and Drano."

"Don't know what those are." She sniffed. "But you're wearing it, just the same."

This time, she had a delicate little brush and a porcelain pot of bright red paste. I imagined my cheeks painted with big, circular stains like a china doll. But apparently, *rouge* was their word for lipstick, because she carefully painted my lips with the sticky red stuff, which was brighter than blood. No one but movie stars could pull off that color red in my world. I tried to imagine how it would look against the white powder and the burgundy dress and decided that I was doomed to resemble a playing card. Like the Queen of Hearts.

"All done," she said. "And thank goodness. You're tougher to prettify than a spoiled child."

"I'm sorry to cause you trouble," I said, remembering my manners.

I could tell that she was one of those seemingly inconsequential people who actually hold great power. I didn't want to burn a bridge with her. Plus, she reminded me of my grandmother, who acted gruff just to test your mettle and see if you were worth getting to know.

"I don't know the ways here. Thanks for helping me."

I went to hug her, and she drew back with a gasp.

"Things must be very different where you come from," she said with an odd tinge to her voice, and that's when I finally realized that she was the same thing as Criminy, a blood drinker. I don't know why I hadn't made the connection sooner, like, say, when I saw the black claws. Did Criminy have those, too, under his gloves? That would be one more downside of getting involved with him, no matter that I nearly melted every time he smiled at me.

Mrs. Cleavers selected a bottle from a small table and poofed a big spritz of perfume over my head. I could feel the tiny cold drops settle on my face. The scent of red roses enveloped me, and I sneezed.

She inhaled and said, "That's better. But don't try to huggle a Bludman, eh? And here's your shawl."

She offered me a piece of black netting, but I said, "No, thank you."

"Master might let you refuse paint, but all ladies wear a shawl," she said, scandalized.

"I don't," I said.

As I turned to the door in a huff, some part of my hairdo fell, and my arm shot up to catch it before everything came tumbling down. At the same time, Mrs. Cleavers clucked and reached up to fix the offending ringlet, and somehow her beaky nose grazed across my bare hand, skin to skin.

And I felt a jolt, as if I had been struck by lightning.

6

We both reacted as if we'd been electrocuted, jumping back and breathing heavily. When our skin had touched, an image appeared in my head as if part of a forgotten memory, one that made no sense. I saw a tiny golden monkey in a green top hat opening a window under the darkness of night and pouring something into the powder jar with which Mrs. Cleavers had tried to whiten my skin.

As quickly as it came, the image was gone. Not a second had passed, barely a breath.

"Did you see that?" I said.

"I felt it," she said. "You're lucky I've got two hundred years of self-control, birdie."

"No, not that," I said. "Did you see the picture, the thing with the monkey?"

"What monkey?" she said, her eyes suspicious slits.

"I felt this jolt, and I saw this image of a monkey in a hat putting something in your face powder," I said. "Isn't that why you gasped, too?"

"This monkey," she said, "what did it look like?"

"It was a tiny monkey, smaller than Criminy's, and it was wearing a green top hat."

"Elvis." She spat. "I should have known."

She picked up the jar of powder and sniffed it, then held it up to the lamplight.

"No scent, no color," she muttered to herself. Then she pierced me again with her sharp, dark eyes. "You say you saw it? Just now? In a dream?"

I nodded.

"You ever seen such things before?"

"No, nothing like that," I admitted.

She opened the door and called softly, "Master, she's ready for you."

When Criminy walked in, his face was hopeful in a way that I found very endearing, even if I didn't want to. He saw me, and his eyes lit up. I could have sworn I saw shadows dancing against fire there, and he reached for my now significantly smaller waist and lifted me up in a twirl, then attempted to lead me in a little dance step. I hoped the skirts would hide my lack of skill and prayed that my face would hide the thrill that zipped through me when he touched me, even through all that fabric.

"You're a vision, Letitia," he said.

Jeff had always called me Tish, thinking that "Letitia" sounded old-fashioned and silly. But I liked the way it sounded when Criminy said it, feminine and charmingly formal.

"Well done, Cleavers. You've gilded the rose."

She bobbed a curtsy, but her sly eyes never left me.

"Master, did you know she's a glancer?" she said.

"Really?" he asked softly.

He dropped my hand and stared at me. The combined weight of their regard was crushing.

"Did I do something wrong? I don't know what a glancer is."

"What happened?" he asked us both.

"I didn't mean to, sir, but we got tangled up and touched skin," she said, a little sheepish. "I jumped away right quick, so no worries on that count. But she had a glance."

"Fascinating," Criminy said. "Please elucidate, darling."

I repeated the dream to him in as much detail as I could remember, desperately hoping I wasn't as crazy as I felt. He listened, deadly serious, and said, "Bring me the powder."

She put it in his hand, and he opened the top and smelled it. He grabbed his coat from the floor where I had left it and put it on, straightening his collar and shooting his cuffs. He pulled a tiny vial from an inside pocket, untwisted its top, and let one drop of blue liquid fall on the powder. It sizzled, and a curling plume of green smoke rose into the air, making my eyes burn.

"Damn," he said under his breath. "Cyanote."

Mrs. Cleavers gasped and put her hand to her forehead, as if she might faint. From another pocket in his coat, he pulled a black silk handkerchief. Working quickly, he tied little knots to form a bag, then placed the entire jar of powder in it. He waved one hand over it, said an unintelligible word, and snapped, and the entire package disappeared.

He wiped his gloved hands off on his breeches and then turned back to us. Noting my dropped jaw, he said, "What?"

"I'm just impressed," I said. "I mean, the top hat and handkerchiefs and rabbits and juggling are pretty standard with a few years of practice, but that looked like it really disappeared. You're really good."

He laughed again, and Mrs. Cleavers chuckled, too. "Standard? You think that's all it is? A little practice? It takes fifty years of legerdemain to banish that little jar to my writing desk just a few yards away. It'll be another fifty years before I can actually make it disappear. And have you forgotten that I made you disappear this morning, as well?"

"Are you saying that was real magic?" I said. "That's crazy."

"Well, let's see. Are you telling me you just saw the past in a vision? That a monkey in a top hat was trying to murder my chief costumer and head accountant with the most powerful poison in existence using her makeup jar? If so, perhaps I'm not the crazy one here."

I raised my eyebrows at him.

"Well, fine, I am the crazy one, but I think we're a matched pair," he answered. "This glancing of yours is a lovely surprise."

"So when I touched her skin, I saw . . . the past? Am I psychic?"

"That remains to be seen. We'll have to test your powers before we paint your wagon."

"My wagon?"

"Of course, love. We've been needful of a fortune-teller, and you've just saved me quite a bit of trouble in the hiring process. You'd think a true glancer would know when and where to show up for a job interview, but somehow the old bluffers never do."

"You're being awfully presumptuous," I said.

"Fine," he said with a chuckle. "We'll do it your way. Madame Letitia Paisley Everett, I'm pleased to offer you employment as a fortune-teller in my caravan. Payment will be room, board, and two hundred coppers per annum. Would you care to accept, at least until you manage to gain control of interdimensional travel and return to your old world?"

I thought of the bunnies, the horses, the Coppers, the

other, less gentlemanly Bludmen, and the huge, heavy world outside. I didn't have a choice, but I appreciated his recognition that I needed to *feel* as if I had one.

"I graciously accept your offer, Mr. Stain," I said with an awkward curtsy.

"But sir," Mrs. Cleavers broke in, "what about Elvis?"

"We'll have a chat," he said darkly. His mouth quirked up in a cruel, heartless smile that reminded me of a pit full of sharpened stakes. Whatever he was to me, I was glad he was on my side.

"But first, let's find some gloves," he said, putting his smile away like a gunslinger holstering a pistol. "You were both lucky this time, but it shouldn't happen again."

Mrs. Cleavers opened another chest and brought me a pair of dove-gray gloves with pearl buttons. I could feel her holding herself away, trying to stay apart from me. I wondered what scared her more—the thought of touching me and feeling whatever had shocked her or of me touching her and seeing something else, whether the past or the future. I slipped on the gloves and stretched my fingers and shrugged my shoulders. My outfit was confining, and I couldn't get away from feeling claustrophobic. And trapped.

"I've never been so covered up," I said. "Is it always this way?"

"If you're a smart little Pinky, yes," said Criminy. "You'll get used to it."

He led me out the door and down the steps. People had finally started to appear around the wagons, and it was very hard not to stare, because they were very strange people doing very strange things.

Closest to us, a taut rope hung between two posts, and

a bored young woman painted like a marionette was riding a unicycle back and forth. Her costume was made of lurid purple leather with yellow harlequin diamonds, laced at the neck, wrists, and ankles, with a flouncy leather tutu. With all that lacing, she had to be human. A Pinky, like me. Spotting us, she perked up.

"Good day, Master Stain," she called. "Who's the new girl?"

Criminy nodded politely but didn't answer.

Underneath her tightrope stood a young man with a nest of wavy auburn hair, his blouse undone to show a hairless bird chest. A big-nosed puppet drooped around his neck on invisible strings. Several other puppets were strewn over a trunk nearby. The man's gloves were scarlet, and he was so focused on the cyclist above that he didn't even acknowledge us as we passed.

"He's in love with her," Criminy whispered, his breath tickling the curls that hung in the tender spot behind my ear. "He keeps hoping she'll fall and break her neck, so that he can turn her without guilt and be her knight in shining armor."

I didn't know what to say to that. In the vampire stories I'd read, the vampire usually just did whatever he wanted and damn the consequences. There was an odd balance of power at play in this world, if the blood drinker spent his life gazing longingly at a bored girl on a unicycle.

The next car was an aquarium. Behind the thick, wavy glass, floating in crystal-blue water and framed by softly waving water plants, was a mermaid.

I had to look twice to confirm it. Yep, a mermaid, complete with silvery blue tail.

Beautiful blond hair billowed around her head, and she had white clamshells over her breasts. Her eyes were dark with kohl and pinned to Criminy. When we were right in front of her, she swam up to the glass and kissed it with a saucy wink at my escort.

"Sirena," Criminy said. "The mermaid. Bit of a trollop. Tried to teach her magic once, but she didn't get on at all." She was waving madly, so he waved back with a bored smile, saying, "Yes, yes, we see you. Get on with it."

The mermaid scowled at us and did a backflip, slapping the surface of the water with her tail. I shrieked as cold droplets sprinkled over me, and Criminy pulled me a little closer. My heart sped up as he gently dabbed at my face with a bright red handkerchief.

"Missed a drop," he said, voice quiet and husky. "Just there."

His lips barely brushed mine. I wanted to push him away. I should have turned my head and slapped him for taking advantage of me. But I was too busy keeping my knees from buckling and melting into a puddle at his feet. The touch was brief and searing, and it was all I could do to pull back and clear my throat. Criminy didn't apologize. He just grinned.

Sirena smacked the glass with her hand and went to sulk behind a water plant. Before I could ask if she was fake or real or really magic, Criminy steered me to the next wagon and the strong man, Torno. He was almost a giant, with huge muscles and a waxed black mustache with curled tips. He wore a tan leather suit that extended up his neck into the oddest top hat I had ever seen, molded tightly around his ears and chin. I couldn't imagine how uncomfortable and sweaty it had to be inside his costume.

As he did squats, he held a red velvet fainting couch over his head. Seated primly on it was a two-headed boy of fourteen or so. Both heads had scraggly hair the color of nothing and dark eyes that were crafty and sullen. The open collars told me that they were Bludmen, and I watched as each hand lifted a teacup to a different mouth, which slurped and sucked as only a teenager can. When the cups returned to the saucers, the lips were painted with blood. Both heads grinned luridly at me, showing red-stained teeth. I shuddered, and Criminy yanked me forward, saying, "It's rude to stare unless you've paid, pet. They were born that way."

"I wasn't staring at their heads," I said. "I was staring at the bloody teeth."

"You get used to it."

Just then, a strange woman walking past us caught my attention. She was actually swallowing a python head-first as if it were the most normal thing in the world. Her skin was a deep indigo black, and her hair fell in braids to her waist. She wore nothing but a shiny corset, bloomers, and snakeskin boots that came to her knees.

"I can't tell," I whispered to Criminy when she had walked past. "What is she?"

"Veruca Lindenfain, Abyssinian swallower of swords, fire, and snakes," he said. "Abyssinians are human, but their blood is so powerful that nothing will drink it. Not even a bludrat wants to go blind and mad. Makes a pretty penny for us, you know, draws a huge crowd wherever we go. Not a lot of her type around, able to walk both worlds and swallow fire, too."

Next was the lizard boy, stretched out on a log, asleep. He seemed like a perfectly normal teenager who happened to be covered in scales of a sickly pale green. A long forked tongue flapped as he snored.

"He needs sunlight," said Criminy. "So he says. I think he's just a lazy bugger."

The trailer beside the lizard boy was painted purple and pink. I smiled at the two pretty girls whispering on the roof. Even when doing handstands on chairs ten feet off the ground, they just seemed so innocent and girlish and happy.

"Cherie and Demi. The Twisty Sisters," Criminy mused with a fond wave. The girls waved back—while standing on one hand each. "Don't worry—they're both bludded, so even if they fall, they'll be fine. I found Cherie in a London orphanage, and Demi was a Stranger, bleeding on the moor. Now they're as close as real sisters and the finest contortionists I've ever met. I've a bit of luck about me, you know."

"Maybe it's not luck," I said.

"Perhaps," he murmured, but I could tell that he was pleased with himself and took an almost fatherly pride in his strange carnivalleros. There was more magic about Criminy Stain than what he pulled out of his hat.

More and more people emerged from the caravan to practice, but we stopped in front of a lonely light blue wagon that showed a bit of wear. Painted words had been scraped off recently and violently. Criminy removed a ring of skeleton keys from another of the mysterious pockets of his coat, selected one, and worked the door open. It was musty and dark inside, with broken furniture jumbled about. There was a distinct smell of dog. My nose wrinkled.

"Sorry, love," he said. "The wolfboy left it a bit of a mess before he ran off."

He led me inside and pushed a button on the wall. A

series of lamps buzzed into life, bathing the dark room in flickering orange light and revealing old wallpaper with black velvet stripes over shiny silver.

"It's considered a good size," he said, "for someone just cutting her teeth. We'll beat the rugs, wash the linen, fix the furniture. Good as new by bedtime. Will it suit you?"

I walked around, touching things. A dainty chair had been reduced to a pile of kindling, and the stuffing was popping out of a silk couch in parallel rips. It was going to take a lot of work to make it livable, but I wasn't going to mention my doubts about his powers as a magician or a taskmaster. Everyone we'd passed on our walk had bowed or curtsied with deep and somewhat fearful respect. Criminy Stain was a man who made things happen.

"So long as I have a safe place to sleep, I'll be fine," I said. "Please tell me pajamas here don't lace up to the neck."

"The door locks from the inside," he said, pointing out four different types of locks on the front door. "And that's the only entrance. No windows. Made for Pinkies, you see. But we'll get you a clockwork as soon as possible, too, to stand guard."

His eyes traveled over my dress like those of a dog looking in the window of a butcher shop. "You can sleep in whatever you like," he muttered.

I blushed and pretended to inspect a painting in a gilt frame. It showed a herd of elephants trampling a lion.

He cleared his throat. "Now that we're alone, I'd like you to try glancing," he said. "As your employer, I need to know what you can do."

"I don't know how," I admitted. "It was more something that happened to me, not something I did on purpose. I didn't mean to touch her."

"Try," he said, and he took my left hand, the one with the compass stained on the palm. He looked into my eyes as he slowly unbuttoned the three buttons and pulled each finger of my glove to loosen it. I just stood there, mesmerized and breathing faster. With a sly smile that made my legs feel like jelly, he brought the glove to his mouth and gently bit the tip of the middle finger. As he held my wrist in one hand, he slowly removed the glove with his teeth. I have no idea how I managed to remain standing, as it was possibly the sexiest thing that had ever happened to me. And our skin hadn't even touched.

The glove dropped to the floor, and he guided my bare hand to the open neck of his shirt. He closed his eyes just before I touched him, his head falling back.

And then the jolt.

In a second, I saw it, the image filling my mind and threatening to burst out of me. I gasped and fell to my knees. He followed me to the floor and held me by the shoulders as if I was going to fly apart.

"What? What is it? Letitia, are you all right? What did you see?" he said, searching my face as I blinked with wide eyes.

"Nothing," I whispered.

"You're lying," he said.

I was silent. He lifted me back to my unsteady feet, and we stared at each other, another contest of wills.

He raised his eyebrows. I wasn't getting out of this one so easily.

"I can't tell you what I saw," I finally admitted. "I just can't."

I couldn't tell him that I was shaken to the core.

I shrugged away from his grasp and picked my glove up off the floor. I turned my back as I slipped it on and clumsily buttoned it. It was as intimate as dressing after a one-night stand, and I couldn't face him until my hand was safely covered again. But I felt his eyes on my back, exerting his power. Or trying to.

"Why won't you tell me, love? Was it something bad?"

"I can't tell you," I repeated dumbly.

"Whatever it is, if it's important, I need to know," he said. "Was it the Coppers? A fire? Imprisonment? Poison? Draining? Death?" He paused and, with a defiant tilt of his head, asked, "Or did you see something of my past?"

"I can't tell you."

"I'm not accustomed to being exasperated," he said, his voice ragged with feeling. "I don't want to force you to tell me, but I will, if I must."

"You can't force me to do anything," I said. "You won't."

"Tell me."

"No."

"Tell me!"

He spun me back around to face him, and the look on his face was terrifying and more than a little thrilling. Anger and danger and excitement and desire were eloquent in his sharply cut features. No one ever had power over him, and now I did, an insignificant Pinky. A human.

"Look," I said. "Nothing is going to happen to the caravan. It's my problem, not yours."

He put his hands on my shoulders, and I could feel the tension between us through the gloves and the thick brocade, like magnets that couldn't decide whether to repel or attract.

"Your problems are my problems, for as long as you're in this world," he said. "Don't you see? I brought you here. I'm responsible for you. You're mine."

"Excuse me?" I barked. "You don't own me." I tried to jerk away from him, but he held me tightly, his hands as strong as iron wrapped in velvet.

Jeff had called me his responsibility, his baby, his darling. His, his, his. My instinct was to run away from Criminy, too. Still, I sensed that he meant something different when he said, "You're mine." But whatever those words meant in this world, whatever they meant to him, I wouldn't let myself give in.

I tugged away, but he only held tighter, and my heart wasn't in it. The vision had stolen my fire. Part of me was tempted just to melt into him. Sure, I felt what he felt, the energy and heat and inexplicable longing between us. But underneath it, at the very core of me, was a fierce need for freedom. A stubborn rebelliousness.

And I couldn't forget the constant worry about Nana, far away in another place, waiting for me, needing comfort and care that only I could give. I had a life there, in my other world, a life I was just starting to rebuild. This new, confusing vision of my future was just too much. I closed my eyes.

"I'm not yours. I don't even work for you yet. My name is Tish Everett, and I belong to myself."

"No, pet," he said, taking a menacing step closer. "You belong to me."

"I don't."

"Not yet."

He sighed and pulled his top hat from somewhere inside his coat. He beat it against his leg once and twirled it up onto his head. Then he looked at me with eyes full of secrets and grasped both of my hands. Warmth bloomed between the gloves, a whisper of cloth always between us.

"Think what you will, love, but you know what they say of glancers."

"I don't," I said, looking down to avoid his burning gaze.

"They can see everyone's future but their own."

I closed my eyes and shook my head.

He was wrong again, though. Touching him, I had seen what would happen to me.

And I was scared.

7

It was a long, charged moment, him waiting for me to look up, me waiting for him to let go. When the knock came at the door, his hands dropped, and my eyes opened. We stepped away from each other. I crossed my arms over my chest and tried to compose myself. He smoothed his hair and kicked a chair, reducing it to another stack of scrap wood.

"Come in," he said, composed and commanding once again.

"I'm so sorry to interrupt, sir," came a high, twitchy voice. "But you summoned me?"

The head that poked through the door seemed alien, until I realized that the man was wearing leather aviator's goggles that covered his head and neck. His eyes were rendered huge, and he blinked fearfully and hiccupped like a screech owl on speed.

"Thank you, Vil," Criminy said. "Please see to it that this wagon is made habitable for our newest star. By tonight."

The man pulled a worn journal and a brass pen from his flapping leather jacket and licked the tip of the pen, saying, "And what's to be painted on the side, sir?"

"Have it say, 'Lady Letitia, Fortune-Teller,'" Criminy said grandly. "If that suits you, of course."

I snorted. "I'm not much of a lady, and I don't know if I can actually tell fortunes."

"I say you are and you can," he said to me. "And paint it burgundy to match mine, Vil," he added. "With gold lettering."

"Yes, sir, of c-course," the man stuttered before disappearing.

"It seems like an awful lot of trouble," I said softly. "Especially if I can't be what you want me to be. If I leave."

"You're not leaving," he said firmly. "Unless you have an enormous natural talent for magic or you know how to open a door to your world, which is one of many. I don't think that's going to happen. Not for a few hundred years, at least. Best get comfortable, love. You're a gypsy now."

"But . . . Me? A fortune-telling gypsy? It's laughable," I said, staring at my feet and blushing.

He spun me around by my shoulders and whipped a dusty sheet from a full-length mirror. Claws had raked across the surface, leaving four slashes that gouged across the silver and into the ornate frame. The wolfboy must have been furious.

And there we were.

It was a vision, like those phony portraits tourists have made of themselves dressed as knights or Old West whores, except it was real. He stood behind me, his gloves framing my shoulders, and together we were resplendent. Where I was lush and curved, flush with blood and paint and glitter, he was spare and elegant and hard as glass. The fascinator's skull winked from my piled hair, and my face rose from the high, tight neck of the gown like a full moon over a dark landscape.

" 'Laughable' isn't the word I'd use," he said.

"Wow," I said, turning my head back and forth, trying to convince myself that it was real.

"Whatever you are where you came from," he said, "whatever you think you are, here, you're a lady and a glancer and a gypsy. And true glancers are rare."

"What if I see something when I touch them—something I don't want to see?" I asked. "Something horrible."

"If you can help them avert trouble, like you did with Mrs. Cleavers, then you're performing a vital service," he said. "And they'll pay for it. Not everyone in this world is happy and safe. Most aren't, actually. If you can't see anything or if you see something unavoidably wretched, learn to lie well. You'll pick it up quick, and you can practice on the carnivalleros tonight."

"I've never performed," I said. "I get stage fright."

He pulled a pocket watch from his vest and, after checking and winding it, said, "We don't open for another day. With a little practice, you'll do fine."

"What's my alternative?"

"Your alternative?" He said it slowly, letting the word roll out in a deadly warning.

"Yes. If I don't want to live here and put on a goofy turban and read palms?"

"Having second thoughts, love?"

Hands on hips, he considered his boots. I chose the strongest-looking chair and sat, a puff of dust rising around me.

"If you don't want what I offer—what you've already agreed to—you've got two choices. Strike out on your own and be eaten by the woodland creatures, leaving behind an awfully pretty skeleton. Or I can take you to the next city and turn you over to the Coppers while you're alive."

"And that's a bad thing, right?"

"How to explain it?" He sat down on the ruined chaise and leaned over a low, oval table. With one gloved fingertip, he drew a rabbit in the dust. "This world of ours, it runs on blood. There used to be balance, but now there are too many of us. Something changed, and all of the animals turned on one another until every creature running wild had fangs." He drew fangs on the rabbit and then snapped, and there were suddenly dozens of tiny, fanged rabbits in the dust.

He had made dust bunnies. I grinned. But he was serious.

"So the Pinkies took every normal animal they could catch and put them behind high fences, where nothing could turn them. Cities were fortified, with mazes of walls around their precious cattle and hogs and sheep. Now the city folk spend every second with clothing tightly laced around throats and wrists to keep from rousing the Bludmen they can't avoid and high boots to crush the bludrats that they can never quite eradicate."

"That sounds horrible," I said.

"I happen to agree," he said with a wry smile. "But a few hundred years ago, one of the strongest cities elected a group to maintain the balance between blood drinkers and supposed innocents. The Copper Equilibrium Consortium, they called it. Because, of course, blood tastes of copper and is worth money, which is made of copper. So clever. And it spread from city to city until the Coppers took complete power. They make rules. They punish rule breakers. And they make sure that the blood drinkers, whether animals or Bludmen, never gain control. Of anything."

"So the Bludmen in the city—are they like normal people?"

He snorted. "What's normal, love? They run businesses

and accept vials of blood as payment, as we do. But they're tamed, cowed, perverted, as I see it. The Pinkies love it, because blood is, after all, a renewable resource. But any Bludman found drinking directly from a Pinky is immediately destroyed."

I could hear the disgust in his tone. He leaned over and wrote some strange figures in the dust between the bunnies, and when he snapped, a moth popped into existence and fluttered around my head.

"Domesticated, as colorful and benign as parrots," he muttered.

"What about you?"

"What about me?"

"You're not tame?"

"Never," he said fiercely. "I'm a gypsy. A rogue. Wicked as they come. The caravan has a special certificate that allows us to travel as we wish and stop outside of cities and villages. I make my own rules, save one: None of my people can feed on Pinkies. Customers use money or vials of blood to buy their tickets, and in return, they get to rub elbows with monsters and freaks, walk the fine line of danger absent in their gilded cage. We give them excitement; they give us the food we crave."

He chuckled, low and bitter. "Sometimes I think we're just mutual parasites, feeding on each other in an endless, vicious, flawed cycle. There's a little too much magic in this world, maybe. But shows like ours are one of the last reminders of a life free from control."

Funny. The life he was offering me, the one I resisted so strongly, was based on freedom. We both wanted the same thing, yet he didn't seem to understand that love was itself a cage, and I wasn't ready to hear that gilded door snap shut. I reached out a hand, tentative, and barely brushed his arm. He smiled at me and leaned to kiss my glove.

"Don't mind me, love. Getting all philosophical. I've never had someone to talk to before. I'm glad you're here."

I smiled, too. It was a tender moment, a peek behind his mask. And a glimpse at what my life would be like outside of his caravan. Unlike in my world and my time, I had to admit to myself that in Sang, a woman couldn't be both independent and safe, whether she was full of blood or hungry for it. And then my confined stomach grumbled, making him laugh.

"But enough of philosophy," he said. "Let's feed you."

It was noon, and the dining car was crowded with hungry carnivalleros. Little booths lined both sides of the long wagon. At one end, a short buffet served stew, bread, and little crabapples. At the other end sat a small table, covered with a cloth of mauve paisley. A mysteriously smoking black cauldron squatted on the cloth, and I watched as Criminy reached in for a small glass tube of red liquid.

Blood.

"Is that all you eat?" I asked.

"Mostly," he said mysteriously. "Two vials a day, when possible, but I can subsist comfortably on one, as long as it's human. With animals, it takes much more to satisfy. Without any blood, I could last a few weeks if I had to, although I'd be weak and peevish and eventually wither to nothing."

"How do you know it's not diseased?"

"What's *diseased*?" he asked.

"Surely you have diseases here?" I asked, dumbfounded.

"Colds, flu, rickets, measles. Plain old infections. Any sort of sickness?"

"If a person doesn't eat or drink, he gets sick. Is it different, in your world?"

I, a nurse, had landed in a world without viruses or bacteria. Was that even possible?

Carrying my tray, he guided me to a larger, curtained booth in a corner. We slid in, one on either side of the table, and he fiddled with the curtains until we were in a cozy little nook lit by a buzzing orange lamp, the thick velvet muffling the sounds outside. The king's table.

I had forgotten to get a drink and started looking around for something, but Criminy smiled and said, "You'll be wanting wine, won't you? Just a moment, love."

As he left me alone in the private nook, I pondered a world without illness. How was I going to describe modern medicine to a blood drinker living in a world of clockwork machines and magic?

Goblet in hand, he slid back into our booth.

I took a sip of sweet red wine and said, "Where I come from, people get sick with diseases caused by tiny, invisible monsters called viruses and bacteria. But there are no blood drinkers and no magic."

"Invisible monsters but no magic," he said, thoughtful.

He removed the cork from his vial and poured it into his own goblet, swirling it around. The thick red liquid clung to the glass, and he sipped it politely. My gorge rose, and I dropped my eyes to my stew, which smelled divine.

"No magic," I agreed. "But lots of science. We have huge buildings called hospitals where doctors work, and they can do all sorts of surgery and fix people on the brink of death. When a person loses a lot of blood, they can replace it with someone else's donated blood. And you can get sick by sharing diseased blood."

He seemed charmed. "That's fascinating," he said. "A world where people go around giving each other blood, but no one wants to drink it." Then he gazed at me, a soft light in his eyes. "Were you happy, where you came from?"

"I was starting to be," I said, "although there were always challenges. What about you?"

"I was maybe a little sad, before," he said quietly. He reached out to stroke my hand, a gesture so fast and light that I wondered if I had imagined it. "I'm one who always yearns, in any case."

We ate for a while in companionable silence. Or I ate, and he occasionally sipped at his glass, his lips stained bright red.

"You know, in my world, blood drinkers are storybook monsters," I said.

"Really?" he asked, delighted. "That's marvelous!"

"There are stories about blood drinkers called vampires, who are supposedly dead. Some people think they can turn into bats or fly and that they're afraid of crosses and mirrors and garlic."

"So that's what you called me earlier. But that sounds nothing like a Bludman, apart from the drinking blood bit," he said, then grinned slyly. "Of all the things you could accuse me of, being dead is definitely not one of them."

I sputtered a little and changed the subject. "This stew is delicious," I said. "Do you know what's in it?"

"Vegetables, of course," he said. "Potatoes. And bludbunny. They're the easiest things to catch. Cook just takes off a glove and stands around, and they come running. Bop 'em on the head, and dinner's on the table."

My spoon clattered to the table.

"So I'm eating something that might have eaten a person?"

"Well, yes. Not that it matters. Everything eats living things. Bludbunnies mostly eat each other, when they aren't mating to make more bludbunnies, which is what they do most of the time. Blood is good for the constitution, pet," he said.

I should have been more grossed out, but I wasn't. Maybe it was the hunger talking, but the stew was wonderful, fragrant and thick. If I hadn't been wearing a very restrictive corset, I would have gone back for seconds. As it was, I finished chewing a hard, tart apple as he drank the last drops of blood from his glass, and we smiled.

"The wine is lovely, too," I said. "Sweet, like berries."

"It's a special vintage," he said. "A gypsy secret."

I noticed that before he flipped the curtains back, he did that same move where he shook like a wet dog throwing water, and his entire persona changed from the open, curious, tender but dark man I saw in private to the sly, hard-edged, imperial gypsy he appeared to be in public.

"Right," he said wolfishly. "Time to shine."

As he stood in front of the assembled carnivalleros in the grass outside, I was amazed at the change in his figure. He wasn't actually a large man, but he now seemed larger than life, a born showman. He paced for a moment, lithe as a jungle cat, inspecting the crowd, then stopped, facing us, and threw something invisible onto the ground.

Purple smoke enveloped him, and the audience rustled around me where I stood, front and center. But no one gasped. They were carnies. They weren't easy to impress.

When the smoke cleared, he stood on a colorful pedestal in a sequin-spangled coat, high collar, and tight black breeches, the perfect ringmaster. He removed his top hat, revealing Pemberly the clockwork monkey sitting on his head. She doffed her fez, and fireworks erupted from underneath, showering us with streamers and glitter.

The people around me dusted the little bits of paper off their shoulders with a grumble, but as the paper fell to the ground, each piece flickered into a butterfly. The swarm of color rose around us, quivering, and then flickered into the afternoon sky, spelling, "Welcome Lady Letitia, Fortune-Teller."

The crowd laughed and clapped, and the people around me patted me on the back with gloved hands. Mrs. Cleavers gave me a push, propelling me toward Criminy, who gave me a hand up onto the pedestal. I smiled nervously.

"Friends," he said, his voice booming. "Allow me to introduce Lady Letitia, glancer extraordinaire and world traveler."

Technically, I suppose, it was the truth.

My eyes roamed the crowd, trying to take in all the strangeness. Everyone I had met so far was there, smiling in welcome. There were probably thirty of them, all told, and I had many people left to meet. Oddly, I didn't have a bit of stage fright. Standing before them seemed natural, and I struck a pose, hands in the air, and flashed my most brilliant smile.

And then everything went black.

8

My eyelids fluttered, fighting to stay closed. *So hard to wake up. Impossible.*

The world faded to black. An awful, sulfury smell made my eyes water, and then Criminy's concerned face swam up against the blue sky.

"Letitia, love, where are you?"

Then blackness descended again. I heard an annoying song like mad puppets playing the kazoo. I hadn't asked Criminy—were there fairies or gnomes or other magic creatures roaming around Sang? And if so, did any of them play kazoos?

My body shook, and my teeth chattered together. I needed to find the gnomes with the kazoos and smash them.

Something dug into my chest and prickled before I could breathe again. It was a familiar feeling, and I realized that Mr. Surly had just jumped off of his favorite sleeping perch: me. And in the background, still the maddening music kept repeating.

I blinked again.

My cell phone. Nana's special ring.

The familiar outlines of my bedroom materialized from

the darkness. The foot of the bed, the lamp, the overly large numbers on the alarm clock. 2:21 a.m.

Ring, ring.

I rolled over and groped on the night table for my phone.

"Hello?"

"Tish, are you OK, sugar?" came Nana's worried voice.

Why was she worried about me, when she was the one calling at 2:21 in the morning?

"I'm fine, Nana," I mumbled. "What's wrong?"

"I had a nightmare," she said. She sounded as if she was annoyed with herself. "And I woke up with heart palpitations. Do I need to worry about that, do you think?"

"It's pretty normal to wake up from a bad nightmare feeling like your heart is hammering," I said, trying to sound patient and not worried. When someone was as old as Nana and in such poor health, almost anything could be a bad sign. But I never wanted her to know that. I needed to take her mind off her heart, help her relax. "What was the dream about?"

"Oh, sugar, you were lost, somewhere far away," she said. "And you were lying on a road in an old dress, and these big red rats were eating on you. It was the most horrible thing I've ever seen."

A shiver crawled over my skin. I hadn't asked Criminy what color bludrats were, but now I could guess. I had also never asked him if glancing—or other sorts of prognostication—ran in families.

"Well, Nana, I can give you a one-hundred-percent guarantee that I'm safe in my apartment, asleep with my cat," I said. "I'm just fine. And you'll be fine, too. Do you think you'll be able to go back to sleep?"

"If I could only get up," she said peevishly, "I'd go make me a cup of chamomile tea."

"I'll make you one first thing in the morning," I said.

"Won't need it then," she grumbled, but I could already hear the sleep sneaking up on her. I didn't tell her, but I always slipped a little Ambien in with her nightly meds to help her sleep. "Night, night, sugar," she said, her voice fading.

"I love you, Nana," I answered. "Sleep tight."

As I closed my eyes and tossed the phone onto the comforter, I heard myself say, "And don't let the bludrats bite."

"She's coming around," someone said.

I opened my eyes. The glare was blinding, and I put up a hand to shield myself from the sun. I couldn't breathe, and I clutched at my belly. My hand crashed against brocade, the stiff stays of my corset threatening to puncture me as I gasped.

"I forgot to hang up," I said stupidly, trying to swim back into whichever reality seemed easier.

"Letitia, love, are you with us again?"

A shadow loomed over me. It was Criminy Stain, his stark face whiter than usual and his eyes frantic and fierce with concern.

"I think so," I said. "What happened?"

"Give us space," he barked, and the circle of curious faces hovering over me disappeared. "Go back to practice, you lazy lot."

His eyes traveled up and down my body, checking for damage. I wiggled my toes for him before I realized that he couldn't actually see my toes.

He stroked my face with a gloved finger, saying, "You scared me, pet. You fainted and fell."

"That would explain why my arm is bruised," I said, rubbing my elbow.

In hindsight, I think that was when I finally understood that I wasn't dreaming. You don't get bruises in dreams. You don't ache. And you definitely don't sit around talking about where you went when you wake up, afterward.

"We thought you were asleep, but we couldn't wake you," he went on. "You came back for a moment with Mrs. Cleavers's smelling salts, but your eyes rolled back, and you were gone again."

"I think I remember that," I said. "But it's all fuzzy. Something stank."

He smiled tenderly and said, "I've never seen anything like it. But you've cemented your flair for the dramatic. The nosy buggers think you went into a glancing trance and will wake up with tidings of doom." Then he whispered, "Where did you go?"

"Help me stand," I said. "I need air."

He scooped me up as if I weighed nothing and placed me on my feet. I wobbled a bit. We attempted a dignified stroll toward his trailer. He was mostly carrying me, actually.

"No," I said. "Put me down. I need to walk. My feet are all pins and needles."

He set me down and waited for me to stop swaying, then offered his arm. We set off for the open field in the opposite direction of the wagon tracks. My skirt tangled around my legs, and I had to kick it to make a trail through the grass.

When we were well away from the caravan, I said, "I was back home."

"Back in your original world, you mean?" he asked.

"Yes, in my own bed, in my pajamas, with a big fat cat on my chest, waking from a dream at two twenty-one in the morning. As if this was a dream."

"What woke you?"

"My phone was ringing."

"Your what?"

"Phone. It's a machine for communicating. My grandmother thought she was sick. It was hard to open my eyes, though, and it felt like this world was trying to tug me back. I saw you here, for just a second, but then I was there again."

"So the salts worked," he said to himself. "What did you do?"

I laughed. "I did what I had to. Assessed the situation as a professional, made Nana feel better, and promised to make her tea in the morning. And then I was here."

"Curious."

"Yep."

We walked for a while, each lost in thought, a light breeze stirring the ringlets that had fallen from my hairdo when I collapsed. At one point, he stopped to remove his sequined coat, revealing the black one I had worn earlier underneath. With a coy smile, he folded the sequined cloth again and again until it was the size of a handkerchief, and then he stuffed it into one of the inside pockets of the black coat. I grinned, as delighted as a child, knowing that his magic would never seem quotidian to me, no matter how accustomed I became to his strange world.

"So the real question is, why did you go back?" he finally said.

"No, the real question is, how do I get back to stay?"

"Do you think that's possible?" he asked.

"I don't know," I admitted. "Let's just say, for the sake of argument, that both worlds are real. If every time I sleep here, I'm awake there, and every time I sleep there, I'm awake here, I'm going to go crazy. If there are no real dreams, if my brain can't rest, it'll be torture."

I kicked a rabbit that was sniffing at my boot. Tears welled up in my eyes, and I hugged myself and turned away from him.

"It's not so bad, love. We'll find a way," he said gently, moving close to draw me into a hug. With my back against his body and his arms around me, I relaxed a little. Whether it was his smell or just the closeness of another person, I couldn't stop the words from tumbling out, couldn't help unburdening myself of what I was feeling.

"I'm not crying because I'm sad. I'm just so relieved. If it's back and forth, that means I'll still see my grandmother. I was so scared that I would be trapped here forever, and my grandmother would worry about me and mourn me and die alone. But it looks like I get to live both lives, even though it makes no sense and will probably make me completely insane."

"Insanity isn't too bad." He chuckled. "I know plenty of mad people, and they get on fine."

"But there are so many questions," I said, sobbing. "If I die in this world, do I die in that world? What if I go unconscious while driving? What if I'm asleep there, and a patient dies because I'm here?"

"I don't know, pet. But I'll try to find out. I've got some old books I can check," he said. "Perhaps this has happened before."

"There's no magic in my world," I said. "But there's a disease called narcolepsy. People just fall asleep standing up wherever they are for no good reason. Maybe this is where they go. Maybe I'm a narcoleptic."

"One might think it's the best of both worlds, no pun intended," he said carefully.

"But I want a choice," I said.

I jerked away from him and stumbled, and when he tried to steady me, I swatted him away.

"Look, I have commitment issues, OK? I had a fiancé, and he almost destroyed me. He treated me like a child, or a doll. He hit me. I was barely a person. And then I decided to fight back, never to be controlled again. And now here I am, trapped."

He watched my outburst with concern, hands in pockets and mouth drawn down. I kept expecting him to interrupt and tell me how to fix my problems, the way Jeff would have. Instead, he just listened.

"What if I like it here better? Nothing's ever equal. What if I spend all my time there longing for Sang and every moment in Sang feeling guilty for not wanting to go back to Earth? What if I start to care about someone, what if I start to care about you? I could never make the choice to stay here. My grandmother needs me. Without me, she'll quit fighting, just give up and die. It would rip me in half!"

I plunked to the ground, the skirt of my dress billowing out around me like a burgundy mushroom.

"It's not fair." I sniffled. "I can't win."

Dropping to the ground beside me, he said, "I beg to disagree, love. It *is* fair, and you *can* win."

"Excuse me?"

"You're just too used to playing by the rules."

"In my world, if you don't follow the rules, bad things happen," I said.

"In my world, which is now halfway your world, there are ways around everything. Loopholes. Nudging a toe over the line," he said.

"But I can't nudge a toe over from one world to the other. I don't have a choice."

"Well, as I see it, no one gets much of a choice, and everyone is forced to live between worlds, and you've got it a good deal better than most. After all, if you haven't any choice, you must capitulate, and there's a comfort in that."

"That sounds a lot like being trapped."

"Not necessarily," he said. "Take me, for example. I drink blood. But I'm forced to live in a world that perverts my natural nature, reduces me to measured sips from a cold glass instead of deep gulps of hot, pulsing life. You think that's easy for a creature? It's like giving you a sandwich made of one onion and two pieces of parchment. Keeps you alive, barely. But I've found a way to make the best of things, beat them at their own game. I live by my own rules. You can do that, too."

"How's that?"

"You've got a gift here, a rare one. That gives you power and, as long as you travel with me, prestige. You won't want for the things you need, you won't go hungry. That's a lot more than most people can say. And hell, pet, maybe you'll learn to love me. Perhaps not. But what woman in any world wouldn't give her little finger to have the love of one good man?"

"You're a good man?" I asked, eyebrows raised in surprise.

"Depends on the criteria," he said with a grin. He looked down and said more soberly, "But I've been waiting for you for a long time. Whether you believe it nor or not, you'll discover one day that we're two halves of a whole. I just have to keep you close and alive long enough to learn it."

"Let me guess. You think we're going to live happily ever after, like some stupid fairy tale?"

"Why not?" His stare dared me to laugh or, worse, to argue.

"Because the whole thing is ridiculous," I said. I despised the bitterness in my own voice. I sounded so damaged. *Good*. If he thought I was his soul mate for some mysterious reason he wouldn't let on, let him see the worst of me.

"It's not ridiculous to me. Perhaps that's the difference between predators and prey, love. I'll never stop hunting. But I expect that one day, you'll stop running."

"Because I want to die?"

"Because you want to live."

I stared at him, trying to puzzle out the monster from the man. He looked so confident and graceful, even squatting in the grass. His grin mixed darkness with humor, hunger with promise. Something in me yearned toward him, it's true. But what did he see in me? I was confused, stubborn, rude, naive, untrusting. I was straddling two worlds, and it was getting increasingly harder to separate Tish from Letitia. I had just learned to see myself as something other than what Jeff had made me. Caught between Sang and my other life, what sort of person would I become?

What's more, I hadn't told Criminy what I'd seen when my hand touched his skin, the vision of our future, of my ultimate destiny. Of my doom.

I shivered involuntarily, staring into the distance.

In two worlds, I had seen only one future. And for the life of me, I didn't know how to stop it.

9

As the afternoon sun slunk over the moors, we remained in the grass. We were only three feet from each other but acres apart. I'd kicked more bunnies than I could count. The last one had been brazen, hopping over a dazed comrade to nibble my bootlace. I picked it up by the ears and launched it at the pink clouds with a feral howl.

"Isn't there anything in this world that is what it seems?" I said. "Isn't anything simple at all?"

"Not that I've found," he said. "But you must admit it's colorful."

"It may be colorful, but I'd rather it was easy."

"Easy things are worth nothing," he said. "You should know that. Is your other world easy?"

"Most of the time," I had to admit.

"Do you have a trade, or do you live with your grandmother?"

"I'm a nurse," I said, feeling huffy. "I help sick people."

"So you can stop the diseases?" he asked.

"Not really. I mostly help the people who are already dying, trying to make their last days comfortable."

"You help people die," he mused. "That sounds quite sinister, and that's coming from someone who drinks blood."

"It's not like that," I snapped. "I help people to end their lives with dignity, in their own homes, on their own terms. I change dressings, offer them pain relief, that sort of thing. It's a calling, and it's something I'm good at."

"Are they all old?" he asked.

"Mostly," I admitted. "Although I have one patient who's only a few years older than me. Mr. Sterling was in a motorcycle crash on Christmas Day, and he never woke up. He was a concert pianist, so we always keep music playing for him."

As soon as I said the name, Criminy's attention focused on me, his gaze sharpened. "Your Mr. Sterling," he said. "What's his given name?"

"Jason," I said softly. "Jason Casper Sterling." Thinking about him always made me a little sad.

Criminy glared up at the sunset, his mouth pursed and his fingers drumming on his knee. I watched him, wondering if I would ever know what was going on behind those cloudy eyes. Finally, he said, "You must be peckish, my dear. Shall we find supper?"

He stood and held out his hand. I took it without thinking. We walked slowly, side by side, toward the caravan, silent. I felt we had said too much, but I expect he felt we had said too little. Neither of us had yet brought up what would happen that night, when I fell asleep. Would I dream bland dreams about forgotten tests and flying through the air, or would I wake up in my other world and make my grandmother's breakfast and go to work while my body slept here, insensible and inert?

Oh, and there was another thought. A creepy thought. If my body was here, sleeping, while I was living in my own world, I would be utterly vulnerable. Anyone could do anything to my poor body, and from what it seemed, I might not wake up in response.

"You said I'd have a clockwork guard, didn't you?" I asked nervously.

"Murdoch's been working on it all day," he said. "Do you like snakes?"

"I don't know any personally," I said slowly, then, "Wait—my clockwork is a snake?"

"Monkeys are complicated," he said. "It takes more than a day to fit one. They have personality, you know. But a snake is flexible, fast, and good for protection."

"Please tell me it's not some giant boa constrictor," I said.

I eyed an enormous clockwork bear juggling balls as it rode a unicycle. It was shaped like a polar bear but had copper markings around its eyes like a panda bear. Along with all the clockwork animals, Herr Sigebert had emerged from his wagon that afternoon for oiling and polishing. We had already passed a brass giraffe doing a bizarre contortionist dance and a silver and black ostrich that laid, and then ate, a golden egg. The creatures were surprisingly realistic, beautiful, and more than a little eerie, with softly glowing eyes that actually blinked.

"No, your clockwork will be something small. Wouldn't be useful if it was ungainly."

"That doesn't sound too horrible," I said.

"You're worried about your body, aren't you? While you're away," he said quietly.

"Anything could happen to me," I said. "And I might never know."

"But it won't. I'll be there tonight. I'll guard you myself. Until we know more about how it works."

"I don't want to seem ungrateful . . ." I began, and I trailed my hand along a royal blue car with a brighter, greener version of the lizard boy painted on it. I didn't really have the words to continue.

"But you're worried about locking your unconscious body in a wagon with a known killer and probable lecher?"

"That's one way to put it."

"Is there someone else you'd prefer?" His tone was guarded, but I could hear the dare behind his words.

"No," I said, opting for honesty. "For some strange reason, I trust you."

"Smart lass," he said.

We'd reached the dining car by then, and he held the door open for me. I stepped up and in, and he followed and took my arm. But instead of leading me to the buffet, he escorted me to a man sitting alone in a booth. He was handsome, that man, staring out the window, lost in thought, fingers tapping on the table, his long hair cascading down his back in light brown waves. His poet's blouse was open at the neck, the sleeves pushed up to bare elbows. Instead of breeches, he wore trousers cut off at the calf. He was barefoot, and after one day in Sang, I was a little scandalized. He had to be a Bludman, and a cheeky one at that.

"Letitia, my love," Criminy said affably, "this is Casper, our harpsichordist."

The man blinked away his daydreams and turned with a slightly annoyed smile, saying, "Nice to meet you—"

"You!" I cried, cutting him off mid-sentence.

I'd never seen the sapphire-blue eyes blinking at me from their delicate fringe of auburn lashes. But I knew the mouth, the raven tattoo on his forearm, and especially the long, agile fingers constantly tapping out phantom notes on the booth's table. I'd cut those fingernails back for months.

"Have we met before?" he asked, polite but confused.

"No," I said. "I just . . ." I looked to Criminy, who was irritatingly amused. I was amazed, flummoxed, and more than a little vexed that he had sprung this chance meeting on me. "Does he know?" I asked him.

"Do I know what?" Casper said, starting to get irritated, too.

"That you're a Stranger," Criminy said matter-of-factly with a charming smile.

Casper shrugged. "Everyone in the caravan knows."

"She's one, too," Criminy said. "And she knows you."

With a pat on my arm, he smugly strolled down the dining car and slid into a booth next to a nervous and twitching Vil. Probably getting an update on the trailer he was going to lock me into later, the sly bastard. I could feel his eyes on my back from all the way across the wagon.

"I don't understand," Casper said, gesturing to the empty seat across the table. I slid in. With Criminy out of hearing range, the man before me seemed to open up and relax. And smolder. "You're from America? Because I don't think I know you. I'm sure I would have remembered." He searched my face, and I searched his, too. His face was . . . very searchable.

It was amazing, the difference between a pale, wasting, inert body and a living, breathing man. The Mr. Sterling I knew had a shaved head and scrawny arms and drooled. But the Casper before me was tanned and gorgeous, like a poetic version of Robinson Crusoe. And I couldn't believe how many sponge baths I'd given him, without him even knowing it. I caught my eyes wandering down his open shirt and snapped my gaze back up to his face. I had to tell him something unpleasant, but I didn't want him to stop smiling that gorgeous, movie-star smile.

"There's no good way to say this, but I'm your nurse in our world. You had a motorcycle accident six months ago, and now you're brain-dead. I'm so sorry."

"Brain-dead," he said to himself. "Figures. My mom told me that bike would kill me."

"What happened?" I asked. I had to know.

"I don't remember. I just showed up here on the ground one day, naked. After the first rabbit bit me, I kept a big branch with me. Killed a deer with it, too. And then I came across a body without a drop of blood on it or in it. I put on his clothes and wandered around until I found the caravan. When Master Stain heard my story and saw me play the harpsichord, he offered me a wagon and a job."

"Do you like it here?"

"Are you kidding?" he asked with a laugh. "It's a dream come true. I'm a concert pianist, and these people have never heard of Beethoven or Mozart. They think I'm a god!"

I had to giggle at that. He was gorgeous and charming in a gentle, bluff sort of way—the complete opposite of Criminy's dangerous allure. I liked him immediately and felt at home in his presence, as if we'd known each other forever. I leaned closer.

"So what's your story?" He smiled, showing dimples. Was he actually flirting with me? I was suddenly self-conscious and had to resist the urge to fiddle with my hair.

I told him my own story, from locket to fainting. But I

left out the part about how I was supposed to be Criminy's magic mail-order bride.

"Are you really stuck here?" Casper asked anxiously. I got the feeling he wanted me to say yes.

"Indeed, pet. Are you stuck?" Criminy asked, appearing suddenly at my side and sweeping me out of the booth.

"What choice do I have?" I called over my shoulder as Criminy's arm snaked around my waist and whisked me away to a steaming basket of what looked and smelled like fried chicken but was probably extra-crispy bludbunny.

I was more than a little distracted and kept stealing glances at Casper. He leaned back in his booth, smiling at me with dimples as he flipped a coin back and forth over his knuckles. After I fumbled my fork to the floor, Criminy sighed and took over, filling my plate and guiding me to our private booth. He lashed the curtains closed more forcefully than necessary.

"Lad was acting a bit familiar," he said, swirling the blood in his goblet with narrowed eyes. "He doesn't speak to anyone much. I think I preferred him when he was sulky."

"I know him," I said, still amazed. "I've taken care of his body for months. And he's been here all along—his mind has, at least. What a strange coincidence."

"I don't actually think it's a coincidence, love," Criminy said. "I take in whatever Strangers I find, if I can use them. I like to confound the Coppers, and misfits go well with misfits. He found us quite near here, so perhaps locations in your world coordinate somehow with locations in Sang."

"So you took him in just because he was a Stranger?" I asked.

"And because of his songs. Starting to regret it a bit."

"And did you turn him, too?"

"Me? Turn him? Hell, no." He laughed, one sharp note. "That's not a Bludman. Whatever made you think he was one of us?"

"The way he's dressed," I said, feeling confused and silly.

"Ah, that," he said thoughtfully. "Now, that's a different story altogether. He's a clever boots, that one. You'll have to ask him one day."

By the time we finished dinner, Casper was already gone. For Criminy's sake, I tried to conceal my disappointment. We stepped into the twilight with calls of farewell from the carnivalleros, and I admired the stars as we strolled through the misty night. The constellations were very strange, and, just like the clouds, they seemed impossibly close. The moon hung like a broken dinner plate caught in the branches of a far-off tree.

We stopped in front of a burgundy wagon so shiny with moonlight that I could see myself reflected in the still-wet paint. It didn't look like the shoddy car of the ex-wolfboy, and my name wasn't painted on the side yet, but I knew it was mine.

"Ladies first," Criminy said with a bow.

I opened the door, careful to touch only the knob.

It was lovely inside, freshly scrubbed and smelling of roses instead of old dog. A new carpet on the floor and some scratchless furnishings had turned the little wagon into a cheerful space. Criminy gestured to an open door at the end, and I found a small bedroom with an ironwork bed covered with a patchwork quilt of shimmering silks.

"It was the best we could do on short notice," he said with his crooked smile.

I opened the door of an armoire crammed in beside the bed. Two more dresses hung there, and drawers held gloves and stockings. And, to my horror, a turban.

I held the offending item out to him on one finger, a mauve jumble of layers with a big paste jewel on the front. I raised an eyebrow.

"Costumes," he said with a shrug. "You get used to them."

I tossed it back into the drawer and slammed it shut.

"So what happens while I'm asleep?" I asked.

"I'll be in the other room with my books and grimoires, trying to puzzle out your peculiar condition. I don't need much sleep."

"Lucky you," I said, my gloved hand trailing over the bed. I realized how inviting the gesture might appear and jerked my hand back. He snickered, a surprisingly dark and intriguing sound that made me forget all about the handsome shipwrecked harpsichordist from my world.

"Will it suit you?" he asked me. I took a moment to answer, part of me enjoying his anxiety.

"I think so," I said. "But I don't have much to compare it to."

"It's better than any city, I promise you," he said with a sneer. "Flats jammed together, everyone cheek to jowl. The air is putrid. The streets are filthy. No matter what you do, the muck gets into your pores, under your skin. Inside, it's very opulent and colorful and shiny, to make up for the darkness outside."

"Have you spent much time in a city?"

"I was born in one. Devlin, across the sea from here. I ran away when I was nine and never went back." He paused for a moment with an odd, faraway look. "It's funny. I've traveled with this caravan for decades, but no one's ever asked me where I came from."

"I think they're scared of you," I said.

"And well they should be."

"I don't think you're as vicious as you think you are," I told him.

"I don't think you've seen me on a bad day," he answered. "I have to keep up the show, terrify them, keep them in line. It's a razor's edge, to run a band of misfits, monsters, beggars, and thieves."

"Why do you do it, then?"

"Because I love it. Because it's what I am. And they're not so bad. It's you who's different. You were supposed to be my solace, my heart's ease. Maybe that's why I'm telling you so much. I probably shouldn't."

"I don't understand why I'm supposed to be anything," I said, feeling touched but also weary of his assumptions. "You said you brought me here. Tell me why."

"It's a long story, pet. Why don't you get undressed and into bed, and I'll tell you while you fall asleep? Maybe I can bore you to dreamland."

Grinning, he slipped out the door and closed it, and I heard his footsteps creaking across the wagon. I hunted through the armoire until I found a long white nightdress. Then I realized that I couldn't get undressed by myself. But I'd get as far as I could.

I unlaced the neck first, and it felt wonderful. Then the wrists. Then I was able to tug the various laces loose enough to wiggle the dress over my head. Twisting and turning to untie the corset, I caught myself in the mirror in heavy makeup, black corset, black petticoats, and black boots. I looked like the cancan dancer of the damned. But no matter how hard I tried, I couldn't get the corset loose enough to wriggle out.

How inconvenient.

"Criminy, I need help," I said softly at the door.

His voice came from the other side, saying, "Name it."

"I can't get the damned corset undone," I said. "Can you yank out the laces? Or can you be that close to so much skin? Maybe your monkey could help?"

Whoa. That didn't sound good at all. I felt my cheeks go scarlet and turned my back to the door.

I heard him slip into the room behind me. "Have you forgotten that I found you completely unclothed this morning and managed to get you here in one piece? I told you, pet. You're different. For me."

Without another word, he began pulling at the corset more roughly than I would have preferred. I concentrated on not falling over, and as I felt it loosen, I put up a hand to my chest to hold it there when he was done.

I could hear Criminy breathing, feel his eyes on my bare back. Nana's bathing suit revealed more skin than what he was seeing. But I couldn't forget that it had been three years since any man except Jeff had seen me naked. Well, if you forgot about that morning.

In a world where people were forced to cover everything, I'm guessing a bit of back was considered the height of risqué. I was still trying to regrow my self-confidence, after Jeff's constant complaining that I was ten pounds overweight. But his ragged breath in the small space told me that Criminy Stain had no complaints whatsoever about my body.

"Thank you," I said. "Um, you can go now."

"I'll go when I'm ready," he breathed, his voice low.

I spun around, clutching the corset over my chest. I took a step toward him, trying to shoo him toward the door. He didn't budge. He looked hungry. I took a step back. Then another. His hands were in fists. He licked his lips. If there was a gentleman in there, I was losing him.

"Not this way, Criminy," I whispered. "Please."

His eyes squeezed shut, and he shook himself, then stepped out the door and shut it. I didn't realize until that moment that I was scared. And excited. But I wouldn't admit anything more than that, even to myself.

As quickly as I could, I shrugged into the nightgown, dropping neither corset nor petticoats until I was covered. Still, I felt exposed and vulnerable, and I undid my boots as quickly as possible and sought the protection of the bed's covers. It was chillier in Sang than I was accustomed to.

Part of me didn't trust him, didn't want to let him into the room. The other part knew that there were worse things than Criminy Stain in the world and that he was better protection than two wooden doors and four locks.

"You can come in now," I called, and the door opened just enough to show me his face, which was carefully blank. Reserved.

"Well, you look cozy," he said politely. "Are you ready for a bedtime story?"

"I think so," I said. I felt very much like a child, small and fragile, with the nightgown's bow tied innocently under my neck. "Am I going to like it?"

"Probably not," he said with a shrug. "Doesn't change anything."

"Where does it start?"

He sat on the edge of the bed. "A long time ago, I had my heart broken by a Bludwoman in the caravan. Her name was Merissa, and she did tricks on the backs of a pair of white bludmares. She was a wicked lass, and she used me and left me for a necromancer. I was just a simple magician then, nothing more, and I was distraught. The caravan was parked near a heavy wood, and I ran away to find solace in the wilderness."

His eyes were far away, and I reached out a hand to him. He picked it up absentmindedly and held it in his glove, not noticing that the skin was bare.

"One morning, I woke up to the sound of screaming, and I found a man, naked, being attacked by a bludstag. I chased it off, of course, and nearly made a meal out of him myself, but I was too curious. He had the most peculiar haircut. We got to talking, and he told me that he was under the care of a sort of chirurgeon in his world, and they put him to sleep, and then he found himself here, in Sang. I was fascinated. I had heard of Strangers before, but I thought it was just a trick by the Coppers, an excuse to drag in anyone suspicious."

"When was this?"

"Oh, maybe fifty years ago. Strangers were more rare then. He started to tell me about his world, but then he vanished mid-sentence. I always supposed they woke him back up. Is that normal?"

"Yes, surgeons put people to sleep and wake them back up every day at the hospital. I wonder how many of them end up here for a little while. And do they never remember it or just assume it was a dream?"

And then I had to wonder about all the people who died mysteriously during surgery, their pulses dropping for no good reason. Had they found their own bludstags on the lonely moors of Sang?

"Anyway, I had no idea what had happened. But I was very curious, so I went about making inquiries, doing research. I finally found a witch who wanted to be a Bludwoman, and we made an exchange. I gave her what she wanted, and she gave me a spell called the Drawing. I won't bore you with all the details, but I enchanted the locket and sent it away to find you in whatever world you waited."

"Me?"

"Part of the spell involved describing exactly what I wanted, but a measure of mystery is involved, too. The Drawing is supposed to draw the other half of your soul, wherever it is. But it's tricky. You could have arrived at any time and in any place. I've been looking for you for a long time, you see."

"How do you know it's me? That there's not some other Stranger out there, working her way toward you?" I asked. "What if I was meant for . . . someone else?"

"That's not possible," he said darkly, and I knew that he knew what I was thinking. He sneered at the door, showing fangs. We could both hear the delicate strains of a harpsichord coming from outside. Only I knew it was a nocturne by Debussy, the notes filled with longing, a lullaby just for me.

"But what if—"

"Don't be ridiculous," he said. "Look into my eyes again."

I didn't want to, because I knew what would happen. But I did anyway.

His eyes gave me the same feeling I got on roller coasters, going down the first hill. As if my stomach was being turned inside out but in a good way. Even though I knew he was of a different species, unabashedly wicked, and apparently much older than he looked, I couldn't help but feel the tug.

"Like a magnet," he said.

"Something like that," I had to admit. "But are you saying you brought me here with magic because you were scorned?"

"Not exactly. She just made me realize that what I thought I wanted wasn't necessarily what I needed. I didn't want to spend the rest of my life chasing shadows, waiting for someone to love."

"Why, Criminy Stain," I said. "You're a romantic."

"Oh, no," he said with a grin. "I'm fiendish and unscrupulous, a vicious killer and a thief and a bloodthirsty monster. And maybe a little romantic. But don't tell anyone, or my reputation's shot."

"But what about me?" I said. "Does it bother you that you've reached through to another dimension and pulled out a broken woman just trying to get her life back? I was weak for so long I barely even know who I am anymore. I feel so dull compared to you. I don't understand what you see in me."

"I see you in you," he said, tracing my face. "And as we've already learned, whatever you are in your world, you're something else entirely here. Now, if I can just get you to give up this other life of yours and love me, I'll be a very contented creature."

"You ask a lot," I said, troubled.

"I'm not used to disappointment."

He smiled warmly, gently, and leaned over to kiss my forehead.

"But it's time for you to sleep, love," he said. "And we'll see how you feel when you wake up."

10

I rolled over and snuggled into the down pillow. Criminy turned off the light and left the room, and I heard him rustling around in the other half of the wagon. The dark pressed down on me, as oppressive as the morning sky of Sang, and before I could even think about his confession or daydream about Casper, I was asleep.

An alarm was going off somewhere far away. The insistent bleating was infuriating, and I had a vision of a bludbunny with large red numbers on its side, hopping around and beeping, trying to lure me closer so it could bite me. I wanted to find it and toss it tail over teakettle into the field until the beeping went away.

"Shut up, you stupid rabbit," I muttered.

Then something brushed my face, and I was sure the numerical bludbunny was purring. I opened my eyes and saw Mr. Surly's blue eyes only inches away. The color was eerily similar to that of Casper's eyes, and I smiled. Dream or not, I had to admit that there were two ridiculously cute guys in Sang.

Back to reality. I got out of bed to turn off the alarm and scratch my ankle, which itched like crazy. Right where the bludbunny had nipped me, there were two puffy pink bug bites. Was it evidence that Sang was real, or did Mr. Surly have fleas?

I guess I would finally know for certain the next time I went to sleep. The alarm clock, which wasn't actually a bunny, said 7:32, so I had a little more than twelve hours before I would find out the truth. I was definitely going to bed early. I hated to admit it, but it was going to be a really long day, just waiting to go to sleep again.

All I could think about was Sang. And Criminy. And Casper.

I couldn't wait to visit him on my nursing rounds. Sure, his body in my world was wasted away, the mind empty. But I could look around his house with new eyes, learn more about him. When I thought of his piano and his nimble fingers stroking up and down the keyboard, I had some very unprofessional thoughts.

While I showered and got ready for work, I thought about the way I looked in the mirror after Mrs. Cleavers's ministrations, with the paint and the hair and the heavy layers of clothing. Only the locket remained, and it no longer shone. But I could open it whenever I wanted and study Criminy's face and think of his scent, red wine and vines. I sniffed my usual perfume, but it seemed rank and fake, so I didn't wear it.

While I dressed, I felt exposed in my T-shirt and scrubs. I was amazed to realize that I missed my corset, which molded my least favorite body part into a pleasing shape. I felt downright frumpy, actually.

As I stared at a cabinet full of cereal trying to decide between Wheaty-O's and Oatey-Squares, I got stuck. What was the difference? It was all packaged crap, none of it real. My life felt idle, easy, bland, safe, a neutral-colored apartment crying to be beautiful and interesting. And that brought to mind the estate sale where I had found the necklace. I had to go back to Mrs. Stein's house and see what was in that bloodred book.

When I showed up at 8:30, Nana was her usual sprightly self, her early-morning nightmare and subsequent phone call forgotten. I didn't bring it up. I always took good care of her, but today I took super-extra-great care of her, making sure that she was in the best health possible.

"Sugar, you seem sweeter than usual. Is there something you're not telling me?" she asked in her most innocent Southern-belle voice.

"No, Nana," I said just as sweetly. "Just doing my job for the grandma I love." And I planned on giving her an extra half an Ambien that night, hoping to keep those nightmares away.

When she was all squared away for the day, I backtracked to the estate sale. No signs, no cars in the driveway, no lights on in the house. The sale was clearly over. But I had to get that book and see if it had the answers to my double life in Sang.

I tiptoed up to the house and peeked through the window beside the front door. Lots of the stuff inside was gone. The table where people had paid for their purchases was still there, but the cash box and notebook were missing. I wondered what happened to all the things that hadn't been sold, if they had been trashed or given to Mrs. Stein's greedy kids or sold to the junk man. Surely no one would miss a grungy old book, if it was still there.

Wait, I thought. *You already stole one necklace. Now you're trying to justify breaking into the house and stealing the book. What are you becoming?*

I'm not a thief, I told myself sternly in answer.

You already are *a thief. What's one more thing that no one wants?*

Stop talking to yourself, I thought, trying to shake the voices out of my head.

I walked around the side of the house, hoping to look inconspicuous. When I glanced up and down the street, I couldn't see a single neighbor. Mrs. Stein's neighborhood was always quiet. I felt as if I was alone in a huge world. And I felt as if the house was waiting for me.

Unfortunately, I had already turned in my key. I ran around back and tried the door, which had an old-fashioned keyhole. I jiggled the knob, but the lock held. Beneath the old welcome mat, I found a key. I couldn't believe that a suspicious old biddy like Mrs. Stein had actually kept a key in such an obvious place.

The house was silent, except for the boards creaking under my nursing clogs and my heart pounding in my ears.

I ran past her closed bedroom door and up the stairs, checking every window I passed for movement outside. I could feel the adrenaline pumping through my body, and I could hear every gasp of dust and tiny groan in the ancient house. As I pounded up the dark, rickety stairs to the attic, I realized that I would be cornered up there if anyone showed up. And I'd never been a very good liar.

The bright red book was easy to spot. I didn't even stop to open it, just ran back down the stairs and out the back door, twisting the lock and slamming it shut. Once I was standing in the grass, I allowed myself to breathe again.

Just then, I heard tires crunching on gravel, and I tossed the book behind some big hydrangea bushes fighting for space against the back of the house. I walked around the corner, pretending to inspect the grass.

"Excuse me, young lady," came an annoyed Southern drawl. "Can I help you?" She was built like a ship, in a lavender power suit and black hose. Judging by her makeup, she spent her days lawyering and her weekends pushing Avon.

"Oh, I hope so," I said, my voice steadier than I expected. "I was at the estate sale yesterday, and I think I dropped my wallet outside."

"No one turned in a wallet," she said, her shifty little eyes roving over me suspiciously. "Can you describe it?"

"Sure. It's light blue with flowers and a zipper."

My wallet was actually tan leather. I didn't even know why I lied to her, where the mental image of the nonexistent wallet had come from. It came to me so easily. The lies were just blooming, one after the other.

"Did you buy anything with your credit card? I might have the records," she said with a cloying sweetness that told me I was being hustled. "What's your name, sugar?"

"Valerie Taylor," I said. "But I didn't actually buy anything."

She flipped through her pink leather notebook anyway, muttering "Valerie Taylor, Valerie Taylor" under her breath. As if it might actually be there somewhere.

"No, no record of anything. Sorry I couldn't help you. Perhaps you should take this matter to the police?" She held out her arm toward our cars and put on her best hostess smile. I didn't budge.

"I'd like to keep hunting around the grass, if you don't mind," I said. "I'm sure it's out here somewhere."

"I'm not sure if that's appropriate. Private property and all."

"Oh, I'm sorry," I said with a warm smile. "But I promise not to bother anyone. The house is empty, right?"

She spluttered and turned red right down to the pearls looped around her neck. "Yes, well, um, but yes, well, you see . . . property rights and all . . . transition of owner-ship . . . deeds . . ."

"Great. Don't let me get in your way. I'm just going to be poking around in the bushes. Thanks so much for your help, ma'am."

I turned my back on her. She turned to the door, still blustering, and opened it with her own key. She had to turn sideways to get through the narrow door, and the second she disappeared, I dove for the book and dropped it into the waistband of my scrubs. I poked around in the bushes for a minute before calmly walking back to my car and driving away with Mrs. Stein's spare key still in my pocket.

That was so easy, I thought. I put my hand on the book and grinned from ear to ear.

But then my brief high of smugness was replaced with horror.

I was a thief now, and a liar, too.

Lying had been so . . . natural. And so completely not like me. The normal Tish would have been terrified of the pushy old battle-ax and run back to her car, and she would have worried for the rest of the day, expecting trouble.

Letitia, on the other hand, was a born actress.

It bothered me the whole drive to Mr. Rathbin's house. I was early, so I parked my car in a shady spot down the street and picked up the book. It was very old but in good repair, with gold-edged pages and a bloodred leather cover shiny from years of handling. There was no title on the spine, and a gold compass rose surrounded by vines was embossed on the front, just like on the locket.

I opened it to a random page, and saw . . . nothing.

The book was empty. Just hundreds of age-stained pages with nothing on them.

I flipped to the inside of the front cover. There was a long list of names written in faded ink the color of dried blood. Which it probably was, actually. Names and dates and notations. Every few entries, the handwriting changed, although all of the letters were cramped and ornate, with lots of flourishes.

The first entry read *Vetivern Stain m. Isly Tatters, 1281*. Next came *Crumm Stain, b. 1283*. Births, marriages, and deaths, all down the line. Strange names, all seeming one-offs from anything in my world. And they lived a lot longer than anyone in my world, too. Jerebiah Stain had apparently lasted 343 years before *d. by draining*.

Eek.

But the last entry caught my attention. *Criminy Stain, b. 1793.*

His parents' names were just above it, *Angero Stain m. Frey Pallor, 1793*.

Same year. Interesting.

I reached out to touch the old words, and the moment my hand connected with the page, I felt the familiar electric jolt and saw new words written there in wet, bright red.

Criminy Stain m. Letitia Paisley, 1905.

I jerked my hand back, and the words were gone.

I would have expected such a thing in Sang, but to glance in my world, in my car, in my scrubs, was really scary. What if it happened every time I touched a patient? Would gloves prevent it, as they did in Sang? Thank goodness I never went anywhere without a big box of latex gloves.

Out of curiosity, I put my palm on another page, but nothing happened. I slammed the book shut and slid it under my seat.

I knocked on Mr. Rathbin's door and walked in with a smiling face. Thus began the usual six-hour shift of work that I could do with my eyes closed, familiar rituals of cleanliness and healing. But today all I could think about was Sang and Criminy and Casper. In every room, I checked the clock. Time passed more slowly than usual.

Finally, I found myself at my next-to-last stop. The beautiful historic town home of former concert pianist Jason Sterling. I knocked and was let in by his cousin, a quiet music student who was paid to live in his apartment. He went back to his room, and as soon as I heard his keyboard, I walked softly over the bare wood floors to take the hand of the empty husk of the man I now knew as Casper. It hung limp and pale in my glove, the long fingers topped with nails that needed trimming. His various machines beeped softly in the background, overlying a CD of his own concertos.

Although I'd never done so before, I gently unwound the gauze around his eyes and lifted one eyelid. Bright blue, unfocused, dead. But so beautiful, like a butterfly preserved under glass. I shut the eye and replaced the wrapping, briefly running my hand through the inch-long light brown hair and wondering what it would feel like if it were long and loose. As I changed his IV, I studied the tattoo for the first time, a black circle containing a raven holding a key on a ribbon. It was a little raised, almost like a brand. I'd have to ask him about it in Sang. That is, if Criminy let me get near him again.

His town home was clean and airy. There were photographs of his family, one of him on a black Harley, one of him in a black tuxedo, smiling by a baby grand piano at Carnegie Hall. In each one, he was gorgeous, full of life, exactly the kind of man I would love to bring home to Nana. His bookshelves held loads of books—a respectable collection of classics, music theory, poetry, and some science fiction. In a little glass locking case, he had what looked to be a first-run edition of *Leaves of Grass*, faded green with gold edges. I nearly swooned.

If he were conscious and I had come here after a first date, I would most likely have consented to making out on the couch for a while based strictly on his good taste.

Once my tasks were done, I reluctantly left this version of Mr. Sterling to his comfortable, slow death. He could last thirty years, if he didn't catch an infection. And I hadn't seen a bedsore yet. But I couldn't help but suffer a little shiver, thinking about his body, just lying there in the quiet house, dying slowly as his cousin practiced scales down the hall.

"Where are you, sugar?" Nana asked me as I washed her dishes that evening. I was daydreaming of Sang as I scrubbed her already squeaky-clean plate.

"I'm here," I said. "Just thinking."

"Did you find yourself a beau?" she asked. "I can spot the look of a pining woman, you know."

"Maybe," I said. I could lie to estate-sale clerks, but I wasn't about to try lying to Nana.

"Well, if he's good enough for you, you be sure to bring him by," she said, shaking her old feather duster at me. "A good boy always visits the kinfolk. That's manners."

"I don't know if it's going to work out," I said thoughtfully. "It's long-distance."

And it was true. Both of them were.

"I'll buy the boy a plane ticket, if he's worth your time," she said. "You know how it was with your grandpa and me. Hit me like a truck of watermelons, the first time I saw him. Fifty years of marriage, and we were still in love when I lost him." She sighed wistfully and stared at the picture on the mantel of Grandpa in his judge's robes. "You listen to me, sugar. You go with your gut."

"Yes, ma'am," I said automatically, and she nodded sagely. She had no idea what was going on in my gut, and neither did I.

All of my choices were actually pretty hard to digest.

11

That night, I went to bed early. Just in case it mattered, I brushed out my hair, washed my face, and flossed my teeth. Then I crawled into bed, curled my hand around the locket, and closed my eyes. I was nervous and excited, and if I had been anyone else, I probably would have had trouble getting to sleep.

But I'm me, so I was asleep immediately. I blinked and found myself in total darkness. I gasped in fear. Nothing was familiar. And I was exhausted.

Then a seam of orange light appeared, and a soft voice called, "Letitia, is that you, love?"

"Criminy?" I said, rubbing my eyes and sitting up.

The door opened, and I was bathed in the warm glow of the something-like-electric lamps from the main room. A Criminy-shaped shadow blocked the glare, and as my eyes adjusted, I saw concern and relief on his face. He sat on the side of the bed and held out a gloved hand as if to touch me, but then he stopped at the last moment.

"Are you all right?" he asked gently.

"I think so," I said. "But I'm so sleepy." My eyelids started to droop closed.

"Stay with me, pet," he said. "Stay in this world a while.

It's my turn to have you." He smoothed the hair off my face and said, "How was it?" Just that little touch gave me the tingles. I wondered if I had morning breath and ducked my head.

"It was . . . totally normal. I woke up in my bed, took care of my grandmother, went to work. It felt like I didn't get any sleep, but it was fine." Then it occurred to me that he looked exhausted, too. "Wait. Did you sleep at all?"

"Not much," he said wryly as he rubbed the back of his neck. "I'll admit I fell prey to a little catnap in the early morning, but the door was locked and Pem was on guard. Had the strangest dream. I was watching you through this big glass window, and you were in a giant castle all surrounded by short green grass, like someone had cut it with scissors and a ruler, and it was raining. And I was soaked to the bone, water pelting down my collar, through my hair. And you sat inside in a sort of ugly blue dress on a plaid sofa, watching a glowing box. I yelled and knocked on the window again and again, but you wouldn't look at me."

"Sounds like a nightmare," I said, but it struck me to the heart. He was describing my old house, Jeff's house, the carefully trimmed yard, and my favorite robe.

"It was," he said. Then, with a smile, as if it didn't matter, he added, "If you ever hear me calling you in the rain, let me in, eh?"

"Of course," I said.

But I could tell something in him was unsettled from the dream, and I didn't want to talk about it, either. I may have felt a little strange in his world, but he would be entirely out of place in mine.

"Oh, and I went back to the estate sale where I found the locket. I got the book it was in."

"Oh?" He said it lightly. "And what sort of book was it?"

"An empty one," I said. "Red leather, no title, no words on the pages. Only a family register on the front cover. Your family."

"Really?"

"Yeah, from the twelve hundreds until now. What year is it?"

"It's spring of 1904," he said. "And you're saying the names were there, but the pages were blank?" He leaned toward me, intent on my words.

"Yep."

"How bizarre," he said to himself. "When I sent it out to find you, it was a family grimoire, my most prized possession, full of every spell, incantation, recipe, curse, scam, and joke in the family. And in your world, it's just empty pages. I wonder if you can bring it back with you somehow."

"But the locket is the only thing that transfers. I mean, I'm wearing the same clothes and hairstyle I fell asleep with here. The makeup doesn't even pass over."

"Yes, but the grimoire was enchanted along with the locket. There's a spell on it, a strong one. It wanted to find you, and it wants to come home to me. It belongs in Sang."

"Well," I said, thinking. "It's under the front seat of my car now, but I can try falling asleep with it in my arms tomorrow night. Although that's going to feel a little silly."

"Thank you, love. I wouldn't trade you, but I'd be glad to have both prizes."

Our eyes met, and we both smiled a bit shyly. He began to move toward me, leaning in for a kiss, but I put a hand against his chest to stop him, paying careful attention to be sure that I only touched his shirt. My stomach flipped inside, but I wasn't going to give in.

"Stop right there," I said.

"Why?" he breathed.

"Because I can't," I said. "I've just woken up in another world. I can't go kissing strange men before breakfast."

"I'm a strange man now?" he said, pulling back to pin me with his sharp eyes.

"I've known you for one day," I said, pushing him farther back so that I could get out of bed. I went to the washstand and looked at my bed-rumpled face and hair in the mirror. With the smudged black makeup, I looked a little like a Victorian consumptive. It wasn't entirely unbecoming.

"One day, and still a stranger. How many days until I cease to be strange?" he asked playfully, peering over my shoulder at his own tired but well-groomed image in the mirror. Despite having spent the entire night in my wagon, he didn't have a bit of stubble. His hair was pulled back into a low ponytail, and it made him seem a little less unruly, a little more proper. Whereas I was a mess, but he didn't seem to mind.

I could feel the prey animal within urging me to keep away from his predatory grin. But he was just a person. He could walk in the daylight, he showed up in mirrors, he didn't sleep in a coffin. He wasn't dead. But I somehow kept expecting him to be more of a monster.

"I think you'll always be strange," I said softly, looking down at the red flowers painted on the china bowl. "Where's the pitcher of water?"

"Pitcher of water?" He laughed. "What do you think this is—the sixteen hundreds?"

He reached to a small dial on the side of the washstand and flicked a switch, and water began to pour out of the mouth of a ceramic cherub set into the wood under the mirror.

"We tap the caravan's pump into the aquifer whenever we park, you see," he said. When the bowl was filled, he flicked the switch, and the water stopped. "When you're done, the drain is below the bowl. Just pick it up and dump it down. It's a little old-fashioned, but it's better than beating your stockings against a rock." Seeing the look on my face, he laughed. "Don't you have running water in your world?"

"Yes," I said. "I guess I thought things were less modern here."

"Less modern? You don't even have clockworks where you come from, you said."

"OK, OK. You win. You're more modern," I said. "Can I get dressed now?

"Of course. Do you need any help with your laces?" He said it casually, but there was a hungry curiosity in his voice that amused me.

"Probably," I said. "But I need help with everything. Can you send Mrs. Cleavers over?"

He laughed that high, wild laugh of his and said, "Mrs. Cleavers doesn't make house calls, pet. She's a very important lady. But I'll send a girl over. I'm better at taking the laces off, anyway."

He sauntered out the door with a smile on his face and his copper monkey on his shoulder, calling, "And come to the dining car for breakfast when you're ready, love. Lots to do."

Moments later, someone tapped on my door, and when I opened it an inch, I saw the back of a head plastered in strawberry-blond curls and a riot of purple and yellow leather. A small clockwork bat clutched her shoulder, rubbery wings folded and red eyes blinking bright. It was the girl I'd seen on the tightrope yesterday.

"Hello?" I said.

She spun around and gave me a bright but fake smile. It reminded me of the look a popular girl once gave me in high school right before she asked to borrow my homework.

"Hi, doll," she said with something like a cockney accent. "Master Crim said you needed lacing up and whatnot, so here I am."

She stepped past me into my car and looked around, appraising. I could almost see dollar signs in her light blue eyes.

"Did this up quick for you, didn't they, love? Nice couch, redid the chaise, brought a new mirror. Fixed all the scratches Pietro left behind, poor lad. You must be quite the fancy!"

"Oh, not really," I managed to squeak out before she'd shoved open the door to the bedroom.

"Cor," she said. "Silk bedding, too! I know what Master's thinking there, eh? Lovely little nest for the lovebirds. Where's your corset and pantalettes, now, love? We got breakfast still."

She was like a sparrow, sharp and quick, and her words flowed out in a musical stream. Gone was the bored look I'd seen yesterday, replaced with the cunning eyes of a pickpocket.

"I'm Emerlie," she said. "Emerlie Fetching. Originally from Blackchapel, of course, which you'll notice from the accent, eh? Learned the tightrope and tricks from me pap, he was an old hand at the caravan. I do the unicycle, rope dancing, fiery hoops, the lot. Been with this show for three years now, and it's fine enough, eh?"

"Eh," I said, handing her the black corset and stepping into the petticoats before pulling the nightgown over my head. Her chatter made it hard to concentrate on anything.

"Oh, that's lovely stuff, now. Fine lace on those, must be from Franchia. Now, this cincher's good, thick stuff. That Mrs. Cleavers knows her way about a closet, eh? Sewed this suit for me, said that if I wouldn't dress as a lady, I wouldn't dress as a man, neither." She dimpled and giggled, as if we were best friends sharing a secret. "Got one in the works for me as'll pop your eyes, all lime and magenta. Now, clutch the door frame while I start pulling, and hold in your breath, that's a good lass."

I obliged, and she started yanking, nearly as cruelly as Mrs. Cleavers. When she finally tied off the laces and I exhaled, I felt oddly at home in the tight garment. It was uncomfortable, but everything was in place, right where it should be. Emerlie flung open the armoire and whistled.

"When's the big day, eh, love? That's the fanciest damn wedding gown I ever seen."

"Wedding gown?" I choked.

"Surely, lass, you've noticed, as there's a frothy white confection here in your armoire? Or did it skulk in at night, when you was sleeping?"

"I saw it," I said. "But I didn't know it was a wedding dress. I just thought it was white."

"And for what other reason does a lady wear white?" she scoffed. "It's a dirty damned life, and that's for sure. So the master hasn't asked you, then, eh?" I could see calculations behind her eyes. I guessed that gossip was currency among the small family of the carnival.

"No," I squeaked.

"Oh, well, it's only a matter of time, then, what with him giving you this loverly wagon to yourself and a boxful of fancy dresses. Now, let's see, which dress? Must be this one. The burgundy. Suits you. Let's get it over your head, then."

She held out the dress to me, and I dove into it, just as I had the day before. She continued chattering as she laced all the laces and smoothed the dress down over me, but I was silently shrieking in a corner of my mind. Why had that presumptuous lecher installed a wedding dress in my closet? Was I going to wake up one day from my other life already dressed and standing at an altar? Just like in my glance at the book?

She found some little pots of makeup in a drawer and went to work on my face. It seemed Emerlie never stopped to breathe, her words just tumbling over one another like a box of puppies as she worked.

"I gots me own Bluddy hopeful, I do. And how he ever expects me to love him, I'll never know, the odd bugger. Stands around mooning at me all day, waiting for a word, and what am I to say? *Go away, ye perverted bloodthirsty monster?* I'm not like you, miss, I was raised to be against that sort of thing, and the thought of kissing him, and him wanting to eat me the whole time, it's just wretched, eh? I don't know how you do it, miss, and I'm sure."

"How I do what?"

"Love a Bludman," she said, her nose wrinkled up. "With the strange eyes and the smell and the skin and the blood."

"What's wrong with the eyes and the smell and . . . whatever you said?" I asked.

"Well, don't you smell him? The blood and death, all meaty and coppery?"

"Criminy doesn't smell like that," I said, confused. "He smells like . . . berries. Wine. Something herby and green. Maybe it's cologne?"

"The Bludmen won't wear a fake scent," she said. "And it wouldn't help, as strong as they smell. And the eyes, always looking like there's a flame there, fire and shadows. They look like hell to me, miss, and no offense. Like the devil's eyes."

"I think it's kind of pretty," I admitted shyly.

She looked at me, doubtful, and said, "Well, at least you must agree it's hard to watch them drink the blood. See it coloring their teeth, turning their lips red?"

I shrugged. She was holding a little pot of bright red rouge and a small brush, and apparently she hadn't noticed the irony.

"Food is food," I said. "It's not like they're killing anyone."

She shivered. "They're a heartbeat away from it every second. Like a bludrat gnawing at a carcass and watching you, and you know what it's thinking about."

"That boy, the one who cares for you. What's his name?"

"Charlie Dregs," she said with an exasperated sigh. "And he's not half bad, for a Bludman. Best Punch and Judy show I've ever seen, the way he works them puppets and clock-works. But still. How could it ever work out? My parents would kill me. My grandfather would come after him with a torch. The children would be halfbluds, and *nobody* likes them. Why buy your trouble?"

"What about Casper?" I asked cautiously.

"The music man?" She shrugged. "Right handsome, if he weren't a Stranger, and no offense."

I didn't know how to inquire further without seem-ing nosy, and I sensed that anything I said would soon be on the lips and ears of everyone else in the caravan. She lapsed into a very welcome silence as she finished paint-ing my eyes. Her prejudice confused me. I supposed that if one were raised to hate and fear Bludmen, one couldn't help feeling that way. But I just didn't feel such revulsion around Criminy, and in Sang, I supposed that made me very odd.

"There, now, miss. You look lovely, if I do say so myself."

I considered my reflection in the mirror, and I looked about the same as I had yesterday. Apparently, having thick black rings around your eyes was the height of fashion in Sang. She'd painted a little outside my lips to make a fat cupid's bow, and she'd stuck the fascinator on the top of my head, and I felt ridiculous.

"Is this how makeup and hair are normally done here?" I asked as gently as possible.

"Oh, cor, yes. I forget Master said you was from far away," she said. "All the young ladies wear their hairbobs in front now—Mrs. Cleavers is a little behind on Citydom. And the lips have to be painted this way, if you want any lad to look twice."

Her face was next to mine in the mirror, and she did have her lips done the same way. She had a tiny maroon top hat surrounded by pheasant feathers nestled in her curls, and she smiled at me, showing yellow teeth.

"See now? Master will be pleased," she said. "And if you can put in a spare word about my wagon, I'd be ever so obliged."

"What's wrong with your wagon?" I asked.

"Nothing." She sniffed. "Except as I don't like sharing

it with that Abyssinian. She's a loverly girl, but there're ever so many snakes about, and it always smells of smoke. I had hoped . . ." She trailed off, staring forlornly around my trailer, then glanced at me and smiled that same bright, utterly fake smile. "But that's all well and good. Fortune-tellers come before tightrope walkers, and that's ever the way of things. Shall we get on to breakfast, then?"

Walking arm in arm with Emerlie was painful. She never stopped talking, and most of what came out of her mouth was complaining in a cheerful voice. She whispered about everyone we passed, just loudly enough to make it clear that she was gossiping. I was embarrassed and hoped that being seen with her wasn't turning anyone against me.

Most of the time, I just tuned her out. I had enough to think about on my own.

She threw open the door to the dining car and squealed when she saw two other girls sitting in a corner.

"Later, love!" she called over her shoulder as she trotted to her friends, one of whom had a spectacularly long beard but was still kind of pretty. The other was rail-thin, with buck teeth, and she threw me an evil look as I scanned the room. Criminy raised an eyebrow from his booth, where he was waiting for me. There was no sign of Casper. I was more than a little disappointed.

After I'd collected my breakfast of hot porridge, some little citrus fruits, and a strange amber-colored liquid, he ushered me into the booth and closed the curtains.

"Why the curtains?" I said. "Doesn't it seem weird—us eating in the same room as everyone else but hiding in a tent?"

"Most of what we say is secret, love," he said, sipping his blood. "And it's not healthy for me to get too close to the others. I have to keep control. Once they see me warbling love songs at you, I'm done for."

He flashed me a bloody grin, the sort that probably made Emerlie want to gag, but it didn't bother me anymore.

"So about last night?" he said, making it into a question.

"I was back in my real world. My clock was ringing, my cat was purring. It was just like waking up from a normal dream on a regular morning."

"But you were tired?"

"Yes, exhausted. Still am. No sleep. I'll probably start going crazy soon."

He waved that off. I blew on my porridge and nibbled a spoonful.

"We have to figure out a way for you to sleep without going back to your other world," he said to himself. "Maybe a charmed sleep?"

"Worth a try," I said. "As long as you know what you're doing."

"I know exactly what I'm doing," he said with a smoldering glance that unsettled me.

I fumbled as I picked up one of the little citrus fruits, which was smooth and golden. I dug in my thumbs, and red juice welled up and stained my gloves, dripping on the table.

"Ugh, what is this?" I cried, looking for a napkin.

"It's a tangerine, love," he said. "I thought you knew that."

"But it's all red inside," I said, dabbing at my sleeve. "In my world, they're not all dark and gooey." I sighed. "More blood."

"You're half right," he said, removing his gloves and taking the fruit from me.

I saw his hands for the first time, black and scaled like Mrs. Cleavers's, with clipped white claws halfway between fingernails and talons. I should have been disgusted, but I wasn't. They were really quite pretty, and effective, too, as he sliced open the peel and removed the sections of rich, red fruit with much less mess than I would have made.

He popped one section into his mouth and sucked it, saying, "Tangerine is the only thing besides blood that I like to eat. Tastes a little like blood but sweeter. Not as nutritive, mind you, but better than nothing."

"Like candy," I said with a smile.

He returned the smile, swallowing the fruit and holding out another piece to me. "A little like candy, yes. Try it."

I could see the dare in his eyes, so I popped it into my mouth. Braced for the worst, I found that it was actually lovely, like a cross between a ripe cherry and a clementine.

"It's delicious," I said, "if a bit staining. My gloves are ruined."

"You're a bit of a tangerine yourself, Letitia," he mused, toying with the curled peel. "Sweet, intriguing, ripe, and juicy. But not quite what you seem. Still wrapped up in a bit of a shell."

"Are you saying I'm a-peeling?" I said, and then I started giggling, and he joined me.

"Yes, my sweet tangerine. Very appealing. But it's time to drop the shell," he said. "The show opens tonight, and we've got to get you ready to perform. You need to get your patter down, practice glancing on the carnivalleros. And my hope is that you'll glance on the person who tried to poison Mrs. Cleavers. Be ready for it. Learn to keep your face closed, reveal only what you must. Get comfortable with lying, and do it fast. Do you think you can?"

"That's a lot to learn in one day," I said. "I'm not like you. I'm not a born performer."

"I'm betting you are, pet," he said. "I can see it in you, waiting to come out."

"I'll do my best," I said. I suddenly felt very small and hopeless. Not that I was so worried about the glancing, because it didn't seem as if I could stop it if I tried. I just didn't want to disappoint him.

"You're going to be great," he said. "And I'll be with you to help."

I sighed. "That's what scares me."

12

My first victim was Torno, the strong man.

"My fortune, never has it been read," he said with a galloping sort of accent. "I hope my future, you will see, is a good one." A small clockwork dog sat on its haunches at his feet, still as a statue except for an odd, robotic panting.

I smiled. I had no idea what to say.

I was sitting behind a crystal ball in a colorful little tent outside my wagon. Bold, curling letters in bright gold proclaimed me a fortune-telling gypsy, so it was definitely too late to back out. I was wearing the highly offensive mauve turban, a black net shawl, and a coin-speckled scarf tied around my hips.

I felt like a big old phony.

Criminy stood behind me in the shadows. He was supposed to be feeding me lines. But he was waiting quietly, giving me a chance to try first, I guess. Before we'd sat down, he had told me, "Your accent is very foreign and exciting, so that'll help. But you must learn to ham it up, make it seem more important than it is. Most folk have never seen a real glancer, and they're expecting magic."

That didn't help me a bit. I was still smiling at Torno,

and he was smiling at me. His clockwork dog yipped, and I jumped. My mind was a total blank.

"*I see that you are very strong,*" Criminy whispered in my ear. "*And you are a fighter. You fought in the war?*"

Of course, he was strong, and he did have scars on his face, including a big slash under his left eye. But I repeated Criminy's words, trying to inject authority and spookiness into my voice.

"Yes," Torno said. "But these things, they are known. They are past. What else can you say to me? What of the future?"

Again, silence.

"Touch him," Criminy whispered.

"If you will be so kind as to remove the glove of your right hand," I said as I removed mine and held my bare hand out to him.

Torno was surprised and stared at my hand as if it were something fascinating and scary. Then he blushed. But he removed his glove and held out his hand.

I grasped it. The jolt wasn't so bad when I was expecting it. Torno didn't appear to feel it, though, and he just sat there, staring at me, his face beet red. I supposed that in Sang, he might not have touched another human's skin in years.

It came to me then, and the words rose from my mouth unbidden, deep, and husky. "The boys will betray you," I said. "Not for blood but money. They know the hiding place. If you begin with fists, it will end in teeth. Only the master can bind them."

His bulging shoulders hunched inside the scarred leather suit. "Master?" he said, his deep voice tremulous with fury.

"It will be done," Criminy said softly from behind me.

"Thank you, Lady Letitia," Torno said. He pulled a gold coin from somewhere in his suit and laid it on the table before me, then walked back toward his trailer, clenching and unclenching his gloved fists. The clockwork dog trotted in his wake, doing an occasional backward somersault.

"See?" Criminy said, picking up the coin. "I knew it. You're a natural."

"I barely understand what I said. But I guess he knows what it means?" I asked.

"He knows. And I do, too. Catarrh and Quincy have always looked up to him, but apparently, they were going to steal something valuable from him. I'll give them a firm talking-to. Problem solved."

"You don't mind having attempted thieves here?" I asked, then I laughed. "Oh."

"Yes. Oh," he said. "I trained them myself. But we don't steal from our own. They're young. They'll learn."

The next person stepped up. It was the lizard boy, Eblick. I'd never actually seen him vertical thus far—just passed out in the sunshine. He was thin and sickly-looking, with pale green scales and watery black eyes, and he wore only a brown vest and trousers. He was one of the few people I'd met who let any part of their body show, but he certainly didn't look very tasty.

"Master," he said, bowing respectfully. "Lady."

"Hi," I said, and Criminy shook his head.

"*Hi* doesn't really set the stage, love. Try something more ominous, like *Greetings from the beyond* or *Your future awaits* or something dramatic. Or just skip it and stare them down."

I pinned Eblick with my fiercest stare, and he quaked and gulped. "If you'll be so kind as to give me your right hand," I said, "I will look into your future."

He held out a claw-tipped, scaly hand. The palm was grayish-white, with long scales like a snake's belly. I grasped it with my own hand and waited for the jolt, but nothing happened. I looked at Eblick, and he was braced as if for electrocution, his eyes squeezed shut.

Time to wing it.

"Ah, yes," I said. "You are fearful, but you must over-come this fear to reach your full potential. Claim your power in the world by gaining strength and . . . eating healthfully and . . . using a magical oil. See the master later," I said, trying to imitate the same husky voice that had come over me with Torno.

"Thank you, lady," Eblick said, worship in his eyes. He placed a transparent silvery scale on the table before me. "I will do as you say."

When he had left, staring at his hand as if secrets were written there, Criminy said, "That wasn't a glance, was it?"

"No, I made that one up," I said. "Just give him some sort of nicely scented oil so he won't look so patchy. He needs to bulk up and get some exercise."

"Well done, love," Criminy said with a chuckle. "Now you're getting it."

"What's with the scale? People are allowed to pay with body parts now?"

"They can always pay with blood, but nobody wants liz-ard blood," he said. "That scale is quite a gift, really. Great healing properties there. Or it can be pulverized and added to draughts and spells. Clever girl, to see that power was what the lad wanted most."

"You were right," I said. "It's pretty obvious when you just look at them."

My next customer appeared, the thin, buck-toothed girl I had seen with Emerlie in the dining car. She was wearing a ridiculous floppy hat that barely fit in my tent. She flounced into the chair and said, "I wish to know how to solve my . . . problem."

"If you'll remove your right glove," I said, and held out my own bare hand.

"Nothing doing. I'm a lady," she said with a sniff.

"Would you like to be a lady with or without a job?" Criminy growled over my shoulder.

"Master, I'm twenty-two, and I've never touched anyone outside of my family," she said, disgusted. "And your pardon, sir, but I don't know this . . . person."

"I do," Criminy said. "And I've let her touch me. That should be good enough for the likes of you."

I could almost see her tucking away that bit of gossip for later, but she knew she didn't have a choice. She daintily removed the glove and held out a hand with fingernails chewed to the quick. She huffed and stared into the air over my head.

I grasped her hand and waited for the jolt.

There.

"The answer lies in the city of Bixby. There is a chirurgeon there." I stumbled over the odd word on the sign from my glance. "He's a pioneer. But the price will be very high. Think carefully before striking a deal."

"How much?" she said in a shocked whisper.

I pinned her with my eyes. "High," I said. "The spirits will not allow me to say more."

"Thank you, lady." She absentmindedly set a coin on

the table and wandered away, patting her huge hat. The poor girl had mule's ears hidden under there, and every spell she'd attempted to remove them had backfired. The chirurgeon was apparently a sort of magical surgeon and could fix her. But she was poor, and it was costly. In the end, she'd have to agree to marry him, and he was old and ugly. It was fascinating, my little window into the lives of these bizarre people.

"You're doing marvelously, love," Criminy said.

"How many more are there?" I asked. "It's a little tiring."

"I've required every carnivallero to come," he said. "There will be even more glancing tonight, so you'd better get used to the strain. Relax more. Have some wine. I can see the worry in the lines of your shoulders."

He massaged my pinched shoulders for a moment. I focused on relaxing and took a sip of wine from the flask hidden under my little table. The glancing wasn't as hard as I was making it. Then I felt Criminy's hands slip from my shoulders down my arms, and his chin settled possessively on my shoulder. When I looked up, I saw Casper waiting, even more gorgeous than yesterday, his eyes guarded but hopeful. Was he as glad to see me as I was to see him?

"How does this work, exactly?" he asked with a polite smile.

"You touch her hand," Criminy snapped. "Only her hand. She tells your fortune. You pay her."

Casper held out his hand. I was drawn to his eyes, but he was having a staring match with Criminy over my shoulder.

"I can't really work with you perching on me," I said in a playful tone.

He released me, but not before his black-gloved hand

caressed my face. I could feel him in the shadows of my tent, tense and lurking behind me. "Get on with it, love," he whispered.

I focused on Casper. His poet's blouse was open, revealing a tanned chest with some sparse golden hairs. His hair was brushed to a wavy sheen and pulled back, and he had silver rings in one of his ears, like a pirate. Those long, beautiful fingers were held out to me as if we were going to go on a picnic in a magical meadow. For just a moment, I forgot all about the possessive Bludman behind me. I took Casper's outstretched hand.

There. The jolt, like sunrise piercing the clouds.

Interesting. Such a secret he had, this boy. And now I had one, too.

I had to keep control. I struggled to keep my voice even. I fought to smile, wondering if it came out as more of a grimace.

"You've found what you were looking for," I said. "Your future is long and filled with greatness. You'll find one heart's desire and lose another. Loss will be your salvation. Happiness lies over the rainbow."

"Interesting," he said.

"A mystic, baffling wonder," I answered softly.

"All truths wait in all things, and you like Whitman. Tell me more," he said, leaning closer, blue eyes bright. His other hand grasped our already clasped hands, bare skin wrapped around my fingers, and it felt so intimate an embrace that I blushed and dropped my eyes.

"Pay her and get on," Criminy growled. "Your fortune's been told, boy."

Casper laughed softly, his fingers subtly stroking mine as he released me. "So it has, Master Stain," he said as he stood and dropped a coin onto the table. "But things can always change."

"Not glances, lad," Criminy said from the darkness.

"I hope we can talk more soon. When we're alone," Casper said with a pointed look and a disarming smile before ducking out of the tent.

I watched him walk away, back proud and hair blowing softly in the breeze. I'd keep his secret, and he'd never know mine. I picked up his coin, a simple copper, rubbing it between my bare fingers before tucking it into my blouse. It was the same one I'd seen dancing over his knuckles. This one I wanted to keep for myself.

Then the bearded lady appeared, blocking my view. I pasted my smile back on and reached for her hand. In the hazy distance, I heard someone playing "Somewhere over the Rainbow" tenderly on a harpsichord.

An hour later, I was almost through the line. I'd seen secrets, hopes, dreams, crises, tragedies, and a few strange comedies. Most people seemed to want the same things— love, sex, power, riches, beauty. I supposed it was the same in any world.

The next person in line was Veruca, the Abyssinian. Most people had approached me with either fear or disdain, but she seemed completely ambiguous. I couldn't read her. I hoped a real glance would come, because otherwise, the only thing I would know to say was that she was fearless and unique, which I was betting she already knew.

She wasn't wearing gloves, and it was hard not to stare at the dark, oiled skin of her exposed body. She held out her hand without a word. I took it.

There.

That was odd.

"You have everything you wish," I said quietly. "But still you will have more. You will always find what you seek, and you will perform a great service. But your end will be a grisly one."

"Tell me something I don't know," she demanded. Her voice was high and guttural, and her tongue was pierced.

"There will be a tall, dark stranger," I said. "And something involving a bee."

She chuckled. "That's cryptic," she said. Then she looked over my shoulder at Criminy and said, "I like her."

She tossed a coin onto the table and left.

As I considered the strange and colorful future I had glanced for Veruca, I felt Criminy tense behind me. A small, stiff man hesitated before my tent. His face was scrunched up in disgust under a green velvet bowler hat that extended in faded leather down his throat and buckled under his chin with shiny brass. It was too tight, and his chin bulged with fat wrinkles underneath.

Although every Pinky I'd seen other than Casper kept his skin covered, this man took it to the extreme, with straps, buckles, and flaps crisscrossing his body. I imagined that if he were chopped open, he would have concentric rings of old leather, like a tree.

"I fail to understand why this unholy foolishness is necessary," the man said.

"Because I say it is," Criminy said darkly. "Lose the glove."

"No offense, lady," he said, failing entirely to meet my eyes. "But I was raised to believe that glancing was irreligious tomfoolery. I think you're a charlatan and a bride of the devil. I do not wish to participate."

"You owe me a debt, Elvis," Criminy growled. "And I

don't care if you believe her or not, but you'll play along, just like everyone else."

The man fumed, and I could hear his teeth grinding. With jerky, angry movements, he removed a thin cloth glove. Underneath it was a leather glove, and when he finally managed to yank it off his hand, I could smell his skin. I really didn't want to touch that foul, sweaty hand.

But if he had to, I had to.

As I reached out, he drew back and looked away as if I were going to slap him across the face. The second our skin touched, I felt the jolt.

Oh, this was going to be bad.

Now I remembered where I had heard his name before.

Instead of letting the glance speak through me this time, I fought it. Now my own teeth were grinding, and my hand clutched his in a death grip.

"Say it, love," Criminy whispered. "Don't fight the glance."

"You killed her," I said softly. "While she was dancing in the woods. But she couldn't help what she was. You think it's your holy mission, but you're just a small-minded coward. You want to kill Criminy, too. There will be a reckoning."

"You're a lying bitch!" he screamed, spit flying from his dry lips.

"You're a murderer," I said.

Criminy flashed past me. His hand settled around the man's throat, his arm rigid and his face feral as he lifted the leather-wrapped body from the ground with more strength than I would have imagined. My hand ripped free of his grasp, and I wiped it off on my skirt.

I hadn't glanced this part, just the aftermath.

"Say her name," he growled.

"Who, me?" I squeaked.

"No. Him. I want him to say her name."

"Never," Elvis said. "She was unclean. She deserved worse than anything I could have done."

The hand squeezed tighter. "Say it."

Elvis's face was turning purple. I felt detached from the violence, as far away and uninvolved as someone watching a lion killing an antelope on TV. I had seen what would happen, and I calmly accepted it as fact. He deserved it, and the only justice to be had in Sang was of the vigilante sort.

"Belleen," Elvis whispered.

Criminy dropped him, and the man choked and gurgled as he struggled back to his feet, reaching frantically for his glove. As he shoved his hand back into the safety of leather, the words tumbled from his mouth, staccato and cruel.

"Belleen the immoral temptress, the evil demoness. She preyed on men's souls, flaunted her vile body in depraved gyrations. And then she drank their blood. And they liked it, paid her for the privilege. I caught her in the woods, dancing naked for the moon, and I cut out her heart and burned it. I threw her body in the swamp, watched the crocagators nudge her foul flesh until it sank below the surface."

Criminy watched the confession, silent, his expression unreadable.

Since Criminy made no move against him, Elvis began to shout, his voice filled with an ugly, prideful righteousness. "The gods speak through me. I am their instrument. The Coppers are taking too long. The Bludmen must be destroyed, the earth scoured of their pestilence. Only man is pure, only man can return Sang to the glory of eternity."

"Are you done yet?" Criminy asked.

Everyone nearby had stopped to stare, crowding around my wagon. I could hear whispers and chittering, but I couldn't tell if the crowd was hungry for blood or just entertainment.

"I will never be finished," Elvis said, his voice rising and gaining force like that of a preacher on a roll. "For my path is righteous, and I am protected by a greater power than your vile spirits of blood. And you can't kill me because there are witnesses."

"Fine. You're righteous and special and on a mission," Criminy said, a wicked and sweet smile spreading across his face. He pulled Pemberly from his shoulder and whispered into the monkey's shiny ear. She darted down to the ground and loped along the line of wagons.

Elvis didn't know how to respond to that. He just nodded once as if accepting fealty.

Criminy crossed his arms and rocked back on his boots, humming to himself. "Oh, it'll just be a moment," he said. "But please believe that I'm entirely understanding. Your feelings have been taken into account, and your path is perfectly reasonable."

The crowd twittered. There were a few giggles. Elvis deflated a little and began to cast around for support.

There was a flash of copper, and Pemberly was again on Criminy's shoulder, her tail wrapped around his arm. Criminy took something from her little black hand.

It was the jar of powder from Mrs. Cleavers's trailer, wrapped in his handkerchief. The poison.

"Here's the thing, though, Elvis," Criminy said. "I've been thinking that you deserve a promotion in the caravan. You've been dusting off the clockworks and running the locomotive for years, and it's your turn to take center stage."

"I don't believe——"

"I'm sure you don't," Criminy said, cutting off Elvis. "But you will. You see, I've been thinking we need a clown. A good, old-fashioned Pierrot. And you're going to do your makeup all by yourself. We'll start with pure white, just like your soul."

Elvis took a step back, and the color drained from his face. His mouth opened and closed, but nothing came out.

Criminy unscrewed the top of the glass jar and held it out to Elvis. The terrified man turned to run, but Catarrh and Quincy appeared and held him by the arms. They were stronger than they looked. The crowd stepped in closer, a solid wall of bodies. Half of them were angry, half were curious, but none showed even a hint of sympathy.

"You can't do this!" Elvis shouted. "It's murder! It's against the laws! You'll lose your license! My human brethren will see you punished!"

"Murder?" Criminy said, drawing back in feigned confusion. "My dear sir, I'm giving you a promotion. It's just powder. A simple bit of makeup. Mrs. Cleavers uses it on everyone. Why on earth would you be frightened of powder?"

The crowd had made a tight circle around them by now, and I had a front-row seat from behind my crystal ball. Mrs. Cleavers pinned Elvis with her darkest glare and bared her teeth.

"I use it myself, you silly man," she said. "There's nothing to fear from powder."

Elvis struggled, but there was no escape.

Criminy held out the jar again and said, "Go on. Paint your face, clown. Unless you'd like to tell your friends and coworkers anything special?"

Elvis looked at the powder, then at the crowd. He hung his head, apparently realizing that the Bludmen would end him, one way or another, now that they knew what he had done.

He dipped a gloved finger into the powder and looked at it sadly. He drew a stripe from his forehead down to his chin, then reached for another finger full and drew a line from cheek to cheek. With a cross drawn on his pallid face, he looked up at the crowd.

"I regret nothing," he said, and blood spilled from his mouth. He fell to the ground, eyes open. Dead.

Emerlie screamed, but one of her friends clapped a hand over her mouth. The bearded lady fainted into Torno's arms. One small man just as leathery as Elvis crept forward to close the dead man's eyes with an apologetic nod to Criminy. Shocked whispers and fierce glares darted across the crowd, yet no one seemed all that surprised. I couldn't tell if that was because they knew Elvis was a bad seed or because Criminy's word was accepted as law.

Criminy pulled a long black silk sheet from inside his coat as easily as if it were a handkerchief. He stepped forward to drape it over the still form in the dust, and the whispering reached a frenzy.

"Everybody stop!" Criminy shouted.

The carnivalleros immediately quieted and stilled.

"This is a family, and we take care of our own. Crimes will be punished accordingly. Belleen has been avenged. Now, get on with it." His voice rang with confidence and finality.

The carnivalleros drifted off. The show was over.

13

The pale, lemony sun lingered at the horizon as I watched the caravan come alive for the first time. Barely refreshed by a few quiet hours alone in my wagon, I was now back in my fake tent in front of my fake crystal ball wearing my fake turban while providing one-hundred-percent real fortune-telling.

Strange double-decker vehicles appeared, first as three distant spots spewing smoke. Then their heavy chugging carried over the hills, and finally they arrived, parking a respectful distance away. They were like a cross between English sightseeing buses and tanks, and their treads left ugly scars across the serene green of the moors. City people apparently took safety very seriously on their country jaunts.

Each bus was accompanied by two Coppers, who galloped ahead on feisty bludmares to check our paperwork with Mrs. Cleavers. In addition to the caravan's license and certificates, every carnivallero was required to have papers, and mine had been freshly forged and magically aged earlier in the morning. I was officially Lady Letitia Paisley. I had argued in favor of my last name, but Criminy had explained that Everett was neither a surname nor a word in Sang and might draw questions, so we had gone with the much more common Paisley. I couldn't think of a single argument that wouldn't expose what I'd seen when glancing on his book, so Paisley it was.

I tried to focus on my breathing and ambience. My biggest criticism from the day's customers had been that I seemed perky but shy until I touched them, when I instantly became somber and mysterious. I needed to maintain that same exotic aura consistently instead of depending on the glancing.

My car was between Emerlie and Veruca's and Torno's, and the wagons had been circled to separate the public and private spaces of the caravan. Clockworks inhabited the spaces between the wagons, doing their tricks and ensuring that no outsiders ventured into the circle within. The juggling polanda bear and dancing leoparth on either side of my wagon were more than a little daunting.

To my left, Emerlie rode her unicycle and juggled plates, looking more bored than ever. Her really dangerous stunts wouldn't begin until the crowd was excited and gathered like a flock of leather sheep by Criminy's hawking. Just beyond her, Veruca stood in a booth painted to look like a lush jungle and practiced swallowing a sword. On my right, Torno lifted big blocks of stone and giant barbells, also warming up for his more impressive show later on.

I had asked Criminy why there wasn't a big top, a giant tent with bleachers for the main show.

"They used to have those," he said, thoughtful. "A couple of hundred years ago, before so many were bludded. But in today's world, herding a bunch of Pinkies into a place with only one exit would be like inviting a flock of geese into a cage with a leoparth. Even if you could keep them safe, they'd never relax. The people of Sang need to see what's coming, make sure nothing is sneaking up behind them."

It was also the reasoning behind our circled wagons. It was like fighting back to back, making sure that we were all on the lookout for whatever might be coming. We needed a space of our own. They were a little scared of us, but we were also a little scared of them. I had to admit that the bulk of my own wagon behind me was reassuring. I closed my eyes and leaned back against it, wishing the glancing was already over and I could try the charmed sleep Criminy had promised me.

"Ready for your first show, my lady?"

I startled. As I pushed up my slipping turban, I found Casper standing before me in a spectacular costume, smiling. He wore a billowing white shirt that laced up to his chin, and over that a sequined waistcoat of sky blue dancing with black music notes. His breeches were black, his boots were polished, and his hair was plaited and tied with a bow.

"You look like Mr. Knightley," I said. "With maybe a little bit of Elton John thrown in."

"That might be the nicest compliment I've ever received, and that includes the time the queen of England told me I played like an angel," he replied, flashing even more dimple.

As hard as it was to look elsewhere, I peeked over his shoulder, to where the tanks were parking. I fidgeted with my turban some more.

"You're scared, aren't you?" he said. "Not used to performing?"

"Not at all," I admitted. "And I'm scared of what I'm going to see, too."

"Ah, yes. The glancing." He sat on the stool across from me, the one reserved for customers, and looked around to check that we were alone. "Speaking of which, you know my secret now, don't you?"

"It's really clever," I had to admit. "Drinking a drop from every Bludman you meet so they don't want to feed on you. Criminy never mentioned that their blud could do that. But why'd you start?"

"I couldn't stand the gloves," he said, flexing his bare hands. "Playing the harpsichord in gloves . . . it's like making love with your clothes on. You can't feel the skin under your hands, the electricity. There's no magic there. What's the point?"

Visions of pianos and hands and bodies in candlelight tumbled through my mind, and I had to bite my lip. He definitely had a way with words. It was strange, being a little infatuated with him. Already knowing that he wanted me, having seen it in the glance. Wanting him, too.

"You should take some blud," he said. "It's important to keep yourself safe here."

"I don't think so," I said. I'd already been thinking about it, of course. "I'd rather be free than safe, and drinking someone's blood and becoming something I'm not . . ." I shook my head. "It's not a compromise I'm willing to make."

"No, no—it's all about being free," he argued. Seeing him animated and passionate made me a little breathless, even if I disagreed with him. "That's the point. Do you know any other humans walking around barefoot and gloveless around here?" He looked down at his boots and tugged at his collar with a shrug. "I'm dressed up now for the show, but most of the time, I'm the only person who isn't wrapped up in fear and cloth."

His lip curled up, and his hands were in fists. The old Tish would have apologized and moved on, changed the subject. But Letitia was more willing to argue for what she believed.

"But how long are you a human, when you're drinking from Bludmen? I don't have anything against them, obviously, but when do you start to crave blood? When does it take you over completely? You might be free to dress differently, but you become a slave to your choices all the same."

"I choose to disagree," he said quietly. "But then again, you've never died. I have. And I don't want to do it again. And I don't want you to, either."

We were silent for a moment, watching the Pinkies disembark and mill about in a tight cluster. I subtly studied him. He was just as pretty when he was angry. Criminy was right to call him sulky, but it suited him. It was odd to yearn toward two such different men at once when I wasn't even sure how I fit into their world. Loving either one of them would be easy, if I let myself. Choosing between them would be the hard part. I would have to ignore the glancing and listen to my gut. I trusted Nana's wisdom more than magic.

He caught my eye, and I was lost for a moment in the startling blue. Despite his bravado, there was fear there, and I wished that I had some solace to offer him. But I didn't.

"Is that what you saw for me, then? Becoming a Bludman?" he asked, almost pleading. "Is that the great loss—my humanity?"

"I can't say."

Or I wouldn't.

He put his head down and chuckled sadly. "You can see it, but you won't tell me."

"I do not talk of the beginning or the end," I quoted with a sad smile.

"You can quit quoting 'Song of Myself,'" he said bitterly. "This is Sang. The words were never written here."

He stood up and walked away.

When he was out of range, I muttered to myself, "That doesn't mean they never will be."

The Pinkies cut a path through the grass, moving toward us in a giddy but skittish herd. My skin tingled as a ripple of magic rolled over me. I looked up and smiled. Everything seemed brighter, sharper, more fascinating. Glitter danced in the air, and a calliope began to play. I wondered if that was Criminy's doing, too, or if Casper's fingers were the magic behind the cheery pipes. Emerlie's smile became genuine, Torno's muscles seemed to bulge a little more through his leather suit, the jigging leoparth let out a very genuine-sounding roar. I sought Criminy in the crowd and saw him in front of his wagon, his hands playing in the air as he grinned. Just another one of his talents, this glamour.

The crowd flowed in little groups, and I could feel their fear and excitement. A gaggle of Pinkies approached me in a rustle of skirts and whispers, my first customers for the night.

Oh, great. Teenagers.

They looked like teens from my own time, except for their heavy, suffocating clothes. Frilly, silly, catty, whispery, scared but hiding it with bravado. The boldest of them broke off from the group and stepped up to me with a flounce and a sneer as her friends giggled behind her.

"Can you really tell fortunes?" she said. "My pa says it's a trick."

I lowered my head and looked up at her through my painted eyelashes, trying to appear mysterious. "It's not a trick, miss," I said, my voice husky. "Touch my hand and see."

"How much is it, then?" she said as if bored, but I could tell that she was caught.

"Whatever you think it is worth," I said. "To know your future."

I held out my hand, with the glove already removed. Mrs. Cleavers had filed my nails to talons and shellacked them, bright red as cherries. When the girl saw it, she gasped.

"Remove your glove," I said with a knowing smile.

She looked back to her friends. They urged her on, and she knew she couldn't back down. She removed her glove with a dainty, unwilling tenderness. She likely hadn't shown her hand to anyone but her parents in her entire life.

When I touched her skin, the jolt was quick.

"The lad you love doesn't return the sentiment," I said, my voice low. "But another does. Beware the one with golden eyes, for she will betray you. Tell your father not to bet on the black mare. Listen to your mother, and don't marry the first one who asks, and you will find happiness."

I dropped her hand. Her eyes bugged out unbecomingly, showing me how young she truly was. "Thank you, lady," she said.

She slipped her glove on and dropped some coins onto the table. I whisked them into a little bag at my feet, as

Criminy had told me never to let them see the money. Her circle of friends enveloped her, but she shook her head at their questions.

"She sees true," she said. "That's all I can say."

Of course, her six friends fell into line before me, and my bag of coins grew heavier. Every time I grasped a hand, I was terrified that I would see something horrible, some hideous end that I couldn't prevent with a few well-chosen words. Or even worse, that I wouldn't see anything and would have to make something up on the fly. But life in the city, from what I glanced, was dull and mostly safe. Only one girl's palm held a tragedy, and I was able to help on that one.

"No matter what your boyfriend says, never sneak out at night," I said, my tone dark and foreboding. "Or else your death will come from the shadows of the alleys, and your mother will find your bones nibbled by bludrats."

It sounded bad because, well, it was bad. But it could easily be averted. *Stay inside, stupid.* I hoped I had scared her sufficiently.

Fortunately for business, nothing spread the word like a group of impressed and terrified teenage girls. Soon I had a line, and Criminy's clockwork monkey came by to do tricks for pennies, which she gathered in her little fez. After turning several back flips, she brought me a note in elegant handwriting signed with a C.

Well done, love, you're a star was all it said, but my mysterious mask cracked into the goofy smile of a kid receiving a love note in high school.

"Miss?" said the next customer. "Can we make this quick?"

I looked up into the anxious face of a Copper. I recognized the spade beard and mustache. It was Ferling, the nicer of the two I'd seen on my first morning in Sang while I was invisible.

I discreetly tucked the monkeygram into my sleeve.

His nervous fidgeting told me that whatever Coppers were allowed to do at the carnival, fortune-telling wasn't on the list. With shifting eyes, he yanked off his leather glove, which had already been unbuttoned. He was ready. And he was worried.

"I need to know if my wife is true," he said quietly. "Quick."

I grasped his hand, and the jolt was powerful.

Oh, gracious. This wasn't good at all.

"Your wife is true, but she is being forced," I said. "Proof lies in the spice chest. The baby is yours. Stay faithful, and all will be well. The bones can knit. Seek vengeance, and all will be lost in blood. When the time comes to choose, remember this."

His face was stricken, his hand trembling in mine.

"I'm sorry," I said in my regular voice.

"Thank you, lady," he said, tossing a vial of blood onto the table and disappearing into the crowd.

It was a tough fortune, and I felt sorry for the man. What I hadn't told him was that his wife was being blackmailed by his partner, Rodvey. It was a fast, confusing jumble of visions, but I could see that if he confronted Rodvey, the resulting duel would leave them both dead. In the bottom of the spice chest, he would find the documents that his wife was winning from Rodvey with her body one page at a time, a fake declamation of Ferling's supposed illegal dealings with the Bludman's Guild. She was doing it to protect him from a false accusation and certain execution.

As I had first deduced, Rodvey was a very bad man.

I had seen something else when I touched Ferling's hand, though, something even scarier that I was absolutely positive not to mention. It was a secret meeting of hooded figures, all in copper-colored velvet robes and surrounded by candles in a stone chamber. In the center of their circle lay a Bludman, whiter than white, his blud draining into strange channels carved into the floor. The faces of the cloaked men were in shadow, and I didn't recognize the voice that spoke.

"Another demon drained. But he has many brothers, and we will bring a plague on their kind, sent from the gods to purge the wickedness of Sang," the voice boomed. "We will destroy all the creatures of blud once and for all. The Stranger will come to make our world pure again."

"Amen," came the answering chant.

The Coppers were planning a secret genocide, and I had no clue how to stop it.

My mind was elsewhere, which made the glancing even easier. Everything seemed so petty after Ferling's revelation, and I didn't have any problem seeming mysterious and far away.

It was amazing how many people needed to be told not to go out alone in the dark of night. It just seemed so obvious, like telling people not to jump out in front of cars. But being cooped up in their clothes and their homes seemed to lull the Pinkies into a false sense of safety. It wasn't even Bludmen they had to worry about, swooping in like dark angels to drain them in the shadows. No, it was the stupid bludrats.

Faces blurred together, and glances streamed into

glances. I forgot most of them almost immediately, like passing faces on a busy sidewalk. I'd only been glancing for a few hours, but I was starting to get sleepy. It must have been time to wake up, in my other world.

"Good evening, madam," came a deep, fatherly voice with a cultivated English accent.

I had been drifting off. *Oops.*

With my head still hanging low, I looked up through my eyelashes. A kind-looking old man with a big, gray walrus mustache smiled at me and held out his hand.

"I've heard a great deal about your talent," he said. "I'd like to know my future."

"As you wish," I said, and grasped his hand.

Despite myself, I gasped. His glance was just as jumbled and fast and confusing as Ferling's, but the secret went even deeper.

First, I saw this man in the city, in an office, speaking to a roomful of Coppers. He was wealthy and powerful, something like a mayor. Outside his window, I saw a soaring white church with broken windows and a strange spire shaped like an X.

Next, I saw him throw back the hood of his copper-colored robe in the empty ritual chamber and kick the drained Bludman's body.

"One down, a million to go," he said to himself.

Lastly, and most chillingly, I saw the old man asleep.

But in the vision, he wasn't wearing this tall top hat, buttoned down his throat. He wasn't wearing gloves or boots or a copper-colored, bloodstained robe.

No, he was reclining in an expensive bed, tucked into rich, fluffy blankets. On his right was a small table with a telephone and a clock radio. On his left was an IV stand.

An older woman in nursing scrubs changed out his IV bag, saying, "Well, then, Mr. Grove. That's better, ain't it? Y'all missin' a beautiful spring day, you know."

She looked out the window at a magnificent magnolia tree in full bloom within a high brick wall. In the fancy driveway was a minivan with *Helping Hands Homecare* on the side next to two purple hands forming a heart.

I startled as the old man asked, "Can you see anything?" in a playful, patronizing tone.

The British accent sounded fake to me, and I wondered what his real one was like. I knew that I had to lie, but I had only a split second to decide whether to seem genuine or ham it up. I went with fake and threw in several of the trite phrases Criminy had taught me.

"Oh, sir. You are a very powerful man, a great leader. You will live a long and fulfilling life. Your destiny is cloudy. The spirits watch over you. Beware a dark-haired stranger."

I focused on his mustache as I finished, and it twitched. His eyes narrowed. He was suspicious. Whether he believed me or not, I couldn't say. Most people aren't prepared for a true fortune-teller who speaks lies.

"I see," he said. "I see." Then his eyes traveled over my face and down to my chest. I drew back.

"That's a lovely chain," he said. "You're brave, my dear, to wear so little clothing around these monsters."

Criminy and Mrs. Cleavers had decided to dress me in a Bludman's blouse for the actual crowd, since they would all be Pinkies. It upped the exotic factor and would help draw their attention away from my occasional blunder. The top of the locket barely peeked out from my cleavage, the ruby glinting in the flickering light.

I wrapped my hand around the locket defensively. "Thank you, sir."

His eyes roved over me. I shifted and drew the shawl over my skin, clearing my throat and looking at the ground. At that signal, Pemberly stopped her cavorting and ran up to tug on the man's coat.

"Our time appears to be up," he said in the same kindly voice. "Thank you so much for sharing your talents, my dear."

He dropped a gold coin onto the table and strode purposefully back into the crowd. My next customer stepped up, a middle-aged woman with desperate eyes.

"One moment, madam," I said.

Fortunately, there was a feather quill on my table, along with the crystal ball, skull, and other props. I scrawled on the back of Criminy's earlier note, *Old man big mustache head of Coppers wants to kill Bludmen is really Stranger!!!* I crumpled it up and gave it to Pemberly.

"Take it to Criminy," I told her.

Her eyes clicked closed and open again in acknowledgment, and she scampered into the crowd. I put on a professional smile for the waiting customer and held out my hand.

Then I went unconscious.

14

Even before my eyes opened, I was overwhelmed. The cacophony was dizzying. My alarm was buzzing, my cell phone was jingling, and my cat was meowing.

9:47. *Crap.*

First the alarm. Slept in for more than two hours. *Oops.*

Then the cell phone.

"Nana, I'm so, so sorry," I began.

"Well, sugar, you're the one who has to clean up if I wet myself," she said in her most peevish tone, "Although breakfast would be nice, too."

"I'm on my way, and I'm bringing doughnuts," I said.

"I might forgive you, then," she said.

I was so exhausted that I could barely stand up. I made a beeline for the coffeemaker.

My morning was blurry and heavy, like being drunk without the fun. I showed up at Nana's just in time to prevent a laundry crisis and mutual mortification, served her hot doughnuts and hotter coffee, and sleepwalked through my chores there, barely able to focus on what she said. I was so tired that I was scared to drive to my next patient.

I ran a red light and nearly got T-boned on the way to

Mr. Rathbin's. When I parked in the driveway, I barely registered that two tires were in his grass. I didn't bother to repark.

"Having a good day, Mr. Rathbin?" I asked with a yawn.

He was pretty jolly for a terminal patient—unless I was late. Luckily, I had brought him one of Nana's extra doughnuts, so he was in a great mood. I set up his meds and helped him brush his teeth. Then, as I was carrying his used bedpan to the toilet, I passed out and hit the floor in a puddle of Mr. Rathbin's urine.

As I slowly rose to consciousness, I had the marvelous, achy, breathless feeling that I only got from several hours of uninterrupted sleep. It was completely delicious. I wiggled my toes and stretched my arms and legs and yawned. It was good to feel rested again. I opened my eyes to complete darkness.

I knew immediately that something wasn't right.

I felt around blindly until I found a side table with a button. I pushed it, and orange light filled the room. It was my wagon.

"Criminy?" I called. There was an answering rustle in the other part of the wagon, and the door opened. He looked confused. And sleepy.

"Are you all right, love?" he said, rubbing his eyes. "It's barely morning."

"I don't know," I said. "I was at work, and then I woke up here. What happened?"

He came in and sat down on the bed, his hand warm on my cheek. I was still in the blouse and skirt from my costume, with my corset laces mercifully loosened. And I was scared.

"You fell after nine," he said. "In the middle of glancing. It was very dramatic, and I suspect your line will be doubly long tonight. I carried you here and put you to bed. But you shouldn't be awake now, I don't think. Unless you fell asleep in your dinner."

"It was just after lunch," I said. "I was helping a patient, and . . ."

"And what?"

"I don't know. I just opened my eyes, and I was here. But I feel rested. How is that possible?"

I tried to look into Criminy's eyes, but they were focused on my exposed cleavage.

"Up here, mister," I said with a playful grin.

"My locket," he said simply. "It's gone."

I reached down, and he was right. Both locket and chain were gone.

"Where? How?" I said.

"I don't know," he answered, angry. "I was right outside. I only fell asleep for a moment. No one came near the door. Pemberly's been on guard. There hasn't been a sound. It's impossible."

"Does it mean I'm stuck here? Is that why I'm not exhausted—because I was actually asleep? In Sang?"

"That could be possible," he said slowly.

"So what am I doing in my other world? Am I asleep there? Am I dead?" I said, voice trembling, fearful. "Who's going to take care of my grandmother? Am I on Mr. Rathbin's floor? Oh, my God. What's happening to me?"

Tears coursed hot down my cheeks. Criminy wrapped his arms around me and stroked my head.

"I don't know, love," he said. "I just don't know."

"What are we going to do?" I asked. My nose was buried in his neck, and the scent was calming and powerful. I somehow hadn't imagined him being this warm and comforting.

"I don't know that, either," he said. "But we're going to find out how it happened."

He stood up and whistled, and Pemberly capered in through the door.

"Pem, someone got into this room. Search it. Find a hole, a trapdoor, anything."

The little monkey began to skitter along the walls. Red beams flickered from her eyes, scanning. Criminy watched her, and I couldn't read him. He should have seemed more worried, more angry. But he wasn't. He almost seemed relaxed. I was missing something.

Then I realized why. If the loss of the locket meant that I was trapped here, then he didn't have to share me.

It meant that I was stuck here. I couldn't leave him.

"Criminy," I said, low and flat.

"Yes, love?" he asked calmly.

"Did you take the locket?"

"Of course not. Why do you ask?"

"I know what it means, if you don't find it," I said. "Don't think I can't see. And I'm not playing along. If you don't find the locket, I'm not just going to give up and live here as your personal plaything. It's all or nothing. If I'm trapped here, I'm leaving. I'll never love you. I'll go live in the city. You can't keep me here against my will. I get both worlds, or I get none."

"So that's how it is," he said softly.

"Yes," I said. "It is."

"I suppose I should have expected that," he said. "If you weren't a wild sort of creature, I wouldn't love you. It would be easy if you just gave in, but easy isn't worth anything, is it?"

"You said so yourself," I admitted.

"We'll find it, then," he said. "I promise."

Once Pemberly showed us the perfectly round, rat-sized hole along the baseboard, the story was easy enough to piece together. The culprit had been a clockwork, and it had known exactly what it was looking for.

"Nibbled through the chain's links with titanium teeth, most likely," said Criminy. "Whoever took it must be powerful and rich. And determined."

"Determined?" I said. "Is it worth much?"

"Depends how much your other world is worth to you, pet," he said, thoughtful as he sipped his breakfast from a cup delicately painted with pansies. "The ruby is big enough but not worth such trouble. He must have known it was enchanted. Tell me—has anyone spoken to you about the locket?"

Oh.

Suddenly, it all made sense. The old man, a Stranger himself, interested in my pretty locket. A Stranger who wanted to destroy all of the Bludmen. A Stranger who might want a way back to my world. In between meeting him and passing out, I hadn't had time to piece it together. I told Criminy everything, from Ferling's glance to the old man's curiosity about the necklace.

He went very still as he listened, his lips compressing into a thin white line and his eyes growing hard. "I never got that note," he said. "Someone's been tampering with my clockworks. And planning a secret genocide. Did you get a name?

"No," I said. "But he's the boss of the two we saw on the moor, Rodvey and Ferling. He's an old man with a big, white mustache. And he's a sort of leader—of a city and of all of the Coppers. Like a mayor. And he works way up high, near a big, ruined, white church with an X on top."

"That's Manchester," Criminy said. "Cathedral of Saint Ermenegilda. He must be the Magistrate."

"Why did no one recognize him, though?" I asked. "Isn't he important?"

"Not to me, not until now. I live outside his laws. It's not an elected position, see? He's in power, he makes the rules, and everyone in the city has to live by them. But he's not going to advertise. Still, he shouldn't be hard to find, and I have friends there. Wisest course of action would be to beat him at his own game. Steal the locket back."

We planned to set out after breakfast, traveling the road on foot. There was much to do before leaving, from briefing Mrs. Cleavers on caravan business to gathering up food and blood. We took a little money but not much. It wouldn't pay to appear suspicious or remotely like a target. Besides, we could always earn our supper on the streets with Criminy's magic or my glancing.

While Criminy was talking to Mrs. Cleavers, I sat on the steps of her wagon, gazing at the morning haze hanging over the moors and thinking about my grandmother. I had never felt so far away from comfort and safety.

"Ready to go fetch your wonderful cities?" someone asked, and I looked up to find Casper leaning against the wagon, his smile playful. As if he had forgotten our earlier disagreement. So I played along.

"Maybe, Mr. Whitman," I said coyly. "But I'm a little scared of the contemptible dreams part."

"I know how that feels," he said. "I'm worried about your dreams, too. And I don't like to think of you alone on the moors with *him*." He looked thoughtful and inviting, hair down and smile warm. Being around him made me feel young and special and full of hope, and I liked it. With a quick, guilty thought of Criminy, I patted the wood board beside me.

He sat down next to me on the step, and I was hyper-aware of his hip and shoulder touching mine. The wind blew his hair in my face, and it smelled of soap. Not berries and vines and darkness but good, clean soap. And his skin smelled so human, so manly, of a life lived in the sun.

"Criminy says that glancers can see everyone's future but their own," I said, feeling a blush creep up my cheeks. "But I truly believe that in the end, you'll have what you want."

"All I've ever wanted before now was music," he said. His shoulder pressed against me, and I unconsciously leaned into him. "I was so busy practicing and traveling and writing. I never had time for people. And now I have so much time and no one to share it with."

A breeze came up, and a lock of my hair whipped across my face. He gently tucked it behind my ear, and his fingers left velvet trails of fire on my skin. I closed my eyes, lost in the moment, and his lips pressed against mine, warm and soft and tender. I felt like a teenager having her first kiss on the doorstep, a stolen moment where everything is golden and shimmering and achingly beautiful. And so, so fleeting.

Just when I hoped the kiss would get deeper, he pulled away and stroked my face. "You're so lovely," he said. "Gentle and curving and beautiful, as a woman should be."

My eyebrows rose at the word *should,* and I had to ask, "What else do you think I am?"

"Let's see," he said with a smile. "You're a nurse, so you must be kind and good-hearted. You know *Leaves of Grass,* so you must be educated and poetic. You're beautiful, but anyone can see that. And you've got that monster Stain wrapped around your little finger, which is pretty clever. The girls fawn at him all day, and he ignores them, and here he's already given you your own wagon. But being my girl won't keep you on his good side, I'm sorry to say."

"I'm not anyone's girl," I said, pulling away and peeling my shoulder off his.

"Then why did you kiss me?" he asked, beautiful blue eyes pleading in a way that somehow made me like him less. "You just feel right to me. I feel so close to you, like you're home. And I think you feel that way about me, too."

I couldn't answer. I did feel that way about him, and I longed for closeness and peace. He was my only link to my world, to the future I'd always wanted. But I wasn't sure if this was the right way to get it. There was something in his desperation that reminded me of Jeff. And it wasn't his business how I felt about Criminy. I turned my face away and sighed. The breeze became a chill wind, and a cloud passed in front of the sun. He reached for my hand, but I shrugged away, tucking my hands into the billowing fabric of my skirt. The moment was gone.

"You've seen your own future, haven't you? And you think you can't change it. You're not willing to take a chance on me." He put his head down and chuckled. "It's a little scary, what you do."

His words wounded me deeper than I would have guessed. As I tried to figure out how to respond, Mrs. Cleavers's door gently shut, and with words as sharp and cold as the blade of a knife, Criminy said, "If you're scared of her talent, then you don't truly know what fear is."

"I just wanted to wish you luck," Casper said stiffly. He stood and lifted my limp hand from my lap, kissing my glove with that same pleading look in his eyes. "Let's continue this discussion sometime, Letitia. Under more pleasant circumstances." He nodded curtly and added, "Take care of her, Stain." He walked away into the grasses, glowing in a sunbeam, and I wondered if we would ever find our golden place again.

"That's *Master* Stain to you, maestro," Criminy growled at his back. "And never fear; I'll keep her close enough."

He pulled me to my unsteady feet and gently slipped off my gloves, tossing them into the grass. The wind felt strange and wild on my fingers. With a meaningful look in his stormy eyes, Criminy brought my hand to his face and kissed the palm.

"I'll never fear you," he said softly. "The maestro's a fool." Then he rapped on Mrs. Cleavers's door and shouted, "Cleavers! Bring my lady a clean pair of gloves."

I slipped on the new gloves, which were black like Criminy's. His kiss, so light and soft, still burned against my palm. It was nice to know that at least one man wasn't intimidated by my gifts, but I had to admit that I was maybe a little worried about his own talents. And teeth.

"Are we going alone?" I asked.

"I had assumed so," Criminy said. "Unless you have a special friend besides the maestro? He wouldn't be much good for drawing the bludbunnies off you, but he'd be fine for target practice."

He winked, and I blew a raspberry. "Don't be silly," I said. "For safety, I was thinking. Or help when we get where we're going."

Criminy's mouth quirked up, and he said, "Love, you're traveling with a very dangerous person. I have razor-sharp teeth, I'm difficult to kill, and then there's the whole 'magic' thing. Do you think Licky the Lazy Lizard Boy would be much help?"

"No," I said, feeling stubborn. "But isn't it odd—a Bludman and a woman traveling alone?"

"According to our traveling papers, which Mrs. Cleavers is fashioning now, we're husband and wife. I'm Ecrivan Paisley, and you're my wife, Petula. I took your name," he said with a grin. "I hope you don't mind."

"What if I do?"

"Honestly, my prickly little hedgehog, it's the safest thing for us both," he said. "Traveling together without a proper relationship makes me a predator and you a trollop. It'll be bad enough when they think we're married. And there's still the caravan tonight, so everyone else is needed. It was lucky, you passing out in front of last night's crowd. We'll say you're in communion with the spirits, and no one will dare knock on your door."

Just as we were setting off, Vil galloped into view. "Murdoch says it's ready, sir," he said, and he held out a small wooden box, about five inches square.

"About time," Criminy said, snatching the box and opening it. He held it out to me and said, "Wedding present, Petula. Try it on."

Nestled within on a bed of soft cloth was a brass bracelet shaped like a snake. Copper diamonds shone among the scales, and dull ruby eyes were set in the head.

"Do I just pick it up and slide it on?" I asked.

Vil blinked at me, his twitchy eyes huge behind the goggles. "Never had a clockwork before?" he asked. "Where'd you say you were from?"

"She's from Bruzzles," Criminy snapped. "From good country folk. Don't make her feel self-conscious, you dolt." He picked up the bracelet and handed it to me. I didn't know what to expect as I slipped it over my glove and onto my wrist.

Nothing happened. I looked at it as if it might bite me.

"He's got to imprint on you, love," Criminy said, reaching over to press a raised jewel between the eyes, which lit up. I must have looked distrustful, because he grinned slyly and added, "It won't hurt."

He moved my wrist in front of my face. With an odd whir, the little snake's head turned toward me, blinding me with red light.

"He's scanning you," Criminy said softly. "Don't blink."

I kept my eyes open wide while the light went back and forth, flickering on and off. The snake made a grinding noise, and then the mouth opened and released the tail. I held my other hand underneath, afraid to drop it, and it slithered onto my glove. It was amazing how lithe the little robot was, how the scales flexed like those of a real snake.

"He's a little Uroboros," I said.

"So tell him," Vil said, losing patience.

"Tell who what?"

"Tell him his name, lass, so he'll know."

"Uroboros," I said, putting my mouth near his head. "Uro is what I'll call you."

Another grinding noise, then a click, and the eyes flashed once with red. Then a black tongue made of thick wire flickered out and back in.

"He's all set, then," Vil said. He pulled out a little slip of paper and read, "*Press the head scale to move from rest mode to active and back. All the common commands. Guard, hide, find, and such. He's not nearly as complex and useful as a monkey, but honestly, I only had two days. Oh, and for defensive purposes, he's programmed to bite, and he's loaded with two doses. Signed, the elusive Mr. Murdoch.*"

"Two doses of what?" I asked.

Vil grinned. "Something I cooked up myself. Instant and profuse vomiting, followed by unconsciousness."

"Sounds effective," I said. "Thanks."

He beamed.

I watched the small snake spread out on my palm, red eyes flickering occasionally and small tongue poking out and in. I pressed the head scale, and he curled into a hoop, bit his own tail, and turned back into a very peculiar piece of jewelry. I slid him over my wrist and took Criminy's arm.

We were off.

15

We followed the deep tread marks of the bus tanks that had carried the city folk to the caravan. The brown scars snaked through the hills and disappeared in the distant fog. As we walked in silence, I watched the countryside, comparing it with my world. It was a strange place, and I'd never seen so much wide-open space in my life. No houses or barns or even ruins. Just miles of grass, small copses, and the occasional bludbunny.

When we saw a fawn peeking out from behind a bush, I stopped to stare at the wide, liquid brown eyes. Then a shower of leaves erupted behind it, and a red-eyed doe towered over the little brown form, dropping a mauled rabbit corpse to hiss at me with bloodstained fangs. The placid fawn copied its mother, the vicious hiss ridiculous coming from the tiny, toothless mouth.

"Back away, love," Criminy said. "If you think the bunnies are bad, you haven't met a bluddoe. They're rather protective."

I did back away, and I continued walking backward until the doe closed her mouth and nuzzled the fawn sweetly. Criminy laughed at me, but my eyes were a little sharper from then on, contemplating the dark possibilities of a forest where Snow White had more to fear from her animal friends than from any wicked queen.

Criminy carried most of our things in an old leather satchel, and he looked dashing with his top hat and traveling cloak. I wore a wool shawl and a heavy black bonnet that buttoned under my chin. With my gloved hand in the crook of Criminy's arm, walking across the moors made me feel as if I'd stepped primly out of a Jane Austen book or an Impressionist painting. But I bet even Elizabeth Bennet had never punted a rabbit before, and my current count was 137.

"How far is it?" I finally asked, chewing on an apple from the bag.

He had several chains looping across his waistcoat, and he stopped to pull one out. It was a large brass compass, but it ticked like a wind-up watch. "Walking, I'd say we're half a day away."

"There's a Manchester in my world, too, you know," I said thoughtfully. "I wonder why some of the places here are a couple of letters off from what I know? Bruzzles sounds like Brussels. Franchia sounds like France. And Manchester is the same."

"Different worlds run that way, I suppose," he answered. "I've read enough about them, and there are always similarities. I suppose it's like a slight warp in a mirror. You're still you, just a little fatter or thinner or more wobbly. Just a tiny change with grand repercussions."

And then it clicked.

"Stein. I found the locket in Mrs. Stein's house. And that's just one letter away from Stain. Maybe you guys are related?"

"Not unless she drinks blood, darling," he said with a chuckle.

I couldn't help wondering what tiny catalyst had caused our worlds to split, if that supposition was correct. If it went back to the Big Bang or if something had gone wrong with an overly aggressive paramecium in the primordial soup. "Funny thing is," he continued, "Manchester used to be called Bludchester. It was an old city built by Bludmen, and they took it from us in a grand slaughter centuries ago. The cathedral was originally dedicated to Aztarte, the goddess of Bludmen. But now they say it belongs to the Pinky saint Ermenegilda."

"Are you worried?" I asked. "About going there?"

"Maybe," he said with a grim grin. "But I'm going anyway. It'll take a good bit of acting, but I like acting."

"Why can't you just make me invisible again?" I asked.

"There you go, thinking things should be easy," he said with a fond chuckle. "It's easy to be invisible out on the moors with plenty of space and quiet. But in the city, people will bump into you, carriages could strike you, and bludrats will smell you there, anyway. And if something happened to you, if we were separated or you were hurt, I wouldn't be able to find you again. You would be stuck that way forever, dead or alive."

"Oh," I said with a shudder. "But why can't you just pretend to be human, then?"

He looked at me, his eyes hard and flinty. "I don't mind pretending to be inferior to you personally, and I very much don't mind feigning marriage," he said, "but I'll never betray what I am. The fine people of Manchester may think me a fiend, but prejudice runs both ways. I've a bit of pride about me, if you haven't noticed."

"I don't think there's anything wrong with what you are," I said shyly. "I just don't want to mess up, and you're much better at this sort of thing than I am."

"Don't worry. You'll enjoy playing along. You'll have to be haughty, and I'll have to act beaten down, when we're in public."

"That sounds kind of fun," I said.

"Just don't forget that it's a ruse, love," he said. "Because once we're outside the walls again, you'll be entirely in my power. And I'd hate to have to spank you."

I choked on the apple I was chewing and couldn't quite figure out how serious he was. Or how serious I wanted him to be.

A few hours later, a giant form began to shimmer in the distance. As we walked closer, I could see it, but it didn't make sense. Gravity shouldn't have allowed such a place to exist.

"There it is," Criminy said, handing me a brass spyglass. "Manchester."

I had to blink. The spyglass was incredible. I could see everything in amazing detail. Not that I really wanted to.

The city rose like a tumor on the landscape, like the shell of a hermit crab with extremely bad taste and a powerful glue gun. It was so much larger than I would have thought possible, an enormous mountain covered in stone and brick and wood. Around the base, in a valley, I could see fields and mines and quarries and refineries and factories belching smoke. A high, hideous wall of dirty gray stone surrounded everything. Razor wire curled around the top edge like deadly cake icing.

The empty moors seemed harmless and peaceful by comparison.

Within the wall, the buildings tottered from the mountain and from one another at odd angles, shored up by cables and poles and metal beams. An oily gray fug hung over everything. It was possibly the most depressing place I'd ever seen.

On the very top of the mountain perched a gigantic white church of a Gothic flavor, with flying buttresses and broken stained glass. At the very pinnacle was the large X from my glance, like a cross fallen on hard times.

"That's where our boy will be," Criminy said, reading my mind. "Right in the 'holier than thou' seat, at the very tip top of the broken city, standing on the backs of the suffering."

I had a strong feeling that he was right. And I really didn't want to be inside those walls.

"We'll have to go in through the front gate," Criminy said, taking the spyglass back. "And there are only two gates, so we'll have to leave through the other one right fast, because they'll be looking for us after the deed is done. So try to hide your face and act as normal as possible." He reached up to my bonnet and pulled down a delicate black veil that made me feel like a goth beekeeper. He smiled at the effect and asked, "Can you put on an accent? Try to sound more like me?"

"How will this do, then?" I said, rather proud of myself.

He chuckled. "Nice try, love, but that's a bit much. Tone it down a bit."

"The rain in Spain lands mainly on the plain," I said carefully.

"The rain in Vane never touches the plain," he said with a laugh. "Vane is mostly jungles. Do you have any other accents?"

"Is *annoyed* an accent?" I said.

"Let's just pretend you're a mute."

I stuck my tongue out at him, and he laughed that wild laugh of his. For just a second, I forgot the insurmountable odds we were up against and my worry for Nana. I laughed that way, too, and it felt good.

By that time, the wide treads of the bus tanks had turned into a dirt road. The ground was starting to get muddy as the grasses dwindled, the few straggling tufts by the road stunted and brown. Bludbunnies were fewer and fewer.

And then I learned why.

16

I saw the thing in the road before I smelled it, but the smell was a close second. I couldn't tell what it was. Just enough meat had been nibbled off the bones to remove hair and obscure the details. But it was definitely a carcass. And right on top of it was the biggest rat I'd ever seen, about the size of a house cat and covered with bristly, rust-colored hair.

Criminy didn't even slow down, but I crowded closer to his side as we approached. The rat didn't seem concerned by us, either, not until we were about twenty feet away. Then it looked up, tubes and sinews dripping from its mouth, and hissed. The effect of its bloodred eyes in the maroon fur was disturbing.

Criminy kept walking, dragging me along toward the nasty rat monster. The thing swallowed whatever it had been chewing and jumped off the carcass, hopping toward us with hackles raised. The fur stuck up in spines behind its neck, and it screamed at us. The scream sounded just like that of a human child.

Without breaking his stride or letting go of my arm, Criminy pulled something out of his boot and threw it.

I barely saw the dark blur shoot out of his left hand, and then the rat was twitching on its side, with a black knife sticking out of its forehead.

We kept walking, and just as we reached the dead rat, Criminy withdrew his knife with a jerk. As he cleaned it on a handkerchief, I pondered the pile of meat.

"It was a sheep, if you're wondering," he muttered.

And I could see it now over my shoulder, the fuzzy white wool dangling from the general shape of a very chewed-up sheep.

"How could it possibly get out of the wall?" I asked.

"They have to bring the grazers out for the fresh grass. They can't grow enough inside the wall to feed the animals. So they bring a team of shepherds bristling with weapons. But if the blud creatures swarm, they just leave one animal behind, a sacrifice for the rest of the herd. Fits in with their general philosophy."

The knife disappeared into his boot. We didn't break our stride. I looked back at the giant rat and said, "So that's a bludrat. And the city is full of those things?"

"Oh, they try to kill them all. But they're wily buggers. Bold and clever. No matter what the Coppers do, they always find a way back in. If I didn't hate the things so much, I'd be impressed."

The city loomed bigger and bigger as we approached. The wall had seemed tall from far away, but standing in front of the gargantuan door made me feel helpless and tiny. I couldn't begin to imagine how the two guards could open the two-story metal monstrosity. They each stood in a small building about the size of a closet, one on either side of the door. And they barely looked human, leather top hats laced down the neck, high collars digging into their chins, and bug-eyed goggles obscuring their eyes.

"Papers," barked the guard on the right through some sort of speaker, and Criminy led me to the glass wall of the booth. He slid our folded, faded traveling papers into a metal box and withdrew his hand before the guard jerked the box into his booth with a clang.

Criminy smiled and did his best to look harmless and weak. I stuck my nose in the air and rolled my eyes.

"State your business."

"We're visiting relatives, sir," Criminy said, his voice humble and obsequious. I knew he was an actor, but I was still floored that he sounded nothing like himself. "The wife and I. My cousin Anders and his family want to meet the new bride. He's a clockmaker, sir, and—"

"Toll!" the guard shouted. "Five coppers or one vial each."

The metal box popped violently back out of the booth, and Criminy snatched out our papers and dropped in a handful of coins. The box shot back into the booth.

"Stand back," the man said, and Criminy dragged me backward.

The guard pulled a lever, and with a loud whirring and several clanks, one of the giant doors began to swing outward. I looked at the guard and quickly glanced away. Nothing but his nose and lips was visible under his uniform, but I could read his disgust for me in his sneer. I straightened my shoulders and snuggled my head into Criminy's shoulder, giving the guard a look of disdainful rebellion. Criminy kissed me on the forehead and chuckled, and the guard spit on the floor and shook his head.

"It's only going to get worse," Criminy muttered into

my ear as we walked through the doorway. "Don't worry, darling. Everyone's going to hate us."

As the door clanged shut behind us, my throat constricted. I wasn't sure what I had expected to find within the tall wall, but it was worse than I could have imagined. The cobblestone streets were narrow and dirty, rife with puddles. The buildings towered above, blocking the sky. The windows all had a dirty film on them, and the people rushed from place to place as if they were being chased. They all looked at me with disgust, just as the guard had done.

Head down, Criminy quickly led me through the streets. We were on the main thoroughfare, a winding road lined with restaurants, inns, haberdashers, and milliners, all with painted signs swinging above their doors. Criminy didn't know where he was, but he knew what he was looking for.

We ducked down an alley. Red lights glittered from the shadows, and I heard a familiar hiss. All of the hairs on the back of my neck rose. It was darker there and more narrow, and I had to jog to keep up with him, my boots' staccato tapping echoing in a way that made me think of bones in oubliettes. Finally, we stopped before a sign showing a vial of blood and a pair of scissors, with the words *Arven Ariel, Barber and Letter* calligraphed underneath.

We stepped through the door and brushed past heavy, moldering curtains. I was expecting a cross between a morgue and a medieval barber, darkness and cobwebs and the smell of meat. But it looked more like a Mexican restaurant. Bright colors, fake palm trees, patterned fans and curtains. The walls were a vivid orange, and the floor was a sparkling, patterned mosaic of blue and lime green. Three plush chairs of maroon velvet waited in a row, each with a tasseled ottoman. A purple parrot on a stand squawked, "Master Arven, ye've custom!"

Criminy was smirking at me. "Not what it seemed, eh?" he said. "It's always like that in the city."

A very normal-looking man in a bowler hat brushed through a beaded curtain and approached us with a blank, professional smile.

"Can I help you, sir? Letting, shave, or haircut?" he asked, rubbing his hands together in burgundy gloves.

"A letting," Criminy said cheerfully. "And information, if you please."

"Won't madam have a seat?" the man asked, leading me to the middle chair. On a tray beside it sat a variety of scissors, straight razors, glass tubes, and antique-looking hypodermic needles. They didn't look entirely clean.

"Excuse me, *what*?" I said, planting my feet.

"Your blood, darling," Criminy said. "Three vials, I think."

The man tugged on my hand. I didn't budge.

"Darling," I said sweetly through clenched teeth, "I wasn't aware I'd be donating blood today."

"Darling," Criminy answered me, "we bring different gifts to the marriage, and right now, we need your blood. So won't you have a seat and relax? I'm told it doesn't hurt a bit. Just a pinch."

I glowered at him. He smiled. I plunked into the chair and gripped the armrests. My gloved fingers tapped. I wasn't scared of having blood drawn, and especially not of drawing it myself. But I didn't trust those primitive instruments, even in a world without infection or disease.

"Now what?" I growled.

"If madam would unbutton her necklet? I assure you, my professionalism is unparalleled." He smiled like a gynecologist.

I reached up and struggled with the buttons, and the man gently rolled down the neck of my gown.

"Just a pinch, if you'll hold still, madam," he murmured, and I turned my head and closed my eyes.

Something cold and numbing swept over my skin, and then I did feel just a slight pinch. I heard Criminy's footsteps move away to the other side of the room, and he pretended to be interested in a painting on the wall. I tried to sit very still and forget that a stranger was draining my blood out through my neck. I did the same thing every day for my patients, albeit from the arm. Was it all that different, just because someone was going to drink it instead of testing it?

Mr. Ariel held a soft cloth to my skin, swiped something cold over it again, and applied something sticky. "We're done, madam," he said, and with my eyes still closed, I struggled to rebutton my dress.

Criminy appeared at my side, his nimble fingers gentle on the buttons as he patted my hand.

"I'm wondering, sir," he asked, "where we might find Antonin Scabrous."

The man was fiddling with his instruments, and Criminy chose one of the three vials of blood on the tray and subtly nudged it toward him next to a silver coin. Both items disappeared into the man's vest, and he didn't turn to us as he murmured, "Tailor, West Darkside. Look for the Inn of the Old Black Dog. Watch out as you cross High Street. They won't like the two of you. Coppers here are harder than elsewhere."

"And the Magistrate?"

The man grunted. Criminy shoved over another vial.

"Jonah Goodwill. Lives in the priory beside the church. He's well guarded and dangerous."

"Many thanks," Criminy said.

I tried to get up from the chair, but the man stopped me with a patronizing hand on my shoulder. "You'll want to sit a moment, madam. And have a biscuit."

It was tough not to give him an earful about phlebotomy, but I kept my mouth shut and took one of the cookies from the tin in his hand. I sighed, and the man looked at Criminy with great curiosity.

"Your lady doesn't know much for a Bludman's wife," he said.

Criminy whisked me to my feet and said, "She's of a gentle constitution, and we're only newly married."

Taking the remaining vial of blood, Criminy guided me out the door and half-dragged me through the maze of streets again. I gripped his hand hard, forcing him to slow down.

"What do you think I am, your personal walking blood factory?" I whispered out the side of my mouth. "You could have at least warned me. Was that even sanitary?"

He put his arm around me, and I felt his breath on my ear as he whispered, "We needed information and collateral, and we got them both. And of course it's sanitary. Didn't you feel the alcool? It numbs and cleans at once. We're not aboriginals."

"Where are we going now? Are we off to sell my hair next?"

"Good heavens, why would anyone want your hair? Not that it isn't lovely," he said. "You heard the man. We're going to the Bludmen's district to speak to an old associate of mine."

"I just don't want to be surprised again," I said, feeling a bit prickly.

"You will be, no matter what," he said. "Might as well expect it."

Ignoring my reticence, he pulled me along at a clipped pace, my heels slipping in muck on the cobbles. From time to time, he hugged me to the wall as a horseless carriage went by, leaving only inches to spare between us and the jerky machine. Like the engine of the caravan's train, the odd carriages had machinery and tubes and wires bursting from the place where horses should have stood. The drivers, perched on rickety benches above and pulling levers, all wore aviator's hats and goggles and navigated the narrow roads with little regard for pedestrians.

No wonder the air was so smoggy—the engines puffed green steam out one side and gray smoke out the other. The lack of horse manure was a bonus, but there was also a certain level of disdain inferred by the machines. If a horse stepped on you, it was personal. But if a horseless carriage clipped you, it was indifferent and cruel, and the driver just kept on driving as the snobby faces behind the window turned away.

We were trotting along a broad avenue when we passed two expensively dressed ladies wearing high platform boots and strange rose-colored glasses. Their pink-tinged eyes shot daggers at me, and the older one hissed, "Bludhoney." I felt Criminy tense and snarl, but I kept moving forward, pulling him with me before he tried to defend my honor.

At the next cross street larger than a drainage ditch, he took a right, murmuring, "That's enough of High Street."

We turned onto an alley specializing in foodstuffs. Butchers and bakers and wine shops stood open, while occasional carts offered lackluster fruits and vegetables. No wonder everyone looked either sickly or florid—even the green things weren't green. The broccoli was gray, and the apples were the gold of old urine. The entire rainbow of plants ran from whitish yellow to yellowish brown.

But the bread smelled heavenly, I'll admit that. And the coffee. And something wafting from a store labeled *Choco-vanerie*. I slowed down to sniff.

"You don't want to do that, pet," Criminy said, dragging me along. "Wait until we get somewhere healthy. This stuff is all ersatz."

"What's ersatz?"

"Fake," he said curtly. "No nutritive value. Made of ground-up meal and flavorings, sometimes even sawdust. It's all the poor can afford. Those vegetables are half-rotten."

And then I could smell it, the subtle sickness wafting from the baskets. I rubbed my nose along Criminy's shoulder, trying to drown the stench with berries.

At the next big cross street, he started to take a left and then looped back when he saw a Copper on a bludmare standing sentinel. "Residential," he said. "I'll just make 'em nervous."

So we went, past booksellers and weavers and pet shops crowded with droopy magpies and small, yappy dogs. We wove through poor streets and rich streets, past beggars and dukes and Coppers. I was getting a headache from hunger and thirst and overpowering smells, and my eyes were so full of new things that they were nearly crossed.

"Mr. Paisley," I murmured, "don't forget to feed your pet Pinky."

He stopped to look at me tenderly and murmured, "Sorry, love. I was so busy trying to keep you safe that I forgot how your kind wilts without food and drink."

He sniffed the air and made several turns until we were in a brighter, altogether richer part of town. When he stopped at a shiny green cart with delectable steam rising from a closed bin, I started drooling a little.

"Wrappy and a squeeze," he said, flipping the man a coin.

"Gonner try some real food, eh, Bluddy?" the man said sourly, but he handed over a cup made of thick, waxed newspaper folded origami-style and brimming with golden liquid. With his other hand, he used tongs to select an oblong packet wrapped in the same greasy newspaper. He dropped it into Criminy's hand with a smirk, and we left quickly without thanking him. I could tell that Criminy was furious. That seemed to happen a lot in the city.

"That *is* for me, right?" I said. Whatever it was, it smelled good. Like fast food.

"It's for you, but it's piping hot. Chappy bastard was hoping to burn one of us. I'll hand it to you as soon as it's cool enough to eat, I promise."

He put the cup into my hand, saying, "Drink fast. These cups don't last long."

After a moment of examination, I turned the cup sideways and poured the golden stuff into the side of my mouth.

"Grape juice?"

"That's why they call it a squeeze," he said wryly. "But city grapes don't grow purple or red—only yellow."

I gulped the juice, and he threw my cup onto the ground and handed me the thing he'd called a wrappy. It was a sort of burrito, filled with boiling-hot lava that tasted a lot like shepherd's pie. It was gristly and heavy on the potatoes and beans, but it had a perfectly satisfying oil-to-salt ratio. I thanked him and licked the sauce off my gloves as we walked.

At last, he turned down a dark alley under a riveted sign reading *Darkside*. I could have sworn the temperature was ten degrees lower on the other side of that sign. The road was poorly kept, with missing cobbles and graffiti in white chalk.

Drain U, one said.

Bluddy go home to the ground, said another.

It was a residential area, but the windows were blacked out or covered with neatly nailed boards. The doors were all painted blood red. There were no window boxes or decorations. No one would live this way on purpose, not unless they were forced. The dismal streets and Criminy's tense silence spoke volumes about the oppression of his species by mine.

The next cross street was more open, with wooden signs hanging just like those on High Street—but darker. I saw a jeweler, a pawn shop, an apothecary. Then, up ahead, a sign featuring a black dog on its back, feet in the air, with an X for an eye. That had to be the Inn of the Old Black Dog. Next door, a spool with a needle—Criminy's friend, the tailor.

We ducked through the burgundy door into a bright room painted with harlequin diamonds in light blue and violet. It was just like Mrs. Cleavers's wagon but neater, with mannequins and mirrors abounding and bolts of cloth stacked neatly on shelves. Directly facing us, head down over a tabletop sewing machine of brass and black iron, was the first Bludman I'd seen in the city.

He looked up at us with a mouthful of pins and grinned like a voodoo doll. His skin was light brown, which contrasted oddly with golden hair and ice-blue, piercing eyes. But his face was jolly, and he seemed glad to see us. That was really starting to mean something.

Stashing the pins in a jar, he stood to stretch his back with a series of pops. He locked the front door, then faced Criminy with open arms, saying, "Crim! How long's it been?"

"Too long, Antonin. Too long. How goes it?"

They hugged and beat each other on the back. Apparently, that male gesture crosses world and species lines as the only acceptable way to show masculine friendship.

"Manchester's not what it used to be," Antonin said, running a hand through his curly gold hair and making it stand on end. "The Coppers get rougher every year. Did you ever think you'd see the day when I'd be stuck sewing in Darkside? But the Magistrate's put up new restrictions, and here I am."

"So I noticed," Criminy said, taking in the room. "Nice spot, though. I guess the fine ladies and masters of High Street secretly send their footmen to you with measurements?"

"They do." Antonin chuckled. "No Pinky can make a finer seam than I. Business is good, if society ain't. And who's this lovely creature?"

When his eyes turned on me, I could sense a latent but polite hunger underneath. Criminy's arm snagged my waist, and he drew me close, saying, "My wife, actually. Letitia, this is Antonin Scabrous, formerly of Scarborough and the best tailor in Sang. We started out in the same caravan as lads and bunked together for our apprentice years."

"Ah, yes. The tale of two tailors' sons who ran off to join

the circus. You got the exciting end of the bargain, and I still ended up with a needle in my mouth," Antonin said with a laugh. "How's the caravan, anyway?"

"Good, in general," Criminy said. "That is, until some rowdy bastard stole my lady's wedding present, a fine ruby locket. We think he's in the city." His voice dropped. "And we think you might know of him."

Antonin winked. "Won't you come back to the sitting room, have a drop to drink? I might have a biscuit for your lady somewhere, too."

We followed him through a curtain of jingling beads and down a narrow hallway cheerfully decorated with hundreds of painted thread spools mounted on nails. We sidled through the tall door at the end of the hall, and I had to blink. It was a narrow sitting room so bright and yellow that it was like sitting in a lemon. The velvet chaise was yellow, the chairs were white with yellow spots, and the walls were yellow and white damask. It was so bright that my teeth hurt.

Criminy swung Pemberly off his shoulder and muttered, "Pem, guard the hall." She scampered to the center of the hallway and stood on her hind legs, and her head began slowly spinning, her eyes casting red lights on the walls, dancing over the rainbow of spools. She had become a copper disco ball. I had completely forgotten the sleeping snake on my own arm.

"Nice monkey," Antonin said. "But don't worry. Owlice is always watching in the rafters of the front room."

"You can never be too careful," Criminy murmured. "Not these days."

Antonin pressed a button on a small, white-enameled cube that looked like a safe. The door popped open, and a breath of warm air wafted out. Inside sat rows of blood vials in cartons, much like the containers that held eggs in my world. He picked up a vial, checked the date scrawled on the glass, and split the contents between two demitasse cups. He handed one to Criminy, who took a dainty sip and sighed.

"Refreshing," he said. "Thanks."

The two men sipped their blood, ignoring me. They started talking about eighteen-something-or-other and people with odd names who did odder things. I yawned. I read the spines of books on the yellow bookshelf and gazed at the paintings in yellow frames. Here I was, trapped in a fantasy world, worrying about my grandmother and my real world, tapping my toes as vicious blood drinkers enjoyed teatime.

"Criminy?" I asked.

"Hmm?"

"What are we doing?"

"I'm having a meal with a friend while you squirm like a child," he said serenely.

I glared.

Antonin laughed and said something in a slurry foreign tongue full of s's and z's.

Criminy laughed, too. In the yellow room, their red-stained teeth gave me the creeps.

"You're laughing at me?" I said. "You bleed me and then laugh at me?"

"I'm sorry, love," Criminy said, trying not to snicker. "It's just an old saying. *Humans are like kittens, their teeth tickle when angry.* You do look so very much like an angry kitten."

It was a horrible position to be in. I couldn't storm out; I had nowhere else to go. In Sang, it was too dangerous to risk even a moment out of their sight. But alone with two predators, I felt less like a kitten and more like an object lesson waiting to happen.

I hadn't felt that way with Criminy before. Inferior, and silly. I hated it, having someone outside our little circle laughing at me. I fought tears. Fighting tears made me think about my other world, my fallen body, and my suffering grandmother. Would I ever see her again? And then I was snuffling into my sleeve.

Antonin looked embarrassed and studied the wall. Criminy set down his cup and moved close to put his arm around me.

"There, there, now," he murmured. "Even angry kittens have their claws. We don't mean to be unkind. Old friends sharing a joke, that's all. We'll get your locket back."

"I'm not a joke." I sniffled. "I miss my home. My grandmother."

Antonin cleared his throat and was about to say something when a bell rang, followed by the unmistakable call of an owl. Antonin's eyes went round, and he whispered, "Coppers," and kicked back the yellow rag rug at our feet, revealing a trapdoor. Criminy grabbed the iron ring and pulled it open as Antonin rattled teacups and slammed cupboards, calling, "I'll be there shortly."

I held up my dress as I stumbled down the stone steps into an unlit cellar that smelled of earth and age. Criminy was at my heels. He closed the trapdoor, dousing us in darkness. I heard the shuffling sound of the rug overhead and sighed, pressing back against Criminy.

That's when I felt something heavy and warm on my boot.

17

Whatever it was, I jumped up and down until it fell off. I wanted to punt it, but I had no idea what sort of rakes or glass jars or pipe organs were around us, waiting to make the noise that would betray our hiding place to the Coppers above.

I put my mouth to where I hoped Criminy's ear might be and whispered, "There's something in here with us. It was on my foot. Kill it!"

His lips moved against my cheek, his breath warm against my skin as he said, "You just kicked a very nice house cat, darling. And a forgiving one. Can't you hear her purring?"

When I slowed my own breathing and stopped listening to my heart thump, I heard it. A soft, low rumble from the ground.

"Why does Antonin have an underground cat?" I whispered.

"To keep her safe, I'd guess," he said. "There's nothing the bludrats would love so much as a nice, juicy cat. Probably lets her up at night, when the front door is bolted."

I felt him fold gracefully to the ground at my feet, and the purring intensified. The blood-drinker was petting a cat. And humming.

"What is this place?" I whispered.

"A cellar," he said. "Surely you know what a cellar is?"

"Of course I know what a cellar is," I hissed. "What else is down here?"

He stood and whispered a word, and a tiny blue flame sparked in the darkness. The first thing I saw was his face. The next thing I saw was a skull hovering slightly behind him. As I opened my mouth to scream, his gloved hand sealed my lips.

"Shh," he said.

"Mmph-mm-hm-mph!"

His eyes flicked back. "Yes, it's a skeleton. It's chained to the wall. It was probably a very bad man. Antonin is part of an underground resistance movement against the Coppers. Did you know that they sometimes steal our children off the street and drain them before crowds as abominations? They do. And this fellow has been dead for quite some time, and he deserved it, so I wouldn't worry too much."

I tried to take my mind off the skeleton by looking around the rest of the cellar. It was about ten feet square, with walls of mortared stone like a crypt. Cobwebs and dust were everywhere. If I hadn't known better by then, I would have looked for a coffin.

On the ground by the skeleton, I saw some instruments that made me look away. Clippy things and poky things and something that looked like a golf-cart battery.

And then the door opened above us, and light flooded in. Antonin's face appeared.

"Come on up. They're gone."

I nearly leaped out of the cellar. Criminy followed at a more stately pace.

"I take it you met Anabella and Mr. Rapture," said Antonin.

"A little warning would have been nice," I answered.

"Thought you'd prefer the dead Copper to the live ones upstairs," he said with a shrug. "They're looking for you. Now, why is that?"

"You first," Criminy said, sinking into a chair.

"There's a price on her head," Antonin said. "A female Stranger of bad intentions in a burgundy dress of last year's fashion accompanied by a Bludman in a black cloak and tall hat with a copper monkey. Last seen at the Fleet Street letter."

"Do you mean the *recently deceased* Fleet Street letter?" Criminy asked.

"I do believe that something unfortunate is in the cards for Mr. Ariel, actually," Antonin said with a wicked smile. His innate potential for violence flashed out for just a moment, like a shark's fin breaking water, but then he was just a tailor again, ruffling his curly hair in a lemon-yellow room.

Pemberly appeared, and Criminy swung her back onto his shoulder. "We should be going before we get you into any further trouble."

"You needed information?" Antonin pressed.

"Ah, yes. So much for small talk over a companionable vial. What can you tell us about the Magistrate?"

"Jonah Goodwill. Old bastard with a big mustache and a bigger hatred of anything inhuman. Lives in the priory beside the cathedral at the top of the mountain, has his own little paradise full of gardens and fruit trees. Eden House. All of the things his grateful citizens can never have. We've tried to gain access for years, but no one can get close. They all disappear."

"That's who we're after," Criminy said. "He's a Stranger himself. And he apparently knows we're coming."

"I met him at the caravan, but I still don't understand how he knew I was a Stranger, too," I said glumly.

Antonin's hand shot toward me, but·Criminy intercepted it. Antonin shook him off with a snort and gently stroked my earlobe.

"Do you think anyone in this godforsaken world would purposefully punch holes in their skin?" he said softly.

I reached to my earlobe, feeling the hole that had been there since my eighth birthday.

Luckily, when you're in need of a disguise, the tailor's shop is one of the best places to be. Gone was my beautiful burgundy dress. Now I was in navy-blue taffeta, the shiny ruffles rustling whenever I moved. My black bonnet was gone, too, replaced by a wide straw hat with a spray of feathers. The hat had come from a very nervous old lady, so my betraying ears were snugly covered by a black lace panel that made my neck itch horribly.

Criminy was resplendent in emerald green, his favorite top hat somehow hidden up the sleeve of his new tailcoat. Instead, he wore a wool bowler, which made him look more dangerous and disreputable than usual. His favorite coat, the one with the hidden magic pockets, was hanging in the cellar by the skeleton. Most of the gadgets and doodads had been stuffed into his waistcoat, and I couldn't understand why it didn't bulge more. Pemberly had been sent back to the caravan with carefully coded messages for Mrs. Cleavers, and Criminy's shoulder looked a little empty without her. We were ready.

"Can't you give her some blud?" Antonin asked, leaning close to look into my face. "Just to color her eyes, give her some stamina?"

"Now's not the time," Criminy said gruffly. "And she's not ready yet."

"She's a Bludman's wife, ain't she? Or is she scared?"

"I'm not drinking any blud," I said. "But the fact that I'm here should tell you enough about how I feel."

"The fact that you're after Goodwill is good enough for me," Antonin answered. "If you're against him, you're on my side."

We left with more male back pounding, a chaste kiss on my glove, and a hand-drawn map showing a shadowy route to Goodwill's home in the old monastery. Now that the Coppers were looking for us, we needed to move fast.

"He won't be looking for us to come after him," Criminy reasoned. "Powerful man like that. Won't expect us to bring the fight to his door. Probably too busy looking for us to watch his own back."

"But what if he isn't?" I pressed.

"What choice do we have, love?" he snapped. "You want the locket. I'm trying to get the locket. We'll follow this plan until things change, then we'll follow a new plan. If you need more of an answer than that, I can't give it to you. You're the one who sees the future, not me."

We followed the alleys of Darkside as far as we could up the mountain. When we reentered the brighter streets of the Pinkies, we clung to the shadows and tried not to draw attention to ourselves. At one point, a Copper turned to stare at us, and Criminy spun around, putting his back against the slimy brick wall of the alley and using my huge hat to shield us both in a wild pantomime of passion that managed to leave me a little breathless. I couldn't help it—lips were still lips, and hips were still hips, even if we were pretending. Behind me, I heard the

Copper spit in disgust. By the time he turned again, we were gone.

Near the cathedral, the neighborhoods grew grimier and duller, and the people seemed more downtrodden and pitiful. Their clothes were ragged and patched, their faces hollow and hopeless.

We huddled in the shadow of the church's high roof. Above our niche was a broken stained-glass window of a figure on a cross bleeding into a cup. Oddly, it wasn't Jesus. It was a woman with red hair. And she looked pissed.

"Who's that?" I asked.

"Depends on whom you ask. To me, that's the goddess Aztarte, the first Bludwoman," Criminy said. "To the Pinkies who now run Sangland, it's Saint Ermenegilda. She died to drive the bloodthirsty demons from the land, to make it safe for the second kingdom of mankind." He examined his map for a moment and muttered, "She was a witch and a virago, but the church tries to play that bit down and just remind everyone of her sacrifice. For humanity."

He pulled out Antonin's map. "Goodwill's place is on the other side of the monastery, behind high walls. The inside of the cathedral is guarded, and the walls are patrolled by Coppers with dogs that can sniff through my illusions. I have no idea how we're going to get in without him knowing about it yesterday."

We heard voices coming around the corner, and I froze. Criminy pulled me to his side.

"Hold still," he said, and he tossed some powder from one of his pockets over us both. I suddenly felt very dusty and dry, similar to the feeling of a mud mask right before it begins to flake off.

"Don't move," Criminy said out of the corner of his

mouth. And it would have been very hard to move, even if I had wanted to. My face and body were completely stuck, and the lone corner of my gloved hand that I could still see was the aged gray of old stone. He'd turned us into a statue.

Moving only my eyeballs, I watched a pack of small, filthy children scamper around the corner, giggling. Their exposed necks told me they were Bludmen—or Bludchildren. They all huddled around a brown object except for one who squatted by the corner, pretending to defecate.

"Did he see you, Les?" said one. I couldn't tell by look or voice what gender or age the child might be. They all looked the same, really—huge eyes in gaunt faces wrapped in grime-covered rags.

"Naw, the skinny one was too busy calling Bertie a stinkin' bat-faced bludbag to notice me lifting the fat one's wallet. Stupid Coppers." The child emptied the bag and divvied up the coins within, then wedged the wallet under my stone skirt.

"What do you think them Coppers taste like?" asked a third urchin wistfully.

"I bet they taste like shite," said the tiniest one of all.

"Cheese it—here comes Rudy!" the lookout hissed. They all ran away, melting into the shadows.

Even frozen beside me, trapped by his own magic, I could feel Criminy's fury. The plight of the starving, filthy Bludchildren had touched a nerve. If he could have shot lightning out of his eyes, the people coming around the corner would have been cinders.

Two young Coppers appeared, their shiny uniforms creaking as they walked behind a giant dog on a chain lead. The dog was copper-colored, too, like a cross between a German shepherd and a mastiff, its boxy head as high as my waist. It was slavering and whining, drool dripping down its chops. The Coppers ignored it.

"Someone oughtta drain those brats," said the skinny one. "Cor, I hate church duty."

"Me, too," said the short, fat Copper holding the dog's lead. "Downright spooky, even in the daytime. Nobody believes in ol' Ermenegilda anymore, anyway, do they?"

"Damned if I know," said the skinny one. "My mum always told me she was just a nice story about helping other humans. About making a sackerfice. Back when people cared."

The dog sniffed Criminy and me energetically. I held my breath. The fat one yanked the dog back, hissing, "It's only a statue, Rudy. Some other dog prolly pissed on it. Cut it out." Then he looked up at the naked saint in the window and grinned, showing teeth like crooked tombstones. "I'd let that ripe little plum make me a nice sacrifice, eh, Gerren?"

"That's blasphemy, that is," said Gerren. "But yeah."

He glanced down from Saint Ermenegilda, looked me straight in the eye, and began to untie the leather laces on his pants, if my hearing was correct. Then I heard his stream, and he sighed as he urinated on us.

Talk about blasphemy.

At least I didn't feel any wetness. Thank heavens for magic.

"Dunno why we didn't get to go to the island with everyone else," the fat one whined. "Nothing here to guard, anyway. What, are the poor folk and the Bludmen gonna overrun us for a barrel of apples and one old, runty cow that don't even give milk no more?"

"You're new, so you don't know yet. Got to keep up the image," said Gerren, puffing out his bird chest as he redid his fly. "Make it seem like there's something worth guarding, even if there ain't. It's funny, all the secrets you learn once you're a Copper."

He sighed and stretched, the leather of his new uniform squeaking. The dog danced around us, straining toward me and Criminy. Gerren smacked it on the nose, and it sat, dejected.

"Do you think what they say about Goodwill is true?" the fat one asked.

"What, that he's really a Stranger?" Gerren said mockingly. "The secret society and the underground lair and all that?"

"Yeah."

"That's ridiculous, that is," Gerren said as they ambled off, dragging the huge dog behind them. "He's just an old hypocrite gone to see a doxy on his magic island or handle the trouble at Brighton. Manchester's so dull and horrid that everybody thinks everybody else is up to no good and that there's some better place. There ain't. All the cities is like this, Joff, me boy, and they ain't never gonna change. Not with them Bludmen about. You've got a lot to learn, lad."

"Bluddy Bludmen," agreed the fat one as they turned the corner and moved out of sight.

I was magically petrified, but I was so tense with shock that it would have been hard to move, anyway. Jonah Goodwill wasn't here—he was on an island somewhere far away. We had no idea where the locket had gone, and the low sky was swelling with the purple streaks of evening. I felt a tear trickle inside the weird crust over my skin, and then I fell to my knees, the spell broken.

"Are you all right, love?" Criminy asked, squatting beside me and searching my face.

I wasn't all right, not by a long shot. I put a hand to my cheek, but it was clean and normal. I had expected to feel the slurry mud of dust and tears or some residue from the magic. But there was nothing.

"I want to go home," I said, my voice cracking. "I want my locket."

"And we'll find it, no matter the cost. Both for you and for those children, to stop whatever Goodwill's planned. But for now, we've got to get off the street. We'll talk to Antonin again in the morning," he said. He dusted off his waistcoat and grinned at me. "We're lucky those bastards stopped to take a piss on a holy relic. At least now we know where to look."

"Where?"

"According to gossip, there's a secret island where innocent animals still roam, a paradise free of the creatures of blud. If they say he's on an island, that's got to be the one."

"But how are we going to find it? One island, in all the world, with nothing to go on but rumors? It's hopeless." I threw my arms around his neck and buried my head in his shoulder.

He wrapped his arms around me. "Sweet little kitten," he said as I rubbed my tears away against his jacket . "Don't you know that rumors are almost always true? And I have other ways of knowing."

I sniffled, gazing at the mazelike town unfolding below us. All the way down at the base of the high wall, a flock of ash-gray, sickly sheep was huddled, as tiny as ants. They should have been grazing, but the ground was just a foul mass of mud. Their bleating sounded like crying.

"Everything is so wrong," I said.

"Not everything," Criminy said, stroking my hair. "But

it appears that Mr. Goodwill isn't all that he seems. I can't wait to ask him myself."

Thanks to the prejudice of the city, we were confined to Darkside for the night. No Pinky inn would dream of opening its doors to a Bludman. We stopped at the Inn of the Magi on the opposite side of the mountain from Antonin's shop. Entering the bloodred door under the wooden sign showing three men in turbans, I felt Criminy relax a little. The front room was very elegant, and a dainty teenage Bludwoman stood behind the counter, wearing a very tall hat.

"Good evening," she said with the same bouncy cockney accent I'd heard all over town. "Can I help you?"

"We'd like a room, please, miss. My wife and I," Criminy said with a low bow. "Daggern and Fevrier Blur."

"There's a two-bedder available on the second floor, sir, or the penthouse," she said, bobbing a curtsy. "Five coppers for the two-bedder, ten for the penthouse."

"We'll take the two-bedder, thank you," he said, producing several coins from his waistcoat and sliding them across the counter. He smiled kindly and leaned forward to pluck another coin from her ear. "And look at this! Miss, you must wash more carefully."

She giggled, and I could see that she was younger than she looked despite her low-cut gown. As we bowed and left with our key, she scribbled in a giant black ledger, her tongue sticking out in concentration.

The room was small but bright and neat. Dainty plates in colorful patterns hung from ribbons and clashed cheerfully with the wallpaper, which was white with green vines. Criminy shrugged off his new coat and put out his hand to me. I didn't know what he wanted, but

I held my hand out anyway, with a little flutter in my stomach. He surprised me by reaching for the snake around my wrist.

"Time to see what your little Uro can do," he said.

He pushed the button, and Uro came alive, flattening out on the table. His head swiveled until it found me, and then the lights blinked, and the black tongue shot out once in what seemed like satisfaction.

"Tell him to guard," Criminy said.

"Uro, guard," I said.

The red eyes flashed once, and the snake's head rose as his body went rigid and his tail split into three separate sections. He was now a sort of tripod, and his head slowly spun around, taking in everything. What a handy device.

"I think we're safe here," Criminy said. "New clothes, different names. And I'll wager that little lass at the front counter wouldn't give us away for all the world. Let's sleep, and we'll start over in the morning. I get the bed closer to the door."

I disappeared into the bathroom to change. Fortunately, the new dress unlaced in such a way that I could get out on my own, and I now had enough experience with a corset to handle that myself, too. I splashed water on my face and used a towel to scrub off the makeup, then shyly emerged in my white nightdress.

To my profound surprise, Criminy was already in bed, breathing deeply under the covers. I had forgotten that he had spent the previous nights watching over my body as I slept—he had to be exhausted.

His back was to me, and I was undeniably drawn to him. It was rare to see him when he was still, when he wasn't already observing me or taking firm control of the situation at hand. His bare shoulder peeked from under the blanket, smooth and white, his dark hair falling to either side. There was a small scar there, pink like a burn, and I unconsciously reached out to trace it with a finger, wondering what sort of creature or weapon could actually wound him.

Just as I touched his skin, surprised as ever to find him so warm, his hand closed around my wrist. I gasped as he rolled to his back, pulling me down on top of him on the narrow bed.

His eyes burned into mine, dark and dancing.

"Surely this is a dream. My fair Letitia, coming to me in the night."

"I thought you were asleep," I said. I tried to draw away, but his bare hands settled on my hips. Even through the blankets and my nightgown, I could feel the hard planes of his body and the hint of claws prickling my skin.

"Asleep? With you that close and watchful? A predator like me? Never," he said, voice husky.

"You must be tired. I'm sorry I bothered you."

I was flustered, and I tried to press up with my arms. That just settled my hips more firmly against his. A slow smile spread over his face.

"Keep trying to escape, love. It's heavenly. No bother at all."

He shifted sinuously beneath me as if asking a question I wasn't ready to answer. I let myself collapse forward, tucking my flushed face into his neck before he could see my embarrassment. I couldn't ignore his body and my response to it, but I could avoid his eyes. I sighed into his hair, awash in his scent. With an answering sigh, he shifted me to the bed so that I was nestled against his side, his arm around me. We barely fit on the mattress, but it didn't occur to me to leave.

"You're still skittish, little love. Now, why is that?" he whispered in my ear. Goose bumps rippled down my back, and he groaned as I shifted against him.

"I'm scared," I whispered back into the darkness of his hair.

He firmly lifted my face, his eyes catching mine.

"Of what?"

"I—"

His lips settled over mine, cutting off the list of everything I feared. The city, the Magistrate, the bludrats, the Coppers, people like Elvis, my world, my grandmother, my own sanity, my freedom. It all fell away as his hand gently cupped my face, his thumb stroking my cheek like a whisper. There was nothing in all the world but him and me and the point where we met, mouth to mouth and heart to heart. The kiss was soft and warm, restrained and gentle. An answer and a mercy. A comfort. I relaxed against him, my fingers tangling in his hair.

He pulled away first and looked into my eyes. The fire in his gaze had fled, leaving an endless, cloudy blue.

"So long as you're not afraid of me, I think we'll be all right," he whispered. "Now, go get some sleep."

I took my cue and crawled into my own bed, which was crisp and cool and smelled deliciously of sage. Oddly, the kiss had calmed me. I knew he could have kept me there, whether by force or just with the simple magnetic tug that pulled me to him again and again. But he hadn't. Instead, he had given me exactly what I needed. Not fire. Not flames. Just warmth.

"Thank you," I murmured, just loudly enough for him to hear it a few feet away.

"Anytime," he whispered back.

In moments, I was asleep.

I awoke the next morning feeling a little dreamy. Part of me had still expected to wake up in my own world. Part of me had also expected a certain darkly handsome magician to slip into bed beside me and reignite the passion held tightly controlled in the kiss. I couldn't decide if I was grateful or disappointed that he had kept his distance. The kiss had felt like a promise of things to come, and now that I was awake and rested, I wasn't sure if I wanted them. I sat up and looked around as the weak sun filtered in through the curtains.

Criminy sat on his bed, legs crossed, fully clothed but bootless. He was wearing mismatched argyle stockings. In front of him was an old-fashioned map. I leaned over to examine the painted images so similar to Europe, part of Asia, and the upper bit of Africa. But the borders were all wrong, and the names were peculiar, and I had a feeling that the little creatures by 'Here there be dragons' were an actual threat.

I sat down on the edge of the bed, unobtrusive but close enough to see the map. There were also some strange little gewgaws strewn across the paper—jewels and bones and rocks. Criminy swept these into a velvet bag, which he stowed in his waistcoat.

"So here we are," he said, pointing to what would have been Britain.

Manchester was in the center, right where Manchester would be on my own maps. But lots of the other place names were off. France was Franchia, right next to Vane. There was Bruzzles—in Belgum. London was still London, though, I noted with a smile.

"And here's where I think Goodwill's island is, according to the bones," he said, pointing to a collection of smudges in the sea just south of Brighton. "Somewhere near the Isle of White. Shouldn't be hard to find."

"Why's that?" I asked.

"His will be the one with the wall around it," he said with a grin. "The man's awfully fond of walls."

"But how do we get there?" I asked. "I can't walk that far. Not in these boots, not with bludbunnies chasing me."

"It's a difficult question," he said. "I don't want to get the caravan involved, so that's out. We don't have money enough for a conveyance, and they'll be looking for us to do that, anyway. And we can't trust the banks, of course."

"What's wrong with banks?" I asked, completely confused.

"They move too slowly, and we'd be easy to catch," he explained.

"Where I come from, banks are buildings that store money for you," I said.

"Who on earth would trust someone else to store their money?" Criminy said, horrified at the idea. "Banks are those giant transports you saw on opening night. Bus tanks, you see. But we can't take that route."

"But we can't walk," I said again. "It would take days. We have to move faster. Can we steal something?"

"Already turning to a life of crime, pet?" he said with an affectionate stroke of my hair. "But no. That would be far too easy to track. We need something fast and free that nobody else wants. And there's only one answer."

"That sounds ominous," I said.

He grinned, showing me his pointy teeth. "It is."

18

Once I heard the details of his plan, I liked it even less. I
maintained an irritable silence as we departed the inn, leaving the counter girl with another coin pulled from her ear.
Criminy had a spring in his step, sure that we were on the
right track. But I was determined to think of an alternative
that didn't scare the crap out of me.

Heads down, we sped toward the gates on the opposite
side of the city from those we had entered through the day
before. On the way, he bought me a wrappy brimming with
buttery eggs and white cheese and lavender mushrooms.
We stopped at a strange store called *Apollinaire's Everything
Shoppe,* which did indeed seem to have everything. It was like
a five-and-dime crossed with my grandmother's attic and a
magic store. I marveled at the peculiar array of goods that
Criminy stuffed into his pack. His leather satchel banged
against his back on the way out with a metallic clang.

As we neared the gate, Criminy yanked me into a dark
alley and blew powder into my face, muttering a spell.
I didn't feel a thing, so I shrugged. He stood back and
laughed, saying, "This one won't hold up long, thank
heavens. Let's hurry."

The guards at the back gate were just as unfriendly as

the ones at the front gate. As the guard looked at me, then down at my even newer set of fake papers, he sneered in disgust and, oddly, pity. But he waved us through, and the giant gate squealed open just enough for us to pass through.

Once we were out of earshot, I reached to my face and asked, "What did you do to me?"

Criminy pulled a small brass mirror from his waistcoat, saying, "It's just a glamour, not something you can feel with your hands. I was trying to make you as different as possible from what you really are. It's already fading."

In the mirror, I saw the most hideous woman I'd ever seen. Warts, chin whiskers, a vein-covered nose shaped like a squash.

"Wow, it's like being thirteen all over again," I said. I had to laugh, too. It was awful, but it was a lot better than getting caught.

Criminy took out his spyglass and scanned the moors. With an annoyed *hmph*, he pulled out a different compass, one I hadn't seen before. Instead of having four arrows, this one had tiny pictures all around the outside of the circle. Criminy turned the dial and fiddled with the mechanism, then sighted along the arrow and started walking. I followed, nervous.

We walked through the empty moors for some time before he put a hand out to stop me, right on the edge of an abandoned orchard. We were in the middle of nowhere and hadn't seen a living thing other than bludbunnies since the city gate shut behind us.

"It's probably just over that hill. Now, unlace your gloves and neck, and stand right here, very still. You're going to have to trust me." He kissed my forehead and disappeared up a tree.

I was alone. With a shaky breath, I began shyly unlacing things, releasing the scent of my flesh on purpose for the first time in this dangerous world. I stood there feeling the breeze on my skin but unable to enjoy it, imagining myself as Andromeda, chained to the rock and ignoring the sea. At least we were hunting something a good bit smaller than a kraken.

The bludbunnies were the first to arrive, hopping innocently out of the cool morning and lolloping to my feet, where Criminy dispatched them one by one with a slingshot. I could barely see him through the leaves, perched on a branch with his neatly folded coat beside him.

Soon the ground around my boots was littered with cute, fluffy corpses in white and soft brown and dappled gray. They reminded me of the fur jacket I'd received for Christmas when I was eight, except that my coat hadn't wanted to eat me.

Next came a fox, which was more than happy to snatch up some bludbunnies and run, not picky at all. Then a doe emerged from the bushes, its steps tentative. Criminy pinged it in the bum with a stone, and it hissed and bounded away.

At last, we heard our quarry thundering over the hill, and my heart beat quick in my throat.

It was so hard not to run away. As if that would have helped.

She was a big one, and she was coming right at me.

In my world, she would have been a Percheron, probably. But in this world, she was a bludmare and built to kill. Feet the size of dinner plates, long and flowing mane and tail, foamy mouth full of pointy teeth. Her huge red eyes were fixed on me. And she was drooling.

She stopped to scent the air. Her glossy black sides quivered as she inhaled deeply. With a roar of triumph, the bludmare reared and galloped straight at me. I tensed. She weighed as much as a VW van, and she was going for the kill.

The ground quaked beneath my boots as she pounded toward me. I steeled myself to hold still. It went against every instinct, just waiting for death to strike. But it's not as if I could have outrun her, anyway. I had to trust Criminy.

When the bludmare was so close that I could see the insides of her pink, huffing nostrils, something flew at her feet. She screamed and went down, thrashing on the ground with three of her legs caught in a bolus. The rope had wrapped several times around her thick ankles, and she wasn't happy about it.

I was frozen in place, in shock but fascinated. Criminy appeared in a blur of emerald green and a flash of silver. In his hands was the bridle cap he had bought from Apollinaire's Everything Shoppe. He fit it over the bludmare's nose and mouth, and her screams stopped, replaced by a furious whuffling. He ran the leather trappings behind her ears and buckled them under her jaw. She was effectively muzzled.

He stood up to grin at the bludmare. Her eyes bulged with rage and reproach. I could almost hear her thinking, *We're creatures of blud, you and I. How can you abuse me so?* and I had a moment of pity.

But then I remembered the teeth and said, "Maybe you should tighten that a notch?"

He did tighten it, and the bludmare sighed against the metal. He cut the bolus from her legs and stood back, holding the leather reins tightly as she heaved her great bulk off the ground and shook. He stepped closer, petting her thick, elegant neck.

"She's a beauty," he said. "What should we call her?"

I was scared, but I stepped forward nonetheless. As her eyes rolled down to stare at me, the prey turned captor, I tentatively put a still-ungloved hand out to stroke her neck. Her skin quivered against my touch, as if she was shaking off a fly.

"Her name is Erris," I said gently.

Criminy looked at me, thoughtful. "Didn't know it worked for animals."

"Me, neither," I said.

Such close scrutiny was making her nervous, and the giant black bludmare jigged in place, shaking her head and snorting. Just as I had seen on the Coppers' mares, froth started to drip from the metal cap.

"Have you ridden before?" Criminy asked me.

"A little, at summer camp," I said, looking into her intelligent red eye and finding myself uncomfortable with her own measurement of me. "I like horseback riding. In theory. She's just so big. And wild."

"The journey that would take us two days on foot will take half a day on her back," he answered. "But I imagine it's going to be a bit hard on your fundament. Especially without a saddle. I'm sorry about that."

"If I remember my days on horseback," I said with a wicked smile, "it's going to be even harder on you."

"I think not," Criminy said, patting her broad back. "She's a wide lass. Well fed. And I like a nice, fat bum. I just need to break her to saddle first."

As I put on my gloves and relaced my dress, I watched the quick, handsome man work the horse. The mare tried to back away from him, pawing and snorting. He released the leather rein a little bit, giving her room. Rushing at her flank, he spun the leather strap, whipping her hip. She jumped away, trying to keep her hindquarters away from him. But he kept pushing into her, making her move. And she kept moving. I watched, transfixed by the give and take of man and beast, by his elegant balance of aggression and patience. He caught me staring and winked. I had to look down to hide my blush.

After a few minutes, she lowered her head and blinked, sides heaving. I could hear her licking her lips inside the cap. Criminy smiled and reached out to stroke her neck.

"I would never want her dead broke, a wild spirit like that," he murmured. "Just obliging. She and I have a lot in common."

I smiled to myself, thinking about my own dead-broke years with Jeff. He probably would have put a shock collar on me if it had been legal. Even scared, it felt good to be free now.

The horse followed him willingly to a fallen tree and stood as he helped me swing my heavy, rustling skirt over her back. She crow-hopped, and I grabbed her mane in my gloved hands. I managed to stay on, and Criminy swung up behind me gracefully. It was a shock to feel his body mold around mine, his thighs tense against me and his arms wrapped around me. I would not have guessed that riding a monster horse could feel so intimate and electrifying. Taking the reins in both hands, he murmured, "Hold on, sweetheart," and kicked her in the ribs.

Erris settled back on her haunches before leaping into the air. I squeezed with my knees and clung to the mane for dear life, and she hit the ground running. Since she was pointed in the right direction, this wasn't such a bad thing, and Criminy just gathered me closer to him and let her gallop.

She was big but nimble and very fast. Once I grew accustomed to the rhythm, staying on wasn't hard at all. It reminded me of driving fast on a bridge on the highway, the car seeming to soar between the metal bumps. *Ka-thunk, ka-thunk.* For hours.

We didn't speak. The air would have sucked our words away. The heavy body beneath us was hot and sweaty, and I was more than aware of Criminy's hard thighs behind mine, pressing into the horse's flesh. His arms held the reins, trapping me within, and I could feel his eyes and thoughts hovering, close but miles away.

My own thoughts wove in and out from the reality of galloping on a bloodthirsty horse across a strange world, to the fear of what would happen when we stopped galloping, to the constant ache in my heart for my other life. As refreshing as last night's sleep had been, part of me was horrified not to wake up in my own world, slightly crazy and very sleepy. Just like when you're having a nightmare and you keep expecting to wake up, but you don't. I had taken the locket's magic for granted.

If my guess was correct, my body was unconscious and unresponsive. I was hooked up to monitors, and a nurse I'd never met was turning and bathing me, keeping me clean and without bedsores. The mental image made me shudder. Knowing what I did about Casper and my brief glance of Jonah Goodwill in my world, it seemed to be the only answer. If you were in a coma in my world, I was betting you were in Sang.

I felt naked without my locket. Naked and trapped. Bit

by bit, Criminy was becoming an anchor, the most familiar thing in Sang. And he was full of surprises. When I'd first seen him and thought of him as a naughty Mr. Darcy, I had been close to the truth. He called himself wicked, and I'd seen him kill. But I'd also seen him be fair, kind, brave, merciful, and loyal. For a monster, there was much to admire in him, and that's before you got to his physical presence, which was pressing against me in the loveliest way.

For a while, I even drifted into a little nap, held safe in his arms and lulled by the monotony of pounding hooves and endless, grassy moors. I didn't dream, and my sleep was uneasy. I fought to open my eyes as the smooth gallop eased into a lope, and then my teeth clacked together as our mount dropped down into a trot. Criminy's arm around my waist was the only thing that kept me on horseback.

"Are we there yet?" I asked muzzily.

Criminy chuckled. "Not even close," he said.

19

Once I had wiped the sleep and dust from my eyes, I was surprised to see a small village coming up on either side of the dirt road. It looked like a movie set of a ghost town in the Wild West. False-fronted buildings faced the street, painted in odd, muted tones. Mauve, powder blue, mustard yellow. A few people bustled furtively between buildings but not nearly as many as I would have expected. They were all wearing shades of gray and black, which was unusual in Sang, from what I'd seen.

Criminy steered our mount between two sturdy poles that were driven into the ground on the edge of town. She switched her tail and danced, looking hopefully from me to Criminy, probably hoping that her unwanted master would give her one of my pinky toes as a reward for good behavior. He slid off and helped me down. A young boy darted out from the closest building and clipped Erris's muzzle cap to the poles with a chain. The big horse threw her head, snorted, and tried to rear, but she was surely stuck.

Patting her neck, Criminy said, "Sorry, lass. It's only for a short while. You'll be free again soon," and then he tossed the boy a coin.

When he looked up eagerly to catch the copper, the

boy's open collar and overly pointy grin told me that he, like the urchins at the cathedral, was a Bludman. With a lifetime of movies and books firmly pounded into my head, I still couldn't believe that Bludmen could bear children in this world. That this little lad would grow up knowing nothing but blood—no cookies, no ice cream, no cupcakes. Still, his smile was bright and innocent, even if he wasn't dreaming of penny candy.

"Thankee kindly, sir," he said. "Will you want the inn, then?"

Criminy looked at the sun. It was late afternoon, and the sky was the dull, bruised lavender of the milk in the bottom of the cereal bowl after all of the marshmallows were gone.

"Is there only one?" Criminy asked the boy. "And where are the Coppers?"

"Feverish is a small village, sir. The Coppers come only for the monthly tithe to Brighton. We've just the one inn. And this is our only tie-up."

With an understanding smile, Criminy gave the boy another coin.

"I'll take you there, sir."

The boy trotted ahead of us into town, and I noticed that his clothes had been many times mended, the breeches patched in similar dark colors and the shoes worn in the heel. The buildings were in need of paint—that was why they were such strange colors. They were faded. It was a poor town, a lonely outpost before the big city on the sea.

Stopping in front of the only three-story building, the boy said, "There you are, sir. And please, don't mention the Coppers to Master Haggard. They drained his wife last year, and it puts him in a right mood." And then he ran off.

We looked up at the sea-green storefront. The sign showed a black diamond, outlined in white, with the words *Haggard Inn* below in heavy, serious script. Not the most promising name for a hotel.

Criminy held open the door for me, and a bell rang as we entered. A fluffy white cat sat on the counter, eyeing us disdainfully. Lucky creature—without Pinkies about, the bludrats must have left Feverish alone. The room was sparse but well kept, the floors spotless and the wavy, green glass sparkling in the windows. An old gramophone resembling a giant brass lily was playing a dirge. It felt like a funeral parlor.

A man in a dusty gray suit appeared from the back room, his sad, ancient eyes full of pride and dignity above a frilly tea-stained jabot from another time.

"Have you a vacancy, Master Haggard?" Criminy asked with a stately bow. I'd never seen him so deferential.

"We do, lad," the man said, his voice sonorous and grave. "One room or two?"

It was like listening to a statue, witnessing something so old that it had started to erode, watching bits of itself wash away in the rain. Just being near him made me feel hopeless.

"One, please, sir. For my wife and me," Criminy said.

"Hmph," Master Haggard said, pinning his soulful eyes on me. "That creature is not thy wife. But one room ye shall have, nonetheless, for I do not judge those who succumb to heathen trends."

Criminy bowed again, murmuring, "Forgive me, sir."

The old Bludman nodded. "Life today must be full of lies, youngster. But I see you remember a time when it wasn't so. Born or made?"

"Born, sir, in 1793."

"You're younger than you look," Master Haggard said. "I was born as well, 1438. Right here, when the county seat was Bludshire. Do you remember what it was like, lad, before Brighton belonged to the prey?"

"I do, sir. A lovely place, all parks and springs and gardens. And the opera and dancing every night."

"And what have they done?" the old man moaned. "It's a dark place now. Filthy, dangerous, polluted. Ruled by the Pinky monsters. Our people are starving. The factory workers are on the verge of rioting. The foremen threaten to toss them into the sea. And what does anyone expect, when the Coppers hold sway? No Bludman can live on two drops a day. It's madness."

"We were headed to Brighton, sir," Criminy said carefully. "We have business in the isles."

"Then you'd best hurry, lad," Master Haggard said. "But what of your lady? How came you to love one of *them*?"

"I called her, sir," Criminy said. "She's a Stranger."

Master Haggard gazed at me and snorted. Then chuckled. Then let out a big guffaw.

"Oh, that's grand. That's just lovely. She's special, isn't she?"

"She's a glancer," Criminy said. "But she's mine."

"Take my hand, woman," Master Haggard said to me, and he removed his glove. His scaly black hand was old and shriveled, the nails twisted white talons. I knew better than to show any distaste as I removed my glove and reached for it. He may have looked as slow and melancholy as an antediluvian basset hound, but I could feel his power lurking underneath. Waiting.

His hand was cool in mine. The jolt was gentle, and I was surprised.

"But why do you want to die?" I said. "Things can change. They can get better."

He released my hand and wagged his head. "The things I love are gone. But you saw the flames?"

"Yes, sir," I said solemnly. Then I turned to Criminy and said, "We have to go. Now."

20

Grasping the old Bludman's hand, I had seen Brighton in flames under dark, threatening clouds low enough to scrape the tops of the burning buildings. Screams filled the air, and the lightning was purple and wicked. I wanted no part of the once-lovely seaside resort.

"If we go there, we die," I said again to Criminy as Erris walked down the dirt road toward Brighton, warming up her muscles. "I know we have to hurry, but there's got to be another way to the islands. We can't just run through a riot. Or a fire."

"There is no other way," he said. "We need a boat. You heard Master Haggard say they were threatening to throw the Bludmen into the sea? It's because the sea is deadly to us. The salt makes us sick, and we're too heavy. We sink and drown. I've seen it. And Brighton is the only place with boats for hundreds of miles."

I sighed deeply, leaning back against him.

"I don't like it, either," he muttered.

"But if you'd seen it," I said. "It's going to be horrible. Fire and lightning but no rain."

"We'll skirt the city, head straight for the docks. In all the brouhaha, no one will notice us, especially not the Coppers. It'll be all the easier to steal a boat and be away."

I felt his legs behind me, urging our mare into a gallop. We topped the hill, and the city appeared below us, a gray blot on the landscape. It splayed out like Manchester squashed flat but just as ugly. Smog hovered miserably overhead. Thunder roiled in the heavy sky, and violet lightning sparked between angry black clouds.

"Actually," he mused, "it's a very well-timed riot, for our purposes. It should be easy to get to the harbor."

Standing sentinel on a rocky outcrop was a black-and-white-striped lighthouse, its lamp spinning slowly and flashing across the city and the sea. Underneath it, ships bobbed in a dark gray harbor. Amazing, the weird mix of technology and anachronism in this world. Giant, three-masted wooden pirate ships nudged the docks alongside shiny brass footballs from *20,000 Leagues under the Sea*.

"What sort of ship do you plan on stealing?" I asked.

"Something larger than a dinghy but small enough to pilot with just the two of us," he said. "I don't think you'll be climbing the rigging in that dress. A sub would be ideal."

"You can drive a submarine?" By that time, I didn't know why I was surprised.

"How hard can it be?" he said. "I can drive the caravan's engine. It can't be much different. It's not like it's a bloody zeppelin."

We were getting close enough to see the giant doors set in Brighton's wall. They had a spiked, medieval-looking portcullis, and I was more than happy to go around.

"Hold on, sweetheart," Criminy said, and he jerked Erris's nose to the right. She tossed her head but obeyed, lurching off the packed dirt and finding new speed in the soft grasses of the moor. A picture-perfect gathering of bludbunnies hissed and screamed in terror, diving for cover as the huge hooves tore up swaths of grass in their bucolic meadow. I laughed.

We were headed toward the harbor. But there was a problem. The high wall, topped with barbed wire just like the one at Manchester, extended out into the sea at least a hundred feet. All of the boats were on the other side of the wall.

"Um, Criminy? How do we get around the wall?" I asked.

"I'm going to scale it," he said. "And you're going to swim. You can swim, can't you, pet? I've been told it's as easy as floating, for your kind."

"I don't think I have a choice," I said.

I wanted that locket, more than I'd ever wanted anything. Without it, my old life was gone. I would never see my grandmother again. And according to my own promise, I'd have to leave Criminy behind, too, maybe end up living in one of these wretched cities, ruled by the Coppers and their leader, a man who had taken away everything I loved. What's more, that same man wanted to use my locket to kill thousands of people he wrongly considered monsters, people who had been kind to me. People like Criminy. I watched the dark waves crashing against the wall and breathed in the salt wind.

"I can do this," I said.

"You can do this," he agreed.

A small ball of solid dread began to form in my corset-constricted belly. I could barely walk in this outfit, and now I had to swim. What about the waves, the current, the flotsam, the jetsam, the rocks, the lightning, the wall? What sorts of animals lurked under the foamy brine? Were killer whales actually killers here?

It didn't matter. I was doing it anyway.

Criminy kicked Erris. As we galloped toward the wall, his arm around my waist seemed to anchor me to the world. Surely he could feel my panic. How did he seem so cool and collected? My swimming wasn't going to be easy, but he had to scale a smooth wall expressly designed to prevent said scaling. I knew he wanted the locket to prevent a genocide, but the fire in his eyes told me that part of his fight was for me alone, and I liked him more for it.

The smooth gallop jerked into a trot and then a bouncy walk, and then Erris was blowing against her muzzle before the wall. I looked up. Way up. It was two stories tall and smooth, without a single handhold that I could see.

Criminy slid off the bludmare and helped me down. My legs nearly collapsed, but he caught me and drew me close. Then I felt a rude shove in the behind from Erris's muzzle.

"Fine, lass," Criminy said, pulling me behind him and patting the horse's neck. "You've earned your freedom."

In one motion, he pulled the cap and halter off the wild mare's head and used the leather reins to slap her hind-quarters. She tossed her nose and took off running for the hills, apparently deciding that freedom was better than a solid bite of measly old me.

Criminy watched her go with a crooked smile. My heart was beating in my ears, and my mouth had gone completely dry with fear. He reached out and stroked my face, tucking an errant curl behind my ear. I looked into his eyes and saw the sea behind me reflected there, the unceasing waves topped with foam. Calm descended over me. The pounding of the waves became soporific. I knew that he was using some sort of magic on me, but I didn't care. I needed whatever he could give me.

"Look, love," he said. "You can do this. You'll have to fight your way out, use all your energy to get around the wall. Once you're on the other side, simply float in to shore. I'll be there, waiting for you."

"You make it sound so easy," I said.

"It is easy," he said. "A simple act. And then we're almost done."

"I can do this," I breathed.

"Yes, you can," he said.

And then he kissed me, gently, and his lips were wet against mine. I should have resisted, but I couldn't. I wanted it too badly, wanted to make sure that if I died in the sea, I'd have this last memory burning in my blood. No matter what I told myself, I was attracted to him more than I wanted to believe possible. And he was a really good kisser.

My mouth tingled, my entire body suffused with heat and hunger. For him. I kissed him back, my tongue breaking past his lips, surprising us both. He changed his angle, moved with me, sure and powerful but gentle. The kiss deepened. I realized that I was straining against him, hungry, panting. Lightning arced to the moors, the light flashing violet against his dark hair. As the thunder boomed, I pulled away, my sight sharp again. I felt unconsciously strong and confident, like an animal.

And, finally, I knew I could do it.

He put his forehead against mine for just a second and murmured something that sounded like "Remember that I did this for you," and then he was moving up the wall like a spider, his black hands stark against the stone.

I turned to face the sea.

I was almost ready. I opened my little bag and found the folded knife inside. Criminy hadn't taught me how to use it yet. But I didn't need instructions for what I was about to do.

The dress had a bunched and bustled overskirt, and the first thing I did was cut off the heavy bustle at the waist to reveal the lighter, straight skirt below. I gathered a handful of my skirt and then chopped that off at the knee, just above the tops of my boots. I stepped out of my petticoats and threw my hat to the ground, too. And then I realized that I had to get into the water before something hungry smelled me.

I put the knife back into the bag and tied it around my waist. With a deep breath, I waded in. The heavy gray clouds seemed as solid as the stone wall at my side, pressing down from the sky against the sea, and I imagined that in Sang, it probably was possible to sail off the end of the globe, just as old sailors in my world had feared. The horizon was a flat line broken only by jagged islands far in the distance, a goal as unreachable as my grandmother's kitchen.

When the first waves licked at my boot, I shivered. The water was freezing, and I could feel it through the leather. I waded deeper. Then I felt the cold lapping against my stocking-clad knees and gasped. This was going to be so much worse than jumping into a pool in a bikini on a summer day, corset or not. And I'd forgotten to loosen my corset.

Crap.

It was too late now. I was up to my waist, and the laces were wet. The remains of my dress were tangled around me. I had to use my arms to keep myself steady, to keep the current from tumbling me into the waves, out of control.

I'd never feared water before, but the sea of Sang was just as bloodthirsty as the land.

And then I was up to my shoulders, dog-paddling, the jagged cloth of my dress pulling me down toward the darkness. The waves smacked against me, cold and impersonal, and I found myself flailing, fighting. Criminy had said that Bludmen could only sink, but I could barely keep myself above the water. The salt stung my eyes, and I could taste it in the back of my throat.

I floundered along parallel to the wall, closer and closer to my goal, the open sea. I was twenty feet away, and then ten, and then I could see the barnacles clinging to the degrading stones at the end of the wall, their hungry purple mouths grasping into the water. The little bastards were probably razor-sharp. I paddled away from them, giving myself room to mess up. I was almost there.

And then I felt something that made my blood run cold.

Just as I rounded the wall from ten feet away, something nudged against my leg. Something large and smooth and hard, just brushing by. Almost impersonal, like bumping a stranger's shoulder in a crowd.

But it was cold.

My first thought was *Shark,* and my second thought was *Sea monster.*

Then my caveman brain kicked in, and my third thought was *Swim, run, escape, kick, swim harder, go go go!*

So I did. I started kicking like a frog, putting power behind the sharp heels of my boots. My arms were cutting through the water in a breaststroke, and the current was finally on my side. I rounded the wall, and the waves began pushing me in toward the shore.

Then I felt it again. The nudging.

More insistent this time. Against my thigh.

Despite myself, I looked down. The water was too dark

and roiling for me to see anything, even my own body. I kicked harder, frantically, with every ounce of strength I had. My feet were numb now, my legs burning. I focused on the shore, a hundred yards away. It felt like forever. Impossible. But then I thought of Nana fighting to stay alive every day and realized that I couldn't do any less. I took a deep breath, determined to reach land again.

Then I felt teeth around my calf, almost gentle. Teasing. Like a dog testing a stick to see if it will break or stand up to a little rough playing.

I gasped and got a mouthful of water. With my other boot, I aimed a kick just to the side of where I felt the teeth, and my heel connected with something thicker than a fish. Something rubbery.

SHARK! my brain screamed. *SWIM NOW!*

I kicked again, and the teeth shook a little and released, and then I was floundering, kicking, thrashing, willing myself toward the shore.

Something nudged my belly from underneath. It felt slightly pointy, like the end of a nose. But larger.

A sob rose, choking me.

I was so close.

My fingers sought the tender points of whatever was nudging from beneath me. It felt like a slimy reptile, an alligator covered in a frilly doily. I shuddered and pushed away.

And then it felt like teeth. Fast as lightning, they grabbed my arm and dragged me under, and I inhaled water, and everything was lost in darkness.

21

"You have to *open your eyes,"* I heard in my mind as I floated in the cool blackness. *"You have to swim."*

I obeyed. I opened my eyes to an eerie, floating, greenish-gray darkness. I could see tendrils of something in front of my eyes, and after a moment, I saw my hand, trailing inky blood, the glove half ripped off.

I was underwater.

And there was a gentle, cool glow radiating from the other side of my hand.

A girl.

But she was made of light, floating weightless in the water, her bobbed hair and long dress untouched by the shifting currents. I hung suspended, my lungs cold. I wasn't breathing.

I shouldn't have been alive.

Her mouth moved.

"You have to swim to shore," she said in my mind, her voice musical and sweet. *"Kick up, get above the waves. You're so close."*

Am I dead? I thought.

"Almost," she said. *"But you have to make it to the lighthouse. You have to free me."*

How?

"Open the door upstairs. Find my bones and bury them. I've been waiting for years. Help me, and I'll save you. Will you do it?"

I'll try.

"Promise!"

I promise. Just help me.

"Then kick up. Break the surface. Breathe. Swim. Go now!" she cried.

A burst of white-hot lightning shot through my muscles, shocking me into action. I gave a mighty kick, and my head broke the surface. Water dribbled from my mouth, and then I was gasping for breath, starving for air. My arms churned in the water, my legs kicked, and the waves seemed to help me, pushing me toward the shore.

I hit the sand hard, the waves driving me into the rocky beach. I coughed and dragged myself forward with my elbows, until Criminy lifted me from the sand. He sat on the beach with me collapsed across his body, his arms holding me tight.

"I knew you could do it, love," he said fiercely. "I knew you could."

"I didn't," I said, holding up my ragged glove and ripped sleeve. When he saw the blood running down my fishbelly-white arm, he licked his lips and shuddered, and I tucked it under my armpit and scooted away to a safe distance. "Something dragged me down. But then there was a girl, and she helped me."

"A girl?" Criminy asked, eyes sharp.

"I guess she was a ghost," I said, hugging myself tightly and shaking, the fear finally catching up with me. "Or my mind playing tricks on me. She made me promise to go to the lighthouse and find her bones and bury them. She said she'd been waiting."

"Then we must," Criminy said, patting me from far-ther away than we would both have preferred. "Ghost curses are hard to break. But first you need to wrap up that wound. I can be good, but not that good."

He looked toward the lighthouse, and I followed his glance up the tall building, the upper story lost in thick clouds. More time lost.

As we picked our way along the large rocks and tide pools, I asked, "Ghosts are real here?" I wasn't surprised, not really. But I wanted to know more. Was I going to be seeing ghosts all over the place now?

"As real as they are anywhere, I suspect," he said. "I've never seen one, only the results of their handiwork. It's only natural that a glancer would see such things. You walk the line between the worlds in more ways than one, you know."

He was trying very hard not to look at me, not to smell me. Despite his self-control, it was still difficult for him to ignore my freshly bleeding arm. On the beach, he had tossed me a handkerchief and kept his distance as I tied it around the wound. And then he'd found a vial in his pack and chugged it, his bright eyes never leaving me. I briefly wondered if it was the one taken from my own veins in Manchester.

The lighthouse loomed over us, a sagging tower of loose boards and peeling paint. The stripes that had seemed so fresh and new from the hill, pitch black and snowy white, were faded to light gray and darker gray, desolate and reproachful. I didn't want to get near it, but I was bound by my promise to a dead girl. Criminy said that she had the power to curse me, and I believed him. I didn't want another enemy in Sang, especially not a paranormal one.

Criminy kicked the door open. It smacked against the wall, making the entire building shake. The stark room inside was coated with dust, the furniture leaning and splintered.

"What happened?" I asked.

"No one's come here for years," Criminy said. "The ships have enough instruments and clockworks to tell the navigators where the rocks are. It's crude and outdated technology, shining a light around the darkness."

"But I saw it," I said, puzzled. "Earlier, when we looked down from the hill. It was orange, and it spun slowly and hit the water."

He turned to look down at me, troubled. "You saw a light? Here? In this lighthouse?"

"Yes," I said. "Didn't you?"

"No," he said quietly.

I didn't know what to say. Why was I seeing things that weren't there?

Criminy pointed to the spiral staircase. "If you must do this, that's the only way up," he said. "But I won't think any less of you if you want to walk right back out that door and bugger the ghost. There are ways around curses, although they aren't pretty."

"We're already here," I said. "Let's get it over with."

He sighed and bowed. "After you, love."

My boots squelched up the tight curve of the stairs, and the ancient wood creaked threateningly under my heels. I picked up the pace, eager to be done with this errand and on to my own treasure hunt. The city, the storm, the sea, the ghost—it was high time to be gone from Brighton.

Around and around we went, Criminy's step light behind me. I hadn't asked him much about his own journey over the wall, but he looked as fresh and crisp as if he'd just stepped out of his wagon. But he was missing his satchel.

Finally, the staircase opened up in a smaller, sparse room. It was the living quarters, with one narrow metal bed against the wall, a tiny potbelly stove, and dozens of sharp metal hooks hanging empty from the faded white wood. I felt as if I was being watched, but there was nowhere for a watcher to hide.

"This is where the lighthouse tender lived," Criminy said softly. "One lonely person, tending the flame above."

"I don't think that was her, though."

"I don't see any bones," he said. "Not even a chest or a box or a cupboard."

"She said there was a door upstairs," I offered.

"Only one way to go, love," he said, pointing his chin at the stairs. "You're not scared of heights, are you?"

"Why?"

"Because I think most of the glass has blown out, and it's going to be windy up there."

I stepped gingerly back onto the staircase and clung to the inside rail on my way up. The tight curve opened onto a narrow walkway with a waist-high wooden railing. He was right. It was a long, long way down, and most of the glass was gone. The jagged remains of the windows that had once sheltered the flame invited the wind to whip us with an impersonal, random violence. Thunder boomed, making the lighthouse shake and quiver beneath us.

There was a small, cylindrical room in the very center of the roof, about five steps away. A metal ring that reminded me of a giant cigarette lighter sat on top of the room. She had to be there, in the metal closet under the flame. It was the only place we'd seen where bones might be found, and a sinister place it was for a young girl's eternal rest.

I edged away toward the door. I felt blind and tiny, with nothing to hold on to, and the wind played with me like a cat toying with a mouse. I tried the handle, and it was unlocked. I glanced behind me to make sure Criminy was close. He raised his eyebrows at me but said nothing. When I opened the door to look inside the small room, his hand was on my shoulder.

The room had riveted metal walls, and it was about six feet square. The warm air hit us like a puff of breath, carrying the stale scent of death. The evening light from the open doorway showed a grisly scene.

Rusty bloodstains remained where fingers had once clawed helplessly at the walls. A figure huddled in the corner, mostly preserved by the dry, salty air sealed within. A mummy. The bobbed black hair was intact, and the skull was covered with taut black skin. Her dress was so thin now as to be transparent, white with a high, lacy collar.

"The poor girl," I whispered.

Before Criminy could speak, the door slammed shut behind us.

And we were trapped in the blackness with a ghost.

22

"That little bitch!" Criminy shouted.

I found his hand. "She's here, you know," I whispered.

In response, eerie, girlish laughter echoed off the metal walls. "Three ghosts in a lighthouse," she whispered, and the voice was different from the calm, pleading sweetness I'd heard underwater. Up here, the voice was filled with madness.

She giggled, and Criminy growled, "I'll be damned if I'm going to spend eternity with a little strumpet like you." He pounded on the door. It didn't budge. It was airtight, of course.

"You'll never get out," she sang. "I couldn't. And you won't."

There was a pause, and I could hear myself and Criminy breathing.

And then came the gruesome scratching of fingernails on a chalkboard.

Or bones on metal walls.

"What happened to you?" I asked, my voice flat, guarded.

"He was a Bludman, and I was a maid," she whispered. "We fell in love. But I was betrothed to my brother's best friend. My love and I were going to stow away on a ship, go to Almanica and start over fresh, where people wouldn't hate us for loving each other. But my brother found our letters. He knew where we were meeting. When I came here, he and my betrothed found me, locked me in to die alone. Told me I deserved it for loving a filthy Bludman. Called me an abomination."

She tittered in my ear. "Just like you."

"What happened to the Bludman?" I asked softly.

"I never found out," the voice echoed. "I died here. And I've been lonely."

I felt Criminy's hand on my arm, and it traveled down to my wrist. I could sense his urgency, so I coughed, trying to cover up the furtive noises as he pressed Uro's head and the little snake whirred with gears. I waited to see red lights, but Criminy must have planned ahead and shielded the ruby eyes.

"Your Bludman—what was his name?" I asked, my voice loud in the tiny room.

"His name was Scarab Crumbly," the voice said, dreamy. "We met in the market. His hair was golden and wavy, like a lion. He had eyes as deep as the sea. And he loved me."

"I knew Rab Crumbly," Criminy broke in, his voice booming in the tiny room. Under his words, I heard metal on metal, scraping. "He was drained twenty years ago by the Coppers. They put his head on a pike for killing a girl named Evangel. Was that you, by chance?"

A strangled cry reverberated off the walls. "Drained! Oh, Rab, my love! You were always true!"

A nightmare apparition appeared inches from my face, the ghost girl with the bob, her mouth now a gaping hole into hell. Her strangled moan turned into a shriek, and that made me scream, and our voices merged and echoed in the blackness. I imagined the metal warping, pressing out, ready to explode. My eardrums ached with pressure, and pain shot through my head in bursts of red.

But through her, illuminated by her, I saw Criminy's back, and he was doing something to the door, and so I shrieked louder. Which wasn't hard, because I was terrified. I hadn't feared the quiet ghost under the waves, but this thing was nasty.

As the ghost expanded, her hands became claws, and her eyes sank back into empty black pools. I was forced backward until I felt bones scraping against the heels of my boots, clutching at my ankles. I was still screaming, couldn't have stopped if I'd tried. She loomed over me, mouth open, and something in the back of my brain idly wondered if there was such a thing as a soul, and where hers was, and where mine would go when the ghostly lips sucked it out through my eyeballs.

And then the door flew open, and the ghostly screaming suddenly stopped, leaving only silence and the tang of salty wind behind. I blinked, and there was Criminy, grinning, holding out his glove.

"I think you kept your promise, love," he said, handing Uro back to me. "Thank goodness for clockworks and their lockpicks, eh? Let's leave this place."

"Not yet," I said. "Hold the door open."

I looked behind me, where the sunset let in just enough light to see the sad, moldering skeleton of a mad girl with a broken heart. I reached out to smooth the black hair, and the jolt came, soft as leaves dancing on a summer night's breeze.

"My G-god," I managed to stutter.

"What do you see, love?"

"Everything she said was true. But her betrothed was Jonah Goodwill himself, and Rab Crumbly was the Bludman who incited Goodwill's crusade against your kind. And against women like me. Goodwill still wears Evangel's engagement ring on a chain around his neck. All of this, everything he's done. All of the horrors he committed. It's all because of her." I paused, studying the white dress. A wedding dress. "Because he loved her, and she chose a Bludman instead of him."

"I didn't think it was possible to hate him more," Criminy said, holding out one of his many handkerchiefs, a large square of sea-green silk. "But I do."

As tenderly as I could, I wrapped the body in the cloth and picked it up. Edging toward the railing, I threw it into the ocean.

"You're free," I said in benediction as I watched the bones clatter against the rocks.

23

The city was in flames, and the docks were silent. I was still in shock. I was also half-naked and soaked through and starting to chafe with salt water. Still, there was a lot I didn't understand. And I was in a hurry.

"If the city's on fire, why isn't everyone running to the docks?" I asked. "Boats are a better bet than the city gates, right?"

"Ah, but you don't know the politics here. Brighton is a city ruled by a few rich Pinkies. Beneath them are the poor Pinkies, the servants, and the Bludmen who work in the factories. The people have been oppressed for decades. They're not used to fighting or tactical thinking. They probably didn't plan very well."

"Still, even from the lighthouse, we didn't see a single person," I said.

"I have a theory," he said. "But it's not pretty."

I stopped walking to look at him. He was troubled, more so than I had ever seen.

"The clockworks are getting quite good, you see. The mechanics are reaching a new level of genius and subtlety. Tell me, if you could use machines instead of dangerous, barely restrained workers, what would you do with the workers? You can't let them go—bloodthirsty, penniless, and with a grudge."

I just stared at him, my jaw set.

He looked up at the smoke barreling from deep within the city and said more softly, "Do you smell that? Doesn't it smell like meat?"

"Are you saying that the people in charge locked up the workers and set them on fire?" I said, incredulous.

"In the end, the winner rewrites history. Call it a bloody revolution, become the heroes who made the city safe for innocent, harmless Pinkies. And such a shame that Darkside Brighton was lost in the workers' riotous flames."

"Can we help them?" I said. "Can we do anything?"

Criminy turned to me, the muscles in his face taut with fury and concern. "We *are* doing something," he said. "The man who has your locket is the mastermind behind every atrocity against a Bludman today. He probably planned this riot. He's the leader, and he's just a little farther away, trapped on an island. Getting your locket back isn't my only goal."

There was a fierce beauty in his determination, a strength of purpose that spoke to my own will. For possibly the first time, I looked at him and didn't see a hint of monster or charlatan or trickster—just a man, and a powerful one. In that moment, I would have followed him anywhere. But he turned toward the sea.

Our ramble along the dock took us past cutters and rowboats to a smart brass submersible, about forty feet long. It still shone with polish and didn't have a single barnacle clinging to the hull.

"This is our girl," Criminy said. "The newer the model, the easier to drive."

"But what if someone's inside?" I asked.

"Then they help us or die," he said cheerfully, and I surprised myself by agreeing with him. Sang wasn't a world for middle ground.

The sub was mostly underwater, leaving perhaps two feet of curved metal above the dark gray waves. She was shaped like a pill, with a propeller at the back and a shiny periscope at the front. Just visible under the waves was a glass window with banks of instruments, dark and waiting. The ship appeared empty. And the sky was getting darker.

Criminy leaped onto the roof and began to turn a brass wheel. It creaked and creaked, and then, with a pop, the door opened. I could see a strip of crimson velvet around the edge, and it made me think of a cat's mouth.

I did not want to go down there, get swallowed up by the ship, and ride underwater, where we were vulnerable and trapped. I wanted to take a nice, breezy ship with sails and lifeboats and emergency vests. But for someone who couldn't swim in the sea, like Criminy, I supposed this vehicle was safer. We both had to take risks.

He disappeared down the ladder, and I scanned the docks until he returned. Nervously, I stepped onto the brass hull and then followed him down into the ship. The crimson velvet continued inside and coated the walls and ceilings. The floor was dark wood, with Turkish carpets running down the middle.

"I can't smell a living thing on the ship," Criminy assured me, "but keep your wits about you, just the same. Can't be too careful about stowaways on a submarine."

The sub was more like an apartment than a boat. The walls had paintings, odd sepia-toned photographs, and shadow boxes of bizarre insects, all firmly screwed to the velvet walls. We were in the sitting room, and a little damask sofa with tasseled pillows beckoned my aching bottom. The hours riding bareback were taking their toll on a body that had been through more than its share of fear and pain in the last few days.

Just before I collapsed on the sofa, I stopped. The Nana in my head chided me, and I sighed. I was sopping wet. I couldn't leave a mark on someone else's good furniture.

"Criminy?" I called. He had disappeared further into the ship. "I need a change of clothes."

His head popped around the corner. "I'm setting our course, love," he said. "Poke around and see what you can find. I'm afraid I lost our bag going over the wall when they started shooting at me. My apologies. The bedroom's down the other way."

I squelched down the narrow hallway, passing the tiny kitchen and bathroom. The bedroom was at the back, in the rounded end of the pill. The bed was approximately six feet square, and the room wasn't much bigger. I slid aside a panel in the dark wood wall to find a gentleman's wardrobe. It was rich and new and a bit big. But it would do.

I slid the bedroom door shut behind me, curious to know if the smell of my naked skin would draw Criminy out. I wondered if it bothered him at all, whether it was nagging, like smelling a hamburger when you were starving. Or if it was more like showing a teenage boy a half-clothed woman. Was it hunger, lust, curiosity? An animal instinct or a human longing?

It didn't really matter. He was at the opposite end of the ship, busy, and I had to change. I couldn't infiltrate Jonah Goodwill's lair half-naked.

I sat down on the edge of the bed and heard a whir-ring purr behind me as the engine started. It was surpris-ingly quiet, not at all the unsophisticated grinding I had expected. The ship shuddered and began to move. I slid a little sideways as it changed course. We were under way.

The wet boots were off first, although it was hard to get the swollen laces undone. Then the sopping stock-ings, thank goodness. Then the shreds of the dress, peeled off like a second skin. Then the corset, after I had used my knife to slash the laces, which involved more than a little gleeful revenge. Then Uro and the gloves, cold and moist as frog fingers, one whole and one shredded and bloody. Finally, I was completely naked.

I lay back and exhaled, my eyes shut in bliss. When I opened them again, I was gazing straight up into a mirror set in the ceiling over the bed. Seeing myself there, laid out naked on some strange rich man's red velvet coverlet, I let out a little shriek and scrambled back to the foot of the bed, away from the mirror and toward the dry clothes in the closet. I couldn't help looking again, and that's when I noticed the brass rings set into the ceiling around the mir-ror. And a leather whip on hooks set in the wall.

Whoever owned this bed was a sex fiend. We had stolen a real *Love Boat*. The red velvet everywhere suddenly made sense.

"Letitia! Love, are you all right?" Criminy called from the other side of the flimsy wooden door. Panicking, I wrapped myself in the scarlet coverlet, the tassels tickling my damp skin.

"I'm fine," I said. "I just startled myself."

"What happened?" he said, and the air suddenly seemed very thick and very still. The thin sliding panel between us bent in a little bit, and I could imagine Criminy on the other side, his hand and face pressed against the black wood, his sharp eyebrows drawn down in concern. His nostrils flaring wide, catching my scent.

I heard him inhale and sigh.

I clutched the blanket more tightly around me.

"Nothing happened," I said nervously. "I just saw something that surprised me. And shouldn't you be steering the boat?"

"I've programmed it already," he said, his voice low and soft. "It'll take us to the open water around the islands and stop. If anything shows up on the sonar, we'll hear an alarm."

He inhaled again, then exhaled with a soft hum.

"So we're alone. Love."

Despite myself, I felt drawn to the door. My determination to resist Criminy and Sang itself was crumbling.

I felt as if he were pulling an invisible string, as if there were a golden hook around my spine leading me forward. I stepped lightly off the bed, trailing the red coverlet behind me. It was over my shoulders and crossed in front of me with both arms, like wings wrapped possessively around my fragile skin.

I pressed myself against the door, feeling the tension of his body pressing back through the flimsy wood. I breathed in. I could smell him, too, his scent rising sharp above the brass and new-cloth odors of the sub. Raspberries and blackberries, sweet and sun-warm, but with a fierce herbal undertone, crushed weeds and thorns. Burgundy and wine and the green of shadows. Eyes shut, velvet coverlet drawn up to my chin, I was taking in the scent with such deep breaths that I was starting to get a little light-headed.

The wood bent in against me a little more. I took a step back.

The door slid to the side, and there he was.

We studied each other in stillness. He leaned against the door frame, at ease but focused. He wasn't much bigger than I, but I suddenly felt quite small. The painting of him in the locket had so cunningly captured the intensity of his gaze and the single-mindedness of his will.

His eyes were dark now, as gray and stormy as the sea through the portholes, captured and infinite at once. The eyebrows that had at first seemed cruel now seemed elegant, speaking volumes with the smallest angle. His mouth was just a little open, and I wanted to kiss it.

No, I wanted to bite it, worry it.

I wanted to bite it? That was strange.

But it didn't matter. I inhaled deeply, taking in more of the scent. My eyes were drawn to the open neck of his shirt, so rebellious in its carelessness. His hair had fluttered loose, drifting over his shoulders. It was smooth and fine and dark, and my hand untangled itself from the blanket to reach out and brush it back. He closed his eyes as my naked skin brushed his jaw.

I half-expected a jolt, but none came. The electricity between us had nothing to do with foresight. I didn't need a glance to tell me what would happen next.

My breath caught in my throat as the blanket fell around me, and his hand snatched it just in time. We both stopped, my hand barely touching his face, his hand holding the blanket, the air between us humming like a plucked string.

I looked down and reached to take the blanket back from him. He didn't let go. I tugged a little, still refusing to meet his eyes. And then he tugged back, pulling me to his chest as he let go of the blanket and wrapped his arms around me. I was caught.

My head was tucked under his chin, and as my nose brushed his throat, I found myself nuzzling his neck. I felt drunk, woozy, swooning. As I rubbed my cheek on his collarbone in a daze, he swallowed hard, and I felt his muscles tense. He was like an animal held in check, barely contained.

Then he stepped back a little, his gloved hands lifting my face to his, cradling my jaw. I shivered, but I kept my eyes closed.

"Look at me," he said, his voice husky and low, compelling.

I exhaled, steeled myself, and opened my eyes.

He was gazing down at me, and his eyes were endless, deep pools of pleading and fire and barely restrained something or other, and they were magnetic, like black holes, but full of flames, and yet gray, and yet full of colors and see-through and dancing with little flecks of glitter, and I couldn't look away, and what pretty eyelashes he had, as long and dark as a woman's, as a kitten's, as a panther's, and the smell, oh, the smell, like crushed heather and berries and springtime in the morning and bodies rolling over and over in the grass and everything covered with dew like cobwebs making mandalas of raindrops, and I couldn't stand it, couldn't hold back for one more second.

But I had to know first.

"Are you doing this?" I whispered, head tilted up and lips so close to brushing his that I imagined our molecules dancing in the air together. "Are you doing something to me? Is this a spell or some sort of glamour?"

"I don't have this kind of power alone," he whispered back.

"Is it inevitable?"

My words hung there, suspended, trapped in the spangled amber of the moment. I couldn't see it, but somehow I knew that he smiled, sharp teeth glinting.

"Only if you want it to be," he said.

And then the cool suede of his glove stroked over my lips, and they felt full to bursting and ripe, and I shivered and breathed out, and the blanket slithered off my shoulders and puddled on the floor at my feet as his lips crashed into mine.

I wrapped my arms around his neck, my skin rippling with goose bumps as his hair brushed over my collarbone. The kiss was hungry and determined, and I barely registered the heat of his skin as his tongue slipped past my lips. He tilted his head, and a tiny sigh escaped me as the kiss grew deeper. As I had hoped, as I had expected, he tasted of berries, like wine, dark and deep.

His gloves stroked down my shoulders and back like an artist's brush, skimming every bone and curve with tender force. I pressed against him shamelessly, and the smooth linen of his shirt rubbing over my nipples made my eyes roll back. He shrugged off his heavy coat, and I could feel the imprint of his hands where they had touched me.

I wanted them back. I wanted them lower.

I squirmed closer, rubbing against him, begging for his touch, and he withdrew from the kiss, licking my lips and chuckling low in the back of his throat. He tossed his vest to the floor and drew the shirt over his head, saying, "Fair's fair. Now, come back to me, beauty."

My body was bereft without his touch, and I suddenly

realized that I was completely naked. I was overcome with shyness. I'd never been aggressive in the bedroom, and I hadn't been with anyone but Jeff in years. I had never felt this passion, this fire—not with Jeff, not with anyone.

What did he want from me? What did he expect?

"Come here," he whispered.

I crossed my arms in front of my stomach and muttered, "Why should I?"

He grinned at me, the corner of his mouth quirking up in the way that made me melt. "Because you want to," he said. "Because you must."

"I don't have to do anything," I said, stubborn to the last.

"Of course not," he said, and he reached out to cup my face tenderly. I looked down, because I couldn't meet his eyes. Now I was facing the elegant, muscled skin of his chest and, even lower, the spare, beautiful curves where flat stomach met hipbones. The scent rising from his warm skin was doing strange things to me.

He lifted my face, caught my eyes with his own. I was stuck, struck, hypnotized. Again, his thumb rubbed over my lips, which were now swollen and tender from his kisses. Then it moved down, tracing over my chin and down my throat, where it rested for a moment in the hollow.

"Your heart is beating fast," he said. "I can feel it, just there."

I couldn't deny it. I couldn't stop my heart from beating any more than I could still my breathing or make myself quit aching for his touch.

The hand traveled farther downward, spreading over my chest and lightly skimming over one breast, pressing gently over the nipple. My body surged toward that hand without thought, and I gasped and blinked and pulled back, unsure. His eyes seemed to go a shade darker, and his head tilted toward me as he licked his lips.

Lower still the hand traveled, too slowly for my liking. When it found my arms crossed tightly over my stomach, wrist grasping wrist, it stopped, and he raised his eyebrows and waited. I didn't budge. I had to keep some sort of power from him, had to feel that I had a choice in what I was doing, if not what I was feeling.

One dark eyebrow arched up in challenge. I shook my head, just the tiniest gesture. I smiled slyly.

Then, swiftly but gently, his hands tugged my arms apart and spun me around. I ended up facing the bed, my wrists held together behind my back in one gloved hand as the other continued right where it had left off, stroking my hip, causing tingles to race over my bare skin.

I took a deep breath and tugged my arms, but he stepped closer, pinning them between us. My captured hands were pressed between our bodies, and a little thrill ran down my spine when I realized how badly he wanted me. I felt the warmth of his breath on the tender hollow behind my ear.

"I don't mind if you want to play coy, Letitia," he whispered, his lips brushing my skin just enough to make me buck. He licked a line from the curve of my ear down my neck, and I shuddered. "But I do aim to make you surrender."

His lips nibbled my neck as his hand stroked relentlessly down the crease of my thigh. Without thinking, I arched just a little bit toward that hand, straining toward the touch that I craved. He chuckled again, and I could feel his teeth scrape against the nape of my neck. My nerves were screaming different messages, *Run* and *Stay* and *No, touch here, damn you*. I had never felt so alive, as if every cell of my body was focused and yearning and feeling and hungry.

The teasing hand changed direction, tracing the lines of my body back upward with deliberate slowness. When it reached my breast, I held my breath. The suede over his thumb rubbed my nipple, circling, and I moaned a little.

"Please," I begged.

"Surrender," he said.

The thumb circled lightly, lazy and maddening. I thought I might explode.

I turned my head and nipped his earlobe, whispering, "Haven't I already?"

The hand left my breast to catch my face there, and his mouth sealed over mine, another promise, his tongue seeking and ravenous. I had never kissed anyone like that, reckless and messy and gasping. He released my wrists and spun me back to face him, and then I felt both of his hands on my ass, pressing me against him. I was straining toward his body, trying to rub every inch of my skin against whatever I could reach.

My mouth was in a frenzy against him, but his tongue was slow, deliberate. I was getting desperate. He was holding back, teasing me, enjoying himself. Playing with me, drawing out the torture now that he'd gotten the surrender he wanted. He was treating me like a kitten again.

I'd show him a kitten.

My hands moved to his back as the kiss grew more ferocious, and I lightly trailed my nails up and down his skin. They were still blood red from Mrs. Cleavers's paint, still filed to points to impress the Pinkies at the caravan. He murmured approvingly into the kiss, and I murmured back while softly and sensually drawing one single nail ever so gently up his spine.

And then I made my hand into a claw and ripped my talons down his back.

He drew back from the kiss and hissed at me, teeth bared. I smiled smugly.

"Meow," I whispered.

"Indeed," he growled, his voice dripping with ferocity.

For just a second, I registered that I could smell the blood on his back, and I was filled with a wild desire to run my tongue up the wounds I had made. And then the full force of his body drove me to the bed and pinned me there, pressing me down into the cool sheets.

The studied tension of his kiss was gone, all veils of playfulness dissolved in the blood on my hands. When he kissed me this time, he meant it.

I meant it, too. I wanted him, more than anything I'd ever wanted in my life. My hands held his face right there, daring him to stop kissing me for even a second. Somewhere at the other end of the bed, he was ripping off his boots and stockings with one hand, but his tongue kept lapping at me, pulling me in. I heard things hit the ground, and then he pressed back over me, and I sighed against his lips, arching my back and finding the heavy fabric of his breeches still there, between us. Between me and what I needed.

I didn't want to wait another second to feel the full, hot length of his skin along my body, to find him poised at the brink of me. I wrapped my legs around him and ground my body against the hardness there, whimpering, all pride and modesty forgotten.

He pulled away to whisper raggedly in my ear, "It takes two hands to do this, love," and I understood.

My hands fumbled for the ties on his breeches as he licked down my throat and between my breasts, and I mumbled, "Don't they have kilts in your world?"

Finally, the laces were loose, and I tried to push down the cloth with clumsy fingers. Just then, he started circling a breast with his tongue, and I dropped the laces to clutch the sheet underneath me, gasping as he took my nipple into his mouth and sucked. I threw my head back and moaned, twining my fingers in his hair.

He kissed me as he shucked his breeches, and the kiss built in intensity until the full weight of him finally covered me, skin meeting skin until there was nothing left between us. I could hear myself whimpering again, feel myself wiggling, but still he held back.

"Are you mine?" he whispered in my ear, and his knee nudged my legs apart. His gloved hand teased me, stroking, dipping and caressing. I was so close. So close.

His finger worked faster, and he licked the hollow behind my ear. I threw back my head and looked up at the mirror then, at the dark fall of his hair and the pale, powerful ripples of his back. I saw the four straight red lines where I had clawed him, already healing. It was only a second that my attention wandered, but then the finger was gone, and he was pushing against me, poised at my last barrier, waiting for my word.

"Are you?"

I was panting, wanting, groaning, a beast of emotion and yearning that couldn't be denied. And he wanted words from me, wanted me to think. Wanted me to make a choice.

"Sometimes," I whispered back in his ear.

Then, so quietly, "Now."

And with a chuckle of fierce triumph, he plunged into me, again and again and again, and I was already there, somehow. I cried out in release, fireworks blossoming behind my closed eyes as he touched something inside me that I hadn't known existed. He stroked again, and again, and I kept waiting for him to bite me or draw blood or do something definitively inhuman. But instead, he just kissed me as I came, his tongue tasting every inch of my mouth with the same hotness that burned below.

"Stop, stop. I'm dying," I said. Inside me, everything felt swollen, loud, overtouched, sensitive beyond belief. "Please."

But he rolled to his side, taking me with him, and his hand moved down to caress me even as he kept moving. Forehead pressed to mine, he said, "You don't mean that. You don't want me to stop."

"I can't take any more," I said. "One's all I'm good for. This is too much."

"It's never too much." He chuckled, his finger moving faster again.

And then I felt it, deep inside me, blooming like some bright flower in the darkness, something new and strange. And I was riding it, consumed by it, the pleasure sweet and sharp as a violin note, rocking me to my core. And we both cried out in release, quaking together before collapsing in a heap, laughing.

24

Sometime later, I woke up curled against him under the red velvet coverlet, my head on his chest. And quite surprised at myself. His arm was around me, his dove-colored glove absentmindedly stroking my wrist. His gloves were the only things he was still wearing. I, of course, wore nothing.

"Good morning, poppet," he said with a sleepy grin.

"Poppet?"

"I believe we're technically pirates now. And you smile in your sleep. I probably did, too."

Warm and rested and satisfied for what felt like the first time in forever, I stretched, my knuckles and toes grazing the walls. For someone on an impossible quest, in that moment, I felt marvelous.

"You're going to have to wash that glove," I observed. "Or throw it away."

He examined his hand, grinning, and said, "Perhaps I'll have it framed instead."

"I didn't glance, you know," I said. "When we touched."

"I know," he said. "And I'm glad. I don't want you to see what's in my head when I'm touching you. That would take away all the fun."

"Does it only work once?" I asked. "The glancing?"

"Perhaps," he said. "Every gift is different."

I should have felt shy, and it seemed strange that I didn't. But I was comfortable there, in a rich deviant's bed on a submarine, cradled by the blood drinker who inexplicably adored me.

"Why do you love me?" I asked, lured into candor by the strangeness of the situation.

"Hmm?"

"I'm just curious. I show up out of nowhere, and you all but pledge your undying love to me, even though you don't really know me. Just because of a broken heart and a spell. It doesn't make sense."

"No, I suppose it doesn't," he said, chuckling. I smiled, to feel his chest rumble with it. "But don't you believe in love at first sight?"

"I believe that other people believe in it," I said. "But I'm just too practical for that sort of thing. There are too many variables, too many chemicals and likes and dislikes and shared interests and the timing of it all."

"Ah, a romantic," he said wryly. "But you're wrong."

"Am I?"

"What if you could take everything you were looking for in a person and whisper it into someone's ear, and they brought that person to you? And then, when you saw them for the first time, even if you didn't know they were the one for you, you suddenly knew it anyway?" His finger traced my eyebrows, my cheekbones, as he thought a moment. "What if your heart stopped when you saw that person, and only after that did you realize that they truly were everything you ever wanted?"

"OK, that would be nice," I had to admit.

"That's what happened for me," he said gently.

"What did you ask for?" I needed to know. It was a tall order to live up to the feeling he had described.

"Cleverness, courage, beauty, humor, strength, slyness, curves, magic, talent, understanding. An equal."

"Didn't you ask for someone . . . you know . . . like you?"

"I did."

"But I'm not what you are."

"Oh, that," he said, considering. "That's not a problem. If it ever comes down to it, I can make you like me."

"Does it hurt?"

"I don't really know," he said. "I've only done it once. Whatever it felt like, to her, it was better than dying. Asking another Bludman anything about the process is considered terribly gauche. But as you've seen, there are advantages."

"Such as?"

"Improved strength and healing, longer life. And with all of those, of course, come courage and humor, because you don't have to worry so much. When you're less likely to die and you don't have to fight for food, the main concern is keeping those you love safe."

"Oh, that's all, is it?"

"Well, yes, that can be a tall order." He chuckled again.

"I have other questions," I said, trying to seem uninterested.

"Hmm?"

"What keeps you from draining me dry? I mean, you want to, don't you?"

"Maybe a little. Not as much as I did."

"Explain."

"I took precautions," he said, somewhat defensively.

"Such as?" I could hear myself sounding like a schoolmarm, but I had the feeling that there was a secret somewhere eluding me, swimming under the murky waters of our relationship. Deep down, I knew that he was lying to me somehow.

He gently lifted me off his chest and turned me to face him. He looked grave but hopeful. "When I tell you this, don't overreact. It's important that you hear the whole story."

I straightened, pulling the velvet blanket back up to cover me. "I'm listening."

He looked down, thinking. Then he met my eyes and said, "I gave you some of my blud."

"You what?" I said, backing away a little. "Why? Why didn't you ask me? What about informed consent?"

Of course, I didn't mention my unexplained interest in licking his back wounds mid-coitus. That didn't count.

"I didn't ask for consent for anything else I did with either of our bodily fluids recently," he said with a wolfish grin. "And giving you my blud has probably already saved your life several times over."

"You're going to have to explain it," I said through clenched teeth. "Because I don't get it, and I'm pretty pissed."

"It's simple," he said, but before he could explain what exactly was simple about secretly force-feeding me his magic blud and turning me into an enormous hypocrite, an alarm siren erupted from the other end of the ship. He leaped up to shove his feet through his breeches and lurched down the red velvet hallway, leaving me naked and speechless in a rich man's bed.

"What is it?" I asked from the pilot's room door a few moments later.

The sirens were still shrieking, and a red light flashed on and off from the ceiling. All I could see over his shoulder was hundreds of blinking instruments and gray water through the viewing window—no obvious emergency.

He paused in his frantic button pushing to glance at me and did a double take.

"I've seen a lot of odd things, but I've never seen a woman in men's clothing before," he said with an amused snort before turning back to the panel of lights. "Not that you don't look dashing."

I snickered.

Dashing wasn't the word I'd use. The breeches were baggy, the suspenders didn't work with my B-cup chest, and the frilly shirt was ridiculous. And I was still testy about the blood sharing. But I didn't want to interrupt an emergency with something petty.

I did anyway.

"So about the blood," I said, hating myself a little.

"Can it wait until after I've saved you from this kraken?" he asked, eyes never leaving the screen.

I moved closer to the instrument panel, unconsciously putting my hand on his shoulder. If there was a sea monster, I wanted to see it. Sure enough, there was a round, black sonar screen with a red crosshair on it. And smack dab in the middle of it was a big, squid-shaped blip. And then there was a loud gong and a creak, and we were thrown sideways.

"Bloody hell!" he shouted. "Where's the stunner? He's going to dive soon!"

"What are we looking for?" I asked, holding on to his shoulder with one hand and the captain's chair with the other, trying to stay upright as the ship shuddered and tossed and flashed red around us. I felt like an extra in *Star*

Trek. The ship jerked to the side, and my throat constricted as I realized that this was in no way a movie set. This fairy-tale monster was real.

"The stunner," he said, his fingers dancing over the controls. "To, um, stun it. Most ships have one, I'm told."

He ran his fingers over the switches and buttons on the console, and I began investigating the overhead instruments. The nose of the ship lurched downward, and I was thrown against the ceiling. After banging my head on something, I looked closer.

"This thing has a picture of lightning on it," I said. "Does that help?"

His hand curled over mine where it lay on the brass handle, and he winked at me as we pulled it together. There was a whirring somewhere below us, then a building buzz, and our hair stood on end. A loud crack and a sudden impact smacked our skulls together, and we got all tangled up as the sub shuddered and righted itself. Then the red lights stopped flashing, and everything was back to normal.

We watched the sonar, and the green squid blob dwindled to a speck, which faded away to nothing. I sighed in relief. Being in a submarine under attack by a giant squid was one of those things so far outside of reality that I couldn't digest it. It felt like a ride at Disney World.

"That went well," Criminy said, falling into the brass and leather captain's chair. "We're getting close, sea monsters notwithstanding. I expect we'll be there within the hour."

"Wait. If the ship was moving the entire time we were asleep, how are we just now getting close to the island? It should have only been a few hours, right?"

He smirked. "I never said it was moving the entire time.

I may have slowed it to a crawl for a while. There was business to attend to."

"How could anything be more important than finding Goodwill and getting my locket?"

I was exasperated. After all we'd been through to get here, we'd lost valuable time. Still, his eyes were soft and kind, and he reached out to chuck me under the chin.

"Look, little love. I admire your determination and tenacity, but you can't press on forever. If we'd stormed the island in the wee hours of morning, you would have fallen over from exhaustion and hunger. You needed respite and rest. You needed to be taken care of, if only for a few hours. Even if you didn't know it yourself."

"But we could have been there. We could have already won. We could have avoided that kraken!"

"No matter how much you like control, some things are simply out of your hands," he said. "Still, it was exciting, wasn't it?"

"Yes, it was fun zapping that squid with you," I said, leaning back against the wall to pin him with my glare. "Now stop changing the subject. About the blood."

Criminy leaned back and rubbed his eyes. I tried not to ogle his chest and instead showed an interest in a preserved butterfly in a case on the wall.

"Here's the thing," he said. "My blud saved your life. Not only because it makes me less likely to hurt you but because it gives you strength and resilience. You nearly drowned, you know. Or maybe you don't know. But you did."

"I guess I glazed over that bit, what with the near murder by ghost."

"Once you've had even a drop of my blud, you no longer drive me crazy with hunger," he said. And then he grinned, flashing his teeth. "At least, not in the way that ends up with you drained. The other kind . . . well, there's no hope there."

I blushed and cleared my throat as he went on.

"You'll always entice me, as my smell will entice you, because that's part of the bargain. But unless I smell your actual blood, I won't be a danger to you. My blud is like an antidote. I guess the maestro told you that—he's got an odd sort of cleverness, that one. The droplets on your skin from the locket helped a little, which is how we managed to get to the caravan with you mostly uncovered." He shifted a little. I think a weaker man would have blushed.

"But it was still tempting," he admitted. "So I figured the faster I got a few more drops in you, the better. Plus, that way, if anything happened to you here, you'd have a better chance of surviving it. Of fighting off bludrats or swimming a mile in the ocean, or something even worse."

I tapped my fingers on the burled instrument panel, eyebrows up, waiting.

"But yes, I suppose it would have been gentlemanly to ask first. I apologize."

"When did you do it?"

"That first meal, in the dining car. In your wine."

"Why didn't you ask me?"

"Honestly," he said with a grin, "how would that have worked? *Oh, hello, dream lover. Would you drink some of my blud so I won't murder you in front of all these nice people?*" He chuckled. "So I took a chance. And I think it paid off, don't you agree?"

"Grudgingly."

"And a little more by the Brighton wall," he admitted. "In the kiss."

"I thought there was something going on there," I said.

"And that's why you said something about *Remember, I did this for you,* isn't it? You were trying to give me strength."

"Do you forgive me, then, Letitia?"

He wasn't joking anymore. He needed my forgiveness.

"I forgive you," I muttered, looking down at my baggy pants and adjusting my suspenders. "But I wish you would have asked." I looked up at him. "And don't do it again without telling me."

"If I give you more blud," he said, "you'll damned well know it."

He stroked my face and turned back to the instrument panel and started pressing buttons. I went back to the bedroom and got his shirt and jacket and folded everything and carried the stack up to the control room. And I admit that I sniffed myself dizzy, too, because everything that had lingered near his skin smelled marvelous, all thanks to that unwanted but helpful blud.

It was obnoxious to know that by the time I had condemned Casper for drinking from Bludmen, I had already had a taste myself. Sure, I hadn't known it at the time. But how could I face him again? I was a hypocrite. The blud had saved my life, just as it had probably saved his, even if he had done it for what I considered to be the wrong reasons. I had tasted blud, and I wanted more. Without my consent, being in Sang had changed me.

When I returned to the instrument room, my inhuman lover was leaning intently over a thick leather book, poring over maps. Without looking up, he handed me a tin of cookies. Too ravenous to bother asking where he had found them, I began stuffing them in my mouth as I examined the map. There were several islands clustered just off the coast of Brighton, surrounding the Isle of White. They were too small to have names, and there were at least a dozen. And we hadn't even discussed what to do when we found the damned place.

Something binged above my head, and Criminy hit a button to stop the noise. The sub shuddered to a stop, and we were bobbing, drifting, a different sensation from the smooth forward motion to which I had grown accustomed. I started to feel a little seasick, actually.

Criminy pulled down a sort of goggle contraption hanging from the ceiling and looked through it, then held it out to me, saying, "There they are. The lesser Isles of White."

I put my eyes to the brass goggles of the periscope and blinked at the relative brightness of the morning outside. Through water-spattered glass, I could see one large island that reminded me of Greece. It was settled, with an older, faded white city around a church. To the right were three much smaller islands. One of them had a ribbon of sparkling white around the edge. Blinding glints promised razor wire across the top. *How welcoming.*

"Guess which one we're aiming for," he said.

"The one with the wall?" I asked.

"Of course."

"I wish I knew if the locket worked for him," I said. "If he can get back to my world with it." Then a horrible thought struck me. "Oh, God, Criminy! What if he's broken it? What if I can never get back?" I flung myself against him, and he caught me and stroked my hair, which I'd tied back with a ribbon.

"He has no reason to break it, even if it doesn't work for him," he said. "And if it didn't work, perhaps he won't be guarding it so well. We'll find it, little love. Don't worry."

"What if it's not with him? What if he left it in Manchester?"

"Impossible. A man like that keeps his weapons close at hand. Like Evangel's ring. He'll trust no one."

"Do you think he knows we're coming?" I asked.

"He's looking for you, we know that much," Criminy said.

"Wait," I said, looking around. "How do we get off of this thing and onto the island?"

Criminy's mouth compressed into a thin line. Then his lips started to twitch. Then he started to shake. And then he cackled, head thrown back, as if it was the funniest joke he'd ever heard.

"Darling, I have no idea whatsoever," he said. "I didn't think that far ahead."

"For someone who can't swim, you're awfully cavalier," I said.

"You have to admit it's funny," he said. "And you have to know I'll find a way."

With the sub bobbing cheerfully in place, Criminy left me at the periscope to search the rest of the ship for ideas. I'd have guessed we were half a mile away from the island. I could see red tile roofs and palm trees rising behind the wall, but that was pretty much it. There weren't Coppers or guard towers or machine-gun turrets, but I didn't even know if those things existed in this world. Yet.

Metal and wood and flesh collided in the hallway. Criminy cursed and appeared with a coil of dirty rope around one arm and a big canvas bag dragging behind him. He was bursting with energy, like a little kid on a Boy Scout trip.

"Found a raft," he said. "And a rope."

"Please tell me I'm not going to tow you in to the island," I said.

"Oh, that could be fun," he said with a grin. "But this isn't the 1600s, sweetheart. It comes with a propeller."

"What about weapons?" I asked.

"You think we're going to storm the island, eh?"

"Well, it stands to reason. If there's something worth guarding, they're going to be . . . you know. Guarding it."

He looked through the periscope. "I don't see guards. Or weapons. Not even the glint off a clockwork."

"To me, that makes it look like a trap. Like they're waiting for us."

"Then how do you propose we spring this trap, darling?"

"I don't know," I said, exasperated. "What else do you have in your wacked-out world? Heat sensors? Mine fields? Dirigibles? Booby traps? Machine guns? Shrink rays? What?"

"Aside from dirigibles, which are rather expensive and rare outside of trade routes, most of what you just said made no sense whatsoever," he said, as delighted as a child hearing a foreign language for the first time. "But it all sounds very dangerous. And fun. Especially the part about the boobies."

I waited, eyebrows raised.

He sighed. "Look, love, I know I seem like a tactical genius, but really, I'm just a magician who occasionally kills a bunny or drives a train."

"So we're just going to putter up to the beach in our raft and walk up to the gate and kindly request an audience with Jonah Goodwill?" I asked.

"You keep forgetting our two greatest strengths," Criminy said.

"Which are?"

"My magic and these harpoons."

25

We were still inside the sub when Criminy did his invisibility spell on us both. Just as I remembered from the field on my first morning in Sang, I felt a cold trickle that spread until I could see through myself, my manly clothes, and even Uro on my wrist. It was very strange, seeing a framed luna moth hanging on the red velvet wall through Criminy's half-see-through, grinning face, as if he were made of glass. With another wiggle of his fingers, the raft and the harpoons joined us in near-transparency.

Then we clambered up the ladder and out onto the roof of the sub. Criminy threw the nearly transparent raft into the air, and it exploded into shape and landed in the water with a slap. I was glad that we could half-see each other and our gear, because leaping into a truly invisible raft would have been impossible.

Criminy hopped in with his harpoon and helped me down. With the touch of the propeller's button, we were buzzing toward the beautiful but most likely deadly island. It was a short trip, and Criminy used our time by showing me the simple mechanism for shooting the harpoon.

"We've got one shot each, love," he said, slipping my finger around the trigger in an all-too-intimate manner. "So make it count. And don't forget we're invisible. A nice harpoon butt to the face will do wonders. And then we steal their weapons."

"But what do we do?" I asked. "Besides break teeth and steal things? How do we know where to go?"

"We sneak around until we figure that part out," he said. "Just follow me. It's going to be fun."

When the raft was almost to the sand, I jumped into ankle-deep water and turned to drag it in. I expected Criminy at my side, but he was still sitting in the raft with a funny smile on his half-invisible face.

"Sorry, sweetheart," he said, "but you're going to have to drag me in. I touch that salty stuff, and I'm not going to be much help to you. Might even make the magic waver."

So I lugged the raft in by myself and beached it, marking its place with a large clump of driftwood. Criminy stepped off onto the sand, dry and chipper. I now had sopping-wet boots, sagging socks, and scratchy, damp breeches. But it was worth it to know that my locket was finally within reach.

With a blithe "Shall we?" he ran toward the jungle, faster than I could keep up. We ducked into the shade, dodging droopy tropical trees and flowering bushes. Up close, about twenty feet from our hiding place in the jungle, the wall was actually quite pretty, with glittering shells and sand dollars and bits of sand and mica mixed in. It was warm and breezy and absolutely nothing like any island that had ever existed near Britain. It would have done wonders for the tourist trade in my world.

But the effect was ruined by the skulls lined up along the top of the forbidding wall, right under the razor wire.

Criminy exhaled out his nose the way men do when they're about to return to their caveman roots and beat something unconscious. "They're all Bludmen," he said. "And women. And children."

I couldn't tell the difference at first. But then I saw the teeth. At least the skulls were old, bleached white in the sun. Nothing fresh.

"That bastard's going to pay," he growled under his breath.

Under cover of the jungle, we trotted along the wall, looking for a way in. There were no windows, no arrow slots, no people. Nothing. Not for a long time. Just strange noises from within, crashes and snuffles and the sounds of movement. Finally, when it seemed as if we had run all the way around the island, we came across a set of double doors lashed together with heavy, rusted chains and an enormous lock.

Criminy looked at it and laughed.

"All that, old man? All that, and it's just a lock?"

"But maybe there are guards on the inside," I said. "Maybe it's bolted?"

"Only one way to find out," he answered, and he handed me his harpoon.

Before I could ask him how he expected me to shoot two invisible harpoons at once, he had jogged to the wall and skittered up it like a cat climbing a tree. I dropped his harpoon and set mine to my shoulder, waiting for something horrible to happen, for the trap to spring finally.

He glanced quickly over the wall into the compound and ducked back down. Then he slowly looked back over and cocked his head at a strange angle. He slid under the razor wire and disappeared. I was nearly hyperventilating with worry and curiosity, and my finger was slippery on my harpoon's trigger.

Something boomed inside. The chains fell away, and the door squealed open. Criminy walked out, no longer transparent, with the strangest smile on his face, disbelieving but amused.

"Come along, Letitia," he called. "There's no one here."

Still nervous and distrustful, I picked up his harpoon and tiptoed out from the shade and into the bright glare of the sun. I could not fathom that the island was empty, that someone wasn't waiting to hurt me. Criminy extended his gloved hand. I took it, and he half-dragged me through the door and beyond the white wall.

It was entirely deserted.

We had found Jonah Goodwill's fabled island, that was for sure. But he wasn't there, and neither was anyone else. Just lots and lots of animals, a veritable Noah's ark that explained all of the weird noises I'd been hearing. Some of them were creatures I'd never seen before, and not a single one was a predator.

Criminy shut the door softly behind us, muttering, "We don't want these poor creatures wandering into the jungle or the sea. Might as well tie tags around their necks with 'Eat me' on them."

I smiled to myself at the irony of a vicious, cutthroat predator worrying about the safety of the soft, squishy innocents of the animal world. He was right, though. The animals had no fear. As soon as he'd made me visible again, deer and giraffes and cows and a strange sort of club-tailed porcupine were all nosing and snuffling hopefully at me, and I felt a little sorry that I hadn't brought a bag of bread or bananas for them. They all shied away from Criminy, though, and a llama even spit on him.

"Can't hide the blud," he said with a shrug.

I shoved past the hungry animals, and we headed straight up to the main building, a two-story manor that looked as if it had been lifted straight out of an American's version of quaint Mexico. White walls, dark orange roof tiles, a fountain in the courtyard. It was beautiful, inside and out. But no humans at all. Just echoes and creepiness. Someone had been there recently, as the fruit bowl on the table was filled with fresh mangoes and pineapples. I was too anxious to eat, but I scooped water out of a fountain with my hand after suddenly realizing I was parched.

We checked every room, harpoons at the ready. And we found no one.

Criminy searched the closets and checked under the beds. I sifted through chests and dressers and anything that might conceivably hide treasure. My locket was nowhere to be found.

We tried the cookhouse next. The ashes of the fire were still warm under the spit, which held an abandoned haunch of meat, burned to the bone.

Beyond that, we found a sandy field with a tall tower, several iron rings sunken into the ground, and a windsock.

"Bastard's got a metal cladder," Criminy said grimly. "No wonder he keeps beating us. It's only two hours to Manchester by dirigible."

I felt as if the breath had been knocked out of me.

"From here to Manchester?" I spluttered. "My locket's all the way back in Manchester now?"

"Don't fret, little love," he said softly. "We'll get it back."

He folded me into his arms, harpoon and all, and I started sniffling, then full-out crying. Whether the old man had tricked us, outrun us, or just coincidentally left his island was unclear, but he was undoubtedly very far away, as was the locket.

I clung to Criminy as if he was the only thing between me and madness. Maybe he was. He held me, patted me, and muttered kindnesses into my ear. I couldn't help thinking about my other world, wondering if my body was in a hospital yet and, if so, how long it had taken my proud grandmother to break down and hire a new nurse for her homecare. What if she tried to get out of bed by herself and broke a hip? And who was feeding Mr. Surly? But I wasn't going to sit around, uselessly indulging my own frustration. I needed to act. I took the handkerchief he offered and blew my nose.

"There's got to be a clue here somewhere," I said between sniffles. "There's got to be something else we can do."

"We can eat and sleep," he said. "Because wherever he's gone, we're not going to catch him today. Might as well get dried out and well rested." He chucked me under the chin. "And let your bum rest after that horse ride, eh?"

But I wasn't done. I saw one more building on the other side of the landing strip, and I squelched through the sand, leaving wet bootprints behind me. Criminy caught up with me, holding his harpoon at the ready.

The last building looked like a storage shed, a simple windowless hut with the same smooth white walls and orange tile roof. In my world, it would have held a couple of rusty, nonworking lawn mowers and the neighbor's long-forgotten weed eater.

As we got close, I felt Criminy tense, and he aimed his harpoon at the door.

"What is it?" I whispered, whipping my own harpoon into place against my shoulder much less gracefully and almost smacking myself in the nose.

"There's someone inside," he said. "A Bludwoman. I can smell her."

The island was silent as we crept toward the hut. Well, except for the random mooing and bleating and occasional horn clashing of the animals, but those noises were normal and comforting. No sound came from within the outbuilding.

When we were right outside the door, Criminy barked, "Who's in there?" in his most fearsome voice.

There was a small noise inside, a scraping. Then a cough. Then a word, barely a ragged whisper.

"Help."

"We're coming in!" Criminy shouted, and he kicked in the door.

It was pitch black inside, except for the perfect rectangle of sunshine radiating through the door frame. Tiny motes of dust and sand danced in the air, and we waited.

The cough came again, followed by scraping and rattling. Chains.

"Criminy?" she whispered from the darkness.

"Tab?" he said, rushing into the room. "What have they done to you, lass?"

I stood just outside the door, wishing I could see what was happening within but afraid to get too close. I heard a loud clang and a whooping gasp, and I leaned in through the doorway.

From the darkness, something flew at me too fast to see. I tried to scream, but the sound was choked off as I crashed to the sand with a body driving me into the ground. Claws settled around my throat, pressing down on my windpipe.

So I did what any sensible person would do.

I passed out.

26

"Letitia, love, come back to me."

Criminy's desperate voice buzzed from far away, annoying.

Then I heard a stranger whisper, "What do you see in that thing? It's unnatural."

I heard gulping and a wistful sigh.

I didn't know the voice, but the tone was all too familiar, calling me back to consciousness. There was something to fear there. I kept my breathing even, my eyes closed.

"There's nothing unnatural about loving someone," Criminy said. "You just think it's unnatural that I don't love you."

"It should have been me," she said. "Thirty years ago, when Merissa left you, I was there. And you taught me parlor tricks, chucked me under the chin. I've been here all along, waiting. And then she showed up and started hovering over that stupid glass ball, and you insisted on acting like a lovesick child. It's disgusting."

"You're a sweet girl, Tab, but it's just not to be," Criminy said, then made a slurping noise and cleared his throat. I was touched by his devotion, but it occurred to me that there was only one thing that he ate, and he had left his blood vials in the lost satchel.

What on earth were they slurping?

"It's not too late, you know," the female said, her voice taking on a sprightly but seductive air.

Oh, please, I thought, inwardly rolling my eyes.

"It was too late the day she arrived," Criminy said. "Look, Tab, you're beautiful and lovely and clever and all, but there's never been a spark here. You're going to make some Bludman very happy one day, but it's never going to be me. You've got to get over it, girl. You've got to move on."

"Oh, like you moved on?" she purred. "I remember you, in the days after Merissa left. I remember those nights on the moors. Just you and me on the blud altar under the moon. Those were good times, Crim."

"Yeah, that was fun," Criminy said, and I could hear annoyance creeping into his voice. "But it was nothing more than that."

"It could be. I could end it now. We can both take her."

Quick as a snake, there was the odd slap of a scale-covered hand on a hard face.

"Never speak it," he growled. "Or *I'll* end *you.*"

"Hmph!"

"Speaking of which, Tab, I'm curious. How'd you get here?"

"You didn't even know I was missing, did you?" she cried. "You self-centered bastard! Some gypsy king you are, not even knowing when one of your own is gone!"

"Emerlie said you had a difficult case of ladies' troubles," he said, sounding oddly prissy.

"And you didn't know she was lying? She's always lying!"

"What happens between your legs is none of my damned business," he snapped. "I had other concerns."

"I ran away, if you must know." She sniffed. "Right after

I heard she was to glance on the carnivalleros. I didn't want her to touch me, vile thing."

Criminy chuckled. "Didn't want her to see your true feelings for me, eh? That's understandable. But I'm sure you didn't run away to this charming island on your own."

"I took my carpetbag and followed the tracks back toward Wolvenhampton. I figured I could scratch by for a few decades, wait for your doxy to die off or get old and ugly. But the Coppers found me, just outside the caravan. Two of them and the old man."

She went quiet. Criminy waited. I almost opened my eyes and told her to get on with it, already.

"He's a nasty character, that Jonah Goodwill. Almost drained me, as you can see. Seemed awfully interested in you and your lady." She paused, and I heard something snap. It sounded like a bone. "Didn't mean to tell 'em everything, but I did."

"Torture and draining not your bag, kitten?" Criminy asked, and I imagined the quirk in his lips, the humor in his eyes.

"Not unless I'm on the other side of the whip," she whispered, a seductive purr in her voice. I'd had just about enough of the minx, and I'd never even seen her.

I sat up. But when I opened my eyes, I realized that I *had* seen her before, although she had looked very different then. It was Sirena, the mermaid from the caravan, but she had legs. Quite a lot of leg, poking out from her dress in ripped fishnet stockings and sky-high heels. And, of course, she was sprawled in the sand, giving Criminy quite an eyeful.

Even more disturbing, though, were the dead things strewn around in front of the shack. Cows, goats, sheep, a giraffe with an awkwardly bent neck. Not a drop of blood could be seen, and the deflated bodies were all placed calmly, side by side. It was like a grisly slumber party at the San Diego Zoo. I cringed.

"Letitia, love, how are you?" Criminy asked, reaching to stroke my face.

The recently tortured but gorgeous blond Bludwoman smirked at me from Criminy's side. Reading my face, she grinned, showing me all of her sharp little white teeth colored with animal blood. She reminded me of an ermine, something small and sleek that would curl quietly around your neck for years and then one day rip out your eyeball for no good reason.

"Not so good, actually," I said, pulling myself to standing and backing away from them toward the shade cast by the shack. I felt my neck, which had one of Criminy's scarves tied snugly around it. "Did she bite me?"

"No, pet, or she'd be dead. She bruised you, and I added the handkerchief so she wouldn't try it again." He glowered at her, and she giggled.

"First of all, I heard your entire conversation. Second of all, how is the mermaid walking?" It seemed a ridiculous question, but it was going to bug me until I knew.

"She's not really a mermaid," Criminy said, avoiding both of our gazes. "But little Tabitha Scowl didn't have an aptitude for anything else at the caravan. She had no place else to go, so I gave her a fake tail and a breathing spell and threw her into a tank of pond water to fool the Pinkies."

"I had an aptitude, but you still wouldn't take me as apprentice," she said fiercely, curling her lavender-gloved hands into claws.

"Yes," Criminy said, grinning. "Somehow I felt I couldn't trust you."

"Imagine that," I said, backing away. I tripped over the leg of a dead gazelle. Criminy caught me and drew me down to the sand, tucking me into his side and putting his arm around me.

Across from us, Tabitha stood and dusted the sand off the plum taffeta of her ragged dress. It was ripped at the thigh and burned in places, and the effect was quite alluring. I felt plain and silly in my men's clothes, and I missed my burgundy dress more than ever.

She stomped into the shack, kicking up sand. She was dwarfed by the doorway, tiny, probably not even five feet tall.

"Criminy, is she—"

"A child?" he asked, guessing my question. "She's more than a hundred years old. But she was only fourteen when she was turned. Apparently, she didn't have a glancer to tell her to stay out of dark alleys at night."

She stomped right back out, holding a little beaded bag and a dramatic, floppy hat covered in black plumes. Dropping to the ground, she pulled a compact out of the bag and started doing her makeup.

"Goodwill and his men left to deal with the burning at Brighton," she said without looking up. "So when are we leaving?"

The raft was awfully crowded on the ride back to the sub. For a tiny creature, Tabitha Scowl took up a lot of room.

Before setting off, we looted the house and found some expensive silver and trinkets to steal but, unfortunately, no secret diary outlining Jonah Goodwill's evil plans. We didn't even find a secret door, and, of course, a shallow island couldn't have a basement. My glance of the cabal in the cellar had definitely been in a city.

Criminy opened the hatch on the sub, and Tabitha was the first one down the ladder. Personally, I had half a mind to lock her in and take the raft back to civilization.

"When we get to Brighton," Criminy said to her, "you're on your own."

"Fine," she said. "I've had it with being a talking fish, anyway." Then she smiled slyly and said, "And who knows? You might change your mind. I can be useful."

Then she flounced back into the bedroom and slammed the door shut as loudly as possible, which wasn't loudly at all. Criminy and I both sighed in relief and slid to the floor. The hallway was so narrow that we sat on opposite sides, knees meeting in the middle. I pinned him with my glare, and he rolled his eyes dramatically.

"Can I help it if all the young fillies fall for me?" he said. "It's probably the accent."

"Everyone here has the accent," I grumbled. "It's probably the hair."

He moved to my wall and put his arm around my shoulders. "Honestly, love, I've been fending off that little minx for years. Had no idea she was so diabolical. If I had, I might have liked her more. Or snapped her neck. Could have gone either way."

"Don't even start," I said, nudging him. "She told Goodwill everything. She betrayed us."

"Actually, she betrayed *you* because she loves *me*," he teased. "It's a bit endearing."

"She stays in Brighton," I said. "Or I'm throwing you off at the lighthouse, and you can hang out with that ghost for a while."

"But she could prove helpful," he said.

"She. Stays. In. Brighton."

"Fine, fine. She stays in Brighton," he said, kissing my forehead before standing and moving to the instrument panel. "So let's get there and dump her off on the poor, unsuspecting fools."

The trip back was uneventful, especially compared with our previous hours in the submarine. I felt a bit anxious about what had passed between us, and as much as I disliked our new passenger, I was glad to avoid idle hours in the conspicuously useful bedroom. My feelings about him were even more complicated after giving in to his magnetic pull and my own lust. I felt closer to him, but I also felt less like myself. I didn't know what I needed most: time to think, time to sleep, or time to explore my feelings. Or Criminy's heart. Or his body.

Criminy was unusually quiet. I didn't know if it was because he was worried about me, about finding Goodwill, about dealing with Tabitha, or all of the above. I didn't want to ask.

I knew that Criminy had explored the ship, but the only door I'd opened had been the bedroom. It occurred to me that I had eaten nothing but cookies in the past twenty-four hours. No wonder I was so wobbly and emotionally spent. I went straight to the galley.

A little enameled cube like the one at Antonin's flat was bolted to the wall. The air within was cold, though, not blood-warm. Inside were chilled tins of strange, thick milk and some shriveled fruit. Behind the sliding doors of the cabinets, I found cans of soup and several packages of ship's biscuit, which were apparently an ancient form of Pop-Tart constructed entirely of cement.

I ended up with a bowl of cold, filmy soup, a glass of

heavy cream, and tepid fruit salad. The apple was pink inside, and the tangerine was mostly dry. I wasn't going to try the rock biscuits. I sat down on the stool bolted to the floor and stared at my lunch. My main thought was *ick*. Probably the same thing Criminy thought when he and Tabitha had feasted on Goodwill's menagerie. It tasted like crap, but you could live on it.

After forcing down lunch and finding the bathroom, I curled up on the floor of the hallway and fell asleep. I was only vaguely aware of Criminy gathering me up, depositing me on a small couch, and sliding another paneled door shut, leaving me in the sitting room of the gently purring sub. The kiss I expected on my forehead never came. I slept uneasily the entire way to Brighton.

I awoke several hours later as the sub ground to a halt. The door to the bedroom was still shut, and I found Criminy alone at the instrument panel. I smiled sleepily and put my head against his shoulder, but he shrugged me off irritably and went to the periscope.

"It's still smoking," he said with a frown. "Every ship on the docks is gone, and I can't see a single living creature."

I yawned. "I'm glad they finally had the sense to run away," I said.

"Not necessarily. Someone could have cut the ships loose, set them adrift to deny the people within an egress. Or they might have been sunken. Or burned."

"I can't believe anyone would do that," I said, although I knew very well that even worse things had been done in my world. "And anyway, we'd see chunks of them floating or smoking, and you don't see any of that, do you?"

He stepped back silently to offer me the goggles.

My vision focused, and my jaw dropped. "It's awful," I murmured.

And it was. Heavy smoke billowed up from several large, flaming buildings and a wide swath of devastation on the west side of the city. It was a strategic burning. Black spires of wood stuck up against the gray sky like jagged, broken teeth in sharp contrast to the rest of the city, which appeared unharmed.

"The factories," Criminy said quietly. "And Darkside."

"How many people lived here?" I asked.

"Maybe fifteen thousand," he said. "One-quarter Pinkies to three-quarters Bludmen, almost all working in the factories or indentured. It was a slave city."

"But I don't understand," I said. "I thought that you couldn't be hurt. As easily as humans, I mean."

He laughed bitterly. "Oh, no. We can be hurt, and we can die. We burn just as easily as you do. Our blood may be different, but we're still made of meat. Most of the Bludmen in that city are dead."

We heard the bedroom door slither open, and Tabitha strode down the hallway and snatched the periscope from my hands.

"You're not dropping me off there," she said, glancing up at Criminy with a wicked smile. "It would be tantamount to murder."

"Then we're leaving you in Feverish, which is just a few miles up the road," he said. "I won't doom you, but I won't travel far with you, either. And by the way, you're fired."

"Ha!" She cackled. "You can't fire me. I quit."

Criminy tapped on the instrument panel, turning dials and flicking switches. I felt a soft pull as the sub changed course.

"We're going around the city. We'll walk the moors to Feverish and find a way back to Manchester."

"But what if Goodwill's still in Brighton?" I asked.

"Then we'll beat him home and wait it out," Criminy said firmly. "Something tells me the old codger likes his comfort and his safety. He'll only stay in Brighton long enough to foist the clean-up on somebody else."

It was a good decision. I was grateful that we hadn't tried the docks. Even as our raft neared a lonely beach farther down the coast, I could still smell the smoke of the smoldering city, and it smelled like barbecue and winter fires. I salivated for a second before I remembered the source of the tantalizing smell, then I threw up over the side of the raft before we reached land.

Tabitha snickered. "She's a tough one, eh?"

"Keep it to yourself, lass, unless you want a tender shove," he said, but he grinned.

"I don't think I'd mind a tender shove from you," she purred.

"It isn't tender things I'm picturing, Tab."

She gave him a dazzling smile and licked her fangs. He chuckled.

I was more than a little amazed. Was he actually flirting with the murderous harpy?

I wiped my mouth and huddled in the bottom of the raft, miserable.

Out of irritation, I didn't offer to tow the raft through the deadly salty sea, but the breaking waves did it for me. We were tossed up onto the beach with a crash, and Criminy hopped out to drag me onto the sand. Tabitha leaped nimbly to the ground and strutted toward the moors. His eyes followed her ass as I heaved and choked at his feet.

I apparently had a rival, and Criminy didn't seem to mind as much as before.

I was a lot more bothered than I wanted to be.

It was half a day's walk to Feverish, which was unchanged. No fires, no influx of new citizens or inn visitors, which proved Criminy's point. The Bludmen of Brighton were gone. We were grim and waterlogged when the same young boy ran to greet us. I had remained sullen and silent the whole way as Criminy and Tabitha chatted and flirted. He held the door open for her, and she let it slam on me. I barely had the energy or the will to catch it. And then we stood before Master Haggard.

"Do you have a vacancy, sir?" asked Criminy as if they had never met.

"We do, lad," the old man replied. "How many rooms?"

"Three, please," Criminy said. "If you'll accept this as payment."

I was surprised to feel my heart drop like a stone. *Three?* As Criminy pulled a handful of Goodwill's engraved silver from his waistcoat and Master Haggard nodded solemnly, my mind was racing. Three rooms? What was he doing?

And why did I care so much? Just because he made my toes curl in bed didn't mean that I loved him or that we'd made any promises.

If Tabitha was feeling victorious, it didn't show. In fact, she looked more annoyed than ever. But we both followed resignedly as Master Haggard showed us to three rooms in a row on the long hall. Criminy took the center room. Tabitha and I glared daggers at each other. It felt like a middle-school field trip, and I was the dork in braces.

"Good night," Criminy called softly as he shut his door.

My door and Tabitha's door slammed shut at the same moment.

In the pitch-black early morning, my door shivered open. I rose from my dreams smiling.

He had come back to me.

I moved over on the bed to make room for him, hoping that the darkness hid my relief and girlish giddiness. I didn't want to seem too eager.

The door shut softly. I couldn't see his shadow or hear his footsteps. Had he just checked on me and gone back into the hall?

"Criminy?" I whispered.

And then a glove clapped over my nose and mouth, driving my head into the pillow.

"Did you actually think it would work?" came the fierce whisper.

I struggled, shaking my head back and forth, but the glove's pressure didn't lessen. I whimpered against the soft leather and started to buck and thrash in panic. I couldn't breathe.

Tabitha's face appeared inches from mine, her eyes feral with fury.

"I don't know what spell you used, but I'm going to drain you for taking him away from me," she growled, a sound so low that I could barely hear it. The scent of copper and death and raw meat rolled off her, and I tried not to gag.

I flung my bare hands up, clawing for her eyes and raking across her cheeks with my pointed nails. When I touched her skin, the jolt came unbidden, and the surprise made me bite down on her hand through the glove.

No wonder she hadn't wanted to touch me, before or later. He'd have flayed her alive for this.

She hadn't actually been captured by Jonah Goodwill. She had sought him out as soon as I arrived, a Stranger with an unusual gift. She was helping the Coppers in return for money and leniency when he unleashed his genocide on her people. She was a spy, a decoy, and an assassin.

But she was supposed to kill Criminy, not me.

I sank my teeth in deeper, hoping to hear her bones crack.

"Don't bite me, you little bitch!" she shrieked, and then she gasped when she realized how loudly her screech had rung out in the sleeping inn.

Doors banged open in the hallway, and footsteps pounded to my door. Tabitha scanned the room in terror, ripped the window open, and leaped out, trailing the long bustle of her dress behind her. All I could do was lie on the bed, gulping for air and trying not to pass out, because I had expressly forbidden myself to do that again.

Seconds later, Criminy cradled me in his arms. Master Haggard leaned out the window in a long gray nightshirt, his basset-hound eyes penetrating the dark.

"She's gone," Criminy said with finality, and he held me closer.

"I'm sorry, little love," he said. "I'm so sorry."

I shivered for an hour in his arms before falling asleep against his chest, and I had restless dreams until dawn broke, red and streaky through the open window.

27

Criminy was furious with himself, and I couldn't get him to calm down.

"How did I not know?" he fumed. "Why didn't I see it?"

"I think you were a little focused on me and the locket," I said patiently. "And the ghost, and Brighton, and Erris, and the caravan. And the genocide."

"That's one thing," he said. "But the damned witch put a love spell on me, and I didn't even notice. Slipped it right into my pocket, probably while we were feeding on the island."

He showed me a little bag of plum taffeta, torn from her skirt, tied with long blond hairs. It was light in my hand, and I felt tiny bones inside and something soft.

"Bird bones, moor grass, rose thorns, and my hair," he said bitterly. "Probably skinked a look in my own grimoire when I wasn't looking. A love spell." He snorted. "Three rooms. I should have known then."

"If you'd asked for two rooms and taken her into yours, I would have pitched an unholy fit," I answered. "But I thought . . . Well, it doesn't matter what I thought. It's over now. Let's just get to Manchester as fast as we can. Before she can get to Goodwill."

He seemed more than happy to let it go. Travel was problem enough.

Erris was long gone, of course. Luckily, Master Haggard said that the village had an archaic but serviceable conveyance and that we were welcome to rent it for ten vials of my blood. With Brighton in flames, times were going to be lean in Feverish. I kept reminding myself that ten vials was less than it sounded like, that I had drawn just as much from my infirm patients. Still, as soon as Criminy had drawn the blood, I felt light-headed. I hoped the transportation was worth it.

When Master Haggard threw open the creaking doors to an old stable to show us the conveyance, I couldn't help laughing. I had envisioned tanks, mopeds, miniature trains, even an electric horse. But in a throwback to my own world, there sat an old-fashioned, fairy-tale carriage in silver and rust-dotted light blue. It looked a little like a four-legged octopus. All it needed was a team of white horses and a footman, and I would have felt like Cinderella. But where the horses should have been was air, and on the back was a big brass box with a large key on it.

Criminy and Master Haggard rolled it into the weak sunshine and stood on the box to wind and wind and wind the key, just like a music box. The further it went, the harder it was to wind. Both men were panting and sweating as the tension increased. Finally, they let go, and Criminy helped me through the heart-shaped blue door onto a dusty velvet bench. He hopped in beside me and grasped the brass steering wheel in both hands.

"Thank you, Master Haggard," he called.

The old man stood back with a slow, doleful wave, calling, "Good luck, lad. Keep her safe. And don't forget that spells work both ways, the Drawing included. She'll pay her own price, in time."

I didn't understand his final words, but he made it sound like I was under a curse instead of a charm. Then he lifted a vial of my blood to his lips and drank, eyes closed in pleasure. Which was creepy. I was not at all sad to see the last of the little town of Feverish.

Criminy pulled a lever, and the carriage whirred into life and rumbled along the dirt road on rickety wheels. Through the glass windshield, the road ahead seemed to stretch forever, like a brown ribbon among the moors.

For the first few hours, we chugged along in silence. I was weak from losing so much blood, and Criminy, I think, felt helpless and wounded for having used me as a mule yet again. With his bag lost in the ashes of Brighton and no crowds to amaze for a handful of copper coins, I was the only ATM in the area. And we were both concerned about Tabitha Scowl.

"I still don't understand," I said at last. "Goodwill hired her to kill you and kidnap me. But she was a heartbeat away from draining me and running away to the caravan with you. Like you wouldn't have noticed that I was gone. And like Goodwill wouldn't have hunted her down."

"Love makes fools of us all, darling, and love spells are sneaky," he said. "They prey upon your baser instincts and natural inclinations. Eventually, I would have believed it myself. With you gone, with that in my pocket, with her nearby . . . in time, I would have loved her. Damn her eyes."

"Then why did you get three rooms instead of two?" I asked. "Why didn't you take her with you?"

"I don't know," he said. "Maybe the spell wasn't done correctly. Maybe she was too weak. Maybe you and I, what we have—maybe that's too strong. It's hard to remember now. It was all muddled. Like being drunk, maybe."

"Well I'm glad," I said as evenly as possible. "She probably would have betrayed you, in the end."

"That's true," he said with a sideways smile. "She probably would have. Not that you're jealous or anything."

"Just thinking about the facts," I said. "And she would have smelled like fish."

He burst out with that overly loud laugh, and I had to join in. It was pretty funny, from a certain perspective. A love triangle with a magician, a fortune-teller, and a professional mermaid, two of whom drank blood and one of whom was an alien from another world.

Laughing like that lightened the mood considerably. I think we both felt a little like idiots. One of his hands crept over to hold mine, but then the carriage lurched over a rock, and he needed both hands to keep us on track.

"I don't mean to keep doing this," I said, "but can I take a little nap?"

"Let's see." He chuckled. "You went four days without sleep, then you swam a mile and got gnawed on by beasties, then you were nearly scared to death by a ghost, then you were ravaged by a suitor in a submarine, and then you were nearly murdered twice by a vicious, lying spy. Oh, and then you lost a couple of cups of blood on your way to go face an evil Copper."

I giggled. He had a point.

"Yes, sweet tangerine. I'd say you deserve a nap."

We had to stop several times to rewind the key. The first winding lasted the longest. Criminy alone wasn't strong enough to wind it all the way again, and I was too weak to be helpful. I slept through most of the journey, waking only when the grating noise of the winding key dragged me up from dreams. Each time, I collapsed back onto the seat after swigging some tepid water from my canteen or munching on stale shortbread cookies that Master Haggard had found in some old luggage. I did wake up once with the frantic need to pee, only to run screaming out of the copse with my shirt untucked, trailed by a madly chittering family of ravenous bludsquirrels.

When night fell, we stopped to build a fire. Criminy caught and roasted a bludbunny for me, and I tried not to swallow it whole. We sat on old logs, warming our hands at the merry flames, and Criminy told me Sangish fairy tales and little stories from his childhood in Devlin. He was such a natural entertainer that I nearly forgot my problems. It was easy to lose myself in his words, following along with laughter and tears and imagining him as a child, handsome and mischievous on the streets of a far-off city.

"More," I said. "Please. Don't stop."

With a grin, he danced and did magic tricks and sang a plaintive lullaby in the low, slurry tongue of the Bludmen. He made shadow puppets against the smoke and threw glitter that made the fire glow blue, and when I looked at his eager smile, I was overcome with adoration and gratitude. I was beginning to think that there was nothing he couldn't do. Here we were, on the road, on the run, and he could make me feel as if we were kids on a camping trip. It was a valuable gift, and not his only one.

"Enough, love. Plenty of time for making merry. But tonight you need more sleep," he finally said.

"But I'm having fun," I said. "I don't want tomorrow to come."

"It's easy to pretend, isn't it?" he said, reading my mind. "That this is all there is? To be in the moment, without a care?"

"I know what you're going to say. Easy things aren't worth much," I said with a rueful smile, holding out my hand.

"Your hand in mine is worth a great deal, Letitia," he said, helping me to my feet. "That's what I'll be fighting for tomorrow."

For my own safety, we slept just off the road in our carriage, crushed together at odd angles. I was afraid it would be awkward, but we were so dusty and exhausted that we crumpled into a companionable heap and went insensible after a kiss as brief and bright as a snuffed match.

The next morning, I woke with my head on his shoulder, smiling. My dreams had been peaceful, all twilight and twining vineyards and far-off music like his Bludman's lullaby. In my dream, he taught me how to conjure a butterfly. I didn't want to wake up. But I did anyway, because I felt as if our time was somehow running out.

As I yawned, Criminy's eyes popped open, and he reached out to stroke my cheek. I smiled back at him as he sat up to stretch.

"Time to beat back the bunny hordes," he said gallantly, knowing that any blood-hungry animals in the area would be waiting outside for a taste of me.

He threw open the door, shouting, "Bunnies, prepare to meet your doom!"

He froze.

"What is it?" I asked.

"Stay here," he said, his voice low.

He stepped down from the carriage and shut the door

in my face. I peeked through the curtains and found myself in awe, yet again, that Sang could be so impossibly bizarre.

Dozens of bludbunnies surrounded our carriage, all dead. Parked on the opposite side of the road was an old-fashioned gypsy wagon hooked up to a white bludmare, her grizzled head hanging dejectedly. The sign nailed to the faded red wagon read, *Madam Burial's Snake Oils: Liniments, Salves, Potions, and Tinctures for Ev'ry Malady of Boddy and Spirit.* The wagon was locked up tight, and the driver's box was empty. Someone swung gently in a hammock chair on a little back porch, a thin stream of smoke billowing from a long pipe.

"I've been looking for you," called a rich, husky voice.

"I see you changed your last name, Hepzibah," he answered.

"Merrywell didn't suit," she said. "At least it almost rhymes."

"I'm here, madam," he said, his voice tired and annoyed. "What more do you require?"

"Of you? Nothing," she said. The shape in the chair unfolded and stood in a haze of smoke. I couldn't see her face from my window, but somehow I knew that she was staring right at me. The pipe pointed in my direction. "It's her as needs something. Is it not so?"

Criminy turned to look at me, his face pained and resigned. "Letitia, love. Would you come speak with us, please?"

Another mysterious woman from Criminy's past. How did they all manage to find him? When I had touched him the first time, I had seen only the future, not his speckled history, and I was beginning to think that was a good thing.

With my back straight and my chin up, I walked to Criminy's side. He took my hand and squeezed it. "Letitia, my love, this is Madam Hepzibah Burial. She's the one who gave me the spell for your locket."

Ah, so a late-turned Bludwoman, then. Up close, her face was like that of an old woman whose wrinkles had been erased and softened or maybe smudged with wax. She had drawn sweeping black cat's eyes over her lids, and her lips were deep burgundy. Her hair was in long dreadlocks of black and red, and she was entirely covered by a wool cloak.

"Hello, my dear," she said with a knowing smile.

"Hello," I answered. Criminy squeezed my hand. I said no more.

"You've lost your locket," she said. "That was careless of you."

"It was stolen," Criminy said. "We are currently en route to retrieve it."

"It's not the only way, Stranger," she said to me. "Come."

She ducked into her wagon. With a loud crack, the shutters flew open under the sign. Leaning through the window, framed by shelves of magical-looking bottles and objects, she crossed her arms on the counter and smiled like a hungry crocodile.

"Don't be afraid, little Pinky," she purred. "Madam Burial knows what you need."

I looked at Criminy, trying to project my extreme doubt and bone-deep fear into my eyes.

"Don't worry, love," he said, resigned. "I'm with you."

I walked up to the window and stopped just beyond arm's reach. Criminy leaned against the wagon, feigning amusement, but I could see the tension in his jaw and the anger in his eyes. The man certainly didn't like a foxhole without an emergency exit. We were apparently stuck with the old broad until she decided otherwise.

Madam Burial placed a dainty glass bottle on the counter, and her mouth twitched in grim amusement. "See that, Dorothy? That's your ticket home. Those are your ruby slippers, right there."

"She speaks in riddles," Criminy muttered. "Sometimes I think she actually believes them."

But I knew exactly what she meant, of course. Any Stranger would.

"Before I click my heels three times, what's the catch?" I asked, and she chuckled.

"You learn quickly, Letitia. The catch is this: it takes two people. You can't go alone. The spell only works with two people holding hands, a complete circle. So you can take your fine magician there, or you can take . . . someone else." She said this last bit with a sly wink and added, "I laid out the cards. You've stolen two hearts in our strange land. You work fast."

I was flustered, and Criminy glared at the Bludwoman with disgust.

"So the harpsichordist is infatuated with her," he scoffed. "He's insignificant."

"So say you," she shot back. "But she can give him back his life, take him home to Grandma. She can take back her safe, comfortable world. She doesn't need your land of lies and blood."

"You don't know what she needs," he growled.

"How does it work?" I asked, and Criminy turned to me, taking both my hands.

"Letitia, love, you can't seriously be considering a bargain with this monster?"

"Takes one to know one," she said, puffing on her pipe.

"You bargained with her once," I said. "I just want to know my options."

"It works like this," she said. "In return for a small token, I give you this bottle. When you're ready to go home, you take the potion into your mouth and kiss your chosen companion, sharing and swallowing it while holding both hands. Then you say exactly where you want to go, and you're there."

"And what's the small token?"

"Just this: tell me my fortune."

"You can give me a potion that'll take me to another world, but you can't tell your own future?" I asked.

"One day, you'll learn that power doesn't work that way," she said with another deep chuckle. "Every time I lay my cards, I draw the Witch. Every time I look into my own teacup, I see a tempest. And my palms are smooth as glass."

"Fine," I said quietly. "I'll tell your future."

Criminy broke in, almost pleading. "Letitia, love, there's bound to be a catch. A trick. She won't give you something for nothing."

"Glancing isn't nothing," I said, my hackles rising. "It's a valuable talent. You said so yourself."

"It's very valuable," he agreed. "But there's something else she wants, or it wouldn't be so simple."

We had a little staring contest, each willing the other to give in. I refused to drop my eyes. What Madam Burial wanted seemed a simple enough request. He just didn't want me to have that potion. And it wasn't even that I wanted it so badly, not really. I just wanted my own bolt hole, my escape hatch in case the locket was broken or gone forever. I wanted a choice.

I took off my glove, and Madam Burial smiled like a vulture folding its wings over a carcass.

"Don't touch her!" Criminy snapped. "Don't do this. Love, she tricked me once, and she won't let you go so easily. I promise you."

"Don't tell her what to do, Master Stain," she warned. "Your sweet little kitten doesn't like that."

Caught between the two of them, I was furious. And I wasn't about to back down.

Madam Burial took off her black lace glove, and her scaled hand hovered in the air, waiting. I grasped it and gasped. The jolt was explosive and strange, a black vortex drawing me in deeply. I dropped her hand as if it was on fire and staggered backward.

Criminy was there immediately, his arms around me, asking, "Are you all right, love?"

"And what did you see?" Madam Burial asked, her tone conversational and teasing.

"How much did you take?" I said, my voice low and dark. I had a sudden vision of what it would be like to rip her throat out with my blunt little Pinky teeth.

"Just five years," she said. "A pittance. I'm surprised you even noticed. Yet."

"What's that supposed to mean?"

She giggled, a high, mad sound. The hair on my arms rose.

"Can't you feel it, little kitten? Doesn't time here seem to run fast for you? Haven't you noticed the crow's feet marching across your face? That locket draws the years from you as surely as my hands. You'll wither in his arms yet, if you don't make your choice soon. Or break the locket."

"Is it true, Criminy?" I asked, my ungloved fingers going automatically to my face, to the tiny ridges that I was sure hadn't been there yesterday, that maybe hadn't been there five minutes ago. "Am I really older?"

"There's always a catch, my love," he said. "But you're beautiful to me, no matter what."

So I couldn't have both worlds, both lives. I'd seen it all in that desperately dark and dizzying glance. The locket was stealing my life, taking my time, drawing my youth and transferring it to the witch as I aged supernaturally fast. I was going to have to choose, and choose soon. It all came down to the potion, the blud, or the locket. Every moment I spent in Sang as a human meant that I grew older faster. My dream of having everything was gone, replaced by images of my hair turning gray with a locket around my neck and a forever-young lover in my arms.

And then there was Criminy's glance, which made a little more sense now.

But it didn't matter. The witch was going to pay.

"Let me tell your fortune," I said. "So we'll be even."

"You saw nothing," she said, drawing up and pulling her cloak tightly around her.

"Suit yourself," I said.

Pushing away from Criminy, I rubbed my temples and stretched my shoulders, feeling tired to the bone. When I stepped up to the counter, Madam Burial looked just a little more lively, the lines on her face smoother and her smug smile brimming with joy at having bested me. But underneath it, I could tell that she was just a little bit scared of me. *Good.*

I snatched the little bottle off the counter and looked her dead in the eye.

"I know how you die. It's going to hurt. And you don't have long," I said.

The horror in her eyes made me smile as I grabbed Criminy's hand and dragged him back across the road.

As I stepped into the conveyance, I called over my shoulder, "And watch out for flying monkeys, you old bitch!"

I couldn't stop staring at myself in the mirror Criminy had dug out of his waistcoat. Was that my first wrinkle, or had I just slept on my arm? Were the bags under my eyes from exhaustion or dehydration or something more sinister?

"But I don't want to be thirty-one," I moaned.

Criminy glanced at me lovingly and said, "Darling, you don't look a day over twenty-six."

"I can't believe I fell for it. You told me there would be a catch, but I was just so certain that I knew what I was doing. I let her steal five years of my life. Five years, gone in seconds." I sighed. "And as long as the locket's around, I'm getting older even faster. I didn't even get to have a big party for turning thirty."

"I'm nearly a century older than you are, if it makes you feel any better," he said.

"And you actually *don't* look a day over twenty-five," I said wistfully. "I guess being a Bludman has its advantages."

"I like to think so," he said with his most dashing grin. "But there's still plenty of time for that. The important thing is that you have what you wanted."

I looked at the little bottle. I didn't really want it. But I didn't want him to know that. And I wasn't ready to admit that I had given up five years of my life just to feel independent and strong.

"I guess," I said.

I hoped I would never run into Madam Burial again.

But of course, I knew I would.

After that, we met no travelers on the road. I fell into an uneasy sleep until a giant bus tank passed us. We had to veer off the road in response to its vicious honking. The driver, just a pair of goggles behind the dirty windshield, would have mowed us down without a thought.

"Foolish Pinkies fleeing Brighton, no doubt," Criminy muttered. "Run over their own grandmothers to get to safety."

"Durgoin da Manblaster?" I slurred, still half-asleep.

"Yes, love," Criminy said with a smile. "They're probably going to Manchester. For all we know, Jonah Goodwill is throwing a ball to celebrate, and they want to shake his hand."

I rubbed my eyes and sat up with a jaw-cracking yawn. "Are we there yet?" I asked.

Criminy pulled out his compass with one hand, and the carriage jiggled all over the road.

"Bugger," he said, shoving the little brass object back into his pocket. "I can't tell for certain. I'd guess we're an hour or so from the caravan. It'll be good to be home, eh?"

"Yes," I said archly, "it would be great to be home. With my grandmother and my cat. Which is why we're going to Manchester now."

"Sorry, sweetheart, but our first stop's the caravan." With both hands on the wheel, he gave me a quick grin and shrugged. "I have my responsibilities, and they might have news. And we need to get cleaned up before we head into the city. You'll scandalize the kingdom in that get-up, if the rats don't get to you first."

He had a point. But that didn't mean I liked it.

"Don't sulk, precious," Criminy said. "But speaking of the dangers ahead, there's something I need to ask you."

I waited. His fingers drummed on the steering wheel. It was as close as I'd ever seen him to nervous and fidgety.

"There's no good way to put it. But do you want to be bludded?"

"I've already told you no," I said patiently. "I appreciate the thought, but I'm not ready to go that route yet. No eternal kiss for me."

"Eternal kiss?" he asked. "That's a bunch of poppycock. It's simply practical. It would be so much safer if you were a predator instead of a delicious little morsel. We're about to go into a city where there's a price on your head and try to sneak into the well-guarded house of a very powerful man to steal a magical object—which is all in a day's work for me, of course. But you could be killed. And worrying about you being killed makes me more likely to get us both killed. And there are still plenty of things around here that want to eat you."

"When you put it that way," I answered, "I guess it is pretty practical. But here's the thing. I don't know what would happen when I got back to my world. If I would be my world's first Bludwoman or a vampire or a corpse. I'm not going to risk it, even if it would make life a lot easier here." Aiming for silly, I added, "Besides, blood's icky."

"Oh, Letitia," he mused, but I could hear pain lurking underneath. "Will you ever accept that this is serious? Do you think me a schoolboy, mooning after a pretty lass? I wonder if you even care for me. If you're just toying with my heart."

"Quit acting soft," I muttered. "Quit playing."

"I think you're the one who's playing," he snapped. "What you're seeing is pain. And you're the only one who sees it," he said more softly. "You're the only one who can cut me, and you wound me deep."

I watched him for a moment, his jaw clenched as he gripped the steering wheel, as if his will and his hands were the only things holding the conveyance together and keeping it on the road. His eyes were focused far ahead, and he let out the saddest sigh.

"I can tell you care for me," he said. "Your smile, your touch, your trust. The way you rouse to me. But your feelings are incomplete. Like there's some missing piece I can't puzzle out."

"I do care for you," I whispered. "In my own way."

He closed his eyes briefly, let that sink in. But then his jaw tightened. "And what way is that?" he shot back. "You're not a little girl playing dress-up. You can't just float along, letting things happen to you. You have to choose, Letitia. Once we find the locket, you have to choose."

"I'm not thinking that far ahead," I said. "I need more time."

"Well, I'm thinking about it," Criminy said. "And I want to know. Once you have the locket, will you go back to your world and leave me with a frail, insensible body that will wither and die here? Will you break the locket, will you take my blud? Or will you go back and forth, never sleeping, until you grow old or go mad?"

"You're forgetting that I could leave now if I wanted to," I said. Here he was, trying to force me into making a choice.

How could he know me so well and not understand what he was doing? "I have the potion. I could take you back, or him. It's my choice."

"Yes, it is. And what will you choose?"

I turned away. My eyes scanned the horizon, watching the never-ending grasses flow into hills and mountains, a world hazy around the edges where the sky always hung too low. There was an entire world here at my fingertips, and I'd only seen one small corner. Somewhere, far across these grasses, a beautiful man from my own world waited for me, filled with hope and playing familiar songs on a harpsichord and aching for the life he'd lost. And somewhere, even farther away, Nana waited, her time being stolen even more surely than mine.

"I can't tell you now," I said.

He had given me three choices, and I had added two more. I didn't like a single one of them.

But then again, I'd already seen the future, and it grew darker with every glance.

28

Something was wrong. Criminy had grown more and more agitated as we rumbled north, but now he was downright twitchy. And he wouldn't put down the spyglass, even though he could barely control the jittering conveyance with one hand.

"What is it?" I asked when I couldn't stand the tense silence anymore.

"The wagons are still circled. The caravan hasn't moved," he said. "My orders were to follow the schedule, and they should be on the way to Liverpool by now."

I could see it then, the far-off shadows against the cloudy sky. I had a feeling of homecoming that surprised me, and I thought of the comforts of my wagon. I actually missed the wallpaper. And the thought of my own little basin of water to wash in and a soft, silk-covered bed . . . oh, it was heaven on wheels.

The conveyance, unfortunately, had only two speeds: stop and go. The traveling speed depended entirely on the tension in the winding key, and we were near the end of a round, so it was taking a painfully long time to climb the last hill.

Finally, he jerked the conveyance off the road and

pulled the brake. It shuddered to a halt, and we jumped out and ran through the thick, stringy grass. Not a single figure lurked outside the caravan. It was eerie.

Something dark moved toward us across the moor, and I saw Criminy's arm swing into motion. But he didn't go for the bolus or the knife in his boot. He just held his arm out, palm open. With a coppery flash, Pemberly swung onto his shoulder by her tail.

"Don't just sit there, Pem. Assess!" he said peevishly, and she swung back down and hurtled toward the caravan. It was amazing to me how he always remembered to use her. I guess it was like me and the watch I wore to check a patient's blood pressure or tell time. I was so accustomed to seeing her on his shoulder that he had seemed a little incomplete without her on the last leg of our journey.

My little Uro had only come in handy once so far, and that was all Criminy's doing. I had been too busy peeing myself in the locked lighthouse to think about my robot guardian's door-unlocking capabilities. The bracelet bumped against my wrist, useless for now.

The ground around the wagons was trampled. Big crowds had been there. But no one was practicing now, as they should have been. The clockworks were motionless between the wagons, their eyes open and unseeing. All was quiet. And that wasn't good.

Criminy veered left, and I followed him to Mrs. Cleavers's wagon. He paused in front of the steps, panting, and regained his composure before knocking politely. I was in much worse shape, doubled over, huffing and puffing in my stained, torn men's clothes.

We waited by the door. Nothing happened. Not a sound came from within, and the lack of her customary shrill reception was ominous. Criminy tried the handle, and the door squeaked open.

The room was always a jumble, but it had recently been the site of a struggle. Dress forms were toppled over, pools of fabric and pincushions sprawled in front of the broken mirror.

Criminy closed his eyes and sniffed. "Pinkies," he said. "Coppers."

At that moment, Pemberly skittered into the room, her tail high. Criminy swung her up onto his shoulder, and she opened her mouth. A thin white ribbon inched out and curled under her chin. Criminy ripped the paper and read, "*Living: 19. Dead: 0. Blood: 0 ml. Caravan: Safe.*"

"Well, it doesn't seem bloody safe, and we're missing twelve and a half," he muttered, tossing the paper to the ground.

"Twelve and a half?" I asked.

"Catarrh and Quincy are gone. Two heads, one body."

We poked around the wagon but couldn't find any clues amid the destruction. Without speaking, we walked back outside and headed in the same direction, toward the dining car. As we passed Emerlie and Veruca's wagon, there was a subtle scrape from within, and Criminy had his ear to the lime-green wall in an instant.

"Someone's inside," he said softly, motioning me to the little wedge of space between two wagons next to Cadmus the cassowary. As I hid behind the still form of the giant brass bird, he knocked on the door and called, "Ladies?"

"Who's there?" came the harsh cawing from within. Emerlie, of course.

"It's Criminy Stain," he said. "Open the door, Em."

The door flew open so quickly it almost smacked him in

the face, and Emerlie came very close to throwing herself into his arms. At the last moment, her lifelong prejudice kept her from seeking shelter in the comforting embrace of her boss the bloodsucker.

"Oh, sir, I'm that glad to see you!" she cried. "We don't know what's to be done."

"What's happened?" he asked, but of course, she ignored that.

"Oh, and that lady of yours, sir? Did the Coppers get her? Or is she dead? That poor lass, I told her, I told her to be careful. But she didn't listen a bit."

"Letitia, come out," he called.

When I stepped out from my hiding place in my rumpled men's clothes and waved sheepishly, Emerlie's jaw dropped, but she ran to hug me just the same. Any port in a storm, I guessed. I patted her awkwardly.

"It's awful, what they did," she said, sniffling.

"And what did they do?" Criminy asked impatiently.

"It's the Coppers, sir. They showed up and demanded you and the papers, and they went to see Mrs. Cleavers, and they had a dreadful row. Said our papers wasn't no good. There was an awful fight in her wagon, and she was howling and cursing like mad as they trussed her up and carried her away. And then all the other Bludmen ran off, afeared the Coppers would take them, too. So the show's been closed down, and we've all been hiding in our wagons. Waiting."

"Waiting for what?" he asked with that peculiar ability of his to be furious and amused at the same time.

"Anything," she said, baffled.

Then she spotted something over Criminy's shoulder, and her face went from worried to relieved to excited to ashamed. Criminy and I both followed her glance and saw a slight man walking toward us through the grass.

"Charlie Dregs!" Criminy called. "You old goat! Where have you been hiding?"

The young Bludman I had seen below Emerlie's tight-rope on my first day had eyes only for her, but he clasped Criminy's hand and nodded to me politely.

"I was keeping watch," he said. "In the next copse."

"Anybody else with you, lad?"

"Naw," Charlie said. "Just me. Had to make sure Em was safe. Nasty Coppers. Ain't right, what they done."

"That's kind of you, Charlie," Emerlie said softly. "Thank you."

He just smiled, and nodded.

Veruca appeared in the doorway and raised an eyebrow at the four of us in front of her wagon, saying with her odd accent, "What is this, springtime for odd couples? Go and make love on someone else's porch. It is a troubled time."

Criminy sent Emerlie and Charlie to gather everyone left in the caravan for a meeting in the dining car. The Pinkies were worried, but the food helped to settle us. Criminy deposited me with Emerlie and her friends and went out to search for any other lurking Bludmen. We needed all the help we could get.

As Emerlie chattered on about how upset she was that her new suit hadn't been complete when Mrs. Cleavers disappeared, my wandering gaze fell on Casper, who was sitting alone at the other end of the car. He motioned me over, and, without making apologies, I went. Emerlie didn't even halt in her prattle.

"I'm glad you're back safe," he said with a devastating smile. The warm look in his eyes almost made me forget the misstep of our last conversation. "I was so worried about you. What happened?"

"It was definitely an adventure," I said, feeling my shoulders relax, the tension uncoiling. There was just something about him, like being in the presence of a movie star. Like the sun was shining only on me when he smiled. "We were chased out of Manchester, we saw a ghost, I got bitten by a sea monster, we rode in a submarine. You know, the usual."

"Sang is what would happen if my bookshelf threw up," he said.

I giggled but quickly turned serious. We were short on time, as it always seemed when I was around Casper. These golden moments were all too brief. I had to know his feelings before Criminy came back.

"Would you go back if you could?" I asked him.

He seemed surprised by the question, as if he actually hadn't considered it. "That would depend on what I had to go back for," he said, studying his hands. "I wouldn't want to be paralyzed or anything. It doesn't really matter what world I'm in if I can't play the piano. There'd be no point to life without my music. But sure, I'd go back, if everything could be the way it was before the accident. Or better."

"And what if you had to stay here?" I pressed.

He didn't know how much was riding on the conversation, but I only had a few minutes to solve my existential crisis and make some of the biggest decisions of my life.

"I like it here, I do," he said. "There are different rules. I'm only missing a family, people to care about, and I think I could have that, if everything worked out the way I'd like it to." Another smoldering smile made me blush. "I may say the wrong thing sometimes, but my heart is in the right place."

"So would you rather stay with the caravan or live in the city?" I asked.

"The caravan is fine for me, but the only safe place for women and children is in the city," he said. "And sometimes I think about it, about owning a theater or starting the first piano bar." He chuckled. "I've always loved to travel. I'll find a keyboard wherever I go, but there's no point in being pinned down unless there's someone really amazing pinning me down. Someone like you."

"Casper, I——"

"You know that's not the name I go by."

The warmth and naked longing in his voice drew me in. I leaned closer. Our eyes met.

"Jason," I said as he touched my cheek.

There was a gentle jolt, soft as waking up in a sunbeam.

I saw us holding hands, drinking the potion, waking up. I saw us in his town home enjoying a sunny morning, sharing a pot of coffee and the newspaper, sprawled on the couch with my feet in his lap. I saw him playing "Happy Birthday" on the piano, singing to my grandmother, all of us wearing ridiculous hats, me holding a cake glimmering with candles over a gently swollen belly. I saw his cousin's room painted over blue, a nursery, and a tiny, serious boy with brown hair sitting in his father's lap with a toy keyboard and a stuffed rabbit. I saw myself, an old woman with short hair, standing before a store window, one wrinkled hand pressed to the glass. Inside the store, a gold and ruby locket glinted, and tears of remorse streaked down my withered face.

"What's the matter?" he asked softly.

I realized that my cheeks were wet, and I shook my head. I couldn't tell him. And that was part of the problem. But I had one more question. "So what do you think I should do?" I asked finally. "Assuming I have a choice?"

He didn't even have to think about it. "Stay here with me," he said.

He slid his hands across the table, trapping one of my own. It made me feel claustrophobic, and I tugged at the grimy neck of my shirt with my free hand.

"We can move to London. It's the most metropolitan city, and the safest. The closest to our world. I'll play music, and you can take in washing or be a clerk somewhere. We'll save up some money and open a dinner theater. It's the American dream, just in an entirely different world. We can invent show tunes and pizza. They won't know what hit them."

I looked at our hands on the table, his wrapped possessively around mine. It was hard to breathe. Maybe being near him made me giddy because he sucked all of the oxygen away. He'd already made his plans; he was just fitting me into the puzzle. I wasn't ready to be held captive like that again, even if there was happiness in the bargain.

My glance had been seductive in many ways, and I had seen things there that I had longed for all my life. Things that, until now, I'd thought I wanted. Warmth, comfort, complacency, normalcy. Although it broke my heart to know that I would never meet that small boy with the stuffed rabbit, the thing that struck me to the bone was the look on my face as an old woman. The naked pain there, the longing, the wondering what I had given up. That version of me understood what was lost, and she was broken.

And I knew my answer.

I slid my hand away and dropped it to my lap. I looked back into his eyes, which were beautiful and hopeful and so full of plans. I hated to disappoint him.

"I'm sorry," I said. "But I can't do that."

"Why not?" he said, shaking his head in confusion and making his beautiful wavy hair swirl around. God, he was so gorgeous. But he was so, so wrong about me.

"I don't think I'm the person you think I am," I said softly. "I don't want to be pinned down, and I don't want to pin anyone else down. I don't want to wash other people's clothes or work retail. I don't want to be afraid of my gift. I don't want to do the safe thing anymore. I don't want anyone else telling me what to do. Ever. And I hate show tunes."

As he spluttered, beginning to plead, a shadow fell over us.

"Anything to discuss, my love?" Criminy said to me.

"I was just asking Casper what he thought I should do," I said. "Stay or go. What do you think?"

Criminy threw back his head in that marvelous, booming laugh of his, as if asking Casper such a question was the most ridiculous thing imaginable. Then he caressed my face gently and said, "I think you should follow your heart. Even if I told you otherwise, you'd still have your way."

"There," I said.

A lone tear coursed down the dust on my face. Something in my heart cracked wide with the sound of the door on a birdcage opening, showing blue sky and freedom beyond.

Finally, someone understood.

Casper stood up, turned his back on us, and walked out the door. I watched him go, privately bidding farewell to the possibilities that would never come to be. In my heart, I knew I'd made the right decision, but I worried for him.

My first glance had shown me much darkness in his future, and he would fall quite low before he'd find his way back out. We'd see him again, but I wasn't about to tell Criminy that.

With a kiss on my forehead, the king of the caravan swaggered to the front of the car. All eyes followed him, taking in his bedraggled appearance and confident manner. When he reached the buffet, he turned and smirked. Reaching into the basket of apples, he took two handfuls and began juggling. Mouths began to quirk up. I couldn't help smiling, too; after all of our hardship and worry, his colorful tricks were a welcome reminder of the everyday magic of caravan life.

After leading the seven apples in circles, figure eights, and various other maneuvers, Criminy caught them all in the top of his hat and stuck it on his head. His eyes rolled upward comically, but I was pretty sure that the apples were long gone. When he lifted his hat again, there was an apple pie underneath. He set the pie on the buffet and sliced it open with a finger. Seven parakeets flew out, circled his head, and disappeared out the open door.

There was a moment of polite applause, and he bowed deeply to his people. When he stood, he met every eye in turn, then began to speak.

"Friends," Criminy said, "I'm sorry I wasn't here to lead you. As you no doubt know by now, the Coppers want our newest employee, Lady Letitia. I must escort her to Manchester to answer to them. Without papers and Bludmen, you are vulnerable. So I leave it for a vote. Will you go to Manchester and take cover among your own kind? Will you stay here and wait for our return? Or will you continue on to Liverpool and sell smiles for coppers?"

Hushed whispers rustled through the crowd. Criminy gave them a moment to soak it in before saying, "Torno, take a vote. We're going to gather supplies."

Taking my arm, he dragged me from the car. The moment the door closed behind us, voices exploded within. While the Pinkies chose their communal destiny, we went to Criminy's wagon. I had never been inside it before, and I felt a little like a teenager seeing her boyfriend's room for the first time. It was tidy but spare and clearly not made for socializing, as evidenced by the conspicuous absence of seating. His wagon was a workspace, with walls of bookshelves and a stained worktable and an old wooden roll-top desk full of small drawers and pigeonholes. I was drawn to it. As I ran my hand over the gorgeous antique, Criminy watched me, pleased.

"It's a beauty, isn't it?" he said.

I hooked a finger through a drawer pull, and he reached out to hold the drawer shut, saying, "I wouldn't open that if I were you. Some of my secrets bite."

"Reminds me of your coat," I said, backing away to scan the bookshelves.

He had loads of books and scrolls. Thick leather volumes, journals spilling ink-spattered papers, small novels, and polished animal skulls watched me from the shelves. As I read the spines, he tossed his old waistcoat onto the ground and started rifling through the pockets, making a pile of things on the floor. I kept my back to him, trying to be polite. I heard him open his chifforobe and shrug on a new coat, which he then filled with all of his talismans and instruments and handkerchiefs.

Some of the book titles were surprisingly familiar, one-offs as familiar as the proper names of cities and people.

Dignity and Discrimination. Sagacity and Susceptibility. Peace and War. There was even a thick volume titled *The Collected Works of Willem Sharkspear, including Gomez and Julietta, MacDougal, Harmlen,* and *A Big Kerfuffle over Nonesuch.*

My eyes wandered from the bookshelf. The door to his bedchamber was ajar, and I could just see a soft wool blanket draping from the bed to the floor. I was about to edge over for a better peek, but Criminy touched my shoulder and startled me. I leaned back against the wall to catch my breath, and he put a hand against the wall over my shoulder and leaned in to kiss me, slow and gentle. I kissed him back enthusiastically, finally free to meet him with an open heart. If I hadn't been leaning against the wagon, I would have melted into a puddle on the floor.

"We're ready, love," he said. "Let's go see what they've decided."

I didn't know what to think as Criminy locked the door behind us. Although my heart was set on the locket, I couldn't help worrying about the caravan and the people who had accepted me as one of their own after knowing me for just a couple of days. Because of the price on my head, their lives and livelihood had been thrown into turmoil. And Criminy could lose everything if they chose to disperse.

But I found myself smiling even before I had stepped down into the grass. Emerlie was on her tightrope, Torno was doing squat thrusts with kettlebells, and Eblick was unconscious on his log, shiny with oil. They were practicing, same as ever. When they saw us, they all came to gather around Criminy's wagon. Except for Eblick, who remained asleep.

"Master, we have decided," Torno said as he curled his

kettlebells. His clockwork dog begged at his feet. "We will stay here and practice, try some new tricks maybe. There is nothing illegal about lifting weights, eh?"

"Not that I know of, old friend," Criminy said with a chuckle. "But what of safety?"

"You don't think a strong man can protect a bunch of little ladies?" Torno bellowed. "Also, we are having the clockworks, and crossbows, and Mr. Dregs. And Eblick."

"What on earth can Eblick do?" I asked, stunned. Unless a Copper tripped over him while he was dozing in the sun, I couldn't imagine how he could possibly help.

Sitting up, the lizard boy sleepily blinked his eyes. He seemed a brighter green than before, his limbs less rubbery. The exercise and oil must have helped. He turned to us and, with a placid smile, said, "I've good news, m'lord. Just found out I'm venomous."

And he opened his green-lipped mouth, showing a set of gleaming yellow fangs.

29

My new dress didn't fit nearly as well as my old one. It was an inch too long, and the burnt orange didn't do as much for my complexion, but it still felt good to be decent again. After Charlie Dregs had started staring at my thin gentleman's shirt and unconsciously licking his chops, Criminy had shooed Emerlie and me into Mrs. Cleavers's wrecked wagon, hissing, "Nothing flashy."

Emerlie giggled. "What's the fun in that, eh?" she said, sliding her yellow-and-purple arm through mine and dragging me off.

My options were limited, without a seamstress around and with most of the costumes trampled or half-finished. And thus, the unfashionable pumpkin dress with puffed shoulders and a ruffled placket that made me feel like Beth from *Little Women* instead of Mina from *Dracula*. The droopy bonnet didn't help my ego, either, but at least it covered my ears with their damning holes.

Honestly, I didn't care what I looked like so long as we could get on the road to Manchester. Now that I had made my decision, finding the locket was the next step. But it wasn't just for my own selfish needs anymore. I had to keep Criminy and his people safe, and that meant stopping

Jonah Goodwill, no matter what. With my arm through Criminy's, we set off toward the hideous city on the hill. We left Pemberly behind to help guard the caravan, but Uro was on my wrist, ready to be of service—if only I could remember to use him.

On foot again on the endless moors, it was funny to think of how new and strange it had felt just a few days ago. Now it was like retracing my steps. Except that this time, we knew exactly where we were going. Straight to the enemy's lair. Either he was waiting for us, or we would be there, waiting for him.

"Did you see anything else?" Criminy asked me again. "When you touched Tabitha?"

"Nothing of the future," I said. "Just them striking a deal, him leaving her alone on the island to wait for us."

"I know why he wants the locket, but I wish I knew what he wanted with you," Criminy said, and I could tell that his thoughts were far away. "Maybe there's a way to find out."

"I guess if you found one of his underlings, I could glance him," I said.

"Too risky. They'll be looking for us in the city. There's another way, though. I hate to ask you again, love, but could I have a drop of blood?"

"Just a drop? No problem. Anything for the locket," I said, holding out my arm. It was my new mantra.

"Not yet," he said, patting my hand apologetically. "We need to find a pool first."

Criminy reached into his coat and pulled out the same brass device he'd used to find Erris. He fiddled with the dials and spun slowly in a circle, fixing his eye on the horizon.

Finally, he stopped, and I followed his gaze over the hills toward a thick wood bursting with bright green.

"That's not too bad, then," he muttered. "Not entirely off course."

I had no idea what he meant.

As soon as we were off the road, the bunnies started to plop out of the grass and follow me, but I was so accustomed to their gentle, hungry stares by now that punting them was automatic.

Just as we reached the wood, something startled in the shadows, making the branches and bushes shudder. Birds burst from the trees like feathered fireworks, screeching in terror. Then the thing inside snorted.

"Shite," Criminy said. "It's a bludstag. This is not part of the plan."

"Do I run?" I whispered.

"No. Don't move. Try not to show fear. They can smell it. They like it."

He picked me up and carried me over to a gnarled plum tree on the outskirts of the forest. He handed me his coat and set me on the lowest branch, hissing, "Climb," before he disappeared.

I moved up a few branches until I was out of mauling distance, then settled in a fork to watch. I spotted Criminy creeping through the underbrush, and then I looked at the huge shape in the bushes. The sleekly muscled stag was hunting Criminy in turn, its head low. I was scared for Criminy, but it was fascinating, watching two predators stalk each other.

Criminy threw a large stick just a little to the side of the stag, and it screamed and dove toward the noise, fangs bared. With the elegance of a lion, Criminy ran and sprang. His arms encircled the beast's neck, and the talons of his black-scaled hands sank into the bristling brown fur. His face contorted into an inhuman mask of feral rage as his open mouth, sparkling with his own fangs, sought the stag's throat.

I couldn't look away. His teeth slashed through the fur and flesh, spraying blood as the beast bellowed. The sound died to a gurgle as Criminy ripped out a chunk and spit it out. As his blood-painted mouth closed over the wound and the stag's body began to tremble and jerk, Criminy's cloudy eyes looked up and met mine.

He was an animal. He was terrifying. And he was beautiful.

I realized that I was biting my lip, that my hand was wound into the ruffled fabric at my chest. Something in me was drawn to the carnage. Like so many women before me, I was a slave to the caveman brain, that deep old part of my DNA that whispered that ferocity would keep me safe and fed and alive and that I should most definitely find the fiercest creature around and hump it.

No problem there.

I'd never seen this kind of violence before.

And part of me was disgusted at being . . . my God, was I aroused by this? But part of me understood and accepted this vitality, this necessary savagery. What Criminy was doing to the stag, it would have readily done to me.

He took a last gulp and stood. Eyes never leaving mine, he wiped the blood from his mouth with the back of his bare hand. He stepped over the huge carcass and stalked toward me through the low grass of the copse, pulling out a black handkerchief to clean off the blood. As if hypnotized, I perched in the crook of the tree and watched him.

My senses were high, and I could smell him on the breeze, smell the blood, hear his footsteps crushing the grass. I wanted to climb down to him, but I couldn't pull my eyes away.

In seconds, he was under my tree, looking up to where I stood on my branch, just eight feet off the ground. He held out his arms, the black scales of his hands glistening in the weak sun. Without a thought, I stepped off the branch and fell, my skirts billowing around me.

He caught me, of course, one arm under my knees and one around my shoulder.

"My hero," I said, breathless.

He chuckled once, low in the back of his throat, and then he kissed me, and I could taste the stag's blood in his mouth, meaty and warm, and I didn't care. I twined my arms around his neck and kissed him back, just as fiercely.

Still kissing me, he carried me toward a birch tree and set me on the ground. With a growl, he lunged and pressed me up against the trunk, his hands tracing my face once before hungrily stroking down my neck, my chest, the curve of my corset, the swell of my hip. All the playfulness and teasing from our last encounter was gone. This was pure animal lust.

And I wanted it.

He found the hem of my dress and tugged it up, violent and sure. My hands wound around his neck, through his hair, tugging the queue loose. Just like in the locket, daring me to answer his call.

I strained against him and squirmed as his hands plunged under my skirts and upward, past the foamy black petticoats, caressing my thighs. For the first time in Sang, I was damned glad that they hadn't invented women's undergarments. As his finger moved against me, sure as pulling a trigger, I moaned and rocked into him.

Without thinking, I ripped off my gloves and undid the laces of his breeches, my fingers more nimble than last time. His hand moved more quickly against me under my dress, the texture of the scales strange and delicious as they rubbed back and forth. Some tiny part of me, the old, tame Tish who lurked far off in my brain, was disgusted. The rest of me was triumphant and joyous and fierce and sure. This was what I had chosen, and I would enjoy every second of it.

I freed him from his breeches, and he moaned against my mouth to feel my hands on him, rubbing up and down, reveling in the soft touch of warm skin on warm skin after days of confinement behind cloth.

We were still kissing, tongues hungry and violent, like two dogs snapping at each other. He pulled away to kiss my neck and found more cloth there. Growling, he set his teeth against it, and the pressure through the fabric was exhilarating. I laughed and nibbled his ear, our hands moving together in the tangle of clothing below, building in speed. Then he jerked up my skirts, and his fingers were replaced by something better, and in one savage thrust, he was inside me. I was grunting and panting, my back rasping against the rough bark of the tree.

I wrapped one leg around him, and he growled in my ear as he plunged even deeper into me. I squealed and pulled him closer, and he lifted my other leg around him. I thought I would split in two in the most wonderful way as I rode him, my back pinned to the tree and my arms wrapped around his neck and my legs wrapped around his waist, ruffled skirt trailing to the ground.

He struck that secret place inside me again and again, splitting me like a ripe plum, juicy and ready to burst. It was too soon, but I couldn't stop, couldn't slow down to enjoy it. As I cried out, he caught my breath in another sloppy, deep kiss, and I pulsed in release as I tasted blood and berries. He shuddered inside me, fighting to the last, and I pulled back before he could bite my tongue as he climaxed.

We were both shaking as the savagery of the interlude drained away. He lowered me to the ground and caught me up when I stumbled.

I blushed and turned away to settle my skirts, which were all tangled up over my petticoats. When I felt his hand on my shoulder, I turned in surprise, and he gave me a shy smile and held a red handkerchief out on his glove-clad hand. I returned the smile and mopped myself off under the dress with my back to him, grateful that my clothes hid the aftermath of our lust from the relatively bright light of day.

When I turned back around, holding the stained hanky, he had put his own clothing to rights. How the man always managed to look both dapper and careless was beyond me.

"Just leave it on the ground, love," he said with a teasing grin. "That's going to make some lucky bludbunny very happy. Now, let's see what our fine Magistrate has in store for you."

30

I knelt on the moss by the spring, fussing with my skirts. After what had just happened, I should have been past modesty with Criminy, but he could make me blush with nothing but a grin. And it definitely wasn't shame or embarrassment that I was feeling. Now that I had made my choice, it occurred to me that I wanted him not only to want me but also to esteem and respect me. I had gone from actively avoiding his adoration to trying to win his favor, and I felt more than a little awkward.

"I don't get it," I said, self-conscious as I tucked the orange ruffles around my ankles. "I thought you didn't drink from blud animals."

By my side, Criminy dug through his coat with deft hands, assembling the tools he needed to work his magic. Fidgety and inelegant by comparison, I waited to play my part. Asking him questions helped me forget my physical and emotional discomfort and took my mind off contemplating what had just passed between us, which was really a very muddled experience.

"I can feed from them," he said. "But they don't taste very good. It's the same reason most Pinkies don't eat predators. Grass-fed creatures are much more succulent. But when it's an even fight and a valid kill . . . well, it gets the blood pumping, and winning the war matters more than the gourmet taste."

On a flat rock by the pool, he laid out a dagger and a murky glass bottle.

"You don't mind, then?" he asked softly, playing with the dagger, the same one he'd used to kill the bludrat. He scoured it with sand repeatedly and rubbed it clean on the moss.

"What, watching you kill and eat a deer?" I asked. "Obviously not. It was . . . different. But not bad." I looked down, too, fiddling with my boot lace. "It was fascinating. You were very beautiful."

He laughed at that.

"Oh, yes, nothing more beautiful than watching a stag have its throat ripped out," he said. "Scares the living daylights out of most of your kind. Further evidence that Bludmen need to be locked up. Enslaved. Drained. For we have violent tendencies, you know, and aren't fit for polite society."

"That's just because they don't have to kill their own meat," I said. "People forget what it's like when it's life or death. I have patients who are dying and need help but are scared to have a needle put in their arm. They live such a soft life that they would risk death because they're afraid of a tiny piece of metal."

"Utter balderdash," Criminy said, polishing the knife on his breeches. "I suppose people really are ridiculous, no matter where you go."

He set down the dagger, clearing his throat and straightening the collar of his coat. I wasn't the only one acting fidgety. He wouldn't meet my eyes.

"Something else is bothering you," I said.

"I'm not sure how to ask, but aren't you worried about

the . . . consequences of our actions?" he said. He looked up with a wry grin. "Half-bluds don't lead a merry life here. I'm surprised you're not taking precautions. I can get you the herbs, if you wish."

"Oh, that," I said with a small, sad smile. "No, I'm not worried. I had . . . I had a loss, in my world. It was one of the worst things I've ever experienced, and I decided that I wasn't ready to try again. I get a special shot, special medicine, once a year, to keep that from happening."

"That's handy magic," he said, considering. "Not that I'd be sorry otherwise. Just so you know. And I'm sorry for the things that have pained you in your past." He held my face, rubbing my cheek with his gloved thumb. "Got a bit of stag blood there," he said.

I reached toward the sparkling pool to get some water, but he stopped me.

"The water needs to stay pure," he said. "But if you're ready, I'll take that drop of blood now."

I shrugged. He was already holding my hand, so he just removed the glove. It was businesslike this time, nothing sexy about it. With the dagger, he pricked my finger and squeezed a drop of blood into the pool, where it landed with a plop and swirled around, melting into the currents of the small spring below the surface. He placed my hand back in my lap and reached for the bottle.

Pouring a thin stream of blue liquid into the pool, he said, "Where is Jonah Goodwill?"

The water rippled, and a picture formed, just on the surface, like a reflection in window glass. It was Jonah Goodwill. In an airy room with white walls and dark wood beams, the kindly-looking old man with the walrus mustache sat at a table, eating his dinner. He seemed so harmless, just an elderly gentleman running to fat, slurping his soup. A servant stood nearby with a towel over his arm, framed by a picture window showing the church steeple of Manchester.

On the white wall behind Goodwill, dozens of black eyes glistened on hunting trophies. I could tell that they were all creatures of blud—they looked bigger, meaner, more vicious than their softer counterparts. The moose in the center looked as if it could take the leg off a rhinoceros.

"Well, that's handy," murmured Criminy. "Now we know he's home." Then he waved a hand over the pool, saying, "Where is my ruby locket?"

The water swirled by itself, the vision of Goodwill wavering and shifting to an empty bedroom with the same white walls and ceiling timbers. The locket lay on an elegant dresser. Beside it sat an old black-and-white photograph of a girl with bobbed black hair holding a bouquet of flowers.

"Good," Criminy muttered. "All of our bludbunnies in one burrow. Now, why does Jonah Goodwill want Letitia?"

The pond rippled, and the vision dissipated. A new scene shimmered into being.

It was Darkside in Manchester. All around the streets, dead Bludmen and women and children were scattered, their bodies spindly and pale and riddled with sores. Then the vision spun to another city, another Darkside, more bodies. Then another, and another. It showed us a world where all Bludmen were dead. The world Jonah Goodwill hoped to bring into being.

And at the center of the vision, surrounded by death, was me, the ruby locket hanging around my neck.

The walk to Manchester was both easier and more difficult after that. Easier because Criminy was bloated with stag blood and full of energy and because I was gnawing on a leg bone of quickly roasted, mostly rare venison. More difficult because Criminy was carrying the stag's lopped-off head by its enormous rack of antlers, a humble gift to Magistrate Goodwill, collector of blud trophies. We hoped it would be our ticket into his presence.

"Do you really think it'll work?" I asked, sidestepping random blood droplets that leaked from the severed neck.

"No way to tell," Criminy said. "Maybe he'll take it, maybe not. If not, I'll throw it at him and knock him down, maybe puncture a lung with a lucky antler. He won't be expecting that."

"But wouldn't it just be easier to let ourselves be captured?"

"Not unless you'd like to see exactly how much blud's in my body, love," he said grimly. "They'll drain me without a thought. Always better to sneak in unawares, keep that ace hidden up your sleeve."

"Your sleeve's covered in stag blood, Master Stain. And you deserve some sort of prize for carrying something that heavy on foot," I said, and then it hit me. "Wait. Why aren't we riding in the wind-up carriage?"

"There's two good reasons, pet," he said. "One, if we arrive at their front gate in something that old and unusual, we might as well show up riding a unicorn. And two, it must go back to Master Haggard undamaged. I don't want a Bludman that old and powerful angry at me."

Back on the road, we soon saw Manchester shimmering against the dark, oily clouds. I could smell the storm coming, and just being near the city made me queasy.

Think of Nana, I said to myself. *Think of her chicken 'n' dumplings and how she smiles every morning when you walk through her door. Think of*

*all the Bludmen you can save, all of the children who will have a better life if
you can stop Jonah Goodwill. You're going into Manchester, no matter what.*

Then Criminy grunted and shifted the stag's head onto
his other shoulder, and my thoughts came back to him. I
smiled at the broad shoulders, the unstudied and catlike
grace, the powerful body writhing with wiry muscles and
striding so easily and boldly with a grim smile through a
dangerous world. There was a soft place in my heart for
him. More than that. He wanted me to be exactly who I
was, and he completed a part of me that I hadn't known
existed. I didn't want to lose that, either.

I had chosen him over Casper, but I hadn't yet decided
what to do about the locket and the potion. The choice he
had demanded that I make came closer and closer with
every footfall toward the whited sepulcher of Manchester. If we made it that far. If we got through the gate. If we
found Jonah Goodwill before he found us. If Tabitha Scowl
hadn't found him first. And if the locket wasn't broken,
and we could get it and me to a safe sleeping place.

That was an awful lot of *ifs*.

Criminy glanced over his shoulder with his mouth
quirked up. "You thinking about changing your mind,
love?" he said. "Now's the time. Run away with the caravan, get bludded, have an easy life with a handsome rogue?"

"There's more than my future riding on that locket
now. And easy things aren't worth much," I said.

He laughed. "Then the hard things had better be," he
said.

When we were almost close enough to Manchester's wall
to attract notice, Criminy ducked behind a screen of wild
hedges and boulders. He set down the huge stag's head,

squatted on the grass, and beckoned to me. I joined him, careful to keep my skirts clear of the oozing trophy.

"It'll have to be magic, love," he said. "They're looking for us. So you're going to be invisible, and I'm going to be in disguise. I'm throwing a harder spell this time, one that won't take so much of my energy to sustain. You'll be invisible until I break the spell, but you'll still be corporeal. You'll have to stay right next to me so we don't get separated, and you'll have to be absolutely silent. And you'll have to accept that if you get hurt, you're on your own. Can you do it?"

"I can do anything," I said.

He plucked a fallen hair from my shoulder and said, "That was easier than usual. Didn't even get to make you squeal."

He removed his glove, laid the hair over his black-scaled hand, and set it on fire with a word. As it burned, he sang things in an odd, musical language until it was ash. Then he kissed me swiftly and sprinkled the ashes over my head.

Even though it was impossible, I felt them land in my hair and melt like snowflakes. Criminy smiled as I faded from view. It was my third time being invisible, and it was just as disconcerting as ever. But this time, I couldn't see myself, not even a little bit, not even like glass or water. I was one hundred percent not there, my clothes and Uro with me.

"Now it's my turn," he said. He nipped his finger and drew lines across his face with the blood, murmuring another song. It was his same blood that had brought me here, bursting from the locket and leaving pockmarks on my bathroom counter and permanent stains on my hand. And it was inside me now, too. It had to be very powerful stuff.

He bent down to put his glove back on, and when he looked up, I gasped.

He was now an elderly man with light brown skin and small tufts of white hair behind his ears. His chocolate-brown eyes grinned at me with mischief, and his quirked smile still held the same pointy teeth.

"How do you feel about older men, little pet?" he said with a raspy voice.

"You look like Antonin's grandfather," I said.

He laughed and rose from the ground with an exaggerated stoop. As he shouldered the stag's head and started limping toward the city, I followed in his wake, the grasses parting for my invisible dress.

Right before we got within hailing distance of the gates, I whispered, "Stop to lace your boot, would you?"

He obeyed, dropping the stag's head and kneeling with exaggerated stiffness to fiddle with the high laces of his boot. I knelt next to him, took his face in mine, and kissed him hard. He raised his arms to pull me closer, then remembered where we were and what we were doing. He scratched his head instead, all the while kissing me back fiercely.

"Whatever happens, I think I love you," I whispered in his ear as I pulled away.

The features he wore weren't his own, but the expression of relief and triumph was.

"I knew you'd come around, pet. Whatever happens, I love you, too," he whispered back. "I always have."

Then he rose from the ground a different man in more ways than one. He shuffled to the guard's post, holding the stag's head on his shoulder and fumbling in his waistcoat for the documents we'd forged that morning, before we knew Goodwill's ultimate plan.

"Papers," came the flat voice.

The old man put the papers in the box and waited as the guard examined them.

"Rafael Fester of Nag's Head," the guard barked. "State your business."

"Good evening, sir," the old man said, his voice a mixture of sunshine and subservience. "Heard Magistrate Goodwill collected curiosities and thought he might accept a humble token of esteem from the people of Nag's Head. This monster devoured eight Pinky children at a picnic afore my son kilt it and died in the bargain."

"You have papers for Viviel Fester," the guard said. "Where is she?"

I had an invisible *Oh, shit!* moment. We had both forgotten about our original, two-visible-people plan—the one we'd made up before the spring showed us the truth of things.

But Criminy was clever and quick as ever. The old man's face was pained, and he softly said, "My wife passed last year, sir. I keep her papers with mine out of habit. Lived together two hundred years, we did." A few red tears rolled down his face.

The guard crumpled the extra set of papers and tossed them onto the ground in his booth, the bastard. No wonder everyone hated Coppers.

"Toll has gone up," the guard barked. "Eight coppers or two vials."

The old man set down the stag head and hunted through his pockets, gathering change. He counted out eight copper pennies and set them in the box. It flicked in, then back out with his papers.

The guard cleared his throat. "It is decreed that all Bludmen register for a badge at the House of Holofernes in Darkside upon entering the city. Bludmen without badges will be subject to inquisition and possible draining. Have you seen either of these people before?" He held up inked drawings of Criminy and me. The word WANTED slithered across the top of each image in elegant calligraphy. The drawing of Criminy was spot-on, but the one of me was more than a little imaginative.

I looked like an evil seductress, some sort of vampy witch-queen.

I liked it.

I wanted a copy for my wagon.

"Never seen the devils, sir, but never been out of Nag's Head till this week, neither. I'll be on the lookout, though. And how can I get to see Magistrate Goodwill, sir?"

In answer, the guard pulled his lever, and the giant door squealed open.

Scratching his head and looking up at the huge doors, Criminy was having a marvelous time acting like a country rube. He picked up the stag's head and wandered through the door. I was close on his heels.

After the door slammed shut behind us, he whispered, "You there, pet?"

In answer, I stroked his back softly, right where I had once clawed him.

"Yeah, you're there," he muttered. "Try to keep up."

Keeping up his country-mouse act, Rafael Fester goggled at the shops and the people and generally got in everyone's way, accidentally smacking a grand Pinky dame with his bloody trophy at one point. He asked random people for directions to Darkside, then took pains to go the wrong way.

Still, I knew that he knew exactly where he was going, and I stayed as close to him as possible, trying to remember not to bump into anyone myself. I saw a filthy urchin sidling close to pick his pocket at one point and almost intervened, but Criminy spun around quickly and pegged the kid with an antler, shouting, "What, who said that?" like deaf old men everywhere. The urchin slunk back into the shadows, rubbing a lump on his forehead.

Finally, I could see one of the shadowy entrances to Darkside, although I didn't recognize anything from our earlier venture to Antonin's house. We were in a part of the city that I hadn't seen before. Rafael relaxed a little among his own people and straightened his back before asking a passing chimney sweep for directions to the House of Holofernes.

"It's two blocks up, but you don't want to go there," the Bludman said in a hushed whisper. "The Coppers know everything that happens in that inn, friend. What goes in your mouth and what comes out of it as well."

"But the guard at the gate said I had to get a badge," Rafael said, acting confused. "What happens if I don't go there?"

"Don't be a fool, old man," the chimney sweep hissed. "Get a fake badge underground. Go see——"

He stepped back as a Copper rounded the corner and made a beeline for them. Picking up his bucket and brush, he said, just a little too loudly, "Glad she's doing well, and give her my best, will you?"

The chimney sweep turned to go, but the Copper swung his billy club in a significant sort of way and said, "I don't see your badge, Bluddy. Yorick must have been giving you directions to the House of Holofernes. How kind. I'll take it over from here."

The chimney sweep hurried away as the Copper pointed the billy club to steer Rafael down the darkening street. Of course, he didn't come anywhere close to touching the dangerous Bludman, however old and frail.

"Wouldn't want you to get lost," the Copper said. "Something bad might happen to you."

"I'm grateful for your help, sir," Rafael said. It was almost believable.

I drifted in their wake, as silent as a ghost. It was twilight, with indigo clouds boiling overhead. Shadows loomed as orange gaslights hissed into life. I waited for the first fat, wet drops of smoggy rain to fall, but the sky was holding its breath.

Stores began opening their doors to Bludmen who had spent all day working as the servants of their prey, the warm light making cheerful rectangles across the shining cobblestones. Bludmen of all ages drifted into the streets, the women walking arm in arm, chatting in groups, or going through the open doors to do business. It was shocking, the difference between the relaxed Bludwomen in their showy, open gowns and the cramped, nervous Pinkies so tightly laced and tightly wound. The Copper's constant sneer made his disgust for Darkside all too obvious, and I couldn't help tripping him once. "Damn Bluddies need to clean up after themselves," he muttered to no one in particular as he straightened his coat.

Finally stopping under an awning, the Copper muttered, "Have fun in there," and stood a little away, watching. Making sure that Rafael didn't bolt.

The sign had a stylized flame topped by the calligraphed *House of Holofernes Inn*. I shivered as Criminy grasped the knob. Something wasn't right here.

Before he could open the door, I put my hand on his shoulder.

"Something smells funny around here," Rafael said, sniffing the air. "Smells fishy." Then he shrugged and went inside. I followed, glad that he had picked up on it, too.

"Good evening, sir," said a deep, sonorous voice.

Behind the counter was a very tall, very thin old Bludman with a nose like an eagle's beak. I doubted he had ever smiled in his entire life. I disliked him immediately.

"Good evening, Master Holofernes," said Rafael. "The guard at the gate told me I had to register, so here I am. I've never been in the city before. Do you have a room available?"

"Sign here," intoned the old man, and he slid a new-looking guest register across the counter. Rafael shrugged and picked up the quill, signing *Rafael Fester, Nag's Head* in shaky cursive. Then he looked up expectantly.

"Papers," said Mr. Holofernes, and Rafael handed them over. Mr. Holofernes gave the aged, worn paper a thorough investigation and even tasted a corner with the tip of his tongue before silently returning them. Then he handed Rafael a little brass badge with an ornate B on it and pointed to one on his own lapels to indicate proper placement.

After he rang a crystal bell, Mr. Holofernes glared at Rafael, and the men stood in mutual awkward silence.

Right before Rafael got bored enough to say something that might have been foolhardy, a dark-haired Bludwoman rushed down the stairs and began chattering at him like a demented parakeet, filling the odd silence. Master Holofernes disappeared.

"Well, hello there, now, sir. How do you do, sir? You'll be wanting a room, won't you, sir? And you've just missed the rain, isn't that lucky? And what a loverly stag you've got there. Did you kill it yourself? That'll fetch a pretty penny, that one, such a loverly rack on it. Now, where are your bags, sir?"

Rafael looked completely flummoxed, and I almost tittered.

"I've got no bags, miss, other than this little sack," he finally said. "Didn't plan on staying the night. Just wanted to bring this token to Master Jonah Goodwill from the good people of Nag's Head, thank him for keeping our city safe. But the guard sent me here, so here I am."

"Well, now, a room'll cost you ten coppers or three vials, sir, and that's Pinky blood, if you don't know. And that includes a half vial at dinner, which is quite the affair. Oh, everyone in the inn gathers together in the salon at elevenses for a loverly party, sir."

"That sounds awfully fancy," Rafael said, digging in his waistcoat for coins. "Wasn't expecting it to be so expensive, though. It's my first night in a big city."

"Oh, now, sir, if that's too dear for you, we've got a half room for five coppers, but it's just got a cot and a ewer. The regular rooms have a nice, spacious bed, city views, and running water, you know. Ever so loverly, I assure you."

Rafael's smile quirked in a familiar way, and he said, "That's kind of you to mention, but I guess I'll indulge and give myself room to spread out and enjoy it. You only live once, eh?"

They laughed together. Must have been an inside joke for Bludmen. She handed him a key and gave him directions to his room, all but ordering him to freshen up before the mandatory party.

I followed Rafael up two flights of stairs, careful to step

at the same time he did, lest anyone wonder why an old man was making twice the normal amount of footsteps. He opened the door to the room and tossed the stag's head onto the floor, where it landed with a splat. I followed him inside, and he kicked the door closed and caught me in his arms, whispering, "I can't see you, but I can still smell you, my love."

I tried to wriggle away, but he held tight and nuzzled until he found my face.

"There you are," he breathed, and his lips found mine. I shifted my angle and startled when my eyes caught motion across the room. I glanced up at a floor-length oval mirror, in which an elderly man was passionately making out with the air. He pulled away as I shook with laughter and pointed at the mirror.

Oh, wait. He couldn't see me.

"I was just watching you make love to nothing in that mirror," I whispered. "It was quite a show."

Rafael chuckled, then sat on the bed and started unlacing his boots.

"What are you doing?" I said.

"I'm going to freshen up, like a good little Bludman," he said. "Right after I do something that requires freshening. I seek to commune with the naughty little ghost of Viviel Fester."

He grinned at me, the wolfish grin. My insides melted a little.

Giving myself a moment, I moved to the window and peeped through the curtains. A heavy, greasy rain was splattering across the cobblestones, coating them like slug slime in the orange gaslights. I shut the curtains. Things were much more interesting inside.

"You can't even see me," I said coyly. "And we already did something freshening-worthy this afternoon. And you're an old man. And you still have to go to a party."

"I don't need to see you," he reasoned. "It'll be dark soon, and I can still feel you and taste you. This afternoon is the ancient past. And we're both going to that party, because I need you to get information."

"Even if all that's true, you're still assuming I want to get unfreshened with a silly old man," I countered.

"In the dark, you won't know the difference," he said.

"Maybe you'll have old-man breath."

"Maybe not," he said in his regular voice, low and husky.

He stepped out of his boots and stood, shrugging out of his coat. He was looking right at me, even though he couldn't see me. He walked to me and brought his arms in until they were right on my shoulders. Then he breathed on me, and I inhaled that wonderful scent of his and sighed.

"Maybe not," I echoed.

"Besides," he said, tracing down my shoulder to my hand and leading me to the bed, "I don't think you've made your decision about the locket yet. This could be my last night with you. One of us could die tomorrow. Or you might leave me forever. I want every bit of happiness I can get." He tried to keep his tone playful and light, but I could hear a farewell in his words, and I couldn't have turned him down if I had wanted to.

The curtains were already closed. He switched off the lights. We were both invisible in the darkness. It was Criminy's face I felt, his soft, smooth hair running through my fingers. I traced his eyebrows and cheekbones, sharp features I would have recognized anywhere.

"I just don't know," I whispered.

"I don't want to know, either, not tonight," he answered, and then our lips met and our bodies melded together, neither of us what we seemed.

Our first time together had been exploratory and playful. Our time in the woods had been fierce and raw. But this time, we were slow and pensive, every touch and kiss filled with longing and a strange, vulnerable finality. We took our time.

It was fun, being invisible.

31

Afterward, we turned on a light, and I watched him stretch, fascinated by his darker, sagging skin.

"Is that what you'll look like one day?" I asked. "Or will you ever get old?"

"It'll be a long time until I'm old by your standards, love. You were right—this is what Antonin's grandfather looked like. It's just a simple glamour," he said, his hand moving right through the curly white hair. "Only works on the eyes. I'll have to dab on some cologne before we go down there, in case I see anyone I know. The other Bludmen will think I'm a simple country rube with no taste."

I stretched, enjoying the feeling of being completely naked and still utterly without shame, just like in my dreams. No sucking in the belly or worrying about stubble. It was so freeing.

"Can't we just stay like this for a while?" I asked. "It's nice here."

"I gave you that choice, pet, but you want your locket. That's why we're here in the first place."

"Don't be testy," I said. "You know I have to do this. I've got a responsibility to my grandmother. She needs me.

And it's for the Bludmen, too. What happened in Brighton can't happen here."

"I know, I know," he growled. "Bugger the lot of them."

He rolled off the bed and ran water into the basin, then began scrubbing himself furiously with a wet towel.

"You look like you're trying to scrub me off of you," I said archly.

"Of course I am," he said. "Dammit, woman! Your scent, your stupid bloody delicious scent lingering in every crevice of my body and my wardrobe, driving me nearly mad. Do you know what it's like to want something so badly, to have it so close, and still feel that it's out of your reach? Out of your control?"

Ouch. Despite my invisibility, I was overcome with the need to cover up. To seek shelter. He was like a storm brewing, and I hadn't seen him angry like this before. Not at me. Thunder rolled outside, and I felt it in my rib cage.

"Why are you angry all of a sudden, Criminy? What did I do?"

He began to dress, staring off into space with eyebrows drawn sharply down.

"The powers I used to bring you here—they weren't cheaply bought. You met the witch. I made my bargain with the devil; I paid my dues. And here you are, perfect in every way. Except that your heart's all tied up in another world, another life, these other people. And I can't even duel them for you, can't trick them or glamour them. They're like smoke and mirrors, like fighting a ghost."

He tossed his wrinkled cravat to the floor and turned to me, his shirt open over an old man's honey-colored skin, peppered with little white hairs. Rafael's face was contorted in anger and sadness, but it was Criminy's eyes skewering me through the heart.

"Of course I'm angry. I'm about to risk my life—again—to get my own locket back so that you can leave me behind. And you've set it up so that if we don't get the locket back, you'll leave me anyway."

In a tiny voice, I said, "I'm sorry."

He kicked the stag in his stocking feet, and it rolled over and sagged.

"Of course you're sorry. It's a losing bet, love. What did you tell that Pinky girl at the caravan? 'Tell your father not to bet on the black horse?' I won't be betting anymore."

"I haven't decided yet," I said, my voice low and wracked with more guilt than I would have liked.

"No, you haven't," he said. "Because you don't know what you'll find when you get back there, to your world. You've got to go feel it out, taste it, roll it around on your tongue, and compare it with the taste of Sang. See how it holds up."

I scooted toward the headboard and picked up a pillow, snuggling it against my face to stanch my silent tears. I was glad he couldn't see me crying. He sat on the edge of the bed with his back to me and put his head in his hands.

"I would burn down the world for you," he whispered fiercely. "Your world or my own. I would rip down this entire city with my bare hands without a second thought. I don't need to taste anything else, I don't need a comparison. I always thought that when you came to me, you'd feel that way, too."

"Did you ever think that maybe I wasn't worthy of such love?" I whispered.

"Not until you brought it up, no," he said softly.

I sniffled.

"But it still doesn't change my feelings," he said, standing up and shaking himself back into his flinty, hard mood. "And we'll have to see what happens when your choices are laid bare. Now, wash up and get decent, because we've got a party to attend."

Lacing a corset was difficult and uncomfortable. Lacing an invisible corset on an invisible body was like taking the SAT blind, in Sanskrit, with a stubby crayon, during a hurricane.

By the time we had found all of my clothing and gotten it back on me using only the sense of touch, we were fifteen minutes late for the party, and I was hopelessly mussed. I helped Criminy straighten his shirt and picked the lint off the velvet jacket that stretched over his own shoulders but appeared to droop somewhat over Rafael's hunched body. The difference between what my eyes saw and what my hands felt was disconcerting.

Next, he shook some sort of powder all over me.

"To dull your scent," he said.

"I don't smell anything."

"Exactly."

"But why don't Pinkies use this stuff all the time?" I asked, thinking about Casper and wondering how much blud he'd ingested for just such an effect.

"Because it's expensive, involves complex magic, doesn't last very long, and is made of . . . well . . . you don't want to know," he explained, avoiding my eyes.

"Ew?"

"Letitia, this is important, love," he said, feeling around to grasp my hand. "We're trying to gather any information possible. However they do it, Coppers are at this party. Without Pemberly, I'm flying a little blind. Your job is to stay out of the way and watch people. Listen to side conversations. Lean in if anyone whispers. Look for holes in the wall or eyes in paintings, where they might be watching."

"I can do that," I said through a mouthful of cold wrappy that I had pulled from our sack. I watched in the mirror as the burrito disappeared bite by bite into thin air. I was more than starving and hunted around the bag for tangerines.

"Above all, don't touch anyone. Don't knock anything over. And don't make a noise. Just find a quiet corner and stay there."

"Aye-aye, captain," I said, licking my fingers.

I was actually looking forward to it—being invisible at a party of Bludmen. I didn't have to worry about introducing myself, or figure out what to do with my hands, or talk about the weather with boring people. I could stare and eavesdrop to my heart's content, collecting the information that we hoped would tell us more about Goodwill's game.

I followed Rafael downstairs. The yappy Bludwoman hostess shooed him into a room that reminded me of the Billiard Room in *Clue,* from the white-checkered floor to the wood-paneled walls and bookshelves crowded with leather volumes. A pool table with eight pockets dominated the space. Red velvet drapes bracketed the windows and doorways, and sickly potted plants loafed in the corners. Miniature vials of blood warmed in buckets over braziers on every table.

The people were even more interesting—all Bludmen, of course. Men and women of all ages wore the typical brightly colored clothes and chatted in small clusters. A few of the wealthier lodgers had clockworks, including monkeys, snake baubles both smaller and larger than my own, and a beautiful jeweled peacock. Rafael ventured toward a knot of older men playing poker. I drifted to a corner behind some young dandies playing billiards.

Time to play spy.

A hen party of women stood near me in fashionable gowns, chatting about bonnet styles and ribbons. Not helpful. On a couch a little apart from them, a middle-aged couple in outdated clothes sipped blood from their snifters in bemused silence. Snippets of conversations floated past, but I couldn't pull any meaning from the words.

Instead, I focused on scanning the room for clues. There were paintings, but they were mostly large landscapes of coursing bludmares and fox hunts. Instead of foxes, there were humans cowering in fear before the riders. Not a single fancy portrait had white eyeballs glinting through holes in the canvas.

I was just about to tiptoe across the room when I noticed Master Holofernes sitting in a wing-backed chair, his face impassive and dark. He was one of the few people not drinking from a snifter. People avoided him and cast odd glances at him, but for the most part, he was ignored, so I ignored him, too.

I waited until the nearest young Bludman had made his shot and set down his cue, then darted around the billiard table to the other side of the room. A teenage girl sat down at a harpsichord and began playing a sad, soft waltz. Her music was going to hinder my eavesdropping, so I slid around the wall to a group of older ladies huddled around teacups.

"It ain't right, that's what," said an old biddy in a gown that was worn and several centuries out of style. "My cousin was in Brighton, a milliner, not even a factory slave. No one in my family's drunk from a body in two hundred years. And what's the thanks we get? Fire."

"Hush, Tavia," said her friend, nudging her in the ribs. "Don't say such things."

"I'm a paying guest, and I'll speak free." Tavia sniffed. "Besides, we're all among kin here, are we not?"

"It's dark times," said an old lady with a tall beehive of white curls, "and I plan to live through them. Again." She got up and sashayed to a bookcase, swinging her padded hips.

"Cowards," muttered Tavia.

"We have to be, dear," said her friend, patting her hand.

I looked for Rafael and found him trying to speak to Master Holofernes, who just wagged his head and remained silent. Rafael shrugged good-naturedly and moved toward the harpsichord, but he was waylaid by the talkative desk clerk, who urged him toward the refreshment table.

I moved closer to hear the interplay.

"I brought my own blood from home and already drank, miss," said Rafael. "Waste not, want not, my mother always said."

"Nonsense, then, Mr. Fester. You've paid your coppers, same as anyone, and you're entitled to your blood. Didn't you say you were going to indulge yourself? Half a vial will sit right nicely. And soon Judith will sing!"

"I couldn't possibly——" Rafael began, but he turned to face an opening door and stopped talking for a moment. Then he swallowed and continued in a lower voice, saying,

"Really, I couldn't, miss. You're too kind. Please excuse a peculiar old man's small-town ways."

Ignoring her pleas, he sidled away to the far corner to examine the bookshelf and make polite talk with the old lady with the beehive hair. The girl at the harpsichord finished the waltz and started playing another sad song and warbling along off-key. Casper was right—he could make a killing here, if that was his only competition.

I was blocked by the men at the billiard table and couldn't see what had spooked Rafael. I began to edge along the wall, anxious to get around the screen of bodies. Then a voice rang out over the harpsichord player's softer soprano, and everyone turned to look. The old men parted, and into the room strutted Miss Tabitha Scowl, singing like an angel.

And around her snow-white neck was my locket.

32

I had never hated anyone the way I hated Tabitha Scowl.

She was tiny and effortlessly beautiful. She had an amazing voice, whereas when I sang, it sounded as if I was gargling with concrete. She had poise and style and confidence and passion.

And, most important, she had my locket. And she probably didn't even know how to use it.

Swishing the long teal bustle of her gown behind her, she put on a coquette's smile as she finished the song and approached the two youngest and most handsome Bludmen in the room. They abandoned their game, holding their pool cues nonchalantly as they chatted with the belle of the ball. I moved closer to listen, but it was just ridiculous flirting. Nothing helpful.

But why was she there? Why did Goodwill trust her with my locket? Was she one of the reasons the Coppers always knew what transpired at this party? And if so, why wasn't she saying anything interesting?

I edged closer to her and leaned in, but she was just complimenting a young Bludman's well-muscled arm. Mere feet away, the locket glinted at me, hanging just below her corset-enhanced bosom. She was too small for it to hang over her heart, as it did on me. I was transfixed, watching it sway as she moved, lovingly noting the deep crimson of the ruby and the interesting engravings on the shining gold.

Mine, I thought.

Something nudged me from behind, and one of the old ladies cried, "Pardon me, sir!" and cast a vicious glare at one of the young men, adding, "If you're going to go smacking people with your stick, you'd best learn some manners."

The young man stared at his pool cue in confusion and apologized. I had to be more careful, before someone really bumped into me and caused a ruckus.

I held up my skirts and tiptoed around Tabitha until my back was to the wall behind her. I could see Rafael by the bookcase watching her around the woman's towering white beehive, his old man's brow furrowed in worry. Then he looked frantically around the room, searching for me even though I was invisible.

I flattened myself against the wall as a Bludman pushed past to join Tabitha's circle of admirers. I couldn't help but breathe the air in his wake. *Yuck.* Old-man breath, with an overpowering stench of blood—even worse than Tabitha. No wonder Emerlie thought Bludmen smelled bad.

Tabitha was laughing now, and I could see the chain around the back of her neck, tangling in the loose hairs of her updo. Every fiber of my being yearned to tackle her and rip the locket off and run with it, but I knew that would be a disaster. I just had to stay close and follow her when she left the party. Still, the necklace drew me, and as much as I hated her, I couldn't help creeping closer and closer until I was near enough to touch the glinting gold.

The door behind us opened, and the busy clerk ushered

in a new couple. A gust of air rushed in behind them as the door slammed shut, and my skirts whooshed around me. Tabitha stiffened, and before I could react, she spun around and raked the air with her gloves. I tried to leap backward, but it was too late. Her hands clutched the ruffles on my dress, and she shrieked in triumph.

"I've got her!" she called. "Party's over!"

Master Holofernes leaped up like a much younger man and wrestled with my invisible form, pinning my arms behind my back. I couldn't see Criminy, but I hoped he was already safely hidden and planning my rescue.

I struggled, stomping hard on the boot of Master Holofernes. A young man's voice screeched from his mouth, "She kicked me! The Bludhoney kicked me, Tab!" And then he cuffed me so hard I saw stars. I guessed Criminy wasn't the only magician in town who could craft a disguising spell.

"I've got the other. It's our new Mr. Fester!" cried the talkative clerk from somewhere out of my sight.

The bitch, it seemed, had won.

Back in our room, we watched two Coppers toss our bed and rummage through Criminy's sack, which held nothing but spare clothes and a few vials of blood. I wondered if any of them were mine.

Criminy stood proudly between two more Coppers, still wearing his Rafael disguise, his old man's arms pinned tightly behind his back. I was held likewise. They apparently hadn't invented handcuffs in this world. Outside, the storm raged, the heavy clouds finally unleashing their tempest.

Looking in my general direction, Rafael flicked his

tongue out at me. It seemed a strange time to be rude, and I returned the gesture before remembering that he couldn't see me. Then he did it again, more slowly. Like a snake.

Aha! I had forgotten Uro around my wrist. The Coppers holding my arms probably didn't know that I had my own invisible clockwork protector. I felt along the bracelet and pressed the head scale. At that moment, another Copper joined us, carrying a thin, coiled rope over one arm.

Drat.

Tabitha looked up from her rifling to hiss, "Well? Tie them, idiot."

Rafael's eyes narrowed as he looked at the rope, but Tabitha laughed and said, "You escape, she dies. I'll drain her myself."

That was enough to keep him still with fury as they bound his arms. In addition to being a magician, I hoped he was an escape artist, because I was starting to form a plan. But I didn't know if I could save us both.

The Copper with the rope moved toward me next, looking confused. How, exactly, does one tie up an invisible woman? But he could see where his comrade held my arms, so he aimed for those. I held the uncoiled snake, waiting. The timing had to be just right; he couldn't know what I was doing.

"You're about to feel my bite," I said calmly, but I put a particular emphasis on certain words.

What I'd actually said was "URO bout to feel my BITE."

It sounded ridiculous, but it worked. The little snake struck, cold and hard and quick. I caught him as the bitten Copper screamed and started dancing around and swatting the air.

The other two Coppers turned their attention to his bizarre behavior. I jerked my arms loose and lunged at Tabitha, who was just turning around in irritation. After snatching the locket off over her head, I ran for the door, flinging it open and running for the stairs. I heard tumult behind me, and I imagined that Criminy was doing everything in his power to hinder pursuit.

"After her, bloodbags!" Tabitha shouted.

I heard violent retching in the hall as I slipped on the landing and pounded down the stairs. *Looks like I owe Vil further thanks.*

I shot out through the front door into the driving storm. The street was empty, and I turned left and ran as fast as I could without looking back, the visible locket floating in midair as my boots slipped on the rain-wet cobblestones. Criminy had warned me that only things touching me when the spell was cast would be invisible, and the locket was no exception.

I was soon panting but didn't slow down. I didn't know where I was going, but I knew that I had to get out of Darkside and into a relatively safer area for humans. And then, of course, I had to avoid the bludrats. Judging by my glances at the caravan, that would be no mean feat.

Whenever I came to a bigger crossroad, I turned, angling ever upward with my eyes on Goodwill's church. I soon found myself in a wealthy residential area of the Pinky part of the city, the fine homes locked up tight for the night. I read the store signs as I passed, hoping for inspiration but thinking on a very animal level. *Escape. Run. Live.*

Then a sign caught my eye: *For Sale.* The narrow town house from which it hung was dark and quiet. I stopped.

The street was empty, the sky perilous, the lightning crashing. The rain bounced off me like vindictive gumdrops. I was soaked to the bone.

I looked up and down the street. Every single home had at least one light in a window and a lit gas lamp outside the front door. The *For Sale* house was utterly dark. I put my ear to the door and heard nothing within.

I held my wrist up to the keyhole and said, "Uro, unlock," hoping it would work for me just as it had for Criminy in the lighthouse. I couldn't see what the invisible snake was doing, but I heard a metallic clunk. When I tried the doorknob, it opened. I stole inside and locked the door behind me.

The garish colors were shrouded in darkness, the mosaic fountain empty. Furniture wrapped in white sheets lurked throughout. But it was dry and quiet, and I was alone. I took the grand staircase up to the second level and dripped into the master bedroom, where a heavy four-poster bed waited under a canopy of spiderwebs. I thought about unlacing my boots and getting undressed, but I was too exhausted. Plus, if someone showed up, I'd have to run again, and I didn't want to run barefoot or naked in Sang.

I dragged myself onto the bed and lay down on the white sheet, feeling aches that I had never felt before. I had walked more in the last few days than in my entire previous life, and I had magically aged five years. Or maybe more. But it wasn't only sleep I was after. Now that I had my locket around my neck, I wanted to go home.

I slipped Uro off my wrist and set him on a sheet-covered side table. I said, "Uro, guard," and listened to the sound of my invisible bracelet contorting into a tripod. I was almost too excited to close my eyes as I curled on my side, holding the locket against my heart.

I stroked my thumb over the ruby and smiled. "I'll come back, Criminy," I said.

As I drifted off to sleep, I had a vision of Nana and me sitting at her table in the bright morning sunlight, eating waffles and laughing.

33

Like a kid at Christmas, I wasn't ready to open my eyes yet. I could sense the darkness, but I wanted to savor it, enjoy the delicious comfort and joy of my own bed, or at least a hospital bed. But no—I had to be home. The bed was soft, and there was a weight on the mattress next to me. I stretched and reached a hand out to pat Mr. Surly.

But the thing under my hand wasn't my silky-furred house cat.

It was hairy and prickly, and it hissed at me.

I screeched and smacked the bludrat off the bed, then heard the satisfying pop as it hit the wall.

I groped for Uro on the nightstand. When I finally found him, he was toppled over, broken, a tangle of jagged metal and wires. They'd killed my clockwork, the bastards.

Those bludrats were smarter than they looked.

A crack of lightning lit up a roomful of small eyes focused on me, red and hungry. Perched on the sheet-covered furniture, crouching on the dusty floor, writhing up the posts and canopy of the bed. They couldn't see me, but they could smell me. They knew I was there, and they knew what they wanted to do with me. I guessed Criminy's icky powder had finally worn off.

Another one scrambled onto the bed and chittered, and I kicked it with the heel of my boot. The others grew bolder and started to creep forward. I had to get out before they started swarming. I stood up and ran out the door and down the stairs. Behind me, dozens of sharp claws scrabbled on the mosaic floors as red, furry bodies thumped down the stairs.

I burst through the front door into the cool, damp world of early morning. Slamming the door behind me, I heard their bodies strike the wood. Their claws scritched against it, and then I heard one start to gnaw. I shuddered and kicked the door.

I jogged uphill toward the church, my wet skirts dragging through the puddles. I needed to get off the streets before the early risers noticed a floating locket. A useless floating locket that was either damaged or a clever forgery. As I walked, I pressed the stone to pop the locket open. Inside, where Criminy's face should have been, there was a carefully folded piece of parchment.

Magistrate Jonah Goodwill of Eden House looks forward to seeing you again, said the elegant script.

Well, fabulous. So much for sneaking in.

He probably had Criminy, and now I knew that he had the real locket.

Soon he would have me, too.

The church towered over me in the queasy green light of the storm's aftermath. It was both beautiful and hideous, which seemed to suit whatever gods claimed to rule Sang. And maybe they were watching over me, as I hadn't encountered a Copper or another bludrat since hitting the streets. At least I'd gotten some sleep before the monsters had shown up to claim my dreaming body.

I stood in the same niche where Gerren the Copper had once urinated on me. I was on my own and unsure of the next step, but at least I had found something familiar. Should I attempt some sort of clever subterfuge or just walk right up and ring the old bastard's doorbell? Either way, he knew I was coming.

The choice was made for me when a huge dog barreled around the corner and knocked me over. Joff the Copper waddled after him, shouting, "Oi, Rudy! There's nothing there, you mangy cur!"

Rudy growled and lunged for my legs, grasping a mouthful of taffeta in his slavering jaws. I tugged backward, but the teeth didn't budge.

I was caught.

The animals of Sang had it in for me.

Joff screeched, "Gerren! Gerren! I see the locket. I've got her! Rudy got her!"

I did my best to break free from Rudy's vicious hold, trying to rip my skirt and run. Joff's eyes followed the movement of Rudy's head, and he saw what I was trying to do. He whipped out his billy club and swung it, and I ducked my face and threw up an arm.

But it wasn't enough. The solid wood club thwacked off the side of my head, and I crumpled to the ground in an invisible heap. The last thing I saw as I went unconscious was Rudy's drool-covered teeth.

He seemed to be laughing.

It was a bad wake-up. My head was pounding, pain radiating from a tender spot just above my left ear. I blinked, and dull light stabbed my brain. I tried to lift a hand to my head, but my arm was pinned to my side. I looked down, and there was my body again, lumpy and stained in wet orange taffeta. It was a relief, being visible again, even if I looked awful. I was on a narrow bed, and leather straps held me at armpit, waist, thigh, and calf. My soggy gray stockings showed through a rip in my skirt, which was extra-wet with Rudy's tooth marks.

I looked around the room, but I was alone. It was a guest room, a place where a maiden aunt would expect to stay for a long visit. Rocking chair, dresser, mirror, a ewer and basin like the one in my wagon, embroidered throw pillows, doilies sprouting everywhere like unwanted mushrooms. Several horrible oil paintings of flowers hung on the wall, along with a portrait of a much younger Jonah Goodwill. In it, he was about forty and looked hopeful and bright, with just the beginnings of his trademark mustache. He almost looked likable. A gold chain hung around his neck, an engagement ring resting over his heart.

I heard voices in the hallway and closed my eyes as the door swung open.

"Don't pretend to be asleep, dullard," Tabitha said. "You're not a good actress."

She flounced into the room wearing my locket—probably the real one this time. Behind her was Jonah Goodwill himself.

He walked over to me with the same kindly smile and stroked my head, saying, "You've given us quite the chase, Miss Paisley. And then you got yourself a head wound and stubbornly refused to wake up for quite some time. I do hope you won't cause me further problems."

"Where's Criminy?" I growled.

"He's right here, of course," Mr. Goodwill said. Something about his friendly, understanding manner repulsed me, like that of a preacher with very bad intentions. Which was kind of what he was.

Two Coppers dragged Criminy into the room, his arms bound behind him. The Rafael Fester illusion was gone, and Criminy's own face was pale and drawn. His eyes met mine, and they were frantic and scared and defiant and loving, all at once. He wasn't wearing his coat of magical pockets, and there were patches of blood on his rumpled shirt. I ached for the comfort of touching him and strained against my bonds.

"Letitia," he rasped. "Whatever he wants, don't do it."

"That's enough out of you," Goodwill said lightly. He pulled a white handkerchief out of his waistcoat and stuffed it into Criminy's mouth. Criminy gagged.

"Now, let's have a little talk, shall we?" the old man said. "Mr. Stain, won't you join us?"

He gestured to the rocking chair, and the Coppers tossed Criminy into it and tied a rope around his chest. He struggled weakly, as if there was something wrong with him that I couldn't see.

"Miss Scowl, I'll need that locket now," Mr. Goodwill said, and she reluctantly pulled the chain over her head and dropped it into the old man's glove. He reached to the table beside me and tossed the fake locket to her. She caught it with a smirk and wiped it off on her sleeve.

"A ruby's a ruby, and fair is fair," she said with a curtsy. "And don't forget that her body's mine, after."

"I would never forget our arrangement, Miss Scowl." He chuckled. "Now, go outside and play. You, too, boys. We have business."

Tabitha swished out of the room with a jolly "Tata, lover!" and a blown kiss to Criminy. The Coppers followed her, one looking disgusted and the other intrigued by her back view. The door closed, and any evidence of goodwill left the face of Mr. Goodwill. "Now that we're all cozy, I'm gonna drop that Sangish tone and speak in a language you understand," he said with a deep Southern drawl. "I know your secret, missy. And now you know mine."

"You don't know anything," I said, keeping my voice level and snotty.

"I know that you're from America, and I know that you love that bloodsucking bastard over there," he said. "Tabitha told me what she smelled in the submarine. If you want him alive, you're going to do exactly what I say."

Criminy tried to talk around the cloth. All I heard was whimpering.

"Here's what's gonna happen," he growled. "That locket won't work for me. I can't get back home. Your pet vamp's magic must be tuned just to you. So here's what you're gonna do. You're gonna put on that locket and go to sleep. And you're gonna go back to wherever you came from. And you're gonna bring me back something I've been looking for for a long time."

He leaned close to my face, and his old-man breath washed over me as spit flicked past his gray mustache and onto my cheeks.

"You're gonna bring me back a disease."

34

I snorted.

"You know that's crazy, right?" I said. "You seriously think I'm just going to go infect myself with a disease and slap on the locket and come back here? Do you think I'm an idiot?"

"I think you love this monster," he said with disgust. "And I think you think you're a good person. I got no such illusions about who I am, little lady. That locket was my last chance. I can't get out of here, and I've tried every kind of religion, white magic, and dark magic. You don't do as I say, and I'll torture and drain him. Then I'll go back to that filthy caravan and torture and kill all those people, too."

I could see the lunatic lurking behind his eyes, the one he hid from most of the world, along with that country drawl. Criminy looked horrified. And murderous.

I just stared at the old man, my jaw dropping. "Why?" was all I could muster.

"Because I want more than a handful of dead folks. Because if I'm stuck here, I want the Bludmen gone. I'm on a mission, girly. I can't build Manchester into a wealthy, God-fearing city with these blasphemous monsters running around, infecting everyone. If I can rid Sang of the vampires, I'll be king of everything, forever. A hundred years from now, little kids will sit in church and look at stained-glass pictures of Jonah Goodwill."

"That's sick," I said.

"You're the sick one," he said. "Cavorting with bloodsuckers and freaks. My daddy was a preacher, and he would have had some choice words for a harlot like you. God sent me to this godforsaken place for a reason, and you're going to help me, or I'll destroy everything you care about."

There were some definite flaws in his reasoning, which was one of the benefits of dealing with a crazy person. I mean, if he was going to kill all of the Bludmen, that included Criminy, too, right? So where was my motivation? And how did he even know if a disease could exist here or affect Bludmen at all? But I wasn't about to argue with him about his diabolical plan. I wanted the locket, and I wanted Criminy alive.

"If I do what you want, what do I get in return?" I asked. My eyes flicked to Criminy, hoping that he could trust me. After our run-in with the witch, he probably didn't.

"Your Bludman lives, and you can run off with your heathen caravan and do whatever the hell you want. And you can keep your locket, too."

"That's not going to do me a lot of good if I've got a disease," I said carefully.

"I don't care if you get it yourself. Bring me a Styrofoam cup of blood or a chopped-off drug addict's finger. Just bring me something that'll spread through blood and kill 'em all. This world's got no diseases. The flu would probably destroy half the population. But it's worth the risk."

There were at least three illogical statements in there, but I let it go and played along.

"I won't let you hurt him," I said. "I'll do it."

Across the room, Criminy closed his eyes and shook his head.

Jonah Goodwill smiled, his bright white teeth showing his good American brushing habits.

"Then let's shake on it and get you all fixed up before bedtime, sugar."

He reached down to grasp my hand where it lay, bloodless and still at my side. I did my best to smile and wiggle my fingers enthusiastically.

We had a deal.

True to his word, the old man had me fixed up. My bonds were released, and a bevy of scared Pinky servant girls helped me undress and wash in a copper tub of hot, perfumed water. Despite my reeling mind, it felt wonderful to be warm and dry and clean again. They fixed my hair and dressed me in an overly modest, blousy gray gown that resembled a sailor suit. It was hideous and bland compared with the shimmering things I'd grown accustomed to, and I wouldn't have been caught dead in it, given the choice. The floppy boater hat with long ribbons added insult to injury.

Next, they ushered me into the dining room, where I was forced to sit at the foot of the table and sip soup across from Magistrate Goodwill. I didn't have much of an appetite, although I'd barely eaten in days. The dead, bloodthirsty stares of the stags and antelopes and moose on the wall seemed to accuse me of treachery with every spoonful.

I was thankful that the old man chose not to converse.

From time to time, he spoke kindly to the servants or complimented the food with his cultured Sangish accent. I minded my manners and kept my mouth shut, hoping to appear stupid, or at least dull and uncreative. I had to wonder if Criminy and I were the only people to hear his real accent since his early days in Sang, before he learned to conceal it.

As the servants bustled around and removed my dainty dish of uneaten cherry pie, I fidgeted and looked down, saying, "Master Goodwill, may I please see Criminy?"

"Oh, no, my dear," he intoned. "I do believe that's a terrible idea. That vicious killer is a very bad influence on you. And he might even try to hurt you. I could never allow that to happen."

The maid clearing Mr. Goodwill's dishes wiped a tear from her eye and gazed at him with adoration. I tried not to barf.

"However, I will allow you to sit quietly in the garden for an hour or so before bedtime. The fresh air will be quite invigorating. I do believe a good night's sleep can cure any ill, don't you?"

"Yes, sir," I mumbled, feeling the eyes of the servants judging me. No allies there.

After dinner, a silent and surly Copper escorted me out the French doors into a beautiful garden. Everything but his sharp nose and scowling mouth was hidden by goggles and leather, but I could tell that my guard disapproved of such vibrant frivolity. Or maybe he just disapproved of a bludhoney like me.

Irises and lilies and roses danced against the dull gray sky, and I leaned down to inhale their perfume. I walked the brick paths toward the orchard trees, apples and tangerines and plums planted in neat rows within the high stone walls of the old monastery. Very few people in Manchester knew what wealth lurked in Mr. Goodwill's little Eden, I was willing to bet. He didn't seem like the sort who enjoyed sharing with his inferiors.

A swaybacked cow dozed placidly across the yard, and she lowed at me as I approached. I expected her to hiss and bare teeth, but then I saw her messy pile of hay and remembered what Joff and Gerren had said about a bludless cow. I patted her bony brown flank and said, "Good luck, Bossy."

Under my Copper's watchful goggles, I settled on a wooden bench among the roses and pulled up my knees to watch the spectacular sunset. Clouds so low and thick that I could almost touch them were painted inch by inch with the bright red and orange of the heavy sun. I imagined the sullen city below us, the labyrinthine streets unfolding in their dirty glory beyond the high walls of the garden.

It was an ugly place but not without small beauties, not without things I would miss.

I swiveled my gaze back to the house, the bricks painted stark white like that of a plantation house from my own country. He'd turned the refectory into his own little Tara. The sunset writhed over the bricks, casting orange shadows like fire on the peaceful scene. Cheerful lamps shone from every window, and I tried to imagine Criminy behind one of them, tied to the rocking chair. Hungry, hurt, confused. Not knowing what choice I would make once the locket was in my hands. Stay with him? Kill his people? Disappear forever? And I had to wonder—did he have any faith in me at all?

Had I given him any reason to?

The wind sighed through the trees, and I thought I

caught a whisper of berries on the breeze, a breath released in resignation.

I was glad that I had told him I loved him before we went through the gate.

I hoped he believed it.

After the sun had set, we all returned to our places in the guest room, except that I wasn't bound to the bed this time. Criminy was still tied to the chair, and he seemed even more miserable and sick than before. Mr. Goodwill smiled, smug and righteous, like a cat that had eaten the canary and spit out the wings. The Coppers stood, masked by their uniforms, inhuman as blank walls. At least Tabitha wasn't there to gloat.

I lay back, and Mr. Goodwill draped the locket over my neck. I sighed as it fell over my heart and cupped it with my hands. Relief coursed through me, and it was all I could do to prevent a smile of joy from transforming my face. I was supposed to appear worried and trapped.

Criminy leaned forward in his chair, straining against the rope, his muffled voice choking behind the gag.

"Shall I swat him, sir?" one of the Coppers offered, holding up his billy club.

"No, thank you," Goodwill said. "Let him watch. Let him suffer."

I snuggled down in the bed, and the old man pushed a button to turn off the lamp. We were bathed in near darkness, and the room felt small and pressing and airless. Only the candle at Goodwill's side remained lit, casting a ghostly glow over his hungry eyes.

"I love you, Criminy," I whispered.

And I turned my head away.

35

My eyes flew open as I hit the floor. Something loud clattered beside me and splashed warm liquid over my face.

I saw the side of a bed and a great deal of shag carpet. There was my hand in a latex glove and, a few feet away, a metal bedpan. A yellow puddle spread out around me, soaking into the carpet, and I coughed.

"Tish!" an old man called. "Miss Everett! Are you OK?"

I pushed myself up to sitting and smiled at Mr. Rathbin. "I must have tripped. How silly of me. Let me clean this up."

As quickly as I could, I soaked up the urine with paper towels and sprayed the carpet as if nothing unusual had happened. Inside, though, I was ecstatic.

Of course, I knew exactly where I was and exactly what had happened. I stroked the tarnished locket, putting the puzzle together finally. The whole time I'd been in Sang since Goodwill had stolen the locket, not a single second had passed in my world. It had to be the locket's spell that made time there run differently for me. Time passed for Casper and Jonah Goodwill and everyone else who was brain-dead or under anesthesia or dreaming. But not me. When the locket was off, I didn't lose a single second of my life on Earth. If not for Madam Burial stealing my years in

Sang, if not for the locket aging me faster there, it would have been a perfect arrangement.

I wasn't brain-dead. Nana wasn't killing herself with worry. And now I knew exactly how the locket worked. If I fell asleep wearing it, I would magically wake up in the other world, whichever one I wasn't currently in. If I took it off in either world, no time passed in the other world. But every second I spent in Sang as a human with the locket intact meant that I aged faster and faster in both worlds, my time stolen by the witch.

I could almost have it all, just by taking off the necklace at the right time. I could have Nana and Mr. Surly and hamburgers and pet harmless little bunnies on Earth. And then I could be a part-time fortune-telling gypsy queen in a traveling show with Criminy. I could still be human, be myself. At least for a little while. It all depended on how fast Madam Burial stole my years, how much faster I aged thanks to the locket.

Criminy had said I would always be beautiful to him, but I was guessing neither one of us wanted me to get too old and wrinkly. Still, there was time.

Now all I had to do was save him and his entire race before bedtime.

I could do that.

But first I had to take care of my next patient, Mrs. Henderson. With distinct thoughts of Criminy, I slyly pocketed a bottle from her medicine cabinet. She was sleeping, she was forgetful, and her son would happily run to the pharmacy for her tomorrow when her meds turned up missing for the umpteenth time. No problem.

Then I called in sick, claiming to have a fever. Another

nurse would cover my next three patients, including Mr. Sterling. I would have to be transferred off his case. Seeing him like that, knowing that it was within my power to bring him back and that I had chosen my own happiness instead . . . it was just too depressing.

He would have to find his own future without me. My first glance of him had shown me that loss would be his salvation, and I hoped it came to pass. I had seen pain, but I had also seen adventure and joy and a destiny not unlike my own, far away in Sang. He would be changed, but for the better. The second glance had been a new possibility, a fork in the road, and part of me would always regret not taking it. But I was committed to my path, and there was no time to lose.

When I got to Nana's house, I was in a hurry. It was almost six, and I still had a long way to go.

She caught me glancing at the clock and said, "Sugar, did someone light a fire under your tail?" Her mouth turned down at the corners, but I grinned. Part of me just loved it when she got her dander up—it meant that she was still fighting.

"No, Nana," I said. "I've got a date tonight, and I don't want to be late."

"Ooh, honey," she said, clapping her hands. "Tell me all about him."

"He's really handsome," I said with a coy smile. "He's an entrepreneur and a magician. And he's pretty much the complete opposite of Jeff."

"When do I get to meet him?"

"I'm not sure," I said. "He's really busy. And I need to make sure he's 'The One' before I go introducing him to your cooking."

"Just make sure he takes care of you," she said. "A true gentleman is so rare these days."

"He does," I said, but it weighed heavily on my mind that right now, I needed to be taking care of him, back in his world.

I tucked her into bed and wrapped my arms around her. My heart tugged, as it always did, when I felt how frail she was getting, how narrow her shoulders seemed. She had always been solid, a rock of comfort and warmth who had eclipsed my distant mother and overly busy father in my heart. But I couldn't escape the fact that she was losing her battle, and nothing in the world could help her.

After I walked out her door, I was all business. I drove to the library and waited my turn for a free computer. I typed "helping hands homecare" into the search engine, and on the second page, I found it. The same logo from the van in my glance of Jonah Goodwill, two hands forming a heart. Luckily, they weren't far enough away to get me on a plane, but the two-hundred-mile drive to Greenville was going to take much longer than I would have liked. I scribbled down the number.

Alone in my car, I made the call. The night nurse said, "Helping Hands Homecare, we bring the care to you. This is Terry Ann." She sounded bored. I could almost hear her doing a crossword with her TV on low volume in the background.

"Hi there, Terry Ann," I said with the kind of smile that travels through phone lines. "I'm so sorry to bother you tonight, but I'm a nurse at Grady Hospital in Atlanta, and I've got a patient named Louise Shepherd who's on her last legs, and she's trying to find a Mr. Grove somewhere near Greenville. She said that he's on home care after a head injury, and he's one of your clients. Is there any way you could help me find him?"

"Ma'am, we don't release the personal information of our patients," she droned.

"I understand that, and I'm so sorry to ask, but I promised her I'd try. I've been taking care of her for a few weeks, and her mind comes and goes, and Mr. Grove is all she ever talks about. She can't even remember his first name, and she doesn't seem to understand that he's unresponsive. But she wanted to give him a keepsake, her husband's Purple Heart from the war. Maybe I could mail it to you, and you could give it to him?"

There was a pause, and I could hear her reserve crumbling. That sounded like a lot of work, and she'd like to get rid of me, but as a nurse, I understood how these things worked. Nurses work in nursing because they like helping people, after all.

"Honey, I ain't supposed to do this," she said, her voice low. "But my grandfather had a Purple Heart, too, and I know what a big deal that is to old folks. I believe you're talking about Mr. Jonathan Grove of 1655 Sycamore Lane in Anderson. But you didn't hear that from me."

"Oh, thank you so much!" I gushed. "You have just made my night and her year. She'll be able to go to her eternal rest now."

"Good luck, ma'am, and God bless," she said before hanging up.

I felt a little bad for heartlessly killing the fictitious Louise Shepherd, but it was for a good cause. And I was pretty sure she didn't feel a thing.

I programmed the address into my GPS and started driving. I listened to my favorite CDs and enjoyed the safety and silence of my world, my car a little fortress of solitude. I thought through the plan over and over again in my head, trying to work out every detail. For all of his own planning, Jonah Goodwill had missed a lot of details himself, and I wondered if his mind was slipping. He was a man of power and influence, but doctors didn't seem to exist in Sang. Maybe he was suffering from dementia or Alzheimer's, something they would have caught in my world. Or maybe he'd just started out plumb crazy.

It was pitch dark as I zoomed over the state line. I navigated past fields and strip malls and trailer parks until I turned onto Sycamore Lane. The country road was long and barely lit and lonely, but I eventually saw the brick wall from my glance, lit up by fancy yard lights. The matching brick house was needlessly huge, and I imagined that the lawn-care staff was even more extensive than the one at Eden House in Sang.

All that trouble for a vegetable who'd never wake up. What a waste.

I stopped in a dark spot a hundred yards away and straightened my scrubs. I put my ID badge into the glove compartment and tucked the locket under my shirt. I didn't know who would be in the house, whether a nurse stayed around the clock or Mr. Goodwill had a housekeeper or a housesitter or an entire extended family. I just had to hope that whoever it was wasn't very bright. Or nosy.

For the tenth time, I checked to make sure that I had all the supplies I needed in my tote bag before I rolled the car into the driveway. No Helping Hands van, which was good. A layperson would be much easier to deal with. Before knocking on the door, I put on my brightest smile.

Time to channel the talented and charismatic Lady Letitia Paisley.

The first knock didn't raise anybody, so I rang the doorbell. There was movement within, and the porch lights came on, nearly blinding me. And then I heard a click I'd heard only in movies, and the door opened, and I was staring into the barrel of a shotgun. After all, it was the middle of the night on a lonely road in the country.

"Can I help you?" said a teenage boy in an open bathrobe and boxer shorts. His glasses were smudged, and there were Cheetos crumbs clinging sadly to a couple of hairs above his lip.

I looked over the gun and smiled nervously.

"Hi. Did Terry Ann at Helping Hands tell you I would be coming? I'm Carrie, and I have Mr. Grove's medicine."

The shotgun dropped, and the boy sniffed. "Nobody called. Sorry 'bout the gun. It's late."

"I know it is," I said apologetically. I held my tote bag open and said, "I'm just filling in. His usual nurse forgot to switch out the IV bag, and they also wanted to start him on IV Zosyn. It's an antibiotic. It'll just take me a minute."

The sullen boy opened the door, and I stepped into a beautiful marble foyer with the sort of curving staircase that must come equipped with at least one debutante in a white dress.

"Thanks," I said. "Are you Mr. Grove's grandson?"

"Yeah," he said. "I'm Toby. We all take turns staying over here, because Grampa's lawyer's too cheap to hire somebody. At least he's got good cable."

"You're a good boy to take care of your grandfather," I said.

"I never even met him," the boy said. He shuffled over to

loaf on a long corner sofa in the next room and turned on the TV. "He's been out for, like, twenty years."

He sat down with his back to me and started switching channels, adding, "He's upstairs in the big room."

I walked up the curving staircase and padded down the deep carpet to the only door with a light shining inside. On the way, I didn't pass a single family photograph or heirloom. The house reminded me of something set up for a magazine. Some obsessively neat aunt probably hired a decorator every five years or so to redo the whole place around the softly breathing man in the bedroom, who never even knew what the walls looked like.

The door was ajar, and I slipped in. There he was, lying in the bed I'd seen in my glance. He was propped up with pillows, and his mustache and hair were carefully trimmed. Even his pajamas were crisp, although I thought it ironic that the top button was unbuttoned, which could never happen in Sang. The room was warm and stuffy, and there was nothing personal, not a single memento. In the background, the radio hummed old-fashioned hymns.

No wonder the old man in Sang was crazy.

I walked to the window, which was covered by thick, light-blocking draperies. Peeking out, I had déjà vu, even though it was nighttime. That glorious magnolia reigned over the walled-in garden, sister to the greenspace behind Eden House. The man simply could not let go of his old life. I opened the drapes all the way. The waxy white blooms glowed in the moonlight, and I wondered if Mr. Goodwill shivered in Sang, thinking that a goose had walked over his grave as he kept vigil over my body and Criminy's fury.

Back to my patient. He had a port in his chest for the

IV, and I had to unbutton his pajama top to get to it. Luckily, the IV bag was nice and full, so I had plenty of time;
his real nurse must have left recently. I leaned out through
the doorway and heard Toby open a soft-drink can and collapse on the couch. Then I heard soft moans. Excellent—
careless, hormonal grandson plugged into Cinemax. I
closed the door gently and locked it, then turned on the
overhead light.

With loving precision, I laid out my supplies on the bed.

36

The timing had to be just right.

Step One: Prepare the syringe, draw up 250 units of Mrs. Henderson's pilfered insulin, and inject it into Mr. Grove's IV line.

Step Two: Use the baby butterfly needle to draw a tube of my own blood.

Mr. Goodwill didn't know that nothing translated from world to world except my body and the locket. I couldn't bring over a syringe or a cup or a finger in a baggie, per his instructions.

Step Three: Stuff everything back into the bag, lie down on my back on the floor, and pour the syringe of my own blood into my mouth.

I really didn't like Step Three.

Step Four: Let my complete exhaustion overtake me in sleep.

I'd considered taking meds to induce my rest, but I didn't want to lie around on the floor, drugged up at his bedside, when I came back. Getting out of that house without real-world consequences was going to take my best acting performance yet.

Excited as I was, I knew that sleep would claim me as quickly as ever.

Step Five: Hope that my mouth stayed shut when I went unconscious.

Step Six: Pray that my cockamamie plan worked.

37

My eyes flickered open, and I fought the urge to spew blood all over the place. Somehow I managed to keep my lips together and my cheeks puffed. I sat up and found Criminy across the dark room. The curtains were drawn closed, and brilliant sunlight burned around the edges. Jonah Goodwill slumped at my bedside, snoring through his mustache.

Criminy's eyes were wide and panicky, his mouth still stuffed with a handkerchief. When he saw that I was conscious, I gave him an exaggerated wink and tried to ease myself silently off the bed. It creaked, and Goodwill startled awake. I sank back down and tried to look pained.

"You're back," he said. "Have you got it?"

I nodded my head and pointed to my bulging cheeks. Then I pointed to the door and held my hand up at chest height with a questioning "Hmm?"

He didn't get it, so I tried a pantomime of a slutty lady with fangs. Mr. Goodwill caught on and chuckled. He rang a bell, and when a servant appeared, he said, "Please ask Miss Scowl and Rodvey to join us."

My cheeks burned, and the blood began to seep down my throat a little. I tried not to gag.

A few moments later, Tabitha Scowl swooped into the room, followed by my old, venomous friend Rodvey, who was obviously disgusted with the lot of us.

"Rodvey, please hold Miss Scowl's arms behind her back," Goodwill said conversationally, and quick as a snake, Tabitha was caught painfully and fighting Rodvey's grasp. The fake locket bounced off her chest as she struggled.

"This wasn't part of the bargain, Jonah!" she cried.

"It's just a test of your loyalty, my dear," he said kindly. Then he took my gloved hand to help me up from the bed and ushered me over to the tiny, squirming Blud-woman.

Just as I was about to spit the blood at her, Goodwill said, "And now, Tabitha, if you will, please remove the handkerchief from Mr. Stain's mouth."

Rodvey let go of Tabitha, and she chuckled darkly as she sashayed to Criminy and slowly removed the gag. Then she stood back, arms crossed over her chest, to watch the show.

Criminy took in a big breath and said, "Not to be too repetitive, but this wasn't part of the bargain, Jonah."

"Like you'd ever be peaceable after this," Goodwill snapped. "You'd be at my throat tomorrow, or starting a riot, or telling the newspapers. You're far too dangerous to live."

"Where's my costumer?" Criminy asked.

"She's drained," Goodwill said curtly. Criminy bared his teeth and strained at his bonds, and Goodwill held his hand out to me and said, "Now, Miss Paisley, if you will."

I shook my head no.

"Give him the blood, or you both die."

I gave him my most eloquent look of tortured pain over comically puffed cheeks.

"Now," the old man said.

I walked heavily to the chair and leaned over to put my hands on the sides of Criminy's face. Then I kissed him, parting my lips to let the blood rush from my mouth into his. There was a sort of primal sexuality to it, feeling the hot, red liquid mingle between us, and his tongue lapped it up hungrily. I almost swooned as I pulled away, and he couldn't help licking the drips off his chin afterward, still watching me.

With hands over my face, I jogged to the basin and pushed the button for water, then rinsed my mouth out as well as I could.

"Alcohol?" I spluttered.

"Rodvey?" Mr. Goodwill asked.

"Left coat pocket," Rodvey grunted, still holding Tabitha tightly.

Mr. Goodwill handed me the flask, and whatever was inside burned my mouth with fumes redolent of paint thinner. I spit it out and rinsed again, then rinsed with water. At least it wasn't actually diseased. The rinsing was mainly for show. I was banking on Jonah Goodwill's ignorance of modern infectious disease. Twenty years out of my world, and he'd probably believe we had colonized Mars.

Leaning over the basin, I willed myself to cry and splashed water over my face.

"What was it?" Goodwill asked me.

"Ebola," I said. "It's only communicable through bodily fluids, and I've been vaccinated. I'm a nurse, so I got the blood from a patient who had just succumbed."

"I remember hearing about that one before I came here. That was clever," he said, nodding appreciatively. "What are the symptoms?"

"From fresh blood, and without medication, it'll be spasms, hemorrhage, and death," I sniffled between sobs. "Within minutes."

"Sorry about your man," Goodwill said, in a voice that made it clear that he wasn't sorry at all. "I'll leave you two to say good-bye."

Tabitha and Rodvey turned to go, but Goodwill stopped in the doorway, blocking them.

"That is," he said with a cruel grin, "after he bites Miss Scowl. It's no good if we don't spread it around, eh? We'll drain him afterward and disperse the vials, of course. But it'll be good to have two fresh bodies of tainted blood."

"Jonah——" Tabitha said, backing away.

"My name is Magistrate Goodwill," he said sternly. "Now, bite her quick, boy. I've got a genocide to plan."

Rodvey cut Criminy's rope, and the Bludman stood slowly, focused on Tabitha. He stalked toward her, and she cringed away from him.

"Crim, no," she said. "Remember our good times? Remember the caravan?"

"I mostly remember the island and the inn," he growled, and then he leaped at her. They fell to the ground as he ripped the flesh of her neck, drinking deeply.

"Don't drain her completely," Goodwill said, unholstering a miniature crossbow and holding it up to Criminy's temple. "I need her blud."

Criminy pulled away from the blood frenzy, his pupils engulfing his eyes in black. Tabitha lay there, her skirts in disarray and her chest barely moving. Criminy was panting, and he wiped his face carelessly as he stood. He gave Goodwill an evil, blood-tinged smile.

"Thanks for the last meal," he said, and then he twitched.

"Glad you enjoyed your own taste of death," Goodwill said. "Rodvey, stay until he's gone, then bring Miss Paisley to the dining room." And he shut the door, leaving Rodvey behind with us.

"Die already," the Copper said, with a lazy hand on his own holstered crossbow. "It's nearly time for tea."

Criminy twitched again, then spasmed, then went into a sort of seizure. Frothing at the mouth, he bumped into me, then caromed off the mirror and bumped into Rodvey, who shouted, "Get off me, Bluddy!" and pushed him away. I was trying my best to act distraught and betrayed and confused, but I wasn't sure where to look. Criminy's mad dance was both terrifying and hilarious, and he was spitting blood all over the place. An especially big glob hit the portrait of Goodwill, and I had to turn my laugh into a choked sob.

Then I heard a small *thwack*. When I next looked at Rodvey, there was a short, thick arrow sprouting from his chest. Criminy had stopped jerking around, and Rodvey's miniature crossbow was in his hands, with one bolt missing.

"You're a good shot," I said.

"You're surprised?"

"Not really."

"So is this stuff actually going to kill me? Because that blood tasted delightful. Like you."

"No, it's clean," I said. "But we've got to run. In about five minutes, Goodwill's going to notice something is wrong."

"Can't I just pretend to be dead for a while so you can escape out the window?" Criminy asked. "Pretending to be dead is rather enjoyable."

"No time to pretend," I said, throwing open the curtains. "Back in my world, I injected his body with insulin. If it works the way I think it does, he'll be dead here in ten minutes. It's got some lag time, but he's going to know there's something wrong. We've got to get out of here."

The window was all panes and couldn't be opened, exactly what you'd expect from an antiquated, paranoid lunatic. I turned to search the room, but Criminy's boot shot through the window, kicking out wooden slats and panes of glass into the bed of orange lilies outside. Taking my hand, he led me out into the bright morning sun. The day was gorgeous, glinting with raindrops and prisms and happy plants.

But there was no time to enjoy the rare sight of a nice day in Manchester. We took off running toward the far wall of the priory, and I could only assume that Criminy was going to find a way to boost me over the smooth white stones that rose at least eight feet tall.

"This would be a lot easier if I had enough time for a glamour. Can't you run any faster, love?" he inquired, not even panting.

"It's been a long couple of days," I said, most definitely panting. "You're lucky I haven't fallen and dragged you down with me."

"That sounds like my kind of fun," he said. He laughed as he ran, and my heart swelled with unexpected love.

We were in the orchard then, running in a straight line between two rows of trees. The dappled shade flickered as we flew over the earth, and the cow stopped grazing to watch our progress with interest. It was probably the most exciting thing she'd seen in her entire life.

It felt as if we had been running forever and would run forever, as if the trees would just go on and on, one after the other. But the wall was closer, and my chest was going to burst soon, and Criminy slowed down as he angled toward a giant old oak tree with branches that swung conveniently near the high wall.

"Let me boost you up," he said.

I lifted my boot, and he practically tossed me onto the lowest branch. I landed on my belly, my wind knocked out, and reached for the next branch. The slippery glove was almost my downfall, and I removed both of the stupid satin things and tossed them to the ground. The billowy sailor dress caught on twigs and under my toes and made upward movement almost impossible, but I tugged myself over two more branches and edged out, holding on to smaller branches to steady myself.

I could see the gritty streets of Manchester over the wall. It was amazing how filthy and bustling the world was outside Jonah Goodwill's private Eden. A little girl in a full-body pinafore tugging a wooden duck on a string stopped to point at me, and her nanny scolded her for woolgathering.

"You've got to hurry, love," Criminy urged.

I turned to snap at him, and my hand slipped. I nearly fell, swinging around and ending up with my back to the trunk, scrabbling for purchase on a crooked branch with arms flung outward.

It was no good. I was slipping, and Criminy was too far below me to help.

I felt a sharp tug on my neck as I slipped. My locket. It was caught on the sharp end of a broken branch.

Even before I had registered what was happening, I fell.

A heartbeat later, my boots landed on a lower branch, and Criminy's arms steadied me, pinning me to the trunk. I hugged the tree, with tears squirting out of my closed eyes, trying to make my throat work again. With one hand clinging to a branch, I felt my neck.

The locket was gone.

38

I opened my eyes and looked down.

"Shit," I said softly.

Criminy stood one branch below me, frowning at the ground. The locket lay in a patch of grass, ruby side up and glinting in the morning sun. When he gazed up at me, Criminy's eyes were more fierce and wild than they had been even when he faced the bludstag. Everything in him that wasn't human was written in that glance.

"Criminy, don't."

"I promised," he said.

And then he jumped.

39

My attention was pulled from Criminy's leap by an odd noise, like a lawn mower. Whatever it was, it was getting louder, and fast. I pushed a leafy branch aside but couldn't see what was coming.

Criminy landed on the ground in a crouch, scooping up the locket and tucking it into his waistcoat in one smooth motion. Then he leaped, his lean body arching like a cat's as his gloveless claws sought purchase in the bark. As his feet touched the first branch and propelled him upward, a crossbow bolt lodged in the tree trunk and quivered.

A three-wheeled vehicle skidded to a halt below us, a strange contraption that looked like a golf cart crossed with a sketch by Leonardo da Vinci. A Copper in full uniform was driving, and Jonah Goodwill was slumped in the passenger seat, a large crossbow in his arms. Another bolt whistled through the air by Criminy's hand as the Copper joined the bow fight. Criminy pulled himself up, climbing like a squirrel. As he stood, Goodwill's next bolt rustled the leaves over Criminy's head. I was amazed that the old man was still conscious, and for a terrified moment, I wondered if I had been wrong. Maybe killing his body in my world wouldn't kill him here. Then we'd be in serious trouble.

"I don't know what you've done," the old man shouted in his deep Southern drawl, all Sangish affectation forgotten. "But I'll kill you for it!"

"You have to get over the wall," Criminy grunted as his belly hit the branch by my boots. He held out a hand to me, and I took the locket from his black-scaled fingers and shoved it down the tight neck of my gown.

"Come on," I begged, grasping his hand to pull him up. "You're almost here. We can do it."

He chuckled sadly and looked down.

And that's when I saw the crossbow bolt through his calf, pinning him to the heavy branch below.

"You can do it, Letitia," he said. "Just get over the wall and go to Antonin. I'll find a way. I'll find you again."

"You only have to last another minute," I said, frantic and unwilling to abandon him. "The old man—"

And then I heard a *thwack,* and a crossbow bolt bloomed from his throat.

Blood spattered over my face and my dress, but I was already in shock. His eyes went wide with surprise. He looked down at the metal point dripping with his blud, then fell slowly backward. It was almost graceful, until the bolt in his leg stopped his downward motion. His body jerked around it and spun, leaving him hanging upside down by the arrow's shaft.

For only a moment, he floated in space, his hair blowing in the breeze. Then the arrow broke, and he fell to the ground with a nasty thud.

Goodwill cackled in triumph.

I took one last look at freedom over the wall. Just a few more feet, and I would have been out of the orchard and on my way to the tailor's shop. But I couldn't leave Criminy.

I began to climb down. I skidded and slipped, just as I had going up, and the bark tore at my hands and wrists, where I'd pulled off my gloves to climb. A broken branch ripped open my left palm, but I didn't register the pain. I swung down from the lowest branch and landed in the dirt beside Criminy's still form.

Ignoring Goodwill, I rolled Criminy over so that he was on his back and cradled his head in my lap. It wasn't easy, with the arrow shaft poking out through both sides of his neck. When I saw that he was breathing, I started breathing again, too. Maybe there was still time to save him.

"What'd you do to me, girly?" Goodwill asked, and I could hear the slurring in his voice. I couldn't believe he wasn't dead yet.

"I told you to watch out for dark-haired strangers, Mr. Grove," I said, my voice breaking.

As he struggled to aim his crossbow at me, I bent my head over Criminy and stroked his face with my bare hands. I felt his lips twitch as he smelled the fresh blood on the scratches. When his tongue shot out and started licking the wound on my palm, I cradled his head and shook with sobs, my now loose hair flopping over us both. Whatever pleasure he could get from the blood, I hoped it would help make his last moments better.

"You knew," the old man said, accusing. "All along."

"I knew enough to find you," I said. "And I knew enough to kill you."

Goodwill flopped over, the crossbow in his hands shaking. He was breathing heavily, sweating and shaking.

Finally.

"Keep your crossbow ready. I want answers before she dies," Goodwill said to the Copper, but he was struggling to stay conscious. His head flipped back, his eyes open to the sky.

"Twenty years you've been here," I said. "And your grandson let me in your door with a bottle of insulin. Too bad you weren't around to teach that boy not to open the door to strangers."

"That blood," Goodwill said. "Wasn't even tainted, was it?"

"Nope," I said. "But yours is."

"You can . . . shoot her now . . . Ferling," Goodwill said, panting and fighting for consciousness.

But Ferling put down his crossbow and said, "I don't think I will, begging your pardon, sir. She done me a favor once. Saved my life."

The old man was panting, and his hand shook as he lifted the crossbow and pointed it at me, point-blank range. Before he could shoot, it clattered to the ground. He fell back, clutching something under his shirt, his hand trembling.

"You know why Evangel never loved you?" I said, my voice raw. "Not because you were human. Not because Bludmen have magic." I watched him gasp.

"Because you're a bad person."

I looked up then to watch the moment when Jonah Goodwill left this world. His old body shuddered and went limp, his face to the clouds. I briefly wondered whether he would wake up in Anderson for just a second, just long enough to see the magnolia's shadow dancing on the wall and my body splayed out on the floor.

40

"Excuse me, madam," Ferling said. "But I believe I hear someone calling me from the house."

He got up and walked away, as simple as that. I guess the Copper had taken my advice and found peace with his wife. And Criminy had taken care of Rodvey. My glancing had been helpful all around, and Ferling had indeed remembered my final words. Maybe all Coppers weren't that bad.

But glancing couldn't help me now. The future I'd seen was shattered. I looked down at the pale face in my lap, the arrow quivering obscenely. Just a tiny trickle of blud eased down his neck into his shirt.

"What do I do?" I whispered.

"Pull it out," he wheezed.

So I gritted my teeth and grabbed the red-stained shaft behind the cruel, metal point and gently tugged.

He groaned and hissed. "Pull harder."

I was panicking, and I could feel my heartbeat in my temples. I was a nurse, dammit, but I wasn't trained for a world this hard. I grasped the arrow again, put a hand on Criminy's neck for leverage, and yanked straight up as smoothly as I could.

The arrow caught for a second, then slithered out of his

throat with a wet, sucking sound. He drew a deep breath, but it whistled. I was watching him, evaluating him for signs of anoxia, biting my lip. Waiting for him to die and leave me alone in a strange country, among enemies.

For just a second there, I wished I had had the witch's potion with me. In my world, I could save him. But the little bottle was far away, sitting on the bedside table in my wagon. He would have wanted to die under the heavy sky of Sang, anyway, not trapped in a hospital in my world, far from the touch of magic.

He coughed and spasmed, and blood sprayed from his mouth.

It was the end.

I bowed my head and sobbed, thinking of everything I wished I had told him. I couldn't find the words, couldn't articulate what he meant to me, what he had taught me about myself in such a short time. I hadn't understood, not until just then, how one could be both captured and tamed at the same time. I cried for all of the adventures with him that I was going to miss now and how there was nothing more for me in Sang. I cried for how colorless and bland my own world would seem, endless days of helping people die and eating tomato soup with my cat and knowing that I had held something fine and not understood its value until I lost it.

His chest stopped moving, his eyes open to the sky.

He was gone.

41

Then he lurched up, sitting—and laughed.

"Well, that was fun, eh?" he said.

I choked on nothing, and he smacked my back.

"What the hell?" I shrieked. "I'm watching you die. You're dying!"

"Not any more than usual," he said with a shrug and a grin.

I hiccuped. I sniffled. And then I went back to crying my eyes out, but in relief this time. He whipped out the remaining bit of arrow still in his calf and rubbed the blud off his boot. Tossing the arrow aside, he pulled me against his chest, shushing me and patting me. I felt very much like a lost kitten.

"You nearly died." I snuffled. "Shouldn't I be comforting you?"

"Piffle," he said. "I'm hardier than that. I told you Bludmen are hard to kill. But you, lass! Oh, you were magnificent. You tricked that old bastard right into his grave. You saved thousands of people. And your dress is truly hideous. I demand you take it off at the earliest possible convenience."

I giggled a little and pulled away. He smiled at me, and I put a finger to the ragged hole in his throat.

"Just a flesh wound," he said. It was already starting to close up. He puffed out his cheeks, and a little fizzle of air hissed under my finger and made me laugh.

"Please don't try that trick at the caravan," I sniffed. "I don't like it a bit."

"Same to you," he said, hopping to his feet and pulling me up after him. "Except that bit with the tongue kissing and the mouthful of blood. I rather enjoyed that."

We limped to the tree, but he pulled my hand back and kissed the ragged palm.

"I've got to ask you for a favor, love," he said.

"Name it," I said. But I already knew what he was going to ask.

"I need some blood," he said. "To help me heal, so I can get you over that wall and to safety before the Coppers realize what's happened. I'm half-drained. But I know where his secret cellar is now, so the whole torture thing wasn't a total loss."

I reached up to the high neck of my gown and pulled at the laces as seductively as possible, but the damned things caught, and I felt like an idiot. He chuckled and leaned over me, and I felt like Little Red Riding Hood, caught in the shadow of a wolf.

He unlaced the neck gently and brushed my lips with his before nuzzling my throat.

"I love you, you know," he whispered in my ear, and then I felt the small gash of his sharp teeth in my skin. Not puncture wounds—more like a little rip, like when you rub past a nail. I whimpered and couldn't decide if it hurt or not. He pressed against me, and I pressed into the tree, and I had a little flashback of our time in the copse. Had it really been only two days ago? Once I started thinking about that, it started feeling better. He gulped twice more, then pulled away with a dreamy look on his face, eyes rolled back in his head.

"That's the best thing I've ever tasted in my life," he said. "Lift your skirt."

"No time for love, Criminy Stain," I said, rolling the neck of my ugly dress back up. "Let's get over that wall and out of Eden."

42

It was getting awfully handy, knowing a magician. We wouldn't have gotten across the street without a glamour, not covered with all that blood. Criminy was still limping as we jogged toward Darkside, but the wound in his neck was nearly closed.

"One day, you'll forget it was ever there," he said.

"I don't think I'll ever forget that, actually," was my response.

We were darting through the crowd when we heard the church bell tolling, a dark and dismal sound, ringing again and again. The people all stopped where they were and looked up to the top of the city, where the church's spire rose into the white-blue sky. It was helpful—they were a lot easier to dodge when they all held still.

"What's happened?" an old man said, looking around frantically.

"Someone's died," a young man answered.

"Lucky him," remarked the old man.

We didn't stop, though—we used the weird calm to get farther toward safety. When the bell was done ringing, we could hear shouts, and then all of the Coppers abandoned their posts and rushed uphill toward the church on their bludmares, knocking people aside in their haste.

By the time we reached Antonin's shop, everyone knew.

Jonah Goodwill, Magistrate of Manchester, was dead.

"An apoplexy," whispered a fashionable young matron having her sash fixed. "He passed on in his garden, smiling among the apple trees that fed the poor and brought him so much joy. Such a dear man."

Every customer brought the tailor another juicy tidbit, most of them patently false. But the true ones were even better.

"They'll name the city Goodwill in his honor," said an old biddy.

"He left a will, but his successor was found dead with an arrow in his chest next to a Bluddy doxy in Mr. Goodwill's own guest room," whispered a barrister's overfed housewife. "Ooh, the scandal!"

"You didn't hear it from me, but the Coppers had been planning to kill off all the Bludmen," said a bald, bookish man with glasses. "They even had a secret cabal."

"He was really an alien from another world," said a little boy getting his first breeches, and his mother flicked his ear for lying.

As Antonin knelt at my feet, hemming my new emerald-green dress and grinning through a mouthful of pins, I shook with repressed giggles.

We had a good laugh in the lemon-yellow room that night as my hideous, blood-spattered sailor dress crackled merrily in the stove. The Bludmen clinked their teacups together, and I inhaled a steaming, curry-flavored wrappy fresh from a street vendor. As far as I was concerned, it was a lovely celebration.

Later, curled together in the spare bed in Antonin's attic garret, Criminy rose on his elbow to look at me in the glow of our candle. His smile was warm and gentle, softening the hard lines of his face.

"Of all the ways it could have gone," he said, "I'd say it went pretty well."

"We were lucky," I said.

"There was some luck. But also a good bit of cleverness and lying and placing the right bets," he said, and he kissed the tip of my nose. "You did well, love."

"I did what I had to," I said modestly.

"The way I felt, when they had me tied to that chair and gagged," he muttered, looking into the dark corners of the attic and scowling. "I'm sorry it was *you* who had to save *me*," he said quietly.

"I think we saved each other," I said.

"I'm going to miss you so much, my love." He sighed, lying back down with his hands behind his head. "But I'll guard your body with my life, I promise. I wonder—if you take off the necklace over there, do you disappear here?"

"I didn't even think to check," I said. "I was too worried about you. But I don't think so. I mean, my body stayed there while I was over here, but time didn't move, and I woke up covered in urine, and . . . it's all really confusing."

He traced the chain down my neck and rubbed his thumb over the jewel of the locket.

"It was all worth it," he said to himself. "All the trouble. It was worth it."

I picked up the locket and studied it, then turned it over. There on the back were the words, just as I'd seen them that first night in my bathroom at home.

"*Viernes toa meo,*" I said. "What does it mean?"

He smiled. "Come to me," he said. "In Sanguine."

"What's that?"

"A dead language."

I giggled.

"But it's very magical and romantic," he admonished. "You had to say the words, and touch my blood, and see my picture for it to work. You had to want to come. It was all part of the spell."

I thought about it for a second. Any one of those random choices made differently, and I would be waking up next to Mr. Surly right now, getting ready to go to Nana's house and make scrambled eggs. Changing IVs, driving my car, drinking my coffee, wondering if there was something more out there.

Now I knew.

"Thank you," I said. "For calling me here. For finding the locket. For everything you've done. I know I haven't been easy."

"Easy's not worth anything," he said. "And you knew I'd find the locket or die trying."

"You had to," I said quietly. "To save your people."

"That may be true. But jumping out of the tree, that was just for you. What do I care for freedom if I can't have the only thing I want?"

I smirked. "Liar. You want lots of things."

"I can lie to anyone but you, love," he said with a chuckle. "And I do want lots of things, most of which are under your dress. But I would never break my promise. Especially not with the chance that you'd change your mind."

I fidgeted with the locket, pressing the ruby to open the catch. Holding the limning up to the light, I squinted from him to his painted image.

"It's you exactly," I said, and my voice broke. "The first time I saw it, all I could think was that whoever he was, he was handsome, and he was daring me to do something wild."

"I suppose I was," he agreed. "Loving a caravan man is adventure enough."

"That it is," I said, and he put his forehead to mine as I sniffled.

"You've got your locket on, then. It's bedtime. You're all ready. Let me kiss you before you go," he said softly. "So you'll remember."

Before I could protest that remembering him would not be a problem or even explain how the locket worked, he was kissing me with longing and fire and passion, his hands cradling my face, his gloved thumbs tracing my cheekbones. I kissed him back, trying to capture the moment in my memory forever. But I couldn't think, couldn't capture anything.

He was too immediate. Too real. Too primal.

Criminy Stain wasn't something I could own or tame. And I didn't want to.

He had awakened things in me that I didn't even know were sleeping. He made me feel alive and vital, and his world, strange as it was, called to my heart. He'd never meant to trap me, and I'd never meant to be caught, yet here we were.

But he'd gotten something wrong, and I had my own surprise for him.

I broke from the kiss and pulled away with a sly smile.

"Close your eyes," I said. "I'm going to do magic."

With his mouth quirked up, he indulged me by rolling over onto his back and shutting his eyes.

I silently pulled the locket over my head and hid it under the pillow.

"What's the trick, love?" he said.

I hitched up my new dress and straddled him, then dove back into kissing him. I slowly nibbled my way up to his ear.

"I can make a locket disappear," I whispered.

43

There's always an epilogue, isn't there?

The chapter that tells you what happened afterward, tying up the story in a nice big bow?

I can't exactly do that. My story doesn't work that way, all nice and tidy. I could maybe have some sort of messy raffia bow that looks as if a haystack exploded, like what my Nana uses when wrapping presents in newspaper. Or twine, the kind they use to tie up mysterious packages in brown paper.

But I'll try to make it neat.

I slept that night. Really, really well. After a week of sleeplessness and traveling and starvation and enough squirts of adrenaline to kill a polanda bear, it was good to sink finally into real, deep sleep. If I had dreams, I don't remember them. But I woke up smiling.

And next to me was a Bludman, a blood-drinking creature from another world, where everyone dressed like Victorian prudes and rode around in genuine horseless carriages and submarines. A world where the sky was too low and the names were off just enough to make it interesting.

I've always had colorful dreams, but even I couldn't have conjured Criminy Stain, magician and gypsy king. Whatever forces drew us together seemed haphazard and random. But in each other, we both found that elusive something, the drive that keeps an animal hunting and hoping.

There was still work to do, of course. He had the caravan to tend to, and I had to return to my world to swallow a mouthful of my own blood and report that Jonathan Grove, philanthropist and preacher, had finally succumbed to his condition. My fears about a murder or police questioning were, of course, unfounded. Nurse Carrie just melted away into the night. After twenty-five years of his bleeding the family's inheritance dry, everyone was more than happy to assume that he had died of old age or complications. It was actually a miracle that he had lasted so long.

The political situation of Manchester is still tense. Without Goodwill at the helm of the second-largest city in Sangland, there's hope. With Rodvey gone, Ferling was next in line, and his stance toward Bludmen has been noticeably kinder. Antonin's shop was allowed to move back to High Street, and the latest newspapers say that Bludmen might begin getting votes in London's Parliament. For once, the gossip was true—there was talk of renaming Manchester as Goodwill, but the Bludmen put up a revolt, and it was abandoned.

As we travel the island, I learn more and more about the wonders of this strange world that distorts history as I know it like a carnival mirror. In Freesia, which corresponds to Russia, the Bludmen rule over terrified Pinkies from an icy palace deep in an enchanted forest. In Franchia, colorful daimons dance in the cabarets under the giddy thumb of the Sun King. In Almanica, Sanglish pioneers press ever farther into the frontier of a world ruled by natives described as half-animal warriors. The stories grow only more fabulous, and I want to see it all. The caravan remains a haven from politics and dogma. But in stopping Goodwill, we helped to make Sang a better place, and I think both worlds are better for his absence.

And I know, because I live in both worlds. While I can.

During the day, I take care of my grandmother, doing my best to make her last time on earth warm and loving and comfortable. We play rummy, and I try to talk her into giving me the recipe for her special chocolate pie. I see my other patients, except for Mr. Sterling. I couldn't bring myself to return to the pretty town home and touch the beautiful, wasted body. I couldn't handle the guilt of knowing that I could have given him everything he thought he wanted. I'd seen it in the glance, and even if I'd toyed with the idea of choosing him, I'd always known it wouldn't happen. He left the caravan for London, and the newspapers say he's the most eligible bachelor in town. My own glance tells me that he still has a journey ahead of him, but if he plays the right notes, he'll find love himself before long.

As for me, my days as a nurse are normal and contented, but I'm biding my time.

At night, when I dream, I'm dressed in burgundy taffeta laced up to my chin. I tell fortunes and collect copper pennies and vials of blood. I laugh with the sword swallower and encourage the lizard boy to get more exercise. I sleep in a scarlet wagon, in a bed draped in silk, with a beautiful ruby locket under my pillow. And beside me sleeps my own personal vampire, or the closest thing around.

Sometimes, that's what I do. Who I am. And I know that no time passes in the other world, that I could stay in Sang and in Criminy's arms forever. But then I'll see an old woman in the crowd and touch my own face, feeling the new lines there. Or I'll gently hold a shriveled hand to read a dark future and remember that my grandmother needs me.

And later that night, Criminy will tuck me into a specially made, well-ventilated box in his trailer. He'll kiss me softly and give me his love and call me his gypsy queen.

And then he'll close the door and lock the box with a key he wears on a chain under his undone cravat. He'll set a small copper snake named Boros on the lid, and the creature's ruby-red eyes will cast eerie lights on the walls as it spins around and around, guarding me. I'll lock the inside lock. I'll fall asleep almost immediately.

And then I'll open my eyes to my other life and take off the locket for a while.

I've made my choice, and for now, my choice is both. And I'm happy.

Except for one thing, hovering on the edge of my thoughts like a bludrat waiting to pounce on an innocent sleeper. There's only one dream I have in Sang, when the locket is under my pillow and I'm curled against my beloved Bludman. Again and again, unbidden, his glance appears in my head, torturing me, a secret he's forgotten to unearth.

My glances have always been true.

All except that one.

Yet.

So each morning when I wake beside Criminy, the first thing I do is check my hands, knowing in my heart that one day, they'll be covered in black scales and blood.

Just like his.

Turn the page for a sneak peek
at the next saucy, sexy, Blud novel . . .

WICKED AS SHE WANTS

By Delilah S. Dawson

Coming from Pocket Books
in 2013

I don't know which called to me more, his music or his blood. Trapped in darkness, weak to the point of death, I woke only to suck his soul dry until the notes and droplets merged in my veins. Whoever he was, he was my subject, my inferior, my prey, and his life was my due. What's the point of being a princess if you can't kill your subjects?

His blood was spiced with liquor; I could tell that much. And as I listened, stilling my breathing and willing my heart to pump again, I realized that I didn't know the song he was playing. It wasn't any of the Freesian lullabies from my childhood, nor was it anything that had been popular at court. I could even pick out the sound of his fingertips stroking the keys without the telltale muting of suede gloves. Peculiar. And no wonder I could smell him, whoever he was, if he wasn't protecting his delicious skin from the world. From me.

He stopped playing and sighed, and my instincts took over. The attempt to pounce was painfully foiled by . . . something. Leather. I was trapped, tucked into a ball, boxed and balanced on my bustled bum like a snail. When he started playing again, my hand stole sideways toward the musty leather. With one wicked claw, I began to carve a way out.

The tiniest sliver of light stole in, orange and murky. Fresh air hit my face, and with it, his scent. It took every ounce of well-bred patience for me to remain silent and still and not fumble and flounder out of whatever held me bound like a Kraken from the deep. My mother's voice rang in my mind, her queenly tone unmistakable.

Silence. Cunning. Quickness. That is how the enemy falls, princess. You are the predator's predator, the Bludman's Bludman. The queen of the beasts. Now kill him. Slowly.

My fingernails had grown overlong and sharper than was fashionable in court, and the rest of the leather fell away in one long curve. I lifted the flap with one hand and dared to peek out.

The room was dim and mostly empty, with a high ceiling and wooden floors. Spindly chairs perched on round tables. Across the room, lit by one orange gas spotlight, was a stage, and on that stage was a harpsichord, and playing that harpsichord was my lunch.

Seeing him there, the princess receded and the animal took over. Body crouched and fingers curled, I sidled out through my hole, my eyes glued to my prey. He didn't notice the creature hunting him from the shadows. His eyes were closed, and he was singing something plaintive, something about someone named Jude. I wasn't Jude. So that didn't matter.

The refined part of my brain barely registered that I was dressed in high-heeled boots and swishing taffeta. I knew well enough how to stalk in my best clothes, and had been doing so since my days in a linen pinafore and ermine ruff. As I slipped into the shadows along the wall and glided toward the stage, hunger pounded in time with my heartbeat and his slow keystrokes. It felt like a lifetime had passed since I had last eaten. And maybe it had. Never had I been so empty. So drained.

I made it across the room without detection. He continued moaning about Jude in a husky voice so sad that it moved even the animal in me. I stopped to consider him from behind deep red velvet curtains that had definitely seen better days. But I didn't see a man. Not yet. Just food. And in that sense, he had all but arrayed himself on a platter, walking around with his shirt open, boots off, and gloves nowhere to be seen. Exposed and reeking of alcohol, he was an easy target.

He broke off from his song and reached for a green bottle, tipping it to lips flushed pink with blood and feeling. I watched his neck thrown back, Adam's apple bobbing, and a deafening roar overtook me. I couldn't hold back any longer. I was across the stage and on him in a heartbeat.

Tiny as I am, the momentum from my attack knocked him backward off the bench. The bottle skittered across the floor, and he made a pathetically clumsy grab for it. I had one hand tangled in his long hair, the other pinning down his chest, long talons prickling into his flesh and drawing pinpoints of delicious blood to pepper the air. I took a deep breath, savoring it. The kill was sure. I smiled, displaying pointy teeth.

His red-rimmed eyes met mine in understanding, and he smiled back, a feral glint surprising me. Something smashed into my head, and he rolled me over and lurched backward with a laugh. Red liquid streamed through my hair and down my face, and I hissed and shook shards of green glass from my shoulders. The uppity little bastard had hit me with his bottle. If I hadn't already had plans to kill him, I now had just cause.

As I circled him, I wiped the stinging wine from my eyes with the back of my hand. I was dizzy with hunger, almost woozy, and he took advantage of my delicate condition to leap forward and slice my forearm with the jagged ends of his blasted bottle. I hissed again and went for his throat, but at the last minute something stopped me short. He didn't smell so good, not any more.

The beast within receded, and my posture straightened.

My arms swung, useless, at my sides. His finger was in his mouth, and when he pulled it out with a dramatic pop, his lips were stained red with my blood. Now he just smelled more like me. And less like food.

"Not today, Josephine," he said with a cocky grin.

I struggled to stand tall and not wobble. Now that he had swallowed my blood, the beast wasn't controlling me, and there was nothing holding me up. I was empty as a cloud, light as a snowflake, beyond hunger. My heart was barely beating. And I felt more than a little dizzy.

"Oh my," I said, one hand to my dripping hair. "I do believe I might swoon. And you've ruined my dress as well. Your lord is going to simply draw and quarter you."

I did swoon then. As the world went black, I felt his hands catching me, his delicious—if no longer maddening—blood pumping millimeters away from my own.

"Easy, little girl," he said. I smelled fumes and sadness on him and something else, something deep and musky and not quite right.

I was delirious as he gently helped me fall to the ground. I could barely mumble, "I'm not a little girl, and you're the most badly behaved serf I've ever met."

I fell away, and his laughter and music followed me into my dreams.

Before my eyes were open, before I was actually awake, I was drinking. Four great gulps and I gasped for more. I clawed at the little glass tube held to my mouth and flung it to the ground.

"More," I rasped. "I demand more."

"How long have you been hiding in that old suitcase?" someone asked.

I opened my eyes, suddenly aware of the unladylike nature of my predicament. A man's arm was around my shoulders, his ungloved human hand holding another vial to my lips as I drank the blood as greedily as a child with holiday sweets. My hair had fallen into disarray, and some of the straggling locks around my face were tinted red with what smelled like old wine. I slapped the vial to the ground—after I'd finished the last drop, of course.

"You," I said. My eyes narrowed, focused on him. I'd never seen so much exposed skin on a serf who wasn't being offered as a meal. His eyes were bright blue, regarding me with curiosity and a noticeable absence of fear and respect.

"What did you do to me, offal?"

He chuckled and grinned. He had dimples. "I'm pretty sure I saved your life, right after you attacked me. I don't hold it against you, though. Looks like you were drained."

"Drained?"

"You can't even stand, little girl."

"Let us understand each other," I said, enunciating every word. "I am not little, and I am not a girl. I am twenty-seven years old, and I am a princess. And you, whoever you are, are my subject. You owe me obeisance, fealty, and blood."

"Come and get it, then," he said with unexpected good humor. He held up a sparkling vial, the amber light glinting off the glass.

"You know very well I cannot," I spat, struggling for control. I had never been so helpless, and it was untenable. Once I was strong again, he was going to pay.

"Then, we'll have to strike a bargain, won't we?"

"I don't bargain."

"Then, good luck."

He stood and began walking back to his harpsichord. Long tangled copper hair rippled over his stained white shirt, and I pledged that I would one day make a mop out of it. Rage consumed me. Rage, and hunger.

"Wait," I gasped, my black hands scrabbling against the

ground. I heard my long white talons scritching over the wood, their sharp ends useless against the effects of being drained. He had to be right; only draining could reduce me to mewling like a kitten. To begging and desperation.

"Hmm?" he asked genially, turning around to grin at me again with those hateful dimples.

"Let's make a bargain."

"I knew you'd see it my way," he said. He walked back to me, pulling another vial from his shirt pocket. He sat down cross-legged, just out of reach, and began flipping it over his knuckles. It reminded me of a wolfhound my father used to have, the way she would gulp under her jeweled collar when he forced her to balance a bone on her nose until he gave her the signal to eat it. I gulped, too.

"First of all, who are you *really*?" he asked.

I closed my eyes, fighting for control of my emotions. I had never begged before, never been in any position that didn't involve absolute power. I had definitely never been helpless at the bare feet of a Pinky, a serf, a paltry human. My hands made fists in the wine-colored taffeta of my gown, the talons piercing the ruffles and digging painfully into my palms.

"I am the second princess of Freesia. My name is Ahnastasia Medevna Krovnova. My father is the Blud Tsar of Freesia, and we reside in the Snow Palace of Muscovy."

At mention of my name, his face underwent a strange ripple of emotions, from recognition to understanding to what appeared to be pity.

"Bad news, princess," he said. "I follow the papers. You were declared dead four years ago."

He cocked his head at me, squinting his eyes as he looked me up and down. I was accustomed to seeing awe, fear, and a polite admiration in a Bludman's eyes. I had never had a human look so brazenly into my face, seeming to reach down into my soul and question what was found there. But this man did just that. And the answering look on his face showed pity. I flinched under his scrutiny.

"I don't . . . I can't . . ." I faltered, and closed my eyes. "I need more blood," I whispered. "Please."

With another look of pity, he uncorked the vial and held me up just enough for me to sip it. I allowed him to touch me, and gulped the blood as politely as possible. I emptied the vial and licked the lip of the glass clean.

"I've answered your question," I said, my haughtiness returning with my strength. "Now you will answer mine. Who are you? And what are you? You smell wrong."

"I'm Casper Sterling," he said. It was unsettling, the way his eyes held mine. I refused to blink as I waited for the answers he owed me. "I'm the greatest musician in London. And I'm mostly drunk."

Hips & Curves.

Want more passion?

Hips and Curves knows lingerie for curvy women, and our Steampunk collection will bring you right back to the most romantic of eras, with a modern edge. Because present-day isn't the only time to be seduced.

Explore all of our steampunk looks at:
www.hipsandcurves.com

FREE SHIPPING
enter code
WICKEDSSBA11
at checkout*

Through September 2012*, Hips & Curves is offering free standard shipping on any purchase at www.hipsandcurves.com when you use

offer code WICKEDSSBA11 at checkout.

*Available only to Continental U.S. residents only.

^After September 2012, call Hips & Curves at 800.220.8878 for current promotions